THE RUPA
OF
WICKED STORIES

By the same author:

Angry River
A Little Night Music
A Long Walk for Bina
Hanuman to the Rescue
Ghost Stories from the Raj
Strange Men, Strange Places
The India I Love
Tales and Legends from India
The Blue Umbrella
Ruskin Bond's Children's Omnibus
The Ruskin Bond Omnibus-I
The Ruskin Bond Omnibus-II
The Ruskin Bond Omnibus-III
Rupa Book of Great Animal Stories
The Rupa Book of True Tales of Mystery and Adventure
The Rupa Book of Ruskin Bond's Himalayan Tales
The Rupa Book of Great Suspense Stories
The Rupa Laughter Omnibus
The Rupa Book of Scary Stories
The Rupa Book of Haunted Houses
The Rupa Book of Travellers' Tales
The Rupa Book of Great Crime Stories
The Rupa Book of Nightmare Tales
The Rupa Book of Shikar Stories
The Rupa Book of Love Stories
The Rupa Book of Wicked Stories
The Rupa Book of Heartwarming Stories
The Rupa Book of Thrills and Spills

THE RUPA BOOK
OF
WICKED STORIES

Edited by
Ruskin Bond

Rupa & Co

Typeset Copyright © Rupa & Co. 2005
Selection and Introduction Copyright © Ruskin Bond 2005

First Published 2005
This edition 2010
Second Impression 2011

Published by
Rupa Publications India Pvt. Ltd.
7/16, Ansari Road, Daryaganj,
New Delhi 110 002

Sales Centres:
Allahabad Bengaluru Chennai
Hyderabad Jaipur Kathmandu
Kolkata Mumbai

Typeset in 13 pts. AmericanGaramond by
Mindways Design
1410 Chiranjiv Tower
43 Nehru Place
New Delhi 110 019

Printed in India by
Gopsons Papers Ltd.
A-14 Sector 60
Noida 201 301

Contents

Introduction

In making this selection of stories I was looking for the 'wicked' element. The stories had to be wickedly funny, or bitingly satirical, or masterpieces of black humour, or just plain wicked. Sometimes the protagonists are wicked; sometimes it's the writer who is wicked. But with one or two exceptions, these are not tales of evil-doing; rather, they are tales of how human-beings can invite ridicule or disaster simply by being too clever or too smug or too good!

The best-known masters of the craft of dark humour were Ambrose Bierce (1842-1915?) and 'Saki' (1870-1916), one an American, the other an Englishman. The straight horror story was pioneered by Edgar Allen Poe, but Bierce went a step further— he gave horror and morbidity a satirical, at times hilarious twist. This gift for black comedy also resulted in his most famous—or infamous—work, *The Devil's Dictionary*, a copy of which should be on every writer's desk. There was one on mine until a writer more devilish than me pinched it.

Ambrose Bierce's own life was as strange and macabre as any of his stories. Possibly the loneliest and most reclusive writer in American literary history, he was referred to as dead when he was living, and was mentioned as living when he was undoubtedly dead. In 1914, when he was seventy-two, he wandered into Mexico with the intention of covering the Mexican revolution as an independent correspondent. He was never seen again. Nor was his grave ever found. His last, cryptic note to a friend was typical of his dry wit; 'Pray for me—real loud.'

Bierce was a contemporary of Mark Twain and may have had some influence on the latter. On one occasion he paid the novelist this back-handed compliment: 'Mark Twain has suffused our country with a peculiar glory by never trying to write a line of poetry.'

And in another context: 'Mark Twain ... has got married. It is not the act of a desperate man ... it is the cool, methodical culmination of human nature working in the heart of an orphan hankering for someone with a fortune to love—someone with a bank account to caress.'

Mark Twain's response, if any, is not on record, but he was capable of the same biting sarcasm, as is evident in the story of 'The Great French Duel,' included here.

On the other side of the Atlantic, writing in a similar vein, was H.H. Munro, who assumed the nom-de-plume 'Saki'. As a young man he had served in the Burma Police. During World War I, he served in the British Army. His satirical little tales and vignettes caught the fancy of a reading public bored with the strict Victorian moral code. Witty and original, his writing cut through hypocritical social mores like a knife through butter. Still popular today, his work influenced writers such as Roald Dahl and Poppy Z. Brite.

'Saki', too, had an end worthy of one of his own tales. Only forty-six, he was serving in the trenches in France, when a soldier lit a cigarette in the dark. 'Put that out, you bloody fool—' he ordered, but was cut short by a bullet in the head.

Some of the other writers represented here are not so well-known, but their stories, culled from old magazines and anthologies, are all readable and entertaining and fall into the category of wickedness in one form or another.

Michael Joseph was a famous publisher who wrote the occasional story. He was also very fond of cats, and if you offered him a book on cats you had a good chance of seeing it published. In 'The Yellow Cat' he presents a chilling little story of crime and retribution.

I have always enjoyed reviving the work of neglected writers whose stories have been undeservedly forgotten. One of these was E.H.W. Meyerstein, poet, novelist and biographer of Chatterton—Chatterton the boy-poet, who took his own life after being accused of fraud.

Crosbie Garstin's story about the old gramophone, 'Golden Silence', is one of my favourites. Garstin led an adventurous life as a horsebreaker on Western ranches, sawyer and miner in British Columbia, and ranger in Matabeleland, where this story is set.

'The Room on the Fourth Floor' is said to be based on an actual incident. In modern terms, this story would be called faction instead of fiction.

'And did your Uncle Bill really try to poison you?' is a question I have often been asked.

'Only in the story,' I have to say. 'But he did poison one or two other people.'

Ruskin Bond
April, 2005

Mr Swiddler's Flip-Flap

Ambrose Bierce

Jerome Bowles (said the gentleman called Swiddler) was to be hanged on Friday, the ninth of November, at five o'clock in the afternoon. This was to occur at the town of Flatbroke, where he was then in prison. Jerome was my friend, and naturally I differed with the jury that had convicted him as to the degree of guilt implied by the conceded fact that he had shot an Indian without direct provocation. Ever since his trial I had been endeavouring to influence the Governor of the State to grant a pardon; but public sentiment was against me, a fact which I attributed partly to the innate pigheadedness of the people, and partly to the recent establishment of churches and schools which had corrupted the primitive notions of a frontier community. But I laboured hard and unremittingly by all manner of direct and indirect means during the whole period in which Jerome lay under sentence of death; and on the very morning of the day set for the execution, the Governor sent for me, and saying 'he did not purpose being worried by my importunities all winter,' handed me the document which he had so often refused.

Armed with the precious paper, I flew to the telegraph office to send a dispatch to the Sheriff at Flatbroke. I found the operator locking the door of the office and putting up the shutters. I pleaded in vain; he said he was going to see the hanging, and really had no time to send my message. I must explain that Flatbroke was fifteen miles away; I was then at Swan Creek, the State capital.

The operator being inexorable, I ran to the railroad station to see how soon there would be a train for Flatbroke. The station man, with cool and polite malice, informed me that all the employees of the road had been given a holiday to see Jerome Bowles hanged, and had already gone by an early train; that there would be no other train till the next day.

I was now furious, but the station man quietly turned me out, locking the gates. Dashing to the nearest livery-stable, I ordered a horse. Why prolong the record of my disappointment? Not a horse could I get in that town; all had been engaged weeks before to take people to the hanging. So everybody said, at least, though I now know there was a rascally conspiracy to defeat the ends of mercy, for the story of the pardon had got abroad.

It was now ten o'clock. I had only seven hours in which to do my fifteen miles afoot; but I was an excellent walker and thoroughly angry; there was no doubt of my ability to make the distance, with an hour to spare. The railway offered the best chance; it ran straight as a string across a level, treeless prairie, whereas the highway made a wide detour by way of another town.

I took to the track like a Modoc on the war-path. Before I had gone a half-mile I was overtaken by 'That Jim Peasley,' as he was called in Swan Creek, an incurable practical joker, loved and shunned by all who knew him. He asked me as he came up if I were 'going to the show.' Thinking it was best to dissemble, I told him I was, but said nothing of my intention to stop the performance; I thought it would be a lesson to That Jim to let him walk fifteen miles for nothing, for it was clear that he was going, too. Still, I wished he would go on ahead or drop behind. But he could not very well do the former, and would not do the latter; so we trudged on together.

It was a cloudy day and very sultry for that time of the year. The railway stretched away before us, between its double row of telegraph poles, in rigid sameness, terminating in a point at the horizon. On either hand the disheartening monotony of the prairie was unbroken.

I thought little of these things, however, for my mental exaltation was proof against the depressing influence of the scene. I was about to save the life of my friend—to restore a crack shot to society. Indeed, I scarcely thought of That Jim, whose heels were grinding the hard gravel close behind me, except when he saw fit occasionally to propound the sententious, and I thought derisive, query, 'Tired?' Of course I was, but I would have died rather than confess it.

We had gone in this way about half the distance, probably, in much less than half the seven hours, and I was getting my second wind, when That Jim again broke the silence.

'Used to bounce in a circus, didn't you?'

This was quite true! In a season of pecuniary depression I had once put my legs into my stomach—had turned my athletic accomplishments to financial advantage. It was not a pleasant topic, and I said nothing. That Jim persisted.

'Wouldn't like to do a feller a somersault now, eh?'

The mocking tongue of this jeer was intolerable; the fellow evidently considered me 'done up,' so taking a short run I clapped my hands to my thighs and executed as pretty a flip-flap as ever was made without a springboard! At the moment I came erect with my head still spinning, I felt That Jim crowd past me, giving me a twirl that almost sent me off the track. A moment later he had dashed ahead at a tremendous pace, laughing derisively over his shoulder as if he had done a remarkably clever thing to gain the lead.

I was on the heels of him in less than ten minutes, though I must confess the fellow could walk amazingly. In half an hour I had run past him, and at the end of the hour, such was my slashing gait, he was a mere black dot in my rear, and appeared to be sitting on one of the rails thoroughly used up.

Relieved of Mr Peasley, I naturally began thinking of my poor friend in the Flatbroke jail, and it occurred to me that something might happen to hasten the execution. I knew the feeling of the country against him, and that many would be there from a distance who would naturally wish to get home before nightfall. Nor could I help admitting to myself that five o'clock was an unreasonably late hour for a hanging. Tortured with these fears, I unconsciously increased my pace with every step, until it was almost a run. I stripped off my coat and flung it away, opened my collar, and unbuttoned my waistcoat. And at last, puffing and steaming like a locomotive engine, I burst into a thin crowd of idlers on the outskirts of the town, and flourished the pardon crazily above my head, yelling, 'Cut him down! —cut him down!'

Then, as every one stared in blank amazement and nobody said anything, I found time to look about me, marvelling at the oddly familiar appearance of the town. As I looked, the houses, streets, and everything seemed to undergo a sudden and mysterious transposition with reference to the points of the compass, as if swinging round on a pivot; and like one awakened from a dream I found myself among accustomed scenes. To be plain about it, I was back again in Swan Creek, as right as a trivet!

It was all the work of That Jim Peasley. The designing rascal had provoked me to throw a confusing somersault, then bumped against me, turning me half round, and started on the back track, thereby inciting me to hook it in the same direction. The cloudy day, the two lines of telegraph poles, one on each side of the track, the entire sameness of the landscape to the right and left—these had all conspired to prevent my observing that I had put about.

When the excursion train returned from Flatbroke that evening the passengers were told a little story at my expense. It was just what they needed to cheer them up a bit after what they had seen; for that flip-flap of mine had broken the neck of Jerome Bowles seven miles away!

An Imperfect Conflagration

AMBROSE BIERCE

Early one June morning in 1872 I murdered my father—an act which made a deep impression on me at the time. This was before my marriage, while I was living with my parents in Wisconsin. My father and I were in the library of our home, dividing the proceeds of a burglary which we had committed that night. These consisted of household goods mostly, and the task of equitable division was difficult. We got on very well with the napkins, towels and such things, and the silverware was parted pretty nearly equally, but you can see for yourself that when you try to divide a single music-box by two without a remainder you will have trouble. It was that music-box which brought disaster and disgrace upon our family. If we had left it my poor father might now be alive.

It was a most exquisite and beautiful piece of workmanship—inlaid with costly woods and carven very curiously. It would not only play a great variety of tunes, but would whistle like a quail, bark like a dog, crow every morning at daylight whether it was wound up or not, and break the Ten Commandments. It was this last-mentioned accomplishment that won my father's heart and caused him to commit the only dishonourable act of his life, though possibly he would have committed more if he had been spared: he tried to conceal that music-box from me, and declared upon his honour that he had not taken it, though I knew very well that, so far as he was concerned, the burglary had been undertaken chiefly for the purpose of obtaining it.

My father had the music-box hidden under his cloak; we had worn cloaks by way of disguise. He had solemnly assured me that he did not take it. I knew that he did, and knew something of which he was evidently ignorant; namely, that the box would crow at daylight and betray him if I could prolong the division of profits till that time. All occurred as I wished: as the gaslight began to pale in the library and the shape of the window was seen dimly behind the curtains, a long cock-a-doodle-doo came from beneath the old gentleman's cloak, followed by a few bars of an aria from *Tannhäuser*, ending with a loud click. A small hand-axe, which we had used to break into the unlucky house, lay between us on the table; I picked it up. The old man seeing that further concealment was useless took the box from under his cloak and set it on the table. 'Cut it in two if you prefer that plan,' said he; 'I tried to save it from destruction.'

He was a passionate lover of music and could himself play the concertina with expression and feeling.

I said: 'I do not question the purity of your motive: it would be presumptuous in me to sit in judgment on my father. But business is business, and with this axe I am going to effect a dissolution of our partnership unless you will consent in all future burglaries to wear a bell-punch.'

'No,' he said, after some reflection, 'no, I could not do that; it would look like a confession of dishonesty. People would say that you distrusted me.'

I could not help admiring his spirit and sensitiveness; for a moment I was proud of him and disposed to overlook his fault, but a glance at the richly jewelled music-box decided me, and, as I said, I removed the old man from this vale of tears. Having done so, I was a trifle uneasy. Not only was he my father—the author of my being—but the body would be certainly discovered. It was now broad daylight and my mother was likely to enter the library at any moment. Under the circumstances, I thought it expedient to remove her also, which I did. Then I paid off all the servants and discharged them.

That afternoon I went to the chief of police, told him what I had done and asked his advice. It would be very painful to me if the facts became publicly known. My conduct would be generally condemned; the newspapers would bring it up against me if ever I should run for office. The chief saw the force of these considerations; he was himself an assassin of wide experience. After consulting with the presiding Judge of the Court of Variable Jurisdiction he advised me to conceal the bodies in one of the bookcases, get a heavy insurance on the house and burn it down. This I proceeded to do.

In the library was a bookcase which my father had recently purchased of some cranky inventor and had not filled. It was in shape and size something like the old-fashioned 'wardrobes' which one sees in bedrooms without closets, but opened all the way down, like a woman's nightdress. It had glass doors. I had recently laid out my parents and they were now rigid enough to stand erect; so I stood them in this book-case, from which I had removed the shelves. I locked them in and tacked some curtains over the glass doors. The inspector from the insurance office passed a half-dozen times before the case without suspicion.

That night, after getting my policy, I set fire to the house and started through the woods to town, two miles away, where I managed to be found about the time the excitement was at its height. With cries of apprehension for the fate of my parents, I joined the rush and arrived at the fire some two hours after I had kindled it. The whole town was there as I dashed up. The house was entirely consumed, but in one end of the level bed of glowing embers, bolt upright and uninjured, was that book-case! The curtains had burned away, exposing the glass doors, through which the fierce, red light illuminated the interior. There stood my dear father 'in his habit as he lived,' and at his side the partner of his joys and sorrows. Not a hair of them was singed, their clothing was intact. On their heads and throats the injuries which in the accomplishment of my designs I had been compelled to inflict were conspicuous. As in the presence of a miracle, the people were silent; awe and terror had stilled every tongue. I was myself greatly affected.

Some three years later, when the events herein related had nearly faded from my memory, I went to New York to assist in passing some counterfeit United States bonds. Carelessly looking into a furniture store one day, I saw the exact counterpart of that bookcase. 'I bought it for a trifle from a reformed inventor,' the dealer explained. 'He said it was fireproof, the pores of the wood being filled with alum under hydraulic pressure and the glass made of asbestos. I don't suppose it is really fireproof—you can have it at the price of an ordinary bookcase.'

'No,' I said, 'if you cannot warrant it fireproof I won't take it'—and I bade him good morning.

I would not have had it at any price: it revived memories that were exceedingly disagreeable.

The Blind Spot

SAKI

'You've just come back from Adelaide's funeral, haven't you?' said Sir Lulworth to his nephew; 'I suppose it was very like most other funerals?'

'I'll tell you all about it at lunch,' said Egbert.

'You'll do nothing of the sort. It wouldn't be respectful either to your great-aunt's memory or to the lunch. We begin with Spanish olives, then a borsch, then more olives and a bird of some kind, and a rather enticing Rhenish wine, not at all expensive as wines go in this country, but still quite laudable in its way. Now there's absolutely nothing in that menu that harmonises in the least with the subject of your great-aunt Adelaide or her funeral. She was a charming woman, and quite as intelligent as she had any need to be, but somehow she always reminded me of an English cook's idea of a Madras curry.'

'She used to say you were frivolous,' said Egbert. Something in his tone suggested that he rather endorsed the verdict.

'I believe I once considerably scandalised her by declaring that clear soup was a more important factor in life than a clear conscience. She had very little sense of proportion. By the way, she made you her principal heir, didn't she?'

'Yes,' said Egbert, 'and executor as well. It's in that connection that I particularly want to speak to you.'

'Business is not my strong point at any time,' said Sir Lulworth, 'and certainly not when we're on the immediate threshold of lunch.'

'It isn't exactly business,' explained Egbert, as he followed his uncle into the dining-room. 'It's something rather serious. Very serious.'

'Then we can't possibly speak about it now,' said Sir Lulworth; 'no one could talk seriously, during a borsch. A beautifully constructed borsch, such as you are going to experience presently, ought not only to banish conversation but almost to annihilate thought. Later on, when we arrive at the second stage of olives, I shall be quite ready to discuss that new book on Borrow, or, if you prefer it, the present situation in the Grand Duchy of Luxemburg. But I absolutely decline to talk anything approaching business till we have finished with the bird.'

For the greater part of the meal Egbert sat in an abstracted silence, the silence of a man whose mind is focussed on one topic. When the coffee stage had been reached he launched himself suddenly athwart his uncle's reminiscences of the Court of Luxemburg.

'I think I told you that great-aunt Adelaide had made me her executor. There wasn't very much to be done in the way of legal matters, but I had to go through her papers.'

'That would be a fairly heavy task in itself. I should imagine there were reams of family letters.'

'Stacks of them, and most of them highly uninteresting. There was one packet, however, which I thought might repay a careful perusal. It was a bundle of correspondence from her brother Peter.'

'The Canon of tragic memory,' said Lulworth.

'Exactly, of tragic memory, as you say; a tragedy that has never been fathomed.'

'Probably the simplest explanation was the correct one,' said Sir Lulworth; 'he slipped on the stone staircase and fractured his skull in falling.'

Egbert shook his head. 'The medical evidence all went to prove that the blow on the head was struck by someone coming up behind him. A wound caused by violent contact with the steps could not possibly have been inflicted at that angle of the skull. They experimented with a dummy figure falling in every conceivable position.'

'But the motive?' exclaimed Sir Lulworth; 'no one had any interest in doing away with him, and the number of people who destroy Canons of the Established Church for the mere fun of killing must be extremely limited. Of course there are individuals of weak mental balance who do that sort of thing, but they seldom conceal their handiwork; they are more generally inclined to parade it.'

'His cook was under suspicion,' said Egbert shortly.

'I know he was,' said Sir Lulworth, 'simply because he was about the only person on the premises at the time of the tragedy. But could anything be sillier than trying to fasten a charge of murder on to Sebastien? He had nothing to gain, in fact, a good deal to lose, from the death of his employer. The Canon was paying him quite as good wages as I was able to offer him when I took him over into my service. I have since raised them to something a little more in accordance with his real worth, but at the time he was glad to find a new place without troubling about an increase of wages. People were fighting rather shy of him, and he had no friends in this country. No; if any one in the world was interested in the prolonged life and unimpaired digestion of the Canon it would certainly be Sebastien.'

'People don't always weigh the consequences of their rash acts,' said Egbert, 'otherwise there would be very few murders committed. Sebastien is a man of hot temper.'

'He is a southerner,' admitted Sir Lulworth; 'to be geographically exact I believe he hails from the French slopes of the Pyrenees. I took that into consideration when he nearly killed the gardener's boy the other day for bringing him a spurious substitute for sorrel. One must always make allowances for origin and locality and early environment; 'Tell me your longitude and I'll know what latitude to allow you,' is my motto.'

'There, you see,' said Egbert, 'he nearly killed the gardener's boy.'

'My dear Egbert, between nearly killing a gardener's boy and altogether killing a Canon there is a wide difference. No doubt you have often felt a temporary desire to kill a gardener's boy; you have never given way to it, and I respect you for your self-control. But I don't suppose you have ever wanted to kill an octogenarian Canon. Besides, as far as we know, there had never been any quarrel or disagreement between the two men. The evidence at the inquest brought that out very clearly.'

'Ah!' said Egbert, with the air of a man coming at last into a deferred inheritance of conversational importance, 'that is precisely what I want to speak to you about.'

He pushed away his coffee cup and drew a pocket-book from his inner breast-pocket. From the depths of the pocket-book he produced an envelope, and from the envelope he extracted a letter, closely written in a small, neat handwriting.

'One of the Canon's numerous letters to Aunt Adelaide,' he explained, 'written a few days before his death. Her memory was already failing when she received it, and I dare say she forgot the contents as soon as she had read it; otherwise, in the light of what subsequently happened, we should have heard something of this letter before now. If it had been produced at the inquest I fancy it would have made some difference in the course of affairs. The evidence, as you remarked just now, choked off suspicion against Sebastien by disclosing an utter absence of anything that could be considered a motive or provocation for the crime, if crime there was.'

'Oh, read the letter,' said Sir Lulworth impatiently.

'It's a long rambling affair, like most of his letters in his later years,' said Egbert. 'I'll read the part that bears immediately on the mystery.

' "I very much fear I shall have to get rid of Sebastien. He cooks divinely, but he has the temper of a fiend or an anthropoid ape, and I am really in bodily fear of him. We had a dispute the other day as to the correct sort of lunch to be served on Ash

Wednesday, and I got so irritated and annoyed at his conceit and obstinacy that at last I threw a cupful of coffee in his face and called him at the same time an impudent jackanapes. Very little of the coffee went actually in his face, but I have never seen a human being show such deplorable lack of self-control. I laughed at the threat of killing me that he spluttered out in his rage, and thought the whole thing would blow over, but I have several times since caught him scowling and muttering in a highly unpleasant fashion, and lately I have fancied that he was dogging my footsteps about the grounds, particularly when I walk of an evening in the Italian Garden.'

'It was on the steps in the Italian Garden that the body was found,' commented Egbert, and resumed reading.

' "I dare say the danger is imaginary; but I shall feel more at ease when he has quitted my service." '

Egbert paused for a moment at the conclusion of the extract; then, as his uncle made no remark, he added: 'If lack of motive was the only factor that saved Sebastien from prosecution I fancy this letter will put a different complexion on matters.'

'Have you shown it to any one else?' asked Sir Lulworth, reaching out his hand for the incriminating piece of paper.

'No,' said Egbert, handing it across the table, 'I thought I would tell you about it first. Heavens, what are you doing?'

Egbert's voice rose almost to a scream. Sir Lulworth had flung the paper well and truly into the glowing centre of the grate. The small, neat handwriting shrivelled into black flaky nothingness.

'What on earth did you do that for?' gasped Egbert. 'That letter was our one piece of evidence to connect Sebastien with the crime.'

'That is why I destroyed it,' said Sir Lulworth.

'But why should you want to shield him?' cried Egbert: 'the man is a common murderer.'

'A common murderer, possibly, but a very uncommon cook.'

Laura

SAKI

'You are not really dying, are you?' asked Amanda.

'I have the doctor's permission to live till Tuesday,' said Laura.

'But today is Saturday; this is serious!' gasped Amanda.

'I don't know about it being serious; it is certainly Saturday,' said Laura.

'Death is always serious,' said Amanda.

'I never said I was going to die. I am presumably going to leave off being Laura, but I shall go on being something. An animal of some kind, I suppose. You see, when one hasn't been very good in the life one has just lived, one reincarnates in some lower organism. And I haven't been very good, when one comes to think of it. I've been petty and mean and vindictive and all that sort of thing when circumstances have seemed to warrant it.'

'Circumstances never warrant that sort of thing,' said Amanda hastily.

'If you don't mind my saying so,' observed Laura, 'Egbert is a circumstance that would warrant any amount of that sort of thing. You're married to him—that's different; you've sworn to love, honour, and endure him: I haven't.'

'I don't see what's wrong with Egbert,' protested Amanda.

'Oh, I dare say the wrongness has been on my part,' admitted Laura dispassionately; 'he has merely been the extenuating circumstance. He made a thin, peevish kind of fuss, for instance, when I took the collie puppies from the farm out for a run the other day.'

'They chased his young broods of speckled Sussex and drove two sitting hens off their nests, besides running all over the flower beds. You know how devoted he is to his poultry and garden.'

'Anyhow, he needn't have gone on about it for the entire evening and then have said, "Let's say no more about it" just when I was beginning to enjoy the discussion. That's where one of my petty vindictive revenges came in,' added Laura with an unrepentant chuckle; 'I turned the entire family of speckled Sussex into his seedling shed the day after the puppy episode.'

'How could you?' exclaimed Amanda.

'It came quite easy,' said Laura; 'two of the hens pretended to be laying at the time, but I was firm.'

'And we thought it was an accident!'

'You see,' resumed Laura, 'I really *have* some grounds for supposing that my next incarnation will be in a lower organism. I shall be an animal of some kind. On the other hand, I haven't been a bad sort in my way, so I think I may count on being a nice animal, some thing elegant and lively, with a love of fun. An otter, perhaps.'

'I can't imagine you as an otter,' said Amanda.

'Well, I don't suppose you can imagine me as an angel, if it comes to that,' said Laura.

Amanda was silent. She couldn't.

'Personally I think an otter life would be rather enjoyable,' continued Laura; 'salmon to eat all the year around, and the satisfaction of being able to fetch the trout in their own homes without having to wait for hours till they condescend to rise to the fly you've been dangling before them; and an elegant svelte figure—'

'Think of the otter hounds,' interposed Amanda; 'how dreadful to be hunted and harried and finally worried to death!'

'Rather fun with half the neighbourhood looking on, and anyhow not worse than this Saturday-to-Tuesday business of dying by inches; and then I should go on into something else. If I had been a moderately good otter I suppose I should get back into human shape of some sort; probably something rather primitive—a little brown, unclothed Nubian boy, I should think.'

'I wish you would be serious,' sighed Amanda; 'you really ought to be if you're only going to live till Tuesday.'

As a matter of fact Laura died on Monday.

'So dreadfully upsetting,' Amanda complained to her uncle-in-law, Sir Lulworth Quayne. 'I've asked quite a lot of people down for golf and fishing, and the rhododendrons are just looking their best.'

'Laura always was inconsiderate,' said Sir Lulworth; 'she was born during Goodwood week, with an Ambassador staying in the house who hated babies.'

'She had the maddest kind of ideas,' said Amanda; 'do you know if there was any insanity in her family?'

'Insanity? No, I never heard of any. Her father lives in West Kensington, but I believe he's sane on all other subjects.'

'She had an idea that she was going to be reincarnated as an otter,' said Amanda.

'One meets with those ideas of reincarnation so frequently, even in the West,' said Sir Lulworth, 'that one can hardly set them down as being mad. And Laura was such an unaccountable person in this life that I should not like to lay down definite rules as to what she might be doing in an after state.'

'You think she really might have passed into some animal form?' asked Amanda. She was one of those who shape their opinions rather readily from the standpoint of those around them.

Just then Egbert entered the breakfast-room, wearing an air of bereavement that Laura's demise would have been insufficient, in itself, to account for.

'Four of my speckled Sussex have been killed,' he exclaimed; 'the very four that were to go to the show on Friday. One of them was dragged away and eaten right in the middle of that new carnation bed that I've been to such trouble and expense over. My best flowerbed and my best fowls singled out for destruction; it almost seems as if the brute that did the deed had special knowledge how to be as devastating as possible in a short space of time.'

'Was it a fox, do you think?' asked Amanda.

'Sounds more like a polecat,' said Sir Lulworth.

'No,' said Egbert, 'there were marks of webbed feet all over the place, and we followed the tracks down to the stream at the bottom of the garden; evidently an otter.'

Amanda looked quickly and furtively across at Sir Lulworth.

Egbert was too agitated to eat any breakfast, and went out to superintend the strengthening of the poultry yard defences.

'I think she might at least have waited till the funeral was over,' said Amanda in a scandalised voice.

'It's her own funeral, you know,' said Sir Lulworth; 'it's a nice point in etiquette how far one ought to show respect to one's own mortal remains.'

Disregard for mortuary convention was carried to further lengths next day; during the absence of the family at the funeral ceremony the remaining survivors of the speckled Sussex were massacred. The marauder's line of retreat seemed to have embraced most of the flowerbeds on the lawn, but the strawberry beds in the lower garden had also suffered.

'I shall get the otter hounds to come here at the earliest possible moment,' said Egbert savagely.

'On no account! You can't dream of such a thing!' exclaimed Amanda. 'I mean, it wouldn't do, so soon after a funeral in the house.'

'It's a case of necessity,' said Egbert; 'once an otter takes to that sort of thing it won't stop.'

'Perhaps it will go elsewhere now that there are no more fowls left,' Suggested Amanda.

'One would think you wanted to shield the beast,' said Egbert.

'There's been so little water in the stream lately,' objected Amanda; 'it seems hardly sporting to hunt an animal when it has so little chance of taking refuge anywhere.'

'Good gracious!' fumed Egbert, 'I'm not thinking about sport. I want to have the animal killed as soon as possible.'

Even Amanda's opposition weakened when, during church time on the following Sunday, the otter made its way into the house, raided half a salmon from the larder and worried it into scaly fragments on the Persian rug in Egbert's studio.

'We shall have it hiding under our beds and biting pieces out of our feet before long,' said Egbert, and from what Amanda knew of this particular otter she felt that the possibility was not a remote one.

On the evening preceding the day fixed for the hunt Amanda spent a solitary hour walking by the banks of the stream, making what she imagined to be hound noises. It was charitably supposed by those who overheard her performance, that she was practising for farmyard imitations at the forthcoming village entertainment.

It was her friend and neighbour, Aurora Burret, who brought her news of the day's sport.

'Pity you weren't out; we have quite a good day. We found it at once, in the pool just below your garden.'

'Did you—kill?' asked Amanda.

'Rather. A fine she-otter. Your husband got rather badly bitten in trying to "tail it". Poor beast, I felt quite sorry for it, it had such a human look in its eyes when it was killed. You'll call me silly, but do you know who the look reminded me of? My dear woman, what is the matter?'

When Amanda had recovered to a certain extent from her attack of nervous prostration Egbert took her to the Nile Valley to recuperate. Change of scene speedily brought about the desired recovery of health and mental balance. The escapades of an adventurous otter in search of a variation of diet were viewed in their proper light. Amanda's normally placid temperament reasserted itself. Even a hurricane of shouted curses, coming from her husband's dressing-room, in her husband's voice, but hardly in his usual vocabulary, failed to disturb her serenity as she made a leisurely toilet one evening in a Cairo hotel.

'What is the matter? What has happened?' she asked in amused curiosity.

'The little beast has thrown all my clean shirts into the bath! Wait till I catch you, you little—'

'What little beast?' asked Amanda, suppressing a desire to laugh; Egbert's language was so hopelessly inadequate to express his outraged feelings.

'A little beast of a naked brown Nubian boy,' spluttered Egbert. And now Amanda is seriously ill.

He Said It with Arsenic

RUSKIN BOND

Is there such a person as a born murderer—in the sense that there are born writers and musicians, born winners and losers?

One can't be sure. The urge to do away with troublesome people is common to most of us, but only a few succumb to it.

If ever there was a born murderer, he must surely have been William Jones. The thing came so naturally to him. No extreme violence, no messy shootings or hackings or throttling; just the right amount of poison, administered with skill and discretion.

A gentle, civilised sort of person was Mr Jones. He collected butterflies and arranged them systematically in glass cases. His ether bottle was quick and painless. He never stuck pins into the beautiful creatures.

Have you ever heard of the Agra Double Murder? It happened, of course, a great many years ago, when Agra was a far-flung outpost of the British Empire. In those days, William

Jones was a male nurse in one of the city's hospitals. The patients— especially terminal cases—spoke highly of the care and consideration he showed them. While most nurses, both male and female, preferred to attend to the more hopeful cases, nurse William was always prepared to stand duty over a dying patient.

He felt a certain empathy for the dying; he liked to see them on their way. It was just his good nature, of course.

On a visit to nearby Meerut, he met and fell in love with Mrs Browning, the wife of the local station-master. Impassioned love letters were soon putting a strain on the Agra-Meerut postal service. The envelopes grew heavier—not so much because the letters were growing longer but because they contained little packets of a powdery white substance, accompanied by detailed instructions as to its correct administration.

Mr Browning, an unassuming and trustful man—one of the world's born losers, in fact—was not the sort to read his wife's correspondence. Even when he was seized by frequent attacks of colic, he put them down to an impure water supply. He recovered from one bout of vomitting and diarrohea only to be racked by another.

He was hospitalised on a diagnosis of gastroenteritis; and, thus freed from his wife's ministrations, soon got better. But on returning home and drinking a glass of *nimbu-pani* brought to him by the solicitous Mrs Browning, he had a relapse from which he did not recover.

Those were the days when deaths from cholera and related diseases were only too common in India, and death certificates were easier to obtain than dog licences.

After a short interval of mourning (it was the hot weather and you couldn't wear black for long), Mrs Browning moved to Agra, where she rented a house next door to William Jones.

I forgot to mention that Mr Jones was also married. His wife was an insignificant creature, no match for a genius like William. Before the hot weather was over, the dreaded cholera had taken her too. The way was clear for the lovers to unite in holy matrimony.

But Dame Gossip lived in Agra too, and it was not long before tongues were wagging and anonymous letters were being received by the Superintendent of Police. Enquiries were instituted. Like most infatuated lovers, Mrs Browning had hung on to her beloved's letters and billet-doux, and these soon came to light. The silly woman had kept them in a box beneath her bed.

Exhumations were ordered in both Agra and Meerut.

Arsenic keeps well, even in the hottest of weather, and there was no dearth of it in the remains of both victims.

Mr Jones and Mrs Browning were arrested and charged with murder.

'Is Uncle Bill really a murderer?' I asked from the drawing room sofa in my grandmother's house in Dehra. (It's time that I told you that William Jones was my uncle, my mother's half-brother.)

I was eight or nine at the time. Uncle Bill had spent the previous summer with us in Dehra and had stuffed me with bazaar sweets and pastries, all of which I had consumed without suffering any ill effects.

'Who told you that about Uncle Bill?' asked Grandmother.

'I heard it in school. All the boys were asking me the same question— 'Is your uncle a murderer?' They say he poisoned both his wives.'

'He had only one wife,' snapped Aunt Mabel.

'Did he poison her?'

'No, of course not. How can you say such a thing!'

'Then why is Uncle Bill in gaol?'

'Who says he's in gaol?'

'The boys at school. They heard it from their parents. Uncle Bill is to go on trial in the Agra fort.'

There was a pregnant silence in the drawing room, then Aunt Mabel burst out: 'It was all that awful woman's fault.'

'Do you mean Mrs Browning?' asked Grandmother.

'Yes, of course. She must have put him up to it. Bill couldn't have thought of anything so—so diabolical!'

'But he sent her the powders, dear. And don't forget—Mrs Browning has since....'

Grandmother stopped in mind-sentence, and both she and Aunt Mabel glanced surreptitiously at me.

'Committed suicide,' I filled in. 'There were still some powders with her.'

Aunt Mabel's eyes rolled heavenwards. 'This boy is impossible. I don't know what he will be like when he grows up.'

'At least I won't be like Uncle Bill,' I said. 'Fancy poisoning people! If I kill anyone, it will be in a fair fight. I suppose they'll hang Uncle?'

'Oh, I hope not!'

Grandmother was silent. Uncle Bill was her stepson but she did have a soft spot for him. Aunt Mabel, his sister, thought he was wonderful. I had always considered him to be a bit soft but had to admit that he was generous. I tried to imagine him dangling at the end of a hangman's rope, but somehow he didn't fit the picture.

As things turned out, he didn't hang. White people in India seldom got the death sentence, although the hangman was pretty busy disposing off dacoits and political terrorists. Uncle Bill was given a life sentence and settled down to a sedentary job in the prison library at Naini, near Allahabad. His gifts as a male nurse went unappreciated; they did not trust him in the hospital.

He was released after seven or eight years, shortly after the country became an independent Republic. He came out of gaol to find that the British were leaving, either for England or the remaining colonies. Grandmother was dead. Aunt Mabel and her husband had settled in South Africa. Uncle Bill realised that there was little future for him in India and followed his sister out to Johannesburg. I was in my last year at boarding school. After my father's death, my mother had married an Indian, and now my future lay in India.

I did not see Uncle Bill after his release from prison, and no one dreamt that he would ever turn up again in India.

In fact, fifteen years were to pass before he came back, and by then I was in my early thirties, the author of a book that had become something of a best-seller. The previous fifteen years had been a struggle—the sort of struggle that every young freelance writer experiences—but at last the hard work was paying off and the royalties were beginning to come in.

I was living in a small cottage on the outskirts of the hill-station of Fosterganj, working on another book, when I received an unexpected visitor.

He was a thin, stooped, grey-haired man in his late fifties, with a straggling moustache and discoloured teeth. He looked feeble and harmless but for his eyes which were pale cold blue. There was something slightly familiar about him.

'Don't you remember me? He asked. 'Not that I really expect you to, after all these years....'

'Wait a minute. Did you teach me at school?'

'No—but you're getting warm.' He put his suitcase down and I glimpsed his name on the airlines label. I looked up in astonishment. 'You're not—you couldn't be....'

'Your Uncle Bill,' he said with a grin and extended his hand. 'None other!' And he sauntered into the house.

I must admit that I had mixed feelings about his arrival. While I had never felt any dislike for hi, I hadn't exactly approved of what he had done. Poisoning, I felt, was a particularly reprehensible way of getting rid of inconvenient people: not that I could think of any commendable ways of getting rid of them! Still, it had happened a long time ago, he'd been punished, and presumably he was a reformed character.

'And what have you been doing all these years?' he asked me, easing himself into the only comfortable chair in the room.

'Oh just writing,' I said.

'Yes, I heard about your last book. It's quite a success, isn't it?'

'It's doing quite well. Have you read it?'

'I don't do much reading.'

'And what have you been doing all these years, Uncle Bill?'

'Oh, knocking about here and there. Worked for a soft drink company for some time. And then with a drug firm. My knowledge of chemicals was useful.'

'Weren't you with Aunt Mabel in South Africa?'

'I saw quite a lot of her, until she died a couple of years ago. Didn't you know?'

'No. I've been out of touch with relatives.' I hoped he'd take that as a hint. 'And what about her husband?'

'Died too, not long after. Not many of us left, my boy. That's why, when I saw something about you in the papers, I thought—why not go and seem my only nephew again?'

'You're welcome to stay a few days,' I said quickly. 'Then I have to go to Bombay.' (This was a lie, but I did not relish the prospect of looking after Uncle Bill for the rest of his days.)

'Oh, I won't be staying long,' he said. 'I've got a bit of money put by in Johannesburg. It's just that—so far as I know—you're my only living relative, and I thought it would be nice to see you again.'

Feeling relieved, I set about trying to make Uncle Bill as comfortable as possible. I gave him my bedroom and turned the window-seat into a bed for myself. I was a hopeless cook but, using all my ingenuity, I scrambled some eggs for supper. He waved aside my apologies; he'd always been a frugal eater, he said. Eight years in gaol had given him a cast-iron stomach.

He did not get in my way but left me to my writing and my lonely walks. He seemed content to sit in the spring sunshine and smoke his pipe.

It was during our third evening together that he said, 'Oh, I almost forgot. There's a bottle of sherry, in my suitcase. I brought it especially for you.'

'That was very thoughtful of you. Uncle Bill. How did you know I was fond of sherry?'

'Just my intuition. You do like it, don't you?'

'There's nothing like a good sherry.'

He went to his bedroom and came back with an unopened bottle of South African sherry.

'Now you just relax near the fire,' he said agreeably. 'I'll open the bottle and fetch glasses.'

He went to the kitchen while I remained near the electric fire, flipping through some journals. It seemed to me that Uncle Bill was taking rather a long time. Intuition must be a family trait, because it came to me quite suddenly—the thought that Uncle Bill might be intending to poison me.

After all, I thought, here he is after nearly fifteen years, apparently for purely sentimental reasons. But I had just published a best-seller. And I was his nearest relative. If I was to die, Uncle Bill could lay claim to my estate and probably live comfortably on my royalties for the next five or six years!

What had really happened to Aunt Mabel and her husband, I wondered. And where did Uncle Bill get the money for an air ticket to India?

Before I could ask myself any more questions, he reappeared with the glasses on a tray. He set the tray on a small table that stood between us. The glasses had been filled. The sherry sparkled.

I stared at the glass nearest me, trying to make out if the liquid in it was cloudier than that in the other glass. But there appeared to be no difference.

I decided I would not take any chances. It was a round tray, made of smooth Kashmiri walnut wood. I turned it round with my index finger, so that the glasses changed places.

'Why did you do that?' asked Uncle Bill.

'It's a custom in these parts. You turn the tray with the sun, a complete revolution. It brings good luck.'

Uncle Bill looked thoughtful for a few moments, then said, 'Well, let's have some more luck,' and turned the tray around again.

'Now you've spoilt it,' I said. 'You're not supposed to keep revolving it! That's bad luck. I'll have to turn it about again to cancel out the bad luck.'

The tray swung round once more, and Uncle Bill had the glass that was meant for me.

'Cheers!' I said, and drank from my glass.

It was good sherry.

Uncle Bill hesitated. Then he shrugged, said 'Cheers', and drained his glass quickly.

But he did not offer to fill the glasses again.

Early next morning he was taken violently ill. I heard him retching in his room, and I got up and went to see if there was anything I could do. He was groaning, his head hanging over the side of the bed. I brought him a basin and a jug of water.

'Would you like me to fetch a doctor?' I asked.

He shook his head. 'No I'll be all right. It must be something I ate.'

'It's probably the water. It's not too good at this time of the year. Many people come down with gastric trouble during their first few days in Fosterganj.'

'Ah, that must be it,' he said, and doubled up as a fresh spasm of pain and nausea swept over him.

He was better by evening—whatever had gone into the glass must have been by way of the preliminary dose and a day later he was well enough to pack his suitcase and announce his departure. The climate of Fosterganj did not agree with him, he told me.

Just before he left, I said; 'Tell me, Uncle, why did you drink it?'

'Drink what? The water?'

'No, the glass of sherry into which you'd slipped one of your famous powders.'

He gaped at me, then gave a nervous whinnying laugh. 'You will have your little joke, won't you?'

'No, I mean it,' I said. 'Why did you drink the stuff? It was meant for me, of course.'

He looked down at his shoes, then gave a little shrug and turned away.

'In the circumstances,' he said, 'it seemed the only decent thing to do.'

I'll say this for Uncle Bill: he was always the perfect gentleman.

Hanging at the Mango-Tope

Ruskin Bond

The two captive policemen, inspector Hukam Singh and Sub-Inspector Guler Singh, were being pushed unceremoniously along the dusty, deserted, sun-drenched road. The people of the village had made themselves scarce. They would reappear only when the dacoits went away.

The leader of the dacoit gang was Mangal Singh Bundela, great-grandson of a Pindari adventurer who had been a thorn in the side of the British. Mangal was doing his best to be a thorn in the flesh of his own Government. The local police force had been strengthened recently but it was still inadequate for dealing with the dacoits who knew the ravines better than any surveyor. The dacoit Mangal had made a fortune out of ransom: his chief victims were the sons of wealthy industrialists, moneylenders or landowners. But today he had captured two police officials; of no value as far as ransom went, but prestigious prisoners who could be put to other uses....

Mangal Singh wanted to show off in front of the police. He would kill at least one of them—his reputation demanded it—but he would let the other go, in order that his legendary power and ruthlessness be given a maximum publicity. A legend is always a help!

His red and green turban was tied rakishly to one side. His dhoti extended right down to his ankles. His slippers were embroidered with gold and silver thread. His weapon was no ancient matchlock, but a well-greased 303 rifle. Two of his men had similar rifles. Some had revolvers. Only the smaller fry carried swords or country-made pistols. Mangal Singh's gang, though traditional in many ways, was up-to-date in the matter of weapons. Right now they had the policemen's guns too.

'Come along, Inspector sahib,' said Mangal Singh, in tones of police barbarity, tugging at the rope that encircled the stout Inspector's midriff. 'Had you captured me today, you would have been a hero. You would have taken all the credit, even though you could not keep up with your men in the ravines. Too bad you chose to remain sitting in your jeep with the Sub-Inspector. The jeep will be useful to us, you will not. But I would like you to be a hero all the same—and there is none better than a dead hero!'

Mangal Singh's followers doubled up with laughter. They loved their leader's cruel sense of humour.

'As for you, Guler Singh,' he continued, giving his attention to the Sub-Inspector, 'You are a man from my own village. You should have joined me long ago. But you were never to be trusted. You thought there would be better pickings in the police, didn't you?'

Guler Singh said nothing, simply hung his head and wondered what his fate would be. He felt certain that Mangal Singh would devise some diabolical and fiendish method of dealing with his captives. Guler Singh's only hope was Constable Ghanshyam, who hadn't been caught by the dacoits because, at the time of the ambush, he had been in the bushes relieving himself.

'To the mango-tope!' said Mangal Singh, prodding the policemen forward.

'Listen to me, Mangal,' said the perspiring Inspector, who was ready to try anything to get out of his predicament. 'Let me go, and I give you my word there'll be no trouble for you in this area as long as I am posted here. What could be more convenient than that?'

'Nothing,' said Mangal Singh. 'But your word isn't good. *My* word is different. I have told my men that I will hang you at the mango-tope, and I mean to keep my word. But I believe in fair-play—I like a little sport! You may yet go free if your friend here, Sub-Inspector Guler Singh, has his wits about him.'

The Inspector and his subordinate exchanged doubtful puzzled looks. They were not to remain puzzled for long. On reaching the mango-tope, the dacoits produced a good strong hempen rope, one end looped into a slip-knot. Many a garland of marigolds had the Inspector received during his mediocre career. Now, for the first time, he was being garlanded with a hangman's noose. He had seen hangings; he had rather enjoyed them; but he had no stomach for his own. The Inspector begged for mercy. Who wouldn't have in his position?

'Be quiet,' commanded Mangal Singh. 'I do not want to know about your wife and your children and the manner in which they will starve. You shot my son last year.'

'Not I!' cried the Inspector. 'It was some other.'

'You led the party. But now, just to show you that I'm a sporting fellow, I am going to have you strung up from this tree, and then I am going to give Guler Singh six shots with a rifle and if he can sever the rope that suspends you before you are dead, well then, you can remain alive and I will let you go! For your sake, I hope the Sub-Inspector's aim is good. He will have to shoot fast. My man Phambiri, who has made this noose, was once executioner in a city jail. He guarantees that you won't last more than fifteen seconds at the end of *his* rope.'

Guler Singh was taken to a spot about forty yards. A rifle was thrust into his hands. Two dacoits clambered into the branches of the mango tree. The Inspector, his hands tied behind, could only gaze at them in horror. His mouth opened and shut as though he already had need of more air. And then, suddenly, the rope went taut, up went the Inspector, his throat caught in a vice, while the branch of the tree shook and mango-blossoms fluttered to the ground. The Inspector dangled from the rope, his feet about three feet about the ground.

'You can shoot,' said Mangal Singh, nodding to the Sub-Inspector.

And Guler-Singh, his hands trembling a little, raised the rifle to his shoulder and fired three shots in rapid succession. But the rope was swinging violently and the Inspector's body was jerking about like a fish on a hook. The bullets went wide.

Guler Singh found the magazine empty. He reloaded, wiped the stinging sweat from his eyes, raised the rifle again, took more careful aim. His hands were steadier now. He rested the sights on the upper portion of the rope, where there was less motion. Normally he was a good shot, but he had never been asked to demonstrate his skill in circumstances such as these.

The Inspector still gyrated at the end of his rope. There was life in him yet. His face was purple. The world, in those choking moments, was a medley of upside-down roofs and a red sun spinning slowly towards him.

Guler Singh's rifle cracked again. An inch or two wide this time. But the fifth shot found its mark, sending small tuffs of rope winging into the air.

The shot did not sever the rope; it was only a nick.

Guler Singh had one shot left. He was quite calm. The rifle-sight followed the rope's swing, less agitated now that the Inspector's convulsions were lessening. Guler Singh felt sure he could sever the rope this time.

And then, as his finger touched the trigger, an odd, disturbing thought slipped into his mind, hung there, throbbing: 'Whose life are you trying to save? Hukam Singh has stood in the way of your promotion more than once. He had you charge-sheeted for accepting fifty rupees from an unlicensed rickshaw-puller. He makes you do all the dirty work, blames you when things go wrong, takes the credit when there is credit to be taken. But for him, you'd be an Inspector!'

The rope swayed slightly to the right. The rifle moved just a fraction to the left. The last shot rang out, clipping a sliver of bark from the mango tree.

The Inspector was dead when they cut him down.

'Bad luck,' said Mangal Singh Bundela. 'You nearly saved him. But the next time I catch up with you, Guler Singh, it will be your turn to hang from the mango tree. So keep well away! You know that I am a man of my word. I keep it now, by giving you your freedom.'

A few minutes later the party of dacoits had melted away into the late afternoon shadows of the scrub forest. There was the sound of a jeep starting up. Then silence—a silence so profound that it seemed to be shouting in Guler Singh's ears.

As the village people began to trickle out of their houses, Constable Ghanshyam appeared as if from nowhere, swearing that he had lost his way in the jungle. Several people had seen the incident from their windows; they were unanimous in praising the Sub-Inspector for his brave attempt to save his superior's life. He had done his best.

'It is true,' thought Guler Singh. 'I did my best.'

That moment of hesitation before the last shot, the question that had suddenly reared up in the darkness of his mind, had already gone from his memory. We remember only what we want to remember.

'I did my best,' he told everyone.

And so he had.

Helping Mummy

NORAH C. JAMES

It was so hot in the cabin that it was difficult to breathe.
Tommy, who was seven, sat watching his mother washing
Baby. He looked round the cabin for the hundredth time.
There was hardly a thing left that he wasn't tired of looking
at. Of course, there was still the electric fan. It was fun to
watch it whirling round and round so fast that it looked like
a film of water. The porthole too, that was interesting, because
he hadn't found out what the two big screws at each side were
for. The porthole was wide open this morning, and the sky
outside a burning blue.

Tommy began to fidget as he sat on the edge of his berth.
He'd been a good boy this morning and dressed himself quickly
when Mummy had told him to. He'd been sitting still for ages
and ages and he was tired of it.

'Mayn't I go on deck now, Mummy?' he asked.

'No, darling. Wait till I've given Baby his bottle.'

Ruth, who was Tommy's younger sister, looked up from her picture book.

'Mayn't we go now, Mummy? I'm so hot.'

'Not yet, Ruth. You heard me just tell Tommy to wait till Baby's ready.'

Mrs Rogers was terribly tired. First there had been the heavy nursing of her husband through his long illness and then this nightmare of a voyage. It was worse even than she had anticipated, bringing three small children back from the Philippines alone. The shock of her husband's death was passing a little and she was beginning to realise her loss. It would have been quite different if he had been with them. He was so good with the children. Anyway, it was better not to think about him or she'd only start crying and that was upsetting for the children. She wondered what was wrong with Baby, he was awfully fretful. Half the night crying and crying. It must be maddening for the people in the next cabin, but she couldn't do anything about it. She'd walked up and down till she could have dropped with weariness.

Tommy was watching his mother. She wasn't smiling or anything. It was a horrid morning. It was mean of Ruth not to let him look at her picture book. There wasn't a thing he could do to amuse himself. Why didn't Baby stop crying? The noise began to irritate him. He put his hands over both his ears and began to clap them rapidly. The sound of the baby's screams changed in quality then. It became a queer up-and-down broken sound, something like the sea breaking on the shore. It was quite a change to hear it that way.

'Ruth,' he called. His sister looked up and stared at him.

'Do what I'm doing and hear how funny Baby sounds.' Ruth imitated him and both the children sat there with their hands clapping their ears.

Mrs Rogers felt almost distracted.

'Oh, whatever is the matter? If you don't stop crying I'll put you through the porthole. There, there, Mummy's own, there.' She got up and began to walk up and down the narrow space between the berths, rocking the baby as she did so. Once she nearly tripped over Tommy's legs which were sticking out straight as he sat on the berth. She saw his wide blue eyes staring at her, and she smiled.

'Darling, I think I'd better go and ask Mrs Green if she'll watch Baby for me just while I get his bottle ready.'

'Can't I fetch her, Mummy?' asked Tommy.

'No, be a good boy and wait here. I don't like you going down those stairs. They're so steep.'

She put the baby down, who was now quiet, and went out of the room. As soon as she had gone it began to scream again.

'Shall I pick him up?' said Ruth.

'No, I don't think you'd better,' Tommy answered.

'Why does he go on crying and crying?' his sister asked.

'I don't know. Ruth?'

'Yes.'

'Did you hear Mummy say that if he didn't stop she'd put him through the porthole?'

'Yes. He mightn't like it!'

'Oh, I don't suppose he'd mind or Mummy wouldn't have told him she'd do it.'

He got off his berth and went over to the cot where the baby lay. Its little red face was crumpled up as it yelled. Tommy made up his mind suddenly.

'Help me lift him,' he said to Ruth.

A little doubtfully she did what he said and they carried him over to the trunk that stood beneath the porthole.

'Hold him carefully, while I climb up,' he said to Ruth. When he was on top of the trunk he said:

'Now give him to me.' His sister stretched her arms until Tommy was able to take the baby from her. Then he stood upright. The porthole was on a level with his eyes. He rested the bundle on the edge for a second.

While he stood there the ship rolled slightly, and he lost his balance and let go of the baby. When he was upright again he saw that it had disappeared.

There was a blessed stillness in the cabin. He got off the trunk and went and sat down again on his berth.

Mrs Rogers came back into the room. She went over to the empty cot.

'Where's Baby?' she said. It was the tone of her voice that prevented Tommy from answering. Ruth said:

'He wouldn't stop crying, Mummy, so Tommy did what you said.'

'Did what I said? What d'you mean? Tell me?' Her voice rose and she shook the little girl. Tommy answered then:

'I put him through the porthole, Mummy.'

Really Was a Bluetit

E.H.W. Meyerstein

'He was *not* fooling Schindler,' the young man in flannels asserted hotly, pacing up and down the glaring white of the *aia*, the large platform of cement specially built for agrarian rites, while the host, his disputant, in a vermilion blaze, spread out the newly picked tomatoes on wicker tables to dry in the fierce Ligurian sun; 'I won't have that. I know it's said by almost everyone, but it's flat nonsense.'

'You cannot get away from the fact that the song of the yellow-hammer cannot be twisted into an arpeggio.'

'I don't try to. It is not the intervals but the rhythm that is in point, and that arpeggio' (whistling) 'is quite near enough *a little bit of bread and cheese* to satisfy any normal person's hankering for programme.'

'What *does* it matter,' came a happy languid voice from the dense protecting foliage of a fig tree, 'what was intended *anywhere* in the "Pastoral Symphony"? Beethoven only meant you to enjoy it, and nobody will ever be able to prove whether he was fooling his biographer about the yellow-hammers in the *Andante* or not; so why get warm?'

Lucia Carpa, the speaker, was a Spanish Jewess who had married an Italian naval officer with a perfect knowledge of English and a penchant for gardening and the Georgics on his leaves. She had no offspring, and to her race's gift for discerning talent when it has got its head just above the water she added a genuine strain of pity, more indigenous to Ireland than Israel, for young people with childlike minds. No one could class Denzil Straker's mind among these. His latest symphonic poem, *Budgerigars*, had been given with circumstance and praise at the first week of the Promenades, and, sure of his ground, he had flown to Nervi for rest and inspiration. The prospect of an early *vendemmia* had set a theme already in his brain, and he was in the throes of argument for argument's sake, which is the surest sign that a creative mind is not fatigued.

'No one agrees about the songs of birds,' she went on. 'Some people will tell you my vivacious little unmelodious friend the bluetit, or billy-biter, as a Lancashire man I met once called him, says *chica chica chee chee*; others are equally emphatic that his message is *zit zit tzitee*, or *tsee tsee tsirr*; and somebody, I forget who, told me once it was some Latin words. It wasn't you, Hippolito, and I have forgotten what the words were, but certainly not in the least like the other versions.'

'Give me the gannet,' said her husband, flicking a wasp off a tomato with supreme unconcern; 'he is the only bird who can pronounce the name of a Roman emperor—Caracalla.'

'You seem to know a lot about birds, Signora Carpa. Is it true that at Verona I shall see little live owls chained to posts in the market-place looking down on heaps of dead becaficos?'

'Quite true! Don't remind me! I always try to avoid the Piazza dell' Erbe, but it is so hard. I hate the sight of a dead bird. Why, as a child, a great oval pastelle of a dead dove had regularly to be taken down from the room I used to have when I stayed with my grandmother in Prince's Gate. No, I don't know a lot about birds, but the bluetit comes into my life in a curious way. Shall I tell him now, Hippolito, or wait till the evening? In this golden sunlight it will seem less nightmarish.'

'It is always that, my dear. He won't enjoy his coffee, if you tell it later, and I shall have to listen. Now I can get the tomatoes laid out. Tell him now.'

'I can't imagine anything nightmarish about a bluetit,' said the young man, squatting on the bright cemented space.

'No more could I, at your age.'

'Neither can I *now*,' said the naval man, 'but Lucia has a Semitic *morbidezza* all her own. Don't let her infect you!'

'Isn't that like a man? To queer one's pitch at starting! Well, if you promise not to interrupt, either of you—Hippolito won't; he's done *his* worst—you shall hear.'

'I promise *I* won't interrupt,' Straker exclaimed boyishly.

'Well, when I was a young woman I had a great and sudden disappointment, which I can't go into; it was many years before I met Hippolito, and for a time it completely embittered me. All the joy went out of people and of everything I did or looked at. I suppose it was what you call disillusionment. A writer we know here tells me it is the sort of phase hard-working creative people go through about forty, and you'll find something not unlike it in John Stuart Mill's *Autobiography*. Anyhow it took me very badly, and it was more than eighteen months before I regained—what would you say?—poise. That began to come through the events I am telling you. My people had tried everything short of getting me certified. I didn't talk wildly; I was completely listless. Books and papers would be offered to me, and I would just take them up and drop them again. One morning at breakfast my father pushed the paper towards me with the illustrated page uppermost. There was no particular news that day, so far as he was concerned, but my eye fell on the photograph of a young man in a trilby hat, and something stirred in me. I looked at it again and read the caption. Then I turned to one of the inner sheets, and knew there was something I must do. It was nine o'clock. After the meal I went upstairs, put on my hat, and walked to Marylebone Police Court.

'I won't tell you his name. I'll call him Oswald. He was not one of our people, but a Roman Catholic, the seventeen-year-old son of a baker and confectioner. It was a good photograph. He had cut his sweetheart's throat with a pocket-knife while she was eating an apple at a street-corner, a little girl of twelve. The whole proceedings only took an hour and a half, and he was committed for trial at the Old Bailey. I judged him *then* to have been insane. There was apparently no motive. The deed had taken place in broad daylight in the neighbourhood of the homes of both parties, and Oswald, if his mother's evidence was to be believed, had run back home immediately afterwards, with a bright smiling face, and the bloodstained knife, closed in one hand, and shouted, "Come and see! Really was a bluetit!" The injured child had staggered to her home, and died an hour after being removed to hospital 'Boy loved me,' was all she could, or would, say.

'I had reached the court before the case was called, and sat behind the dock. I had a perfect view of the young man as he entered and as he left it. How shall I describe him? There was the same look of childlike attention on the face as in Lady Stanley's famous picture *His First Offence*, though, of course, he was some years older than its subject; but nobody could have said it was a bad face; on the contrary it was stamped with candour and simplicity. I was glad I had come, and not disobeyed the summons of that Press photograph. But the moment the mother, a reddish-haired virago, came out with her only boy's ("our roundsman's") remark, I realised, in a sort of vision, that, whatever was meant by it, Oswald was the very image of a bluetit, a bird I particularly used to notice as a child in the winter, when we stayed with my grandfather at Alresford. His fidgeting, where he sat, put me in mind of one that regularly disported itself on a maple just outside the drawing-room window, and that quaint puckish, or perhaps I should say Mongolian, setting of the black lustreless eyes, I cannot tell you why, seemed birdlike and titlike beyond the rest. Once I grasped this, everything else seemed to fit into the picture; his shabby olive-green suit was the bird's back; he wore a yellow pull-over, crown-blue tie and socks; and a very white shirt showed, I liked to think, where the secondaries should. Although the case was of the most tragic type, and, quite clearly, there was neither money forthcoming to brief counsel with a flair for obtaining lunacy verdicts in capital issues, nor the element of sensational disclosure that spurs the Press to support a defence, I felt curiously elated and bright, certainly not as a result of morbid curiosity—you must take my word for that—though desperately aware that if my family knew where I was they would regard my malady as almost beyond cure. The moment the prisoner stepped down, a police officer standing ready in case he should faint, his eyes caught mine, and I felt—oh, how shall I put it!—as if a reviving draught were being poured down my parched throat. No! I know what you are thinking. Love? It wasn't that at all. I had been in love. This was something quite different; but even then, with the emotion fresh and obscure, and the future unseen, I knew instinctively that I was on the path of health.

'I drifted out of the court with the crowd, and made my way home in a dream. My absence had not been noted. I had bought a newspaper going along, and now I cut out Oswald's photograph. Questions might have been asked had the house copy been found mutilated. The next step was obvious, as soon as I drank in the now known features. I must call on his family; I knew the address; it had been stated in court, a mean street in Kentish Town. I could combine the visit with one to the Zoo, and look at the bluetits there. I slept well that night—my nights had lately been restless—and the suggestion of the Zoo at breakfast gave pleasure. Lucia was beginning to take an interest in something, you see. Nor were objections raised to my going alone, since my lethargy or stupor had worn out the patience of every companion. When I got up to my room I clapped my hands and danced for joy in my secret.

'Of course, I might be mistaken for a journalist or worse and turned away from the door; yet I believed that saturation in that photograph and the birds at the Zoo would make me not unwelcome. At first I thought I would say I came to help, and wondered if I should put so much money by to ease the legal expenses, which must be heavy, even if the boy were hanged. But I decided against this while at the Zoo; I would say I came for *their* help, that I could not rest for thinking about their son, and leave it at that. Here was the shop! The family lived over it, and the tragedy had taken place at the next street corner. A woman was standing inside behind a twin pile of eclairs and cream buns, the woman who had given evidence yesterday. The braveness to carry on! I found it not hard to speak:

' "I am not a reporter, but I was in court yesterday. I felt it would help me to come and say how sorry I am. I have known trouble."

' "You are one of them probation women, I'm thinking. Very glad, I'm sure. What did you say I could do for you?"

'My brain suddenly went blank. I had fired my shot. I had not quite expected to encounter this self-sufficient pride. What I should have said next, I don't know, but the father came in, a squat white-faced man with tortured grey eyes. The woman turned to him with: "This lady's a stranger; not from the newspapers."

' "What is it, lady?" he said gently.

' "I cannot help thinking about your son. I want to help him, or rather I want you to help me. I don't think there is anything I can do, unless I gave something towards the defence."

' "Don't you trouble," he said; "I see you are genuine. Come in! You mind the shop," he added, to his wife.

'That was the beginning. He saw I was genuine. I suppose nobody had seen that before, or, at any rate, made me feel it; and when I tell you that these people would not accept one penny of mine, and were quite content that I should have tea with them now and again, you will readily understand that a new beauty came into my life, and I felt that sleep was not the best that life could give. That afternoon they told me that their boy (he was their only child) had always been childish with regard to birds, which from his earliest years, would come to him, and feed out of his hand, not only sparrows and robins, but shy wayward creatures like the wren, and even, so they averred, a kingfisher. Until his fourteenth year they had lived at Horsham, and it was his uncle's business that they took over in Kentish Town, on his death, and now they rued the day they came to London. I asked if Oswald had ever had a pet bluetit; they said not, but they did not know of a country bird on which he was not on good terms. He had no violent habits, and would not watch a fowl being killed. His deed was inexplicable. I should go and see the mother of the poor little girl. They were still friendly with her. I asked if he had many girl friends, and was surprised to receive the answer "Only this one."

' "None in the country?"

' "No, none at all, till now. He didn't take to girls, or they didn't to him," the father said; "any amount of boy pals!"

' "You see," said the mother, who interrupted at this point, "he was always a good boy. Plenty of spirit, but we never had to correct him."

' "How do you explain what he said about the bluetit?"

' "I can't," she said, tearful for the first time, "can't no how. You understand, miss, *he's not mad.*"

'I had to understand that; both parents were firm there. With the curious illogicality of their class they would prefer what was dearest to them to be executed rather than confined as a lunatic. "So you see," the father ended; "we don't want no expense for a great lawyer to make judge and jury say he weren't in his senses, nor does the boy want that. We don't want to lose him, but if he's to live he must be right-minded like us. If his father and mother were rich, steps would be taken to prove him mad, no doubt. We *may* be poor, but we've set our faces agin that."

'I left that house exalted; there is no other word.

'Tea I had had there, and found my parents and elder sister sitting over the remains of theirs. They had had visitors, the Gollers. Vanessa Goller and her father, Sir Luke, the fashionable surgeon, had been over two prisons. They were full of the self-devoting energies of an art master and his wife who taught the juvenile-adult 'star' class to make leather and silver objects. "There, Lucia," said my father, "there's an occupation for you! I dare say I could write to Major Greathead—where did they make him Governor, Wandsworth or Pentonville?—and see about your going in one day a week. You haven't done any leather-work for a long while now, but I don't expect your fingers have lost their cunning." This was meant considerately, and my mother chimed in, "Yes, dear; think about that, do! Vanessa said some of the young men looked quite refined. At the remand prison they showed them a young murderer, waiting his trial, only a boy. That is what you want, contact with all different kinds of humanity. I think it so brave of Vanessa; she offered to go with her father."

' "She hasn't thought of going to the murderer's *home*," I said.

' "No, of course not! Nothing morbid like that. Just her large interest in the world—see everything, that's what I always say; see everything, but don't *touch* everything."

' "How *could* you think that of Vanessa?" my only sister added, and my father clinched the matter with, "I will say that about the Gollers, they watch life sympathetically at close quarters, but they never pry too deep, *never*."

'Thus I realised that I must on no account speak of my experience at home; it simply would not be understood. Neither did my family refer again to the prison matter, though they dined with the Gollers next week. Nor did I attend Oswald's trial. It didn't last five minutes. He pleaded guilty, and his parents were grateful for escaping the attentions of the Press by this simple step. The judge, after passing sentence of death, said the facts of the case would be before the Home Secretary, and a reprieve was granted actually before the petition, got up in the neighbourhood of the crime, was sent in. It was considered possible, I learnt, that the parents would regain their only child in ten years. I visited them regularly, and they showed me his letters, queer inexpressive formalities. I never wrote to him, but one Saturday afternoon in his second year in prison, when, by the way, I had almost entirely lost my listlessness, and behaved outwardly like any other young woman, I went with them to visit him.

'It was a cold, bright day, and the hills round Maidstone were covered with snow. After entering by a postern gate in a side street we waited in a room adjacent to it, which contained a number of newly baked loaves. Then we were led across the yard to a classroom, where the young man was brought in by an officer, and allowed to embrace his people. He had been apprised of my coming, and shook hands frankly. As I took his hand, the whole scene before me was blotted out, and I seemed to look on a bluetit twisting itself round a twig, like the little acrobat it is. I ought to say that I had not worked myself up into this state; on the contrary, I was eagerly taking note of the immediate surroundings. The vision was somehow forced upon me. When I came back to myself we were all seated, we on one side of a table, he and the warder on the other. I took little part in the home talk, though occasionally a glance was made in my direction, as to a friend of the family. After half an hour the officer rose, and we followed suit to say good-bye, and I wondered if I should have the same experience when we shook hands, as we did after the parental kisses. I *saw* nothing, except the red healthy cheeks and the dark lustreless eyes, but (could I have imagined it?) he didn't say "Good-bye," but "Really was a bluetit!"

'As soon as we were outside the prison I put my doubt to the test by asking his mother why he said that. "Oh," she said, without hesitation, "that was his way of telling you what he was in for," "As it were the number on his arm," her husband added. This might be the reason, yet I was not wholly satisfied. In Oswald's next letter home there was a message of thanks to me for coming to see him, but no desire expressed that I should come again; neither did I do so. Three years later, just a month before I first met my husband, he was released on licence.

'I had now completely gained poise, and went everywhere. I am, in any case, tenacious of old associations, and I had continued to visit the parents, who were greatly respected in their neighbourhood for staying where they were and living down their notoriety. One incident, and only one, happened in that long interval with any bearing on my own secret little fund of pleasure. Sir Luke Goller, who always liked my handwriting and hated typescript, asked me to catalogue the books in his country-house at Studland, while Vanessa, who had had a breakdown, was abroad. Among them was Baptista Porta's *Physiognomonia*, with its curious engravings showing the resemblance between human and beast-and-bird faces. I was sitting with this on my lap, by the open library window, in front of which extended the branch of a copper-beech, when I heard a scuffling noise, and, looking up, observed two bluetits fighting, or rather one attacking the other on the end of this branch, the ferocity of the one uppermost being astonishing; he seemed bent on digging his beak into the throat of the other, which, with wing outspread, was clinging by one foot to the oscillating twig. I jumped up and clapped my hands. Both flew away, and were out of sight in a second. Then I looked down and saw the old book open at the picture of the ape and the ape-faced man. I cannot explain; it seemed a warning somehow, and both Sir Luke and Lady Goller remarked on my silence at lunch (it was early autumn) al fresco under that tree.

'That November Oswald came out of prison and resumed his employment as baker's roundsman. I purposely did not put in an appearance at his home for some months, though I sent my usual Christmas gift to the parents, and something for him, which he acknowledged in a manly note written in a minute hand; but in February his father wrote that he was in bed with a dislocated thigh, owing to a collision with another baker's boy, and would like to see me. He was sitting up in bed eating an apple off a plate with a knife on it, and started talking about the bearded woman at Barnum's whom his mother had seen as a little girl; "We're not old enough to remember her, are we, miss?" Then he went on to say that *Dead Man's Rock*, which he had just finished, looked to him as if it had been written after *Treasure Island*, which he had read "in there," but there were "points about it." At this moment his mother, who had been standing behind my chair, went out to make me some tea, and he took occasion to thank me again for thinking of him, adding, rather illogically, that the mother of Eva (the little girl he had killed) had sent him this apple, and was coming in that afternoon. Opposite the bed, placed longways to the wall, was a window looking out on the yard at the back of the house, and over it a birdcage containing two canaries. I looked up at them, as a ready way of turning the subject, and had got as far as "The birds are still your friends, Oswald," when his nose was on my cheek, and I saw a glint somewhere near my throat. I don't know to this day what I did; I don't think I either screamed or fainted. The horror was too intense. I heard a voice say, "Bless me, I've forgotten the matches. *Oswald!*" There was a clatter of steel on china, and the face fell back on the pillow. The kind pressure of a woman's arm was round my shoulders; oh yes, the mother was hurrying me out of the room. I am sure I said "I think I'll go away. Let me go!" "He didn't mean you any harm, dear. I was close by." "Oh, let me go, please! I shan't speak of this." "We know that; we trust you. But he didn't mean you any harm. Here's Eva's mother; *she'll* tell you so." Then I saw that we were on the stairs, and another woman, with a younger, thinnish, freckled face, confronted us. "Has anything happened?" she asked. "No, I only forgot there was a knife with that apple." "Oh!" she said. "Never you mind, lady! There's no vice in him, as I hope for heaven there isn't, and my little Eva was taken. *We don't all kiss the same.*"

'There was no answer to this. I told the mother I understood; I would write; really I did not want any tea, nor to speak to Oswald's father, who was in the shop. She insisted that I should let the other woman see me to my bus. I had to do this. I noticed my escort had a bag. I entreated her to let her friends know that I bore none of them any ill will; if they understood that, I need not write, and they need not write to me. "I'll make it right," she said; "They asked me to-day on purpose to meet you. They wanted you to see this." She opened the bag, and took out a small photograph: "This is Eva," she said. I started back as I looked at it; it might have been *my* face at twelve. "Ah" she went on, as if reading my thoughts, "but you're like that *now.*" "This wasn't in the newspapers at the time," I managed to say. "No," came the reply, "they put in one that wasn't a bit like Eva." I couldn't speak; it was as if the knife were at my throat again. I saw that kind lean face, that had somehow won through its anguish, peering into mine, and a voice from—oh!—ever so far away: "Don't bother, dear, but let them or me know when you get married. Only that! Here's the bus.

Remember, I said I'd make things right. I've lost my only little girl through him, and I'm a woman of my word." She helped me in, and stood smiling on the pavement. I can see her now.

'In the bus I remembered in the early days Oswald's people had told me I should go and see this woman. Who knows? If I had, this dreadful experience might not have come my way; but again, if I had, I might never have entirely recovered from my apathy or decline. There's a price to be paid for everything in life.

'That's about all. I received no letters from any of the parties, and I wrote none then. As I told you, I had already met Hippolito, and it may well be that day's event precipitated our engagement. On my wedding-day we both sent Oswald's family a telegram, announcing the fact. It was answered by unsigned telegram thus: *"Happy days to both from us four."*'

'Her suggestion, not yours, to send that wire?' commented the young composer, and the Italian naval man took mock aim at his gleaming flannels with a tomato, and then suddenly dropped it.

Pendlebury's Trophy

John Eyten

I

Arthur St John Pendlebury—known to his intimates as 'Pen'—
was the beau-ideal of the cavalry subaltern, with plenty of
friends, money, and self-assurance. Before he had been in the
country a year, India was at his feet; this is not to say that he
had overstudied her languages or customs, but that he had
sufficient means for fulfilling any of his aspirations, which were
limited to picnics, polo ponies, and shikar trophies. To the latter
his first long leave was devoted. To one who has stalked the
Highland stag under the eye of an experienced man the stag of
Kashmir seems easy game, and satisfaction was in Pendlebury's
eye as he ran it over his pile of kit on Rawalpindi station: new
portmanteau; new gun-cases, containing his twelve-bore, his
Mannlicher Schonhauer, his Holland and Holland High Velocity;
fieldglasses and telescope; kodak, for recording triumphs; new

tent, fully equipped with every device for comfort and cooking—
altogether a capital outfit, pointing to an interesting addition
to the Scotch heads in the hall at Pendlebury, for he could not
fail to bag a Kashmiri stag or two in three weeks. To this
sentiment Ali Baksh, his Mohammedan servant, agreed in perfect
English ... capital man, Ali Baksh—a real treasure.

The drive from Rawalpindi to Srinagar was quite pleasant,
the scenery being almost English, though the road was only so-
so. On arrival Pendlebury resisted the tame temptations of
picnic-making, and got down to business at once. He was not
going to be bothered with consulting the old local bores in the
Club, because the obvious thing to do was to get hold of a native
fellow who could talk English a bit, and knew the ropes from
A to Z, and such a man was known to Ali Baksh, who would
find him out quietly and persuade him to accompany the saheb.
His friend, he said, was the best man in Kashmir, who being in
constant request, would accompany only noted shikaris. Ali
Baksh tactfully insinuated that Pendlebury belonged to the
latter category, and Pendlebury of course believed him—for
even the finished product of Eton and the Bullingdon is often
singularly artless in the experienced hands of an Indian bearer.

At eleven o'clock on the morning after arrival, Ali Baksh
produced the paragon, whose name was also something Baksh—
Pir Baksh, Pendlebury believed him to say. He was a fine-
looking, well-set-up fellow, with fierce moustaches and glittering
eyes; nicely turned out too, with a khaki suit of military cut,
mauve shirt, and neat puttees; he carried a long mountaineering
pole, and had glasses slung in a leather case over his shoulder,
and was altogether the type of what a shikari ought to look,

and indeed does look in magazine illustrations. To the experienced old bores in the Club he might have appeared to overdo the part, but to Pendlebury he was the very thing. Besides, he knew all the likely spots, had excellent chits from officers in quite good regiments, indicating invariable success, and, lastly, got on well with Ali Baksh.

So Pir Baksh was engaged on the spot—for the modest sum of one hundred rupees, paid in advance, for the three weeks' trip, and on the understanding that he would waste no time over uncertainties, but would lead on direct to the spot where an astounding stag had been marked down. About this stag there was no doubt whatever, for Pir Baksh himself resided in its neighbourhood, and knew its haunts and habits so well that the stag might almost be said to be one of the family. He had been keeping it, he said, for a General, but could not resist the temptation of seeing it fall to the rifle of so noble a saheb as Pendlebury. They parted quite effusively, after payment had been made, and Alki Baksh accompanied Pir Baksh to make the *bandobast*. Pendlebury washed his hands of these matters, so naturally did not see Pir hand over the stipulated thirty rupees to his friend Ali outside.

As Pendlebury remarked in the mess on his return from leave. 'What I like about this country is that you only have to get hold of a good servant, tell him what you want to do and how you like it, and say '*Bazar chalo, bandobast karo.*' He'll do the rest. Now I had a first-class *bandobast* up in Kashmir—never had to say a word myself; no use messing a good man about.'

And so it was—his two men certainly were not messed about, for between them they did everything, and ran

Pendlebury—engaging ponies and carriers on the basis of a twenty per cent commission for themselves; leading in men from the shops, who staggered beneath a vast weight of stores, some of which were destined for Pendlebury's consumption; making a great show of polishing things and cleaning clean rifles. There was nothing wrong with that *bandobast*, and Pendlebury could well afford to pay the hundred and fifty odd rupees which it was found necessary to disburse. In fact, the charm of the whole thing was that Pendlebury believed throughout that he was saving money—a fact which redounds to the credit of the astute pair.

The start for the first camp was worth watching; first rode Pendlebury, every inch a cavalry officer, his blue eyes full of good humour, and his cheeks quite pink with excitement; his shooting suit was good to look upon, and Ali Baksh could certainly polish boots. At a respectful distance behind him rode Pir Baksh, resplendent in Jodhpur breeches, while, last of all, Ali marshalled the kit, a fine staff in one hand, and in the other that emblem of the bearer, a brass hurricane lamp. It was a procession to be proud of, and successful shikar was in the very air.

The haunt of the famous stage was ten marches away, and Pendlebury beguiled them with small-game shooting and the taking of snapshots. The marches were very well run, and it was not the fault of Pir Baksh that a leather suitcase, the telescope, and a cartridge bag got lost in process of crossing a river. In fact Pendlebury thought Pir Baksh had behaved very openly about the whole thing, and had seemed to regard the matter as a personal loss—whereas, in truth, it was exactly the opposite. But for this mishap all went swimmingly.

They reached the little village at the edge of the forest in the evening, and Pendlebury's tent was pitched under delightful chenal trees near a little stream which looked first-class for trout. He could hardly sleep for excitement, and lay awake picturing the record stag and its record head, and hearing the sound of a high-pitched song in the bazaar, where, had he but known it, Pir and Ali were entertaining the local shikaris at his expense. Finally he shouted, '*Choop. Choop karo ek dam*!' and lay back with the satisfaction of one whose commands are obeyed.

Next day it was arranged that Pir Baksh should go for *khubr* of the stag, while Pendlebury fished the river for trout. So Pendlebury sallied out with his split-cane and fly-boxes, and a man to carry his net, and another man to bear his lunch, while Pir Baksh, with his glasses and pole and preposterous jodhpurs, departed in the opposite direction. It was curious that so confident and so famous a shikari should require the assistance of a local man, a stranger of ragged and unkempt appearance—but we will suppose that he too needed some one to carry his lunch.

Pendlebury had a pleasant enough day by the bright, clear stream, and brought home several minute trout for his dinner. Of the movements of Pir Baksh little is known, except that he went quite a distance into the forest, starting at 10 AM and returning at noon, after which hour he sat with Ali and the local talent in the Bazaar. Yet, when he was announced at 8 PM, he entered the tent wearily enough, with much bazaar dust on his boots and puttees—so much that Pendlebury could see that the fellow had had a pretty stiff day of it. Pir Baksh was mysterious and confidential; in response to Pendlebury's eager inquiries he allowed that he had seen the stag, but when Pendlebury whooped with delight, he qualified this intelligence with the remark that the stag was *bahut hoshiar*, and had only arrived on the scene in the late evening, after a complete day of tireless, lonely watching on the part of Pir Baksh. He had heard the stag at intervals and had not dared to move for fear of making it nervous. It would be as well to let it rest, under due observation, for a day or two, and then make certain of it. Incidentally he had heard in the bazaar on his return that another saheb, a well-known hunter, had set his heart on this stag and had hunted it for a month, but, since he had not seen fit to engage the services of Pir Baksh, he had not had a shot. It was finally suggested that Pendlebury would do well to visit a noted pool three miles down stream for the next day or two, and this Pendlebury agreed to do. After all Pir Baksh knew the ropes, and this stag was worth waiting for.

So for the next two days Pendlebury lashed the stream for trout, while each morning Pir Baksh started with a set face for the jungle and spent the day in the bazaar, arriving each evening at a later hour and more visibly weary and dusty. Each evening, too, the antlers of the stag had grown with its cunning. Rowland Ward's book, which Pendlebury of course carried, had no record in it to touch this head, as described by Pir Baksh; to Rowland Ward the head should go for setting up—none of your local *mochis*. Pendlebury saw the footnote in that book—

'Shot by A. St J. Pendlebury, Esq, the Blue Hussars, Kashmir, 1920. A remarkable head, with record points, length and span.'

On the third evening Pir Baksh was very late indeed. Pendlebury had turned in, and had long lain listening to a perfect orgy in the bazaar, when, about midnight, Ali Baksh gave that deprecating cough whereby the Indian servant makes known his humble presence, and announced Pir Baksh.

A tired, grimy, dusty picture he made in the light of the electric torch, and a pitiful tale he told. He had sat up without food for a day and half a night—

'*Bahut kam kiya, saheb. Main bilkull bhuka ho gya—bilkull. Kuchh nahin khaya gya.*'

Great indeed had been the sufferings of the worthy man (considering they had been experienced in the bazaar), but he had seen the stag at close quarters, and something told him that the saheb would shoot it tomorrow.

Such a stag—a Barasingha indeed, with antlers like trees, and a roar like a river; such a stag had not been seen for twenty years, when 'Ismith' Saheb had missed just such a one, and had given him, Pir Baksh, his new rifle and a hundred golis, vowing he would never shoot again.... '*Kabhi ham aisa Barawala nahin dekha.*' Pendlebury was, of course, half out of his mind with excitement, and, had it been feasible, he would have gone out there and then and tried conclusions. As it was, he contented himself with lauding Pir Baksh to the skies, an honour which the latter accepted with sweet humility. He would make the *bandobast*; they would start out after tiffin, and would lie up till the evening. Let the saheb have no doubts; he would slay that stag, and his name would be great in Kashmir.... '*Kuchh shaqq nahin hai; qaza zarur hoga ... zarur.*'

Like an echo outside the tent, Ali Baksh repeated the comforting '*zarur.*'

II

Pendlebury arose at 6 AM for the stag which he was to see at 6 PM, and spent the most nerve-racking morning of his life. He cut himself shaving; he fiddled with his rifles, and asked a dozen times whether he should take the High Velocity or the little Mannlicher; he counted out ten rounds of ammunition and laid them ready ... then decided to take the other rifle, and counted out twenty more; then, finally changed his mind and decided to take both, with about thirty rounds; he stuffed his pipe too full, and broke the vulcanite stem in tapping it out; changed his boots three times; smoked quantities of cigarettes, and burnt a hole in his copy of Rowland Ward with one of them; and he ate neither a good breakfast nor a sufficient lunch.

In fact Pendlebury did his utmost to spoil his eye and his hand, instead of strolling out with a rod and forgetting the great stag in the excitement of landing a pound trout, as any of the old bores at the Club would have advised him to do.

At last the great moment arrived, and Ali Baksh whispered, 'Pir Baksh here, sir.' With an immense effort Pendlebury assumed the nonchalance he did not feel, and strolled out of the tent, where he found Pir Baksh carrying a rifle and looking very businesslike in ancient garments; a ragged, disreputable stranger had the other rifle. When Pendlebury, who was feeling nervous enough already, objected to the latter's presence, Pir Baksh pointed out the advantages of having a man on the spot to help skin the shikar, and so had his way. On the way Pendlebury did a great many things which the old bores at the Club would have deprecated: he smoked too many cigarettes— 'to steady his nerves'; he slogged along instead of walking quietly, thus laying up a clammy shirt for himself in the evening; also, he cursed the men for not hurrying, and then cursed still more when, half-way, he discovered that he had forgotten his second-best pipe, his flask, and his sandwiches. However, it was too late to do anything then.

They climbed uphill through thick forest bordering a little hill stream till they came to an open glen, with green moss at their feet and tall trees around them. Half-way up the glen Pir Baksh whispered a halt, and Pendlebury was led behind the trunk of a fallen tree, where he was asked to wait, without moving, while Pir Baksh and the stranger moved furtively off under cover of the trees.

Hours seemed to pass as Pendlebury fingered his Mannlicher, the final choice, expecting every moment to see the dark shape loom in the glen. Time and time again he opened his breech to see if the thing were working, and feverishly moved the backsight up and down the slide, finally leaving it at five hundred yards, when a sudden sound startled him.

It was booming, long-drawn ... the unmistakable roar of a stag far above him. He was at once certain that Pir Baksh had messed up the whole show, and that he ought to be farther up the glen; it would be dark for a certainty before the stag moved down; it was getting dark already. A twig cracked behind him, and he turned to see Pir Baksh behind him, holding his finger to his lips.

'Barawala ata,' whispered Pir Baksh, while Pendlebury got into a position of readiness; there was no doubt about the approach of the stag, for it roared more than once, and was evidently moving down the little stream.

A quarter of an hour passed—the sun sank—still no view of the stag; in five minutes it would be too dark to see the foresight. Pendlebury began to fidget, when suddenly Pir Baksh touched his arm, and pointed ... a dark shape was moving under the trees by the stream.

'*Woh hai, saheb,*' whispered Pir Baksh. '*Maro. Maro. Zarur lag jaega.*'

Pendlebury aimed his wavering piece in the direction of the dark shape, and squeezed the trigger....

There was a flash and a kick—then a commotion under the trees, as a big animal splashed with a snort through the tiny stream and crashed into the undergrowth beyond—farther and farther away.

'Damn!' said Pendlebury—not so Pir Baksh, who sprang to his feet with a wild '*Lag gya. Lag gya. Zachmi hai,*' and, motioning to Pendlebury to stay where he was, ran towards the stream, throwing out a parting '*Milega zarur.*'

It was quite dark when Pir Baksh returned and informed the ecstatic Pendlebury that the stag '*sekht zachmi ho gya. Khun bahut hai. Aiye, saheb.*' Up jumped Pendlebury and followed across the glen and the stream, where Pir Baksh borrowed his electric torch and searched the ground ... yes, there was blood ... first a mere drop on a leaf; then, five yards on, a bigger splash; farther still, a regular patch dyeing the ground. Pir Baksh explained that the beast had been hit forward—a truly wonderful shot—and had carried on to die. He would be found quite dead in the morning—till then there was nothing to be done.

On the way home, Pir Baksh, in the intervals of exultation, promised to make an early start, dissuading Pendlebury from accompanying him by remarking that this was only poor shikari's work, unsuitable for the Saheb Bahadur. Pendlebury was fagged out, and let him have his way; before he went to bed he had a last loving look at the Mannlicher, which he found sighted at five hundred yards! This he put down to carelessness in carrying, and congratulated himself that he had not had it at five hundred when he fired; good shot as it had been, he would not have put the beast at over seventy yards ... funny how he had felt certain that he had hit him before Pir Baksh spoke!

III

Pendlebury's next morning was almost as bad as the last. He clung to the camp, springing out of his chair at the slightest sound; he had occasion to throw his boots at Ali because the latter had made a noise like Pir; once more he failed to do justice to his meals, and spent the day alternating between triumph and despair. But the hours never brought Pir Baksh, and at last he turned into bed and lay awake, listening. Presently he heard a hubbub, then saw lights outside. As he sprang out of bed he was greeted with the welcome 'Mil gya, saheb,' in the dulcet tones of Pir Baksh; he rushed out, and there, amid a crowd of admiring servants, stood Pir Baksh himself, grimed with mud and dust from head to foot, his clothes artistically torn, blood on his coat ... but in his hands great antlers, branching out from a draggled mask.

Pendlebury whooped; the servants sucked in their breath with wonder; and Pir Baksh, in shrill tones, raised his pæan of victory. Twenty miles had he toiled; fifteen hours without food;

but for the saheb's honour he would have dropped with fatigue and died. Even in death the great stag had been wondrous cunning, and would never have been brought to book but for the superior cunning of Pir Baksh; there had been a personal encounter, in which danger had been gladly braved for the saheb, and a valuable life risked. Great was the name of 'Pendlebari Saheb,' who gives life to poor men, even to the humble shikari beneath his feet....

This stirring recital—composed that day in the bazaar—was followed by that little lull which tactfully indicates baksheesh to the least imaginative of us, and Pendlebury rose to the occasion nobly. There was a hundred-rupee note for Pir Baksh; twenty for the disreputable stranger who had given *bahut madad*, and who was described as a '*sidha admi ... kam kernewala bhi*'; twenty more for Ali Baksh for being a good fellow; and *mithai* for all the camp. Pendlebury did things handsomely.

The old Club bores might, with reason, have sniffed at that head had they seen it; but, as it happens, it was packed straight off to Pendlebury's agents in Bombay, for shipping to London, on the advice of Pir Baksh—so there was no one to call attention to a resemblance between these antlers and a pair produced by the disreputable stranger aforesaid on the occasion of Pir Baksh's first visit to the bazaar. In point of fact both pairs had a similar chip off one of the brow points.

The stranger had asked twenty rupees for this pair ... but who can fathom the mind of the East?

Another trivial detail ... Pir Baksh and the said stranger had slain a young stag on the second day; while Pendlebury was fishing, for they had feasted the village with fresh venison that night. It was also on record that Pir Baksh had retained the mask, and had bottled a small quantity of blood.

One more fact—Pendlebury had been mistaken about his sighting, and the stag at which he fired in the dusk was not a warrantable one; at least, so the stranger informed me afterwards. Not that it matters, for the shot went well over its back.

But what matters? The great head has the pride of place at Pendlebury Hall, and Pendlebury is happy whenever he sees it. And, anyway, Pir Baksh was an artist.

The Yellow Cat

MICHAEL JOSEPH

It all began when Grey was followed home, inexplicably enough, by the strange, famished yellow cat. The cat was thin with large, intense eyes which gleamed amber in the forlorn light of the lamp on the street corner. It was standing there as Grey passed, whistling dejectedly, for he had had a depressing run of luck at Grannie's tables, and it made a slight piteous noise as it looked up at him. Then it followed at his heels, creeping along as though it expected to be kicked unceremoniously out of the way.

Grey did, indeed, make a sort of half-threatening gesture when, looking over his shoulder, he saw the yellow cat behind.

'If you were a black cat,' he muttered, 'I'd welcome you— but get out!'

The cat's melancholy amber eyes gleamed up at him, but it made no sign and continued to follow. This would have annoyed Grey in his already impatient humour, but he seemed to find a kind of savage satisfaction in the fact that he was denied even the trifling consolation of a good omen. Like all gamblers, he was intensely superstitious, although he had had experience in full measure of the futility of all supposedly luck-bringing mascots. He carried a monkey's claw sewn in the lining of his waistcoat pocket, not having the courage to throw it away. But this wretched yellow cat that ought to have been black did not irritate him as might have been expected.

He laughed softly; the restrained, unpleasant laugh of a man fighting against misfortune.

'Come on, then, you yellow devil; we'll sup together.'

He took his gloveless hand from his coat pocket and beckoned to the animal at his heels; but it took as little notice of his gesture of invitation as it had of his menacing foot a moment before. It just slid along the greasy pavement, covering the ground noiselessly, not deviating in the slightest from the invisible path it followed, without hesitation.

It was a bitterly cold, misty night, raw and damp. Grey shivered as he thrust his hand back into the shelter of his pocket and hunched his shoulders together underneath the thin coat that afforded but little protection against the cold.

With a shudder of relief he turned to the shelter of the courtyard which lay between the icy street and the flight of stairs which led to his room. As he stumbled numbly over the rough cobblestones of the yard he suddenly noticed that the yellow cat had disappeared.

He was not surprised and gave no thought whatever to the incident until, a few minutes later, at the top of the ramshackle stairs, the feeble light of a hurricane lamp revealed the creature sitting, or rather lying, across the threshold of his door.

He took an uncertain step backward. He said to himself: 'That's odd.' The cat looked up at him impassively with brooding, sullen eyes. He opened the door, stretching over the animal to turn the crazy handle.

Silently the yellow cat rose and entered the shadowy room. There was something uncanny, almost sinister in its smooth, noiseless movements. With fingers that shook slightly, Grey fumbled for matches, struck a light and, closing the door behind him, lit the solitary candle.

He lived in this one room, over a mews which had become almost fashionable since various poverty-stricken people, whose names still carried some weight with the bourgeois tradesmen of this Mayfair backwater, had triumphantly installed themselves; and Grey turned it skilfully to account when he spoke with casual indifference of 'the flat' he occupied, 'next to Lady Susan Tyrrell's.'

Grey, although he would never have admitted it, was a cardsharper and professional gambler. But even a cardsharper needs a little ordinary luck. Night after night he watched money pass into the hands of 'the pigeons,' ignorant, reckless youngsters, and foolish old women who, having money to burn, ought by all the rules of the game to have lost. Yet when playing with him, Grey, a man respected even among the shabby fraternity of those who live by their wits, they won. He had turned to roulette, but even with a surreptitious percentage interest in the bank he had lost. His credit was exhausted. Grannie herself had told him he was a regular Jonah. He was cold, hungry and desperate. Presently his clothes, the last possession, would betray him, and no longer would he be able to borrow the casual trifle that started him nightly in his desperate bout with fortune.

His room contained a wooden bed and a chair. A rickety table separated them. The chair served Grey as a wardrobe; on the table stood a candle with a few used matched which he used to light the cheap cigarettes he smoked in bed; the grease had a habit of adhering to the tobacco when the candle was used, and Grey was fastidious. The walls were bare save for a cupboard, a pinned-up *Sporting Life* Racing Calendar and two cheap reproductions of Kirchner's midinettes. There was no carpet on the floor. A piece of linoleum stretched from the empty grate to the side of the bed.

At first Grey could not see the cat, but the candle, gathering strength, outlined its shadow grotesquely against the wall. It was crouched on the end of the bed.

He lighted one of the used matches and lit the small gas-ring which was the room's sole luxury. Gas was included in the few shillings he paid weekly for rent; consequently Grey used it for warmth. He seldom used it to cook anything, as neither whisky (which he got by arrangement with one of Grannie's waiters), bread nor cheese, which formed his usual diet, require much cooking.

The cat moved and, jumping noiselessly on to the floor, cautiously approached the gas-ring, by the side of which it stretched its lean yellowish body. Very softly but plaintively it began to mew.

Grey cursed it. Then he turned to the cupboard and took out a cracked jug. He moved the bread on to his own plate and poured out the little milk it contained in the shallow bread-plate.

The cat drank, not greedily, but with the fierce rapidity which betokens hunger and thirst. Grey watched it idly as he poured whisky into a cup. He drank, and refilled the cup. He then began to undress, carefully, in order to prolong the life of his worn dinner-jacket.

The cat looked up. Grey, taking off his shirt, beneath which, having no vest, he wore another woollen shirt, became uncomfortably aware of its staring yellow eyes. Seized with a crazy impulse, he poured the whisky from his cup into the remainder of the milk in the plate.

'Share and share alike,' he cried. 'Drink, you——'

Then the yellow cat snarled at him; the vilest, loathsome, sound; and Grey for a moment was afraid. Then he laughed, as if at himself for allowing control to slip, and finished undressing, folding the garments carefully, and hanging them on the chair.

The cat went back to its place at the foot of the bed, its eyes gleaming warily in Grey's direction. He restrained his impulse to throw it out of the room and clambered between the rough blankets without molesting it.

By daylight the cat was an ugly misshapen creature. It had not moved from the bed. Grey regarded it with amused contempt.

Usually the morning found him profoundly depressed and irritable. For some unaccountable reason he felt now almost light-hearted.

He dressed, counted his money and decided to permit himself the luxury of some meagre shopping in the adjacent Warwick Market, which supplied the most expensive restaurant proprietors with the cheapest food. Nevertheless, it was an accommodating spot for knowledgeable individuals like Grey.

The cat, still crouching on the bed, made no attempt to follow him, and he closed the door as softly as its erratic hinges would allow, aware that the cat's eyes still gazed steadily in his direction.

In the market, he obeyed an impulse to buy food for the cat, and at the cost of a few pence added a portion of raw fish to his purchases. On the way home he cursed himself for a fool, and would have thrown the fish away, the clumsy paper wrapping having become sodden with moisture, when he was hailed by a voice he had almost forgotten.

'Grey! Just the man I want to see!'

Grey greeted him with a fair show of amiability, although, if appearance were any indication, the other was even less prosperous than himself. He, too, had been an *habitué* of Grannie's in the old days, but had long since drifted out on the sea of misfortune. Despite his shabby appearance, he turned to Grey and said:

'You'll have a drink?' Then, noting Grey's dubious glance, he laughed and added: 'It's on me all right. I've just touched lucky.' A little later Grey emerged from the public-house on the corner the richer by five pounds, which the other had insisted on lending him in return for past favours. What exactly the past favours had been, Grey was too dazed to inquire; as fare as he could recollect he had always treated the man with scant courtesy. He did not even remember his name.

He was still trying to remember who the man was when he climbed the stairs. He knew him well enough, for Grey was the type who never forgets a face. It was when his eyes alighted on the yellow cat that he suddenly remembered.

The man was Felix Mortimer. And Felix Mortimer had shot himself during the summer!

At first Grey tried to assure himself that he had made a mistake. Against his better judgment he tried to convince himself that the man merely bore a strong resemblance to Felix Mortimer. But at the back of his mind *he knew*.

Anyway, the five-pound note was real enough.

He methodically placed the fish in a saucepan and lit the gasring.

Presently the cat was eating, in that curious, deliberate way it had drunk the milk the night before. Its emaciated appearance plainly revealed that it was starving; yet it devoured the fish methodically, as though now assured of a regular supply.

Grey, turning the five-pound note in his hand, wondered whether the cat had after all changed his luck. But his thoughts kept reverting to Felix Mortimer....

The next few days left him in no doubt. At Grannie's that night fortune's pendulum swung back unmistakably. He won steadily. From roulette he turned to *chemin de fer*, elated to find that his luck held good.

'Your luck's changed with a vengeance!' said one of the 'regulars' of the shabby genteel saloon.

'With a vengeance,' echoed Grey, and paused; wondering with the superstition of the born gambler if there were significance in the phrase.

He left Grannie's the richer by two hundred odd pounds.

His success was the prelude to the biggest slice of luck, to use his own phrase, that he had ever known. He gambled scientifically, not losing his head, methodically banking a proportion of his gains each morning; planning, scheming, striving to reach that high-water mark at which, so he told himself with the gambler's time-worn futility, he would stop and never gamble again.

Somehow he could not make up his mind to leave the poverty-stricken room in the fashionable mews. He was terribly afraid it would spell a change of luck. He tried to improve it, increase its comfort, but it was significant that he bought first a basket and a cushion for the yellow cat.

For there was no doubt in his mind that the cat was the cause of his sudden transition from poverty to prosperity. In his queer, intensely superstitious mind, the yellow cat was firmly established as his mascot.

He fed it regularly, waiting on it himself as though he were its willing servant. He made a spasmodic attempt to caress it, but the cat snarled savagely at him and, frightened, he left it alone. If the cat ever moved from the room he never saw it go; whenever he went in or came out the cat was there, watching him with its gleaming amber eyes.

He accepted the situation philosophically enough. He would talk to the cat of himself, his plans for the future, the new people he met—for money had speedily unlocked more exalted doors than Grannie's—all this in the eloquence derived from wine and solitude, he would pour out into the unmoved ears of the cat, crouching at the foot of the bed. And then, without daring to speak of it, he would think of Felix Mortimer and the gift that had proved the turning-point of his fortunes.

The creature watched him impassively, contemptuously indifferent to his raving or his silence. But the weird ménage continued, and Grey's luck held good.

The days passed, and he became ambitious. He was now within reach of that figure which he fondly imagined would enable him to forsake his precarious existence. He told himself that he was now, to all intents and purposes, safe. And he decided to move into more civilised and appropriate surroundings.

Nevertheless, he himself procured an expensive wicker contraption to convey the yellow cat from the garret to his newly acquired and, by contrast, luxurious maisonnette. It was furnished in abominable taste, but the reaction from sheer poverty had its effect. And then he had begun to drink more than was good for a man who required a cool head and a steady nerve for at least part of a day which was really night.

One day he had cause to congratulate himself on his new home. For he met, for the first time in his thirty odd years of life, a woman. Now Grey divided women into two classes. There were 'the regulars'—soulless creatures with the gambler's fever and crook's alphabet—and 'pigeons,' foolish women, some young, most of them old, who flourished their silly but valuable plumage to be plucked by such as he.

But Elise Dyer was different. She stirred his pulses with a strange, exquisite sensation. Her incredibly fair hair, flaxen as waving corn, her fair skin, her deep violet eyes and her delicate carmine mouth provoked him into a state of unaccustomed bewilderment.

They talked one night of mascots. Grey, who had never mentioned the yellow cat to a soul, whispered that he would, if she cared, show her the mascot that had brought him his now proverbial good luck. The girl agreed, with eager enthusiasm, to his diffident suggestion to go with him to his flat; and he, in his strange simplicity, stammered that she would do him honour. He had forgotten that Elise Dyer knew him for a rich man.

Elated by his triumph, he paid her losses and called for champagne. The girl plied him skilfully with wine, and presently he was more drunk than he had been since the beginning of his era of prosperity.

They took a cab to the flat. Grey felt that he had reached the pinnacle of triumph. Life was wonderful, glorious! What did anything matter now?

He switched on the light and the girl crossed his threshold. The room which they entered was lavishly illuminated, the lights shaded into moderation by costly fabrics. The room, ornate and over-furnished, reflected money. The girl gave a gasp of delight.

For the first time the cat seemed aware of something unusual. It stretched itself slowly and stood up, regarding them with a fierce light in its eyes.

The girl screamed.

'For God's sake take it away!' she cried. 'I can't bear it! I can't be near it. Take that damned cat away!' And she began to sob wildly, piteously, retreating towards the door.

At this Grey lost all control and, cursing wildly, shouting bestial things at the oncoming animal, seized it by the throat.

'Don't—don't cry, dearie,' panted Grey, holding the cat; 'I'll settle this swine soon enough. Wait for me!' And he staggered through the open door.

Grey ran through the deserted streets. The cat had subsided under the clutch of his fingers and lay inert, its yellowish fur throbbing. He scarcely knew where he was going. All he realised was an overwhelming desire to be rid of the tyranny of this wretched creature he held by the throat.

At last he knew where he was going. Nor far from Grey's new establishment ran the Prince's Canal, that dark, sluggish stream that threads its way across the fashionable residential district of the outlying west. To the canal he ran; and without hesitation he threw the yellow cat into the water.

The next day he realised what he had done. At first he was afraid, half hoping that the superstitious spasm of fear would pass. But a vivid picture swam before his eyes, the broken surface of a sluggish dream....

'You're a coward,' she taunted him. 'Why don't you act like a man? Go to the tables and see for yourself that you can still win in spite of your crazy cat notions!'

At first he refused, vehemently; but it gradually dawned on him that therein lay his chance of salvation. Once let him throw down the Gauntlet *and win* and his peace of mind would be assured.

That night he received a vociferous welcome on his return to the Green Baize Club.

It was as he feared. He lost steadily.

Then suddenly an idea came to him. Supposing the cat were still alive? Why hadn't he thought of that before? Why, there was a saying that every cat had nine lives! For all he knew it might have swum safely to the bank and got away.

His feverish impulse crystallised into action. He hurriedly left the club and beckoned urgently to a passing taxi-cab.

After what seemed interminable delay he reached the spot where he had madly flung the cat away from him. The stillness of the water brought home to him the futility of searching for the animal here. This was not the way to set to work.

The thing preyed on his mind in the days that followed. Exhaustive inquiries failed to discover the least trace of the yellow cat.

Night after night he went to the tables, lured there by the maddening thought that if only he could win he would drug the torment and be at peace. But he lost....

And then a strange thing happened.

One night, returning home across a deserted stretch of the park, he experienced a queer, irresistible impulse to lift his feet from the grass and make for the gravel path. He resented the impulse, fought against it; he was cold and worn out, and by cutting across the grass he would save many minutes of weary tramping. But the thing—like a mysterious blind instinct—persisted, and in the end he found himself running, treading gingerly on the sodden grass.

He did not understand why this had happened to him.

The next day Grey did not get out of his bed until late in the afternoon.

He crossed the room in search of his dressing-gown and caught sight of himself in the glass of his wardrobe. Only then did he realise that he was clambering over the floor with his head near the carpet, his hands outstretched in front of him.

He stood upright with difficulty and reached a shaking hand for brandy.

It took him two hours to struggle into his clothes, and by the time he was ready to go out it was nearly dark. He crept along the street. The shops were closing. He saw nothing of them until he reached the corner where he halted abruptly, with a queer sensation of intense hunger. On the cold marble before him lay unappetising slabs of raw fish. His body began to quiver with suppressed desire. Another moment and nothing could have prevented him seizing the fish in his bare hands, when the shutters of the shop dropped noisily across the front of the sloping marble surface.

Grey knew that something had happened, that he was very ill. Now that he could not see the vision of the yellow cat, his mind was a blank. Somehow he retraced his footsteps and got back to his room.

The bottle of brandy stood where he had left it. He had not turned on the light, but he could see it plainly. He dragged it to his lips.

With a crash it went to the floor, while Grey leapt into the air, savage with nausea. He felt that he was choking. With an effort he pulled himself together, to find that it was beyond his power to stop the ghastly whining sound that issued from his lips. He tried to lift himself on to the bed, but in sheer exhaustion collapsed on the floor, where he lay still in an attitude not human.

The room lightened with the dawn and a new day passed before the thing on the floor moved. Something of the clarity of vision which comes to starving men now possessed him. He stared at his hands.

The fingers seemed to have withered; the nails had almost disappeared, leaving a narrow streak of hornish substance forming in their place. He tore himself frantically towards the window. In the fading light he saw that the backs of his hands were covered with a thin, almost invisible surface of coarse, yellowish fur.

Unimaginable horrors seized him. He knew now that the scarlet thread of his brain was being stretched to breaking point. Presently it would snap....

Unless—unless. The yellow cat alone could save him. To this last human thought he clung, in an agony of terror.

Unconscious of movement, he crept swiftly into the street, his shapeless eyes peering in the darkness which surrounded him. He groped his way stealthily towards the one place which the last remnant of his brain told him might yield the secret of his agony.

Down the silent bank he scrambled headlong, towards the still water. The dawn's pale radiance threw his shadow into a grotesque pattern. On the edge of the canal he halted, his hands embedded in the sticky crumbling earth, his head shaking, his eyes searching in agonised appeal, into the depths of the motionless water.

There he crouched, searching, searching....

And there in the water he saw the yellow cat.

He stretched out the things that were his arms, while the yellow cat stretched out its claws to enfold him in the broken mirror of the water.

Why Herbert Killed His Mother

Winifred Holtby

Once upon a time there was a Model Mother who had a Prize Baby. Nobody had ever had such a Baby before. He was a Son, of course. All prize babies are masculine, for should there be a flaw in their gender this might deprive them of at least twenty-five per cent of the marks merited by their prize-worthiness.

The Mother's name was Mrs Wilkins, and she had a husband called Mr Wilkins; but he did not count much. It is true that he was the Baby's father, and on the night after the child was born he stood Drinks All Round at the Club; though he was careful to see that there were only two other members in the bar at the time he suggested it, because although one must be a Good Father and celebrate properly, family responsibilities make a man remember his bank balance. Mr Wilkins remembered his very often, particularly when Mrs Wilkins bought a copy of

Vogue, or remarked that the Simpsons, who lived next door but one, had changed their Austin Seven for a Bentley. The Wilkinses had not even an old Ford; but then the buses passed the end of their road, and before the Prize Baby arrived, Mrs Wilkins went to the Stores and ordered a very fine pram.

Mrs Wilkins had determined to be a Real Old-Fashioned Mother. She had no use for these Modern Women who Drink Cocktails, smoke Cigarettes, and dash about in cars at all hours with men who are not their husbands. She believed in the true ideal of Real Womanliness, Feminine Charm, and the Maternal Instinct. She won a ten-shilling prize once from a daily paper, with a circulation of nearly two million, for saying so, very prettily, on a postcard.

Before the Baby came she sat with her feet up every afternoon sewing little garments. She made long clothes with twenty tucks round the hem of each robe, and embroidered flannels, fifty inches from hem to shoulder tape, and fluffy bonnets, and teeny-weeny little net veils; she draped a bassinet with white muslin and blue ribbons, and she thought a great deal about violets, forget-me-nots and summer seas in order that her baby might have blue eyes. When Mrs Burton from 'The Acacias' told her that long clothes were unhygienic, and that drapery on the bassinet held the dust, and that heredity had far more to do with blue eyes than thoughts about forget-me-nots, she shook her head charmingly, and said: 'Ah, well. You *clever* women know so much. I can only go by what my darling mother told me.' Mrs Burton said: 'On the contrary. You have a lot of other authorities to go by nowadays,' and she produced three pamphlets, a book on Infant Psychology, and a programme of lectures on 'Health, Happiness and Hygiene in the Nursery'. But Mrs Wilkins sighed, and said: 'My poor little brain won't take in all that stuff. I have only my Mother Love to guide me.' And she dropped a pearly tear on to a flannel binder.

Mrs Burton went home and told Mr Burton that Mrs Wilkins was hopeless, and that her baby would undoubtedly suffer from adenoids, curvature of the spine, flat feet, halitosis, bow legs, indigestion and the Oedipus Complex. Mr Burton said 'Quite, quite.' And everyone was pleased.

The only dissentient was the Wilkins baby, who was born without any defect whatsoever. He was a splendid boy, and his more-than-proud parents had him christened Herbert James Rodney Stephen Christopher, which names they both agreed went very well with Wilkins. He wore for the ceremony two binders, four flannels, an embroidered robe with seventeen handmade tucks, a woolly coat, two shawls, and all other necessary and unnecessary garments, and when he stared into the Rector's face, and screamed lustily, his aunts said: 'That means he'll be musical, bless him.' But his mother thought: 'What a strong will he has! And what sympathy there is between us! Perhaps he knows already what I think about the Rector.'

As long as the monthly nurse was there, Mrs Wilkins and Herbert got along very nicely on Mother Love; but directly she left trouble began.

'My baby,' Mrs Wilkins had said, 'shall never be allowed to lie awake and cry like Mrs Burton's poor little wretch. Babies need cuddling.' So whenever Herbert cried at first she cuddled him. She cuddled him in the early morning when he woke up Mr Wilkins and wanted his six o'clock bottle at four. She cuddled him at half-past six and half-past seven and eight. She cuddled him half-hourly for three days and then she smacked him. It was a terrible thing to do, but she did it. She fed him when he seemed hungry, and showed him to all the neighbours who called, and kept him indoors when it rained, which it did every day, and nursed him while she had her own meals, and when she didn't gave him Nestlé's, And he still flourished.

But what with the crying and the washing that hung in the garden, the neighbours began to complain, and Mrs Burton said: 'Of course, you're killing that child.'

Mrs Wilkins knew that the Maternal Instinct was the safest guide in the world; but when her husband showed her an advertisement in the evening paper which began: 'Mother, does your child cry?' she read it. She learned there that babies cry because their food does not agree with them. 'What-not's Natural Digestive Infants' Milk solves the Mother's problem.' Mrs Wilkins thought that no stone should be left unturned and bought a specimen tin of What-not's Natural Digestive Infants' Milk, and gave it to Herbert. Herbert flourished. He grew larger and rounder and pinker, and more dimpled than ever. But still he cried.

So Mrs Wilkins read another advertisement in the evening paper. And there she learned that when Babies cry it is because they are not warm enough, and that all good mothers should buy Flopsy's Fleecy Pram Covers. So, being a good mother, she bought a Flopsy's Fleecy Pram Cover and wrapped Herbert in it. And still Herbert flourished. And still he cried.

So she continued to read the evening papers, for by this time both she and Mr Wilkins were nearly distracted, and one of the neighbours threatened to complain to the landlord, and Mrs Simpson kept her loud speaker going all night and day to drown the noise, she said. And now Mrs Wilkins learned that the reason her baby cried was because his Elimination was inadequate so she bought him a bottle of Hebe's Nectar for the Difficult Child, and gave him a teaspoonful every morning. But still he cried.

Then the spring came, and the sun shone, and the bulbs in the garden of Number Seven were finer than they had ever been before, and Mrs Wilkins put Herbert out in the garden in his pram, and he stopped crying.

She was such a nice woman and such a proud mother that she wrote at once to the proprietors of What-not's Natural Digestive Infants' Milk, and Flopsy's Fleecy Pram Covers, and Hebe's Nectar for the Difficult Child, and told them that she had bought their things for Herbert and that he had stopped crying.

Two days later a sweet young woman came to the Wilkins' house, and said that What-not's Limited had sent her to see Herbert, and what a fine Baby he was, and how healthy, and could she take a photograph? And Mrs Wilkins was very pleased, and thought: 'Well, Herbert is the most beautiful Baby in the world, and won't this be a sell for Mrs Burton,' and was only too delighted. So the young woman photographed Herbert in his best embroidered robe drinking Natural Digestive Infants' Milk from a bottle, and went away.

The next day a kind old man came from Flopsy's Fleecy Pram Covers Limited, and photographed Herbert lying under a Fleecy Pram Cover. It was a hot afternoon and a butterfly came and settled on the pram; but the kind old man said that this was charming.

The next day a scientific-looking young man with horn-rimmed spectacles came from Hebe's Nectar Limited and photographed Herbert lying on a fur rug wearing nothing at all. And When Mr Wilkins read his Sunday paper, there he saw his very own baby, with large black capitals printed above him, saying: 'My Child is now no longer Difficult, declares Mrs Wilkins, of Number 9, The Grove, SW 10.'

Mrs Burton saw it too, and said to Mr Burton: 'No wonder, when at last they've taken a few stones of wool off the poor little wretch.'

But Mr And Mrs Wilkins saw it differently. They took Herbert to a Court Photographer and had him taken dressed and undressed, with one parent, with both parents, standing up and sitting down; and always he was the most beautiful baby that the Wilkinses had ever seen.

One day they saw an announcement in a great Sunday paper of a £10,000 prize for the loveliest baby in the world. 'Well, dear, this will be nice,' said Mrs Wilkins. 'We shall be able to buy a saloon car now.' Because, of course, she knew that Herbert would win the prize.

And so he did. He was photographed in eighteen different poses for the first heat; then he was taken for a personal inspection in private for the second heat; then he was publicly exhibited at the Crystal Palace for the semi-finals, and for the Final Judgment he was set in a pale blue bassinet and examined by three doctors, two nurses, a Child Psychologist, a film star, and

Mr Cecil Beaton. After that he was declared the Most Beautiful Baby in Britain.

That was only the beginning. Baby Britain had still to face Baby France, Baby Spain, Baby Italy, and Baby America. Signor Mussolini sent a special message to Baby Italy, which the other national competitors thought unfair. The Free State insisted upon sending twins, which were disqualified. The French President cabled inviting the entire contest to be removed to Paris, and the Germans declared that the girl known as Baby Poland, having been born in the Polish Corridor, was really an East Prussian and should be registered as such.

But it did not matter. These international complications made no difference to Herbert. Triumphantly he overcame all his competitors, and was crowned as World Baby on the eve of his first birthday.

Then, indeed, began a spectacular period for Mr and Mrs Wilkins. Mrs Wilkins gave interviews to the Press on 'The Power of Mother Love', 'The Sweetest Thing in the World', and 'How I Run My Nursery'. Mr Wilkins wrote some fine manly articles on 'Fatherhood Faces Facts', and 'A Man's Son'—or, rather, they were written for him by a bright young woman until Mrs Wilkins decided that she should be present at the collaborations.

Then a firm of publishers suggested to Mr Wilkins that he should write a Christmas book called *Herbert's Father*, all about what tender feelings fathers had, and what white, pure thoughts ran through their heads when they looked upon the sleeping faces of their sons, and about how strange and wonderful it was to watch little images of themselves growing daily in beauty, and how gloriously unspotted and magical were the fairy-like actions of little children. Mr Wilkins thought that this was a good idea if someone would write the book for him, and if the advance royalties were not less than £3,000 on the date of publication; but he would have to ask Mrs Wilkins. Mrs Wilkins was a trifle hurt. Why *Herbert's Father*? What right had Paternity to override Maternity? The publisher pointed out the success of Mr A.A. Milne's *Christopher Robin*, and Mr Lewis Hind's *Julius Caesar*, and of Mr A.S.M. Hutchinson's *Son Simon*, to say nothing of Sir James Barrie's *Little White Bird*. 'But none of these children was my Herbert,' declared Mrs Wilkins—which, indeed, was undeniable. So the contract was finally signed for *The Book of Herbert*, by His Parents.

It was a success. Success? It was a Triumph, a Wow, a Scream, an Explosion. There was nothing like it. It was The Christmas Gift. It went into the third hundredth thousand before December 3rd. It was serialised simultaneously in the *Evening Standard, Home Chat*, and *The Nursery World*. Mr Baldwin referred to it at a Guildhall Banquet. The Prince used a joke from it in a Broadcast Speech on England and the Empire. The Book Society failed to recommend it, but every bookstall in the United Kingdom organised a display stand in its honour, with photographs of Herbert and copies signed with a blot 'Herbert, His Mark' exquisitely arranged.

The Herbert Boom continued. Small soap Herberts (undressed for the bath) were manufactured and sold for use in delighted nurseries. Royalty graciously accepted an ivory Herbert, designed as a paper-weight, from the loyal sculptor. A Herbert Day was instituted in order to raise money for the Children's Hospitals of England, and thirty-seven different types of Herbert Calendars, Christmas Cards, and Penwipers were offered for sale—and sold.

Mrs Wilkins felt herself justified in her faith. This, she said, was what mother love could do. Mr Wilkins demanded ten per cent royalties on every Herbert article sold. And they all bought a country house near Brighton, a Bentley car, six new frocks for Mrs Wilkins, and an electric refrigerator, and lived happily ever after until Herbert grew up.

But Herbert grew up.

When he was four he wore curls and a Lord Fauntleroy suit and posed for photographers. When he was fourteen he wore jerseys and black finger-nails and collected beetles. When he left one of England's Great Public Schools he wore plus-fours and pimples and rode a motorcycle and changed his tie three times in half an hour before he called on the young lady at the tobacconist's round the corner. He knew what a Fella does, by Jove, and he knew what a Fella doesn't. His main interests in life were etiquette, Edgar Wallace, and the desire to live down his past. For on going to a preparatory school he had carefully insisted that his name was James. His father, who knew that boys will be boys, supported him, and as he grew to maturity, few guessed that young James Wilkins, whose beauty was certainly not discernible to the naked eye, was Herbert, the Loveliest Baby in the World. Only Mrs Wilkins, in a locked spare bedroom, cherished a museum of the Herbert photographs, trophies, first editions, soap images, ivory statuettes, silver cups, and Christmas cards. The Herbert vogue had faded, as almost all vogues do, until not even a gag about Herbert on the music hall stage raised a feeble smile.

But Mrs Wilkins found the position hard to bear. It is true that the fortunes of the family were soundly laid, that Mr Wilkins had invested the profits of his son's juvenile triumphs in Trustee Stock, and that no household in South Kensington was more respected. But Mrs Wilkins had tasted the sweet nectar of publicity and she thirsted for another drink.

It happened that one day, when (Herbert) James was twenty-three, he brought home the exciting news that he had become engaged to Selena Courtney, the daughter of Old Man Courtney, whose office in the city Herbert adorned for about six hours daily.

Nothing could have been more fortunate. Mr Wilkins was delighted, for Courtney, of Courtney, Gilbert and Co., was worth nearly half a million. Herbert was delighted, for he was enjoying the full flavour of Young Love and Satisfied Snobbery combined, which is, as everyone knows, the perfect fulfilment of a True Man's dreams. The Courtneys were delighted, because they thought young Wilkins a very decent young man, with none of this damned nonsense abut him. And Mrs Wilkins—well, her feelings were mixed. It was she, after all, who had produced this marvel, and nobody seemed to remember her part in the production, nor to consider the product specially marvellous. Besides, she was a little jealous, as model mothers are allowed to be, of her prospective daughter-in-law.

The engagement was announced in *The Times*—the reporters came, rather bored, to the Kensington home of Mrs Wilkins. She was asked to supply any details about her son's career. 'Any adventures? Any accidents? Has he ever won any prizes?' asked a reporter.

This was too much. 'Come here!' said Mrs Wilkins; and she led the reporters up to the locked spare bedroom.

What happened there was soon known to the public. When (Herbert) James, two evenings later, left the office on his way to his future father-in-law's house in Belgrave Square, hoping to take his fiancée after dinner to a dance given by Lady Soxlet, he was confronted by placards announcing 'The Perfect Baby to Wed'. Taking no notice he went on to the Tube Station; but there he saw yet further placards. 'The World's Loveliest Baby now a Man', and 'Little Herbert Engaged'.

Still hardly conscious of the doom awaiting him, he bought an evening paper, and there he saw in black letters across the front page: 'Herbert's Identity at last Discovered', and underneath the fatal words: 'The young City man, Mr James Wilkins, whose engagement to Miss Selena Courtney, of 299 Belgrave Square, was announced two days ago, has been revealed by his mother, Mrs Wilkins, to be Herbert, the Wonder Baby.' There followed descriptions of the Perfect Childhood, stories taken from the Herbert Legend; rapid advertisements rushed out by What-Not's natural Digestive Infants' Milk, Flopsy's Fleecy Pram Covers, and Hebe's Nectar for the Difficult Child, illustrated by photographs of the Infant Herbert. The publishers of the *Book of Herbert* announced a new edition, and a famous Daily Paper, whose circulation was guaranteed to be over 2,000,000, declared its intention of publishing a series of articles called 'My Herbert is a Man, by Herbert's Mother'.

Herbert did not proceed to Belgrave Square. He went to Kensington. With his own latchkey he opened the door and went up to his mother's boudoir. He found her laughing and crying with joy over the evening paper. She looked up and saw her son.

'Oh, darling,' she said. 'I thought you were taking Selena to a dance.'

'There is no Selena,' declared Herbert grimly. 'There is no dance. There is only you and me.'

He should, doubtless, have said: 'You and I,' but among the things a Fella does, correct grammar is not necessarily included.

'Oh, Herbert,' cried Mrs Wilkins, with ecstatic joy. 'My mother instinct was right. Mother always knows, darling. You have come back to me.'

'I have,' said Herbert.

And he strangled her with a rope of twisted newspapers.

The judge declared it justifiable homicide, and Herbert changed his name to William Brown and went to plant tea or rubber or something in the Malay States, where Selena joined him two years later—and Mr Wilkins lived to a ripe old age at the Brighton house and looked after his dividends, and everyone was really very happy after all.

Golden Silence

CROSBIE GARSTIN

I met Hepplethwaite two miles west of the river drift. He was homeward bound to his store at Mokala, sitting on a waggon, nursing a large square box on his knees as if it were his only child and uninsured at that.

We passed the time of day, agreed that *veld* was scarce, and water scarcer.

Said I: 'Wouldn't you find it less warm if you could persuade that packing-case to get off your lap and sit somewhere else?'

''Fraid of breaking it, it's a gramophone.'

'Where did you get it'

'Took it over from the railway gauger, Kreige, in part payment for some sheep.'

'Any records?'

'Only four, but I'll get some more up from Cape Town. I'm rather glad I've got it now; a fellow gets fed up with the everlasting silence out in the bush and the sound of his own voice talking to nobody, don't he?'

'He do,' I agreed.

'This'll be a bit of variety—drop out my way some day and we'll let her rip off a tune or two.'

I accepted the invitation and we parted. I didn't envy him his seventy-mile tramp to Mokala cuddling that cornery crate all the way; still, music hath charms, and one has to make some sacrifices. I was out near Mokala buying goats a fortnight later, so I called in on Hepplethwaite. We had supper and sat outside his hut afterwards, smoking our pipes and watching the moon rise over the bush.

He asked if I would care to hear the gramophone, and I said I should.

He bawled to his cook-boy who cranked up the engine and let it get a record off its chest.

'I've taught Mackintyre to work the thing,' Hepplethwaite explained, 'it saves me having to jump up every minute or two to put on the brakes and reload, etc; he's tickled to death with it, calls it the "Fairy in the box." '

'Home Sweet Home' finished and 'Annie Laurie' commenced.

'Great invention, when you come to think of it,' Hepplethwaite observed. 'Great invention, the gramophone. Have your potted Caruso after coffee; tired of him, open a tin of Melba; weary of Melba, uncork a jar of Lauder; and so. Great idea.'

'Annie Laurie' wailed to a close and the versatile machine rang a chime on the 'Blue Bells of Scotland.'

'Great idea, when you come to think of it. Nowadays you don't have to dedicate half your life to sawing at a fiddle or plunking a piano, don't have to let your hair grow and all that to get a respectable noise when you want it, you just sell an ox, buy a gramophone, and have the whole boiling lot at your nod— marvellous business, when you come to consider it.'

'Half a moment,' said I, interrupting his unsolicited testimonial. 'That boy of yours is putting on "Annie Laurie" Again; we've just had her.'

'I know, can't be helped. I only have three records now. The fourth, "Mary of Argyle," fell off a table into a scrap between my bull-terrier and Bob St John's mastiff. "Mary" got the worst of it.'

'You're going to get some more records though, aren't you?'

'Rather. I've sent down to the coast for a catalogue. I'll get some Gilbert and Sullivan, I think. 'Yeomen of the Guard,' 'Dorothy,' and so forth, also some Gaiety pieces and some rag-time; there are great possibilities in gramophones. You must drop out some day when they arrive, and we'll have a blooming Queen's Hall concert.'

He turned and shouted again to Mackintyre, the cook-boy, who obediently slipped the engine into the low gear.

'Told him to play them over again, slowly this time, by way of variety.'

Later on in the evening we had the three pieces over again at full speed this time by way of more variety. By permutations and combinations Hepplethwaite had worked out how many varieties there were to be got out of those three pieces.

You, gentle reader, may work it out for yourself, if you are given to combination and permutations; anyway, there are quite a lot, and we had them all that night before we turned in.

At breakfast next morning Mackintyre, who gloried in his new accomplishment, served us up 'Annie Laurie' with the porridge, 'Home Sweet Home' with the goat ribs, and 'The Blue Bells of Scotland' with the marmalade. I rode away after that.

If anybody had asked me to sing (which they never do) any of these three songs backwards, forwards, sideways, or upside down during the next month I could have done so, yea, even in my sleep. Sometime later I got a letter from Hepplethwaite. He had sundry heifers for sale, would I come out and look at them?

I reached Mokala in the late afternoon; Hepplethwaite was in the store, so also was Jopie Ziervogel. Jopie Ziervogel, along with his *vrouw*, a lady built on very much the same lines as a Baltic *galliot*, inhabits a wattle and dab hut in Chaka's Stadt, where he repairs the native ploughs and waggons in return for stock and fair promises.

'Hello,' said Hepplethwaite, 'that you? Sit down and make yourself at home, heifers will be in at sundown. Cup of tea? Jopie, a cup of tea?'

Jopie squirmed about in his chair, shuffled his *velschoen* (in which he sleeps) over the floorboards, coughed, smiled, and said he didn't mind if he did. 'S'cuse me a moment,' said Hepplethwaite. '*Lo batlau?*'

The two native girls addressed produced black cones of Makalaka tobacco, which they exchanged after much haggling for some beads, brass wire and the inevitable *barsella*, or tip, of two cotton reels.

Mackintyre brought in three cups of tea, grinned a white grin that looked like dawn breaking through pitchy night, and went off to cook the evening's meal.

Jopie squirmed about in his chair, blushed and stammered out an opinion that the weather was hot but that he thought we'd have more rain.

A nude native entered bearing two mangy fowls upside down by the legs, which he sold for some kaffir corn and a *barsella* of a handful of sweets. Jopie laid down his empty cup, shuffled his *velschoen* violently, squirmed on his chair in a paroxysm of embarrassment, went scarlet in the face, and gasped out:

'Mis-ter 'Epplethwaite, could I year a chune on the gramy-phone, please, Mis-ter 'Epplethwaite, please?'

Hepplethwaite put down his pen and looked at Jopie as if that gentleman's sudden and immediate demise would make a happy man of him. He picked up a heavy ebony ruler and grasped it, bludgeon-wise in a tense fist; then his hand relaxed and he sighed. 'Mackintyre, bring the gramophone,' he shouted wearily, and strode out of the store to bargain for an ox that a spindle-shanked ancient had for sale.

To be a successful Kaffir storekeeper one must be equally at home among ploughs, patent medicines, and peppermint drops, beads, blankets and bovines, one must combine the patience of a Job with the commercial acumen of a Scotch Jew of Yankee extraction, one must be all this and then some.

Mackintyre appeared bearing the music-maker, wound it up and set the 'Blue Bells of Scotland' ringing the old familiar tune.

Jopie sat back in his chair, his ears wide open, a smile of æsthetic ecstasy nearly splitting him in half.

We had 'Home Sweet Home' after that, and the 'Blue Bells' again after that, after that we had 'Home Sweet Home'. I went out to where Hepplethwaite and the ancient were endeavouring to bluff each other under.

'Where's "Annie Laurie"?' I asked.

'Bust. Bob St John felt suddenly tired here one night and sat on her.'

Inside the store Jopie had got the 'Blue Bells' at it again. Hepplethwaite shivered and jerked his head towards the noise.

'He comes here about once a week and sits playing those two darn tunes over and over, back and forth the whole blessed afternoon, until I'm nearly off my blooming head.'

'Why do you let him?'

'Oh, well, he's a customer, you know. Buys a tin of coffee and a pound of sugar once in a way, and a packet of sweets on Christmas Days and blue moons. Got to oblige customers, you know.'

At this point the ancient teetered up and said that seeing it was his old college chum Hepplethwaite, he'd take three pounds fifteen shilling for the ox—he had demanded eight pounds earlier in the afternoon. Hepplethwaite burst into cackles of well-simulated mirth—I forgot to say that to be a successful Kaffir storekeeper one has also to be an actor of no trifling ability.

'Ha, ha! Three pounds fifteen for that ox! Why, it was so old it would probably die a natural death before nightfall, and so thin it would do nicely as a hat rack, wheeled into the front hall.' Another cackle of well-simulated mirth. 'Ha, ha! M'purru' (M'purru being the ancient) 'must be cracking a joke at his'

(Hepplethwaite's) 'expense, a humorist, a funny man, what? Three pounds fifteen, ha, ha, very amusing!'

The ancient said there was no joke intended, and in that case he and the ox must go home.

'Go!' said Hepplethwaite, winking at me, and the ancient drove the ox off round the corner of the store. Inside the tin building the gramophone was singing 'Home Sweet Home' to the entranced Jopie. Hepplethwaite groaned, 'It isn't only Jopie but Bob St John and his crowd from the "Eland"; they stop here on their way back and forth from the mine, tumble whooping off their Cape cart, haul out the gramophone, and keep it grinding away until the last survivor drops flat somewhere in the thin hours of morning—it's the limit, believe me.'

'Why do you stand for it? Are they customers, too?'

'Yes, pretty good customers, too, confound 'em!'

'Where are those new records you were talking about— "Dorothy," the "Yeomen of the Guard," and all?'

Hepplethwaite snorted. 'My confounded transport manager drank his back teeth awash on Kaffir beer in at the siding, pulled out at midnight with the case of records on top of a load of grain and lashed the span lickety split down into the Bongola River in flood—being hopelessly drunk he was about the only thing saved.'

The ancient poked his corrugated face round the store corner.

'I am going, Baas.'

'All right.'

'Three pound and a half, Baas?'

'Three pound, I told you.'

'Good-bye, Baas.'

'Good-bye, M'purru.' The face withdrew slowly.

'So you're still harping along with "Home Sweet Home" and the "Blue Bells"—eh?'

'No, I'm not, Bob. Jopie, Mackintyre & Co. are though.'

'Going to try again?'

'Sure enough. I've sent for another case, it should be up next week.'

Jopie, having played the 'Blue Bells of Scotland' to a lingering finish, rolled out of the store, insisted on shaking hands with both of us, took off his hat, mounted a rusty yellow mare, and tripped off home to his *vrouw*.

We turned back to the store, at the door of which we discovered the ancient, squatting on his lean hams.

'Three pound five shillings, Baas,' said he.

'*Ociami*,' Hepplethwaite graciously agreed, and paid him in goods at the retail value of three pounds five and the wholesale value of one pound ten. There is something in commercial life that appeals to me.

That night after supper Mackintyre attempted to give us 'Home Sweet Home,' but we choked the machine at the first whoop, and kicked the impresario swiftly in the direction of his hut. Time passed on, and one day I was in Knox's store at the siding buying myself some tea to mix with a little water I had at home.

Knox was reading a letter that a native runner had just brought in; it seemed to annoy Knox, he mumbled sourly from time to time.

'What's rowelling you?' I asked.

'Hepplethwaite, I do his forwarding from the railway, y'know, also for Hergesheimer, up at Nyoriliwe. One's case marks are

H.M., t'other's H.N. In the dark the other night I made a mistake and sent some of Heppy's stuff up to Hergesheimer— Heppy's got snotty about it,' he wagged that merchant's letter; 'don't see why, perfectly reasonable mistake.'

'Let me see,' said I, 'Nyoriliwe is about six hundred miles away, isn't it, across the desert? When will Hergesheimer's waggon be back?'

'In about ten weeks if his spans are fit and he bustles 'em back immediately, which he won't—still, I don't see why Heppy should rear up and paw the air like that, it was only some footling gramophone records, anyhow.'

'Some *what?*'

'Gramophone records—what are you laughing at?'

'Nothing,' said I. 'Gimme my tea and lemme go.'

Hepplethwaite was in his little fenced-off patch of a garden when I rode up, drenching his budding pumpkins with his morning's bath water—one learns the economics in our country.

'*Dumela,*' said he, jerking the last soapy dregs over up aspiring lettuce, 'You've come just in time for scoff; hang an your horse and walk right into the *kya.*'

Supper over, we dragged our deck-chairs out of doors and sat smoking our pipes and talking 'beef on the heel' as ever.

'Like to hear the gramophone?' he asked.

'Well, if you've got any new records——'

Hepplethwaite chuckled grimly.

'No, I haven't got any new records, half my new records are floating downstream towards the Indian Ocean and t'other half must be getting pretty near the German West African border by now. Moreover, I haven't got any gramophone; you've come just two hours too late, my son.'

'What's happened?'

'A whole lot of things; one of them was that I got fed up to busting point with gramophones. The gramophone is a noble invention, but I've been unlucky and determined to get rid of mine.'

'Did you sell it to Jopie?'

'I tried to; he rose to it like a trout at first but afterwards he thought he'd better talk it over with his *vrouw*. They were closeted in solemn conclave for about a month; at the end he rode over and said he was afraid they couldn't afford it just then, but if the Chief Chaka paid up for the shortening of four waggon tyres, and Intaemer broke his iron plough beam which was already cracked and paid Jopie for welding it, if I would take half a bag of seed oats and some fowls in part payment, and if the old spotted cow had a heifer calf at Christmas then they would go into conclave again and let me know the result sometime about Easter.

'The "Eland" Cape Cart, homeward bound, rolled up just after Jopie had gone; Bob St John was abroad with two miners and a case of "Dop". They stayed up most of the night. Bob St John teaching one miner the Argentine Tango to the strains of "Home Sweet Home," lugging the poor, half-strangled blighter round and round the hut, smashing into the furniture, while the other miner beat time with two tin plates, kept the engine running and accompanied it with song and hiccoughs. A kind of tired feeling began to steal over me about dawn.

'When they departed next day, the gramophone was lashed to the cart's rack unbeknown to them.

'Now, thought I, if they want "Bluebells" and "Home Sweet Home" all night and day they can have it to their souls' content out on the "Eland" without troubling me. I don't know the fellow who said "Silence is golden," but he spoke the word that time all right; it is not only golden, but strung with pearls, festooned with diamonds and plastered with mitres; anyway, that's how I felt the night after the Cape Cart left.'

I laughed. 'So that ended the gramophone.'

'No it didn't, wait a bit—this afternoon I went out to see if I could hit a buck, and coming home I saw the spoor of a Cape Cart and six mules; there is only one in this district and that's the "Elands." When I got to the store I found they had not stopped, but gone on; they meant to camp at the *Bongola* water-holes tonight, my boy said, they had left a parcel for me, however.

'Yes, it was the gramophone, of course, sitting on my table, wrapped up in sacking, come back like a cat, like a bad ha'penny, like a ruddy boomerang. There was also a note thanking me for the *loan* of my instrument which they herewith returned along with one record, "Home Sweet Home" having unfortunately committed suicide by hurling itself from a shelf.

'What did you do then?'

'What did I do, what did I do?—I took the whole box of tricks and thrust them into Mackintyre's arms. "Take 'em," I said, "miles away from here, miles and miles; take 'em to some desolate corner of the world and smash 'em into little, tiny, small smithereens, smash 'em into powder, into nothing at all."'

'Finish,' said I.

'Finish,' echoed Hepplethwaite, lounging contentedly back in his chair and puffing lazy smoke-rings towards the tropic stars.

'And golden silence cometh to her own again.'

Hepplethwaite nodded.

Suddenly I jerked upright in my chair both ears pricking, from somewhere out in the dark bush came a faint whirr, a tinkle and the distant nasal intoning of a familiar, a very familiar tune, the indomitable Bluebells of invincible Scotland.

'*Mackintyre!*'

Hepplethwaite bounced from his seat, poised rigid for the moment like a pointer pointing, whirled on his heel and dashed into the hut.

Another second and he raced past me, brandishing a native battle-axe that ornamented his walls, and the darkness engulfed him.

A minute later a startled yell pierced the night air, followed by a metallic crash and a whirring as if all the clock-springs on earth were tearing out.

Then silence, golden silence, I lay back in my chair and laughed and laughed—which is a silly way I have.

The Cat-Lovers

E.H.W. MEYERSTEIN

Mr Justice Grist and Mr Justice Leanjer had been friends from the days when they confronted one another as advocates in assize courts. They had played into one another's hands then, through the strength of their joint atachment to cases of robbery with violence, and now, exalted to the Bench, they had earned the pleasure of pronouncing those sentences, of which, by means best known to practitioners of the Criminal Bar, it had previously been their earnest wish to ensure a good annual return.

Both were of the type that regretted the obsolescence of the good old judicial harangue before the death sentence. As youths, not crueller than most, they had married masterful women earlier in life than their careers warranted, and groaned under the lashes of tongues for which their professions allowed no unpunishable redress. Being childless, they could not 'take it out of' their offspring. Nagging breeds severity in the nagged;

the severity of these went into their profession, and was ultimately wreaked on the backs of the judged.

They were now getting old, and, like the retired naval officers of the 1840s, deplored the milk-and-water discipline of the modern penitentiary. Seldom, very seldom nowadays, they were treated to an offender who would plead: 'I know what punishment to expect—the cat; it is the only punishment for such a cowardly action,' and have the precious opportunity of replying: 'You are perfectly right, and I am going to sentence you to twenty strokes with the cat.' This, for them, had been the high-water mark of delight, to *agree* with the delinquent, by preference a strapping young miner of, say, twenty-two, and actually *to order him what he asked for*. Far more often today it was their fate to observe: 'The medical report states that you are not fit for a flogging with the cat-o'-nine-tails. I therefore reluctantly award you (so many) strokes with the birch.' Latterly, indeed, the power of the medical profession had become so menacing that they were reduced to prescribing the longest term of imprisonment allowed by statute, with no corporal hors-d'œuvre whatever.

Both were in the public eye, and the Sunday papers, as often as they could, published their awards together, so as to impress their readers with the survival of the Middle Ages.

But one circumstance alone was wanting to cement their friendship; it had not yet fallen to the lot of either to sentence to imprisonment, with a whipping, a man who had already undergone such a sentence on the recommendation of the other. Though many a prisoner had been flogged twice, or even three times, by Grist's or Leanjer's orders, there was, oddly enough, no instance of a Grist victim's back smarting under Leanjer or a Leanjer victim's back smarting under Grist. The learned brothers had often commented in talk or correspondence on the queerness of this fact. Had they been literary critics matters might have been arranged to suit their convenience, but the divine impartiality of the English judicial system subjected them to the divagations of chance. They had come to the philosophical conclusion that the hand of Providence was shown here; life had still something more to offer, and dreary hours on the Bench or opposite a partner for life were sustained by the hope of the right permutation occurring at last.

It came and, as neither could have anticipated, in double strength. In the same month, and on the same day, Edward Round and Derek Bollow, aged twenty-four and twenty-six, were sentenced to fifteen strokes with the cat and eighteen months' hard labour at the Old Bailey, Round for a post-office raid with pepper, Bollow for robbing an impatient landlord of his gold watch and chain after bruising him. Their judges obtained remission from their wives for that evening, and at their club over a bottle of Anjou '24 celebrated the astonishing coincidence.

'I recall your man very well,' said Mr Justice Leanjer. 'He brought up the rear of a very dismal day some five years ago. He was reported fit for modified Borstal treatment, but I had the satisfaction of prescribing a modified whipping.'

'And I recall yours,' said Mr Justice Grist. 'Not quite so long ago that was. Every attempt was made to prove that the assault on the girl was unaccompanied by robbery, but I put a question to her before she left the box; it convinced the jury that the shilling missed from her purse was picked up by the prisoner.'

In prison, a few days before undergoing the corporal part of their sentences, Round and Bollow during exercise snatched a word or two about their careers. Idleness and a doting mother had propelled each to crime, but the inspiration of the birch and the anticipation of the cat made them avengers, though outwardly respectful and subservient. Moreover, as readers of a Sunday paper, they appreciated the relation in which they stood to their judges, though they had not seen the report of their trials.

'I should like to get Leanjer when I'm out,' said Round, a squat, snub-nosed, ruddy ironmonger's assistant with black hair and hazel eyes.

'I'm with you,' said Bollow, a tall, freckled, cocksure, blue-eyed plumber with huge red hands and a ginger crest. 'You should have just seen his face when he ordered me that dose. I wonder he don't come and have a look at us here. I suppose you can't be a judge *and* a visiting magistrate.'

'The papers would probably get wind of it if our judges stood by while we were being bashed. It will be next week, I think. The cruellest part is not letting us know when it's coming.'

Round was not far out. Three mornings later, at about 10.30, an officer popped his head into Bollow's cell (and into Round's some few minutes later) with: 'Bollow, get your coat on, and come with me.'

The doctor was waiting, and two more officers were in the offing. After an examination of throat, lungs, and heart, the officers marched in, each seizing an arm, and conducted Bollow to an isolated part of the prison, where the triangle and the volunteer flogger, a 'screw' who earned an extra pound that day, stood, strap in hand, ready to receive him. 'Bollow,' remarked the Governor later, 'did not cry out more than men generally do under punishment. Round didn't take it nearly so well, I thought. Short men seldom do. Doctor, you stood the ordeal very creditably.'

On some natures the cat acts as the law requires it should. They are ashamed of themselves, only wish to skulk for the rest of their lives, and, like the women whom Pericles addressed, be heard of neither for evil nor for good. Some few anticipate the law's purpose by taking their lives in the interval between their sentence and its performance. But Round and Bollow fell into neither of these categories. For them their bashings were dramatic inspirations. They looked forward now to the execution shed— 'cold meat shop' they styled it—but only after a double murder that would be completely satisfactory to their now thoroughly warped intellects. Lest tender domestic influences should wean them from their joint decision, they found on their release (they were 'model prisoners,' and obtained remissions) that their partners had left them for good. Round's wife had gone off with her lodger, and Bollow's girl had married his first cousin. They obtained plumbing and bricklaying jobs in the same district, thanks to the nervousness of the prison authorities, who did not wish to shoot two such persons out on to the world without occupations, and set up house together in one room, saved from quarrelling by the force and urgency of their mission.

The two judges lived on different sides of the same street, not a dozen streets away from the small newspaper shop over which the ex-convicts lodged. Scarce a day passed but the latter took a stroll down that respetable privet-bordered thoroughfare, and often they were rewarded with a sight of the elderly gentlemen walking side by side. Their wives' appearance they knew quite well after a few days in that neighbourhood. Every Tuesday Lady Grist went to Lady Leanjer's for Bridge, and the players could be seen in the front room from the pavement. Their husbands did not play, and in vacation would sometimes join forces at Mr Justice Grist's, while the ladies were thus engaged. More often than not, when the rubbers were over, Lady Leanjer would leave the house with her friend to bring the judge back to his evening meal. She would not trust her friend to send him home, as she felt uneasy if he was out of her sight and in another woman's company for even five minutes.

True to type, as some who have frequented lawyers' chambers will be aware, the judges were extremely averse to making the fabric of their domiciles more secure. This was the one point on which no conjugal nagging could be brought to bear effectively. But at last something really had to be done. There was a great fissure in the porch of Mr Justice Leanjer's, and there were loose bricks above the study window at the back of Mr Justice Grist's, and it was there that pointing operations were first begun. The building firm chosen was not that which employed Bollow, but it was not hard for him to scrape acquaintance with one of the men on the job, and learn a little about the internal economy of Number 18. Every Tuesday, the day of the Bridge party, one of the two servants had the afternoon off, so it was evident that for a successful battue a Tuesday afternoon in vacation when the two judges were alone in the house, with either the cook or the house-parlourmaid in charge, must be selected.

Worked had ceased at 18, and had begun at 23. It was a raw drizzly twilight when Round and Bollow, in appearance two lounging capped and belted working men, with the corner of a white card peeping out of the torn coat-pocket of either, appeared at the front-door of Mr Justice Grist's, taking their stand one behind the other. Bollow knocked and rang, according to the instructions on the brass plate, and the cook appeared.

'Me and my mate have called for a bag of tools what we left here a day or two back.'

'I don't remember *your* face,' the cook began. 'Where's the other one?' But while she spoke Round had been pushing his mate forward, and now both were in the hall, the door was shutting, and the chloroformed gag being applied by Bollow. Round cut the telephone wire. During this joint procedure not a word was spoken. Then, still one behind the other, they advanced quickly towards a room at the back of the long hall.

The judges, both a little deaf, were sitting at a table in full view of the garden, playing chess. An open box of cigars, a sherry decanter, and two glasses stood on the projecting rim of a large mahogany bookcase with double doors in the lower section opposite the fire-place. 'I have moved,' said Mr Justice Grist.

'It is your last move,' said Bollow audibly, and Round removed the key of the door to his pocket.

The elderly gentlemen turned spectacled eyes simultaneously on the intruders. They did not rise from their chairs; they were lifted from them. By a preconcerted arrangement each man took a victim. Though the owner of the house was not so spare as his colleague, he was a baby in the grip of Round.

'This is an outrage,' spluttered short-sighted Mr Justice Leanjer, as his glasses fell on the floor. Bollow trod on them. The owner of the house was tongue-tied—he had recognised the men at once. 'We're not going to waste words on you,' said Round; 'You're going to be killed first, and flogged after. But you'll know *what a bashing is like* before you get one. Steady him, pard! Ready! Now kiss your learned brother! "*Kiss*," I say!'

With tremendous force the heads of the judges were driven against one another; Mr Justice Grist's glasses broke on the side of his colleague's nose.

'Won,' roared Round.

The dazed and shaking forms were placed again in position, 'Kiss!' Another resounding crack.

'Tew,' roared Bollow.

Three, four, five, six followed in sharp succession. The two heads were now dangling, the floor prickly with broken glass. At the eighth impact Round called 'Enough! Strip them!'

A scuffling noise was heard in the passage, 'She's waking up,' said Round.

'Never mind her! She'll have to go out for the police. Get to with the work!'

In a quarter of an hour's time Round unlocked the door and tok his place opposite Bollow at the chess table. So neatly had the affair been handled that not a piece was overturned. The men had swept them aside, poured themselves out sherries, taken a cigar apiece, and sat, wine-glasses before them, contemplating their work. Each smoked, his stout leather belt hanging across his knees.

Lady Grist, accompanied by her friend Lady Leanjer, let herself in with her key before the cook returned with four policemen. The two ex-convicts were not the first things the ladies saw before they fainted. They saw the naked plum-coloured backs of their husbands side by side on the library carpet. Neatly balanced on the nape of each neck was a card. These were inscribed in block capitals:

Exhibit 1   Exhibit 2
Cat-Lover Grist   Cat-Lover Leanjer

Merrily laughed Round and Bollow three months later, as each stood on the drop.

The Women Avenge

EDGAR JEPSON

Lady Northwold gazed across the big drawing-room at Lady Mosenheim and hated her. She hated her big, sleepy brown eyes; she hated her broad, white, waxen, impassive face; she hated her big, heavy figure; she hated the feline relaxation with which it sprawled in the easy chair.

But nowadays she hated so many things. Before Charles had been killed at Neuve Chapelle and Jack at Loos she had not even taken the trouble to despise Lady Mosenheim. She had considered her a creature of another sphere, whose appearance and attributes were of no importance. Now she hated her: she was a part of this new, dreadful, desolate life. She could not even give her credit for the firmness and skill with which she handled the committee of women, checked their chatter, drove them along and dealt efficaciously with the heavy tale of work. They were in earnest: no doubt of that. But they were a pampered, feckless crew, used to gabble and to have their gabbling listened to, incapable of sustained effort. Often she helped Lady Mosenheim, supporting her with a few incisive, frequently contemptuous, words which hushed and abashed the time-wasters. But she hated her. She was part of this welter of death into which the world had fallen, in which she herself went on living, if indeed it could be called living.

Between them they drove another motion through and chose three women to see to the carrying out of the work it involved, one of them capable, all three in earnest, deadly earnest. They would make mistakes, silly mistakes; but they would learn from them and get the work done; hundreds of wounded men would benefit by it.

In spite of herself Lady Northwold breathed a sigh of satisfaction at the progress they had made. Lady Mosenheim gazed with a faint, pondering frown at her handsome, high-bred face, with its clearly cut features and its disdainful air. The hair under her hat was white. Before Neuve Chapelle it had been a warm chestnut brown. Her face had been smooth; now there were deep lines in it. She looked more than her forty-nine years. But she sat upright in her straight-backed chair. Her face was serene. Lady Mosenheim made up her mind.

The Duchess of Hammersmith was putting forward a proposal that efforts should be made to bring in the country clergy and arrange that wounded officers should become paying guests at their parsonages. Lady Northwold's eyes wandered to Clarissa Leggat. But for the war Clarissa would have been Charles's wife months ago. Lady Northwold had been doubtful about the match: Clarissa had been one of the most extravagant as well as one of the most beautiful girls in London; it had seemed not unlikely that she would ruin Charles. Yes: there was no doubt that Clarissa had kept her beauty; but something of its colour had faded; her violet eyes were duller than they had used to be. Well, she was not extravagant now: that frock was months out of fashion and shabby; she had not bought a new frock since the war began. Hundreds of wounded men were grateful to Clarissa. With her wonderful vitality she never seemed to tire. Sometimes she complained that she never tired. Lady Northwold saw that the change in her also displayed itself in a restlessness; she changed her position half a dozen times while the Duchess of Hammersmith was speaking. No: Clarissa would not have ruined Charles.

A sub-committee was appointed to deal with the proposal of the Duchess of Hammersmith, and the meeting broke up.

As Lady Northwold was going towards the door, Miss Beecher, Lady Mosenheim's secretary, gave her a note. In it Lady Mosenheim asked her to stay to speak to her privately. Wondering, she consented.

The women drifted out slowly; half a dozen of them paused to make suggestions to Lady Mosenheim, foolish, impracticable suggestions. Lady Northwold wondered at the impassive, patient politeness with which she dealt with them.

Clarissa came to her and asked what Lord Northwold was doing now.

'Organising—always organising,' said Lady Northwold. 'You'd better come back with me to lunch and see him.'

'Thanks, I should like to. But Lady Mosenheim wants to speak to me first. I'll come on later.'

'Oh, she wants to speak to me, too,' said Lady Northwold.

Lady Mosenheim came to them. She seemed to Lady Northwold to have lost some of her impassivity; there was a gleam in the depths of her sombre eyes, a suggestion of suppressed eagerness in her tones.

'I shall keep you only a little while. Will you come to my room?' she said.

Lady Northwold and Clarissa followed her. Lady Northwold disliked her smooth, noiseless movement. A woman of her weight ought not to move so silently. There was something feline and foreign in it.

Lady Mosenheim brought them into her room. It was not large; and drawn rose-coloured curtains dimmed the light. There were no chairs in it. Divans covered with cushions were against the walls, which were draped with hangings of a barbaric richness of colour matching the coverings of the divans and cushions. The scent of incense hung heavy on the air. Lady Mosenheim was the daughter of an Eastern banker; her girlhood had been passed in Smyrna and Stamboul.

Lady Northwold disliked the room, its barbaric colour, its dim, scented air.

'Will you sit down?' said Lady Mosenheim, and she sank on to a divan in a half-reclining posture.

Clarissa followed her example. Lady Northwold sat on the edge of a divan, upright.

Lady Mosenheim looked at them thoughtfully, then she said in her deep, soft voice: 'I have chosen you because you are the two strongest women I know. Also you are honourable women. If you do not join in it, you will not breathe a word of my plan to anyone? Is that not so?'

'We shall not,' said Lady Northwold, somewhat astonished at this opening.

'Not a word', said Clarissa.

'My law says: "Breach for breach, eye for eye, tooth for tooth," ' said Lady Mosenheim slowly; and her voice was yet deeper. 'But the men will not avenge and punish. I have talked to them—to your men, politicians and generals—to my men, politicians and financiers. They will not avenge; they will not even punish. The men who have robbed me of my sons are to go scot-free.'

She paused; they looked at her earnestly, with intent eyes.

'Therefore the women must avenge and punish,' said Lady Mosenheim.

She paused again. Clarissa raised herself higher on her elbow; and a sudden fierce gleam shone in her eyes.

'I don't quite understand,' said Lady Northwold.

'The women whose sons and lovers have died must punish the traitors who betrayed them, the murderers who sent them to their death,' said Lady Mosenheim.

'Yes. But how?' said Clarissa a little breathlessly.

'There is only one punishment for traitors and murderers—death,' said Lady Mosenheim in a passionless tone.

'But we women?' said Lady Northwold.

'The women must kill. The men will not. They are busy and forget. How should they remember? Did they endure our travail? Did they rear the children? But we women, we do not forget. We shall never forget. We shall not forgive. We must avenge,' said Lady Mosenheim.

Her deep tones were as passionless as if she were discussing an abstract problem in physics.

'It is true. We do not forget—and as for forgiving—no,' said Clarissa between her set teeth.

'No. We do not forget,' said Lady Northwold.

'Then will you help to avenge?' said Lady Mosenheim.

'But what can we do?' said Lady Northwold.

'We can kill,' said Lady Mosenheim.

'Of course we can!' cried Clarissa; and her eyes were gleaming with a fierce light.

There was a faint flush on Lady Northwold's face; and she said softly: 'If we only could.'

'We can. There are many ways,' said Lady Mosenheim with quiet confidence. 'The question is: will you avenge your dead?'

'Show me how!' said Lady Northwold softly, but quickly.

Her face was changed; the apathy had vanished from it; it was flushed with eagerness.

'Yes. Show us how,' said Clarissa eagerly.

'Good. I will show you,' said Lady Mosenheim.

She half turned, pressed a spring in the wall behind her, pushed back a sliding panel, and drew from it an octavoledger bound in vellum.

'Here is a list of eighty traitors and their crimes. Most of them would have been set against a wall and shot months ago in France, Russia, or Germany. Let us choose the one we will execute first, for with different men, the method will be different,' said Lady Mosenheim.

They rose quickly and came to her side.

The ledger contained a list of names; and written against each name was the crime, or crimes, the traitors had committed. The first names were the names of politicians only.

'Of course, we cannot begin with this man,' said Lady Mosenheim, setting her finger on the first name, 'It would upset things too much at present. He must wait. But what about this one?'

She laid her finger on the sixth name.

'That's the man!' cried Lady Northwood and Clarissa with one voice.

'Yes. I've thought that he was the man to begin with. Every one will know why he was executed. If he hadn't sacrificed his country to his career, this horror would never have befallen the world. He'll make an excellent example. There are, too, a dozen political malefactors who will take warning by his fate. They'll shiver in their shoes. What is more they'll make an awful fuss.'

'What does that matter?' said Lady Northwold contemptuously.

'Then shall we deal with Blagden first?' said Lady Mosenheim.

'Yes,' they said with one voice.

'Then the first thing to do is to get him into our hands. You know him of course?'

'I knew him. But of course he hasn't been in my house since we learnt his treachery. But I haven't actually broken with him. I haven't seen him to cut him. He doesn't give people the chance,' said Lady Northwold.

'If you were to invite him to your house on the river, would he come?'

'He would. He's a snob of the worst,' said Clarissa.

'That's excellent,' said Lady Mosenheim. 'Once we get him there, we can take our time about dealing with him. But I'm afraid we shall have to have the help of a man. We three would not be a match for him physically. We can't afford to bungle. There are eighty names of traitors in this list; we must execute at least forty of them before anyone begins to suspect us.'

'We mightn't be a match for him physically, though he does lead an inactive life. But it seems wrong to have to call in a man,' said Clarissa.

'It does; but——' said Lady Mosenheim; and she shrugged her shoulders.

'We needn't. There's Williams,' said Lady Northwold quickly. She turned to Lady Mosenheim and added: 'She's my cook—a Welshwoman. Her only son was killed in the retreat from Mons. He was one of those who had to fall out because they had been given tight boots; and the Germans murdered him. We lost scores of men through one consignment of boots.'

'I know. The name of the contractor and the name of the man who got them through after they had been rejected are here,' said Lady Mosenheim; and she tapped the ledger. 'They come quite early on the list.'

'If Dinah knew them, she'd murder them, or try to. She was always a fierce creature; and she has been brooding. She'll join us—joyfully. And she's six feet tall, broad in proportion, and stronger than three men out of five. She'd be more than a match for Blagden,' said Lady Northwold. 'Also she has already been fined for asaulting a Labour leader.'

'I expect that he's on the list,' said Lady Mosenheim. 'But is she safe? She can be trusted to hold her tongue?'

'I can answer for her,' said Lady Northwold.

Lady Mosenheim laughed a slow, somewhat chilling laugh and said: 'Good. Things are shaping—things are shaping. I knew that if you two came into my scheme, difficulties would vanish. It looked as if I should have to be content with poisoning off these vermin quietly. But now we can execute them in such a way that the lot of them will be shaking in their shoes before the month is out. I think that we shall hang some of them.'

'We will begin with a hanging. We will hang this man Blagden— at River Court,' said Clarissa. 'Why I know the very tree. Dinah Williams and I will hang him on it. It's an ideal place.'

'Good. I thought you would be an enthusiast,' said Lady Mosenheim smiling at her.

'Why we could almost try him first,' said Clarissa.

'There is no need. The dog will know why we hang him,' said Lady Mosenheim.

'The thing to do is to make a beginning,' said Lady Northwold. 'I will write to him at once inviting him down to River Court and asking him to fix the day. If he accepts, we can make definite arrangements. If he refuses, we must find some other way of getting him into our hands.'

'That's the way to work—no waste of time. Meanwhile I will go on getting information about the boot contractor. We know all about Blagden. But the boot man is another matter,' said Lady Mosenheim.

She came down with them to the door of the house; and they shook hands with her with the friendliest warmth. They went down the steps to Lady Northwold's car changed women: they carried their heads high; their faces were bright with new purpose; the listlessness had gone from their carriage and gait.

Lady Mosenheim did not miss the change in them; a smile of satisfaction wreathed her lips.

After lunch Clarissa went to her canteen work in a munition factory in South London. As soon as Lord Northwold had set out for the Admiralty Lady Northwold sent for Dinah Williams.

She came, a big-boned, broad, thick, tall woman, with reddish hair, green-eyed and freckled. Her lips were set in a gloomy repression; and she wore a somewhat truculent air.

'You half-murdered that Labour man, Bill Tripp, because you thought he was hindering the men who were trying to avenge Bob; and I raised your wages for doing it,' said Lady Northwold gently.

'It's little use wages are to me, m'lady. I've no one to spend them on now Bob's gone; and I'll never have any grandchildren now, so it's no use saving up,' said Dinah in a deep, harsh voice.

'I suppose not,' said Lady Northwold sadly. 'But would you like to help to punish the men who are to blame for Bob's death?'

Dinah looked at her, gasped, and cried: 'Would I like it! Give me the chance, m'lady; and I'll bless your name every day I live!'

'I mean really punish them—kill them—execute them as traitors,' said Lady Northwold in the same quiet voice.

'I'm ready to choke any one of them here and now!' cried Dinah; and she held out her big hands with the fingers working.

'Yes. But we want to hang people, not hang for them,' said Lady Northwold grimly. 'It would spoil our usefulness.'

'Yes, m'lady,' said Dinah more quietly.

'So you see I don't only want you help because you're stronger than most men. I must be able to rely on you. A word to any one about what we do, or are going to do, would make us quite helpless again. And the women have to do this work; the men won't.'

'They're a poor lot,' said Dinah with conviction. 'Not a word will ever come from me, m'lady.'

'I'm sure it won't,' said Lady Northwold.

Dinah rubbed her big hands together and said in an anxious tone: 'An' when do we begin, m'lady?'

'Very soon—next week, perhaps.'

'It'll be something to look forward to, m'lady. I'm thinking I shall sleep better o' nights. It's doin' nothing an' bein' able to do nothing that's so wearing.' She paused and added in a faintly hopeful tone: 'Is there any chance of punishing the man as sold them tight boots to the Government?'

'A very good chance. In fact, I think I can promise you that he will be punished soon, and the man who helped him to sell them, too.'

Dinah laughed a mirthless, bitter laugh, and said in a low, very harsh voice: 'I'd go to hell for that, m'lady, cheerfully!'

'Hush! You mustn't say dreadful things like that,' said Lady Northwold, in a horrified tone. 'Besides, the hangman doesn't go to hell for hanging murderers; he just performs a duty. And we're only going to perform a duty which the men are too slack and timid to perform. But, of course, they don't remember as women do.'

'An' that's true, m'lady. An' how should they? A boy is his mother's ever so much more than he is his father's—all children are, if it comes to that,' said Dinah.

'Yes. That's just it. If our boys were as much to their fathers as they are to us, these scoundrels would have been hanged a year ago,' said Lady Northwold, with a sudden heat.

'Well, we're going to make up for their slackness, m'lady. An' I'm sure you'll see as we make up for it proper when we do start,' said Dinah, in an almost cheerful tone.

'I think we can trust ourselves to make a thorough job of it,' said Lady Northwold, with quiet confidence.

'Yes, m'lady,' said Dinah; and she left the room on brisk feet, smiling.

Lady Northwold went to her writing-table and wrote her invitation to Mr Blagden. Then she went out and posted it herself. She would have liked to register it.

At dinner she told Lord Northwold about it.

'What? Blagden? You've invited Blagden down to River Court?' he cried, in a tone of stupefaction.

'Yes. I thought I would,' she said carelessly. 'Blagden and Lady Mosenheim.'

He stared at her blankly.

'My hat!' he said softly and no more.

Mr Blagden was somewhat surprised and much pleased by Lady Northwold's invitation. As a public man he was well aware that the disfavour of the public is nearly as fleeting as its favour; and he was bearing the disfavor into which he had fallen without great impatience. That disfavour would die down; his disastrous concealment of the unpalatable truth would presently be forgotten; and he could trust his colleagues, the most important of them partners in his secrecy, to help him to return, after a few years, to public life. In the meantime he had his pension and his friends who understood his position.

He was so much pleased with this invitation because it was a sign, a striking sign, that his unpopularity was beginning to wane. Lady Northwold was not only on the opposite side in politics, but she had lost her two sons in the war. If she could forget, who could not? He felt it to be a tribute also to his personal qualities: he had been a figure in society before his resignation; society wanted him back. His large, flabby face was wreathed with a smile almost triumphant as he wrote the answer to the invitation. He wrote it with thoughtful care: he must not show how much he was pleased; he must not show himself too eager; but he must show a cordial readiness to accept the proffered olive branch. He did.

Lady Northwold had asked him to choose the day on which he would come; and out of his desire not to show himself too eager he chose the following Wednesday week.

It seemed a long while to wait to Lady Northwold and Clarissa and Dinah Williams; Lady Mosenheim came of a more patient race. Lord Northwold did not fail to perceive the change in his wife, and he told her that during the last few days she had grown seven years younger.

'It must be this beautiful summer weather after all the rain we've been having,' she said, smiling at him.

It might be. But he wondered. He wondered yet more when she went out of the drawing-room humming 'Tipperary.'

On the morning of the Wednesday chosen by Mr Blagden for his visit, the Northwolds' butler wondered at the cheerfulness of Dinah Williams. She who had been so gloomy and savage for months went so far as to joke with the two maids she was taking with her about the prospect of their findings sweethearts at River Court.

Lady Northwold was motoring down with Lady Mosenheim and Clarissa, who was to drive the car. Clarissa came to the house glowing. In the course of the past week her cheeks had filled out almost to their old contours; they had recovered their old warm colouring. They drove round to Park Lane to fetch Lady Mosenheim. She came down the steps of her house with a lithe eagerness astonishing in one so bulky; and her eyes, usually dull, were shining. They reached River Court an hour before Mr Blagden.

It is a large house, in the middle of beautiful gardens, tended now only by boys and old men. The front is towards the river; and a broad lawn runs from it down to the river's edge. Two cedars stand, twenty yards apart, fifty feet from the house; a shrubbery of tall deodars runs down the left side of the lawn, a shrubbery of taller Wellingtonias down the right side of it. At the bottom of it, on the left, about fifteen yards from the river a group of three great chestnut trees tower above the deodar shrubbery. Their branches reach to the edge of it.

As soon as the three women had washed off the dust of the journey they walked down the lawn to the chestnut trees.

'That's the bough I was thinking of,' said Clarissa, pointing to a great limb which ran out at right angles to the trunk about sixteen feet from the ground. 'It would bear twenty men.'

'Yes. It is an excellent bough,' said Lady Mosenheim, gazing at it with approving eyes. 'And you have the rope?'

'It's at the bottom of Dinah Williams' trunk,' said Lady Northwold. 'She bought it in Birmingham on Friday. I sent her down there on purpose to buy it. It seemed safe. She bought two dozen clothes-pegs, too. It would never have done for one of us to buy the rope, for if there is a great fuss, as there will be, our photographs will very likely be in the papers, especially if we have to give evidence at the inquest.'

'That was an excellent idea. I knew that you and Miss Leggat were the people to work with. I have brought a card with 'For Treachery' typed on it. It is part of an ordinary post-card; and I typed it myself. There'll be no tracing that.' said Lady Mosenheim.

'Dinah is going to cut two lengths off the rope to tie his hands and feet with,' said Clarissa. 'Of course, we'll gag him with his own handkerchief.'

'You think of everything,' said Lady Mosenheim, smiling at her.

'It will give us plenty of time to try him, if he can't shout for help,' said lady Northwold.

'Try him?' cried Lady Mosenheim, in a tone of sharp surprise.

'I should much prefer to try him, if it can be done,' said Lady Northwold.

Lady Mosenheim looked at her with a pondering frown.

'The facts and his guilt are clear enough,' said Clarissa. 'We only want to hear any defence he has to make.'

'Oh, that will be easy enough,' said Lady Mosenheim quickly. 'We can try him without his knowing that he is being tried, for he will make that defence whenever we choose to question him—at lunch—at dinner. He has it ready—always.'

'Why, of course,' said Lady Northwold in a tone of relief.

Mr Blagden arrived at a quarter to five; and at five they had tea under the right-hand cedar at the upper end of the lawn. The politician was in great feather, for he was resolved to make it clearto them how much they had lost by not enjoying more of his society. Moreover, he was stimulated by finding himself among such agreeable people in such delightful surroundings. He talked excellently about people, books, plays, and places. He was far too tactful to breathe a word about the war. No suspicion crossed his mind that not one of his three listeners was really interested in anything else.

Yet there was something abut them that aroused a vague uneasiness in him. After a while he decided it was their eyes. There was, indeed, no hostility in them; but he had a feeling that all the while they were studying him, weighing him. Their lips smiled all the while in response to his pleasant humour; but their eyes smiled not at all.

After a while they rose and strolled about the gardens. He talked about the flowers and plants very pleasantly, displaying a considerable knowledge of gardening. He had words of warm admiration for the three chestnut trees and deplored the passing of the village blacksmith.

Then he asked to go on the river in a Canadian canoe; and Clarissa went with him. She was animated, even gay. He was too busy paddling and steering to observe that her eyes never smiled. He told himself, somewhat cynically, that she was an example of the quickness with which a fashionable woman forgets.

At dinner he was again the agreeable, brilliant talker; and the three women seemed to hang on his lips. Jael was not more pleasant and sympathetic with Sisera. But still their intent eyes never smiled; and now and again the vague uneasiness invaded him. He told himself that it was absurd. Assuredly there was no hostility in their gaze, merely interest, unaffected interest, natural enough but none the less flattering.

Then as they were drinking their coffee under the cedar Lady Mosenheim struck the jarring note.

She said in a deep, almost purring voice, with a note of cynicism in it in utter disaccord with the beauty of the gardens and the night: 'I suppose people are forgetting their dislike of you, Mr Blagden?'

He paused, taken aback by so crude an introduction of an unpleasant personal topic.

'Oh, yes. They never remember anything long,' he said, with a note of impatience in his voice.

They said nothing. They looked at him with those intent, weighing eyes.

A sudden desire came upon him to clear himself of blame in their minds. They were women of the world: they could understand and judge him by the proper standards, the standards which really regulate the actions of a man of the world.

'Of course, people who are not in politics themselves don't understand a matter like that, how carefully one has to move, how impossible it is sometimes to move at all,' he said slowly, almost didactically. 'We could not have acted otherwise than we did without doing the party irreparable damage. We should have had to run counter to the traditions of fifty years. We had always opposed any increase of armaments. We had always kept the Navy even as small as we dared. Had we suddenly turned round and proposed a large increase in the Army we should have stultified ourselves. It would have wrecked the party.'

'Another half-million men would have made the difference though, wouldn't it?' said Clarissa carelessly.

'They would have made a great difference,' said Mr Blagden cautiously.

'Wouldn't they have prevented the war?' said Lady Northwold in the tone of one rather bored by the subject.

'That is a great deal to say—a great deal,' he said quickly.

'Roughly speaking, it would have prevented it,' said Lady Mosenheim in a tone of no great interest in the matter.

'Roughly speaking—probably,' said Mr Blagden in a judicial tone. 'The fact that we were in a position to come to the aid of France effectively would have made a great difference. But I assure you that it would have meant wrecking the party. A considerable percentage of our followers in the House would have revolted; the Irish would have voted against the proposal to a man; and at the next General Election a third of our supporters would have refrained from voting at all. We should have had to make a bargain with the Tories, too; and goodness knows what price they would have asked for their support. And then the Press. Just think of what the Cocoa Press and the *Evening Liberal* and the *Bawchester Guardian* would have said. We should have had to rely entirely on the Tory Press for support. Why, it's unthinkable! No: I talked the matter over with some of my oldest colleagues, men who know the game—

Parliamentary politics, I mean—from A to Z; and they agreed with me that it could not be done.'

'But you might have warned the country,' said Lady Northwold.

'We couldn't do that without enlarging the Army and wrecking the party,' said Mr Blagden quickly. 'One thing meant the other. And as things are nowadays, if a party goes out of office, it stays out of office for years.'

'I see,' said Clarissa slowly. 'It didn't seem worthwhile to save the world at the expense of the party.'

'Dear, dear! That's an unfair thing to say—very unfair. It's—it's so crude!' said Mr Blagden, with some heat.

'And of course the Germans humbugged you. They never let you gather that they were in such deadly earnest,' said Lady Northwold quickly in the tone of one trying to smooth matters over.

'Oh, no: they didn't. You can't humbug me,' said Mr Blagden proudly. 'But we thought it would be quite easy to keep England out of it. And it would have been but for their incredible stupidity in violating the neutrality of Belgium. If they'd only had the sense to violate the neutrality of Switzerland! Of course, in that case the so-called strong men of the party would have resigned. But really it would have been stronger without them—much stronger.'

'I suppose it would,' said Lady Mosenheim. 'And so if it were to do again, you would do just the same.'

'Oh, you can't expect me to say that!' cried Mr Blagden; and he laughed shortly. 'I could not foresee that there would be all this unreasonable fuss abut our having kept our knowledge of the coming danger to ourselves.'

'I suppose it has damaged your career,' said Clarissa in a sympathetic tone.

'To tell you the truth, my dear young lady, it has played the very dickens with my career. I shouldn't wonder if it was seven or eight years before I hold office again,' said Mr Blagden bitterly.

The three women looked at one another with quietly eloquent eyes. There was no need for Lady Northwold to say aloud that she was satisfied; her eyes said it.

'I do not believe that you will ever hold office again,' said Lady Mosenheim, with rather chilling conviction.

He looked at her with keen annoyance and said fretfully to Clarissa: 'Lady Mosenheim is not very encouraging. But I think she overestimates the memory of the British public.'

'I don't know about that,' said Clarissa doubtfully.

Dinah Williams, bringing out whisky-and-soda on a tray, created a diversion. As she mixed a whisky-and-soda for Mr Blagden, she gazed at him earnestly. His flushed face of a man who had dined well and his big cigar did not seem to please her. Her eyes were grim.

Lady Northwold pointed out the beautiful effect of the moon rising through the trees on the crown of the slope beyond the river; and presently Mr Blagden recovered his serenity and again talked easily. The three women kept looking towards the deodar shrubbery on the left, not impatiently, with expectant eyes.

It was nearly twenty minutes later that Dinah Williams appeared in the entrance of a path which ran through it from the lawn to the rose garden. She had taken off her white cap and apron and would hardly have been visible had she not held a white handkerchief in her hand. She did not wave it.

Lady Northwold breathed a short sigh and rose. Dinah Williams disappeared.

'Let us go down to the bank of the river and get really cool,' said Lady Northwold.

'An excellent idea. I shall sleep much better for it,' said Mr Blagden.

'Oh, you'll sleep soundly enough,' said Lady Mosenheim in her deep, soft voice.

He led the way, talking amiably with Clarissa, deploring the fact that he was a bachelor, alone in the world. Lady Northwold and Lady Mosenheim came a few yards behind them in silence. Lady Mosenheim clasped Lady Northwold's hand for a moment. It was cool and quite steady; it did not even quiver to the sudden touch. Their eyes never left the shapeless bulk and clumsy head of the politician.

They came under the chestnut trees.

'A truly delicious coolness,' said Mr Blagden, pausing to look up into the dark roof of interlacing boughs.

Dinah Williams came noiselessly round the great trunk behind him; her big arm went round his neck, half choking him, she swung him off his feet, lowered him, shifted her grip to his throat, and dropped heavily on him, driving the breath out of his body. Clarissa and Lady Northwold seized his wrists; and Clarissa deftly bound them together. Lady Mosenheim, kneeling beside him, took his handkerchief from the pocket of his dinner jacket, and thrust it into his gasping mouth. Clarissa bound his ankles together.

They rose. There had been no struggle, but all four of them were panting softly. Dinah Williams laughed exultantly.

'Hush!' said Clarissa.

They stood gazing down on him.

'Bring him to the place,' said Lady Northwold.

They stooped, lifted him, carried him under the bough, from which the rope was already dangling, and set him on his feet.

'We are going to hang you,' said Clarissa quietly.

'You have confessed that you are one of the persons responsible for this war. On your own showing ordinary courage and honesty on your part would probably have prevented it. So we shall hang you,' said Lady Northwold.

'You betrayed your country and the world, so we hang you,' said Lady Mosenheim.

'You sent thousands to their death and you're going to hang for it,' said Dinah Williams.

None of them spoke with any heat. At the moment they were quite impersonal, mere arms wielding the sword of justice.

He gazed from one to another stupidly. A fat and inactive man he had hardly recovered enough from the rough handling to understand them clearly.

Lady Northwold slipped the noose over his head and drew it tight. Lady Mosenheim pinned the card on which she had typed 'For Treachery' to the lapel of his jacket. All four of them took hold of the rope and hauled.

They felt no horror. In the darkness under the trees they could barely see his body rise from the ground. They could not see that it was a body; it might have been a sack of corn.

When it had risen about six feet from the ground they ceased hauling. Dinah Williams wound the rope round the trunk of the tree and made it fast. They came away.

Twenty yards up the lawn Lady Mosenheim raised her big arms in the air, heaved a great sigh, and said: 'I feel as if a weight were lifted from my soul.'

'Yes. That's exactly it,' said Lady Northwold quietly.

'I shall sleep—oh, how I shall sleep to-night!' said Clarissa.

'I know, miss,' said Dinah Williams.

She took the path through the shrubbery, went round to the back of the house, and in through the back door.

The others went through the long windows of the drawing-room into the hall, and upstairs. On the landing they kissed one another and said good-night.

They slept heavily.

At eight o'clock next morning Mary Bates, the housemaid who brought Lady Northwold's tea, wore a startled air.

When she had set the tray on the little table beside the bed and drawn the blinds she said in a tone of excitement: 'Please, m'lady. Mr Blagden's bed hasn't bin slept in; an' his pyjamas are lying on it just as I left them; an' Hopkins says that the droring-room winders were open all night.'

'Surely he hasn't fallen into the river!' cried Lady Northwold. 'When we went to bed he had gone for a stroll down the lawn. Tell Higgins to make haste down to the river and look. I will get up at once.'

Mary Bates went quickly. Lady Northwold ate her bread-and-butter, drank her tea, and rose. From the window she saw

Higgins, the gardener, Mary Bates, and two boys hurrying up the left-hand side of the lawn with scared faces.

She opened the window, leaned out, and when they drew near, called to them.

'The gentleman 'as 'ung 'isself, m'lady!' cried Higgins.

'Send for the police at once! Don't let anyone go near the spot—there may be a clue!' cried Lady Northwold.

The local police arrived in twenty minutes. Two hours later a high official and three detectives arrived from Scotland Yard. They could find no clue to the perpetrators of the crime. Lady Northwold and her guests could give them no help: Mr Blagden had gone for a stroll down the lawn; they had gone to bed, leaving him to fasten the drawing-room windows. They had heard no cry, no sound of a struggle. Mr Rodwell, the official from Scotland Yard, found them sufficiently shocked and horrified. He suggested that they should return to London; it would only be distressing for them to stay in the house; the police would take charge of it. They accepted the suggestion thankfully. An hour later, having sent Dinah Williams and the maids by train, they drove off in Lady Northwold's car.

On the way, with never a word about Mr Blagden, they quietly discussed which criminal they should execute next.

As Lady Mosenheim went up the steps of her house she turned and said cheerfully: 'It will encourage the others: you'll see.'

Beckwith's Case

MAURICE HEWLETT

The facts were as follows. Mr Stephen Mortimer Beckwith
was a young man living at Wilsford in the Amesbury district
of Wiltshire. He was a clerk in the Wilts and Dorset Bank at
Salisbury, was married and had one child. His age at the time
of the experience here related was twenty-eight. His health was
excellent.

On 30 November, 1887, at about ten o'clock at night, he
was returning home from Amesbury, where he had been spending
the evening at a friend's house. The weather was mild, with a
rain-bearing wind blowing in squalls from the southwest. It was
three-quarter moon that night, and although the sky was
frequently overcast it was at no time dark. Mr Beckwith, who
was riding a bicycle and accompanied by his fox-terrier Strap,
states that he had no difficulty in seeing and avoiding the stones
cast down at intervals by the road-menders; that flocks of sheep
in the hollows were very visible, and that, passing Wilsford

House, he saw a barn owl quite plainly and remarked its heavy, uneven flight.

A mile beyond Wilsford House, Strap, the dog, broke through the quickset hedge upon his right-hand side and ran yelping up the down, which rises sharply just there. Mr Beckwith, who imagined that he was after a hare, whistled him in, presently calling him sharply. 'Strap, Strap, come out of it.' The dog took no notice, but ran directly to a clump of gorse and bramble half-way up the down, and stood there in the attitude of a pointer, with uplifted paw, watching the gorse intently, and whining. Mr Beckwith was by this time dismounted, observing the dog. He watched him for some minutes from the road. The moon was bright, the sky at the moment free from cloud.

He himself could see nothing in the gorse, though the dog was undoubtedly in a high state of excitement. It made frequent rushes forward, but stopped short of the object that it saw and trembled. It did not bark outright but rather whimpered—'a curious, shuddering crying noise', says Mr Beckwith. Interested by the animal's persistent and singular behaviour, he now sought a gap in the hedge, went through on to the down, and approached the clumped bushes. Strap was so much occupied that he barely noticed his master's coming; it seemed as if he dared not take his eyes for one second from what he saw in there.

Beckwith, standing behind the dog, looked into the gorse. From the distance at which he still stood he could see nothing at all. His belief then was that there was either a tramp in a drunken sleep, possibly two tramps, or a hare caught in a wire, or possibly even a fox. Having no stick with him, he did not care, at first, to go any nearer, and contented himself with urging on the terrier. This was not very courageous of him, as he admits, and was quite unsuccessful. No verbal excitations could draw Strap nearer to the furze-bush. Finally the dog threw up his head, showed his master the white arcs of his eyes and fairly howled at the moon. At this dismal sound Mr Beckwith owned himself alarmed. It was, as he describes it—though he is an Englishman—'uncanny'. The time, he owns, the aspect of the night, loneliness of the spot (midway up the steep slope of a chalk down), the mysterious shroud of darkness upon shadowed and distant objects and flood of white light upon the foreground— all these circumstances worked upon his imagination.

He was indeed for retreat; but here Strap was of a different mind. Nothing would excite him to advance, but nothing, either, could induce him to retire. Whatever he saw in the furze-bush Strap must continue to observe. In the face of this Beckwith summoned up his courage, took it in both hands and went much nearer to the furze-bushes, much nearer, that is, than Strap the terrier could bring himself to go. Then, he tells us, he did see a pair of bright eyes far in the thicket, which seemed to be fixed upon his, and by degrees also a pale and troubled face. Here, then, was neither fox nor drunken tramp, but some human creature, man, woman, or child, fully aware of him and of the dog.

Beckwith, who now had surer command of his feelings, spoke aloud, asking; 'What are you doing there? What's the matter?' He had no reply. He went one pace nearer, being still on his guard, and spoke again. 'I won't hurt you,' he said. 'Tell me what the matter is.' The eyes remained unwinkingly fixed upon his own. No movement of the features could be discerned.

The face, as he could now make it out, was very small—'about as big as a big wax doll's,' he says, 'of a longish oval, very pale.' He adds: 'I could see its neck now, no thicker than my wrist; and where its clothes began. I couldn't see any arms, for a good reason. I found out afterwards that they had been bound behind its back. I should have said immediately, "That's a girl in there", if it had not been for one or two plain considerations. It had not the size of what we call a girl, nor the face of what we mean by a child. It was, in fact, neither fish, flesh, nor fowl. Strap had known that from the beginning, and now I was of Strap's opinion myself.'

Advancing with care, a step at a time, Beckwith presently found himself within touching distance of the creature. He was now standing with furze half-way up his calves, right above it, stooping to look closely at it; and as he stooped and moved now this way, now that, to get a clearer view, so the crouching thing's eyes gazed up to meet his, and followed them about, as if safety lay only in that never-shifting, fixed regard. He had noticed, and states in his narrative, that Strap had seemed quite unable, in the same way, to take his eyes off the creature for a single second.

He could now see that, of whatever nature it might be, it was in form and features, most exactly a young woman. The features, for instance, were regular and fine. He remarks in particular upon the chin. All about its face, narrowing the oval of it, fell dark, glossy curtains of hair, very straight and glistening with wet. Its garment was cut in a plain circle round the neck and shorn off at the shoulders, leaving the arms entirely bare. This garment, shift, smock or gown, as he indifferently calls it, appeared thin, and was found afterwards to be of a grey colour, soft and clinging to the shape. It was made loose, however, and gathered in at the waist. He could not see the creature's legs as they were tucked under her. Her arms, it has been related, were behind her back. The only other things to be remarked upon were the strange stillness of one who was plainly suffering, and might well be alarmed, an appearance of expectancy, a dumb appeal; what he himself calls rather well 'an ignorant sort of impatience, like that of a sick animal'.

'Come,' Beckwith now said, 'let me help you up. You will get cold if you sit here. Give me your hand, will you?' She neither spoke nor moved; simply continued to search his eyes. Strap, meantime, was still trembling and whining. But now, when he stooped yet lower to take her forcibly by the arms, she shrank back a little way and turned her head, and he saw to his horror that she had a great open wound in the side of her neck—from which, however, no blood was issuing. Yet it was clearly a fresh wound, recently made.

He was greatly shocked. 'Good God,' he said, 'there's been foul play here,' and whipped out his handkerchief. Kneeling, he wound it several times round her slender throat and knotted it as tightly as he could; then, without more ado, he took her up in his arms, under the knees and round the middle, and carried her down the slope to the road. He describes her as of no weight at all. He says it was 'exactly like carrying an armful of feathers about'. 'I took her down the hill and through the hedge at the bottom as if she had been a pillow.'

Here it was that he discovered that her wrists were bound together behind her back with a kind of plait of things so intricate that he was quite unable to release them. He felt his pockets for his knife, but could not find it, and then recollected suddenly that he should have a new one with him, the third prize in a whist tournament in which he had taken part that evening. He found it wrapped in paper in his overcoat pocket, with it cut the thongs and set the little creature free. She immediately responded—the first sign of animation which she had displayed—by throwing both her arms about his body and clinging to him in an ecstasy. Holding him so that, as he says, he felt the shuddering go all through her, she suddenly lowered her head and touched his wrist with her cheek. He says that instead of being cold to the touch, 'like a fish', as she had seemed to be when he first took her out of the gorse, she was now 'as warm as toast, like a child'.

So far he had put her down for 'a foreigner', convenient term for defining something which one does not quite understand. She had none of his language, evidently; she was undersized, some, three feet six inches, by the look of her, and yet perfectly proportioned. She was most curiously dressed in a frock cut to the knee, and actually in nothing else at all. It left her bare-legged and bare-armed, and was made, as he puts it himself, of stuff like cobweb, 'those dusty, drooping kind which you put on your finger to stop bleeding'. He could not recognise the web, but was sure that it was neither linen nor cotton. It seemed to stick to her body wherever it touched a prominent part. 'You could see very well, to say nothing of feeling, that she was well made and well nourished.' She ought, as he judged, to be a child of five years old, 'and a feather-weight at that'; but he felt certain that she must be 'much more like sixteen'. It was that, I gather, which made him suspect her of being something outside experience. So far, then, it was safe to call her a foreigner: but he was not yet at the end of his discoveries.

Heavy footsteps, coming from the direction of Wilsford, in due time proved to be of Police Constable Gulliver, a neighbour of Beckwith's and guardian of the peace in his own village. He lifted his lantern to flash it into the traveller's eyes, and dropped it again with a pleasant 'good evening'. He added that it was inclined to be showery, which was more than true, as it was, at the moment, raining hard. With that, it seems, he would have passed on.

But Beckwith, whether smitten by self-consciousness of having been seen with a young woman in his arms at a suspicious hour of the night by the village policeman, or bursting perhaps with the importance of his affair, detained Gulliver. 'Just look at this,' he said boldly. 'Here's a pretty thing to have found on a lonely road. Foul play somewhere, I'm afraid'; he then exhibited his burden to the lantern light.

To his extreme surprise, however, the constable, after exploring the beam of light and all that it contained for some time in silence, reached out his hand for the knife which Beckwith still held open. He looked at it on both sides, examined the handle and gave it back. 'Foul play, Mr Beckwith?' he said, laughing. 'Bless you, they use bigger tools than that. That's just a toy, the like of that. Cut your hand with it, though, already, I see.' He must have noticed the handkerchief, for as he spoke the light from his lantern shone full upon the face and neck of the child, or creature, in the young man's arms, so clearly that, looking down at it, Beckwith himself could see the clear grey of its intensely watchful eyes, and the very pupils of them, diminished to specks of black. It was now, therefore, plain to him that what he held was a foreigner indeed, since the parish constable was unable to see it. Strap had smelt it, then seen it, and he, Beckwith, had seen it; but it was invisible to Gulliver. 'I felt now,' he says in his narrative, 'that something was wrong. I did not like the idea of taking it into the house; but I intended to make one more trial before I made up my mind about that. I said good night to Gulliver, put her on my bicycle and pushed her home. But first of all I took the handkerchief from her neck and put it in my pocket. There was no blood upon it, that I could see.'

His wife, as he had expected, was waiting at the gate for him. She exclaimed, as he had expected, upon the lateness of the hour. Beckwith stood for a little in the roadway before the house, explaining that Strap had bolted up the hill and had had to be looked for and fetched back. While speaking he noticed that Mrs Beckwith was as insensible to the creature on the bicycle as Gulliver the constable had been. Indeed, she went much farther to prove herself so than he, for she actually put her hand upon the handle-bar of the machine, and in order to that drove it right through the centre of the girl crouching there. Beckwith saw that done. 'I declare solemnly upon my honour,' he writes, 'that it was as if Mary had drilled a hole clean through the middle of her back. Through gown and skin and bone and all her arm went; and how it went in I don't know. To me it seemed that her hand was on the handle-bar, while her upper arm, to the elbow, was in between the girl's shoulders. There was a gap from the elbow downwards where Mary's arm was inside the body; then from the creature's diaphragm her lower arm, wrist and hand came out. And all the time we were speaking the girl's eyes were on my face. I was now quite determined that I wouldn't have her in the house for a mint of money.'

He put her, finally, in the dog-kennel. Strap, as a favorite, lived in the house; but he kept a greyhound in the garden, in a kennel surrounded by a sort of run made of iron poles and galvanised wire. It was roofed in with wire also, for the convenience of stretching a tarpaulin in wet weather. Here it was that he bestowed the strange being rescued from the down.

It was clever, I think, of Beckwith to infer that what Strap had shown respect for would be respected by the greyhound, and certainly bold of him to act upon his inference. However, events proved that he had been perfectly right. Bran, the greyhound, was interested, highly interested, in his guest. The moment he saw his master he saw what he was carrying. 'Quiet, Bran, quiet there,' was a very unnecessary adjuration. Bran stretched up his head and sniffed, but went no farther; and when Beckwith had placed his burden on the straw inside the kennel, Bran lay down, as if on guard, outside the opening and put his muzzle on his forepaws. Again Beckwith noticed that curious appearance of the eyes which the fox-terrier's had made already. Bran's eyes were turned upwards to show the narrow arcs of white.

Before he went to bed, he tells us, but not before Mrs Beckwith had gone there, he took out a bowl of bread and milk to his patient. Bran he found to be still stretched out before the entry; the girl was nestled down in the straw, as if asleep or prepared to be so, with her face upon her hand. Upon an afterthought he went back for a clean pocket handkerchief, warm water and a sponge. With these, by the light of a candle, he washed the wound, dipped the rag in hazeline, and applied it. This done, he touched the creature's head, nodded a good night and retired. 'She smiled at me very prettily,' he says. 'That was the first time she did it.'

There was no blood on the handkerchief which he had removed.

Early in the morning following upon the adventure Beckwith was out and about. He wished to verify the overnight experiences in the light of refreshed intelligence. On approaching the kennel he saw at once that it had been no dream. There, in fact, was the creature of his discovery playing with Bran the greyhound, circling sedately about him, weaving her arms, pointing her toes, arching her graceful neck, stooping to him, as if inviting him to sport, darting away—'like a fairy,' says Beckwith, 'at her magic, dancing in a ring.' Bran, he observed, made no effort to catch her, but crouched rather than sat, as if ready to spring. He followed her about with his eyes as far as he could; but when the course of her dance took her immediately behind him he did not turn his head, but kept his eye fixed as far backward as he could, against the moment when she should come again into the scope of his vision. 'It seemed as important to him as it had the day before to Strap to keep her always in his eye. It seemed—and always seemed so long as I could study them together   intensely important.' Bran's mouth was stretched to 'a sort of grin'; occasionally he panted. When Beckwith entered the kennel and touched the dog (which took little notice of him) he found him trembling with excitement. His heart was beating at a great rate. He also drank quantities of water.

Beckwith, whose narrative, hitherto summarised, I may now quote, tells us that the creature was indescribably graceful and lightfooted. 'You couldn't hear the fall of her foot: you never could. Her dancing and circling about the cage seemed to be the most important business of her life; she was always at it, especially in bright weather. I shouldn't have called it restlessness so much as busyness. It really seemed to mean more to her than exercise or irritation at confinement. It was evident also that she was happy when so engaged. She used to sing. She sang also when she was sitting still with Bran; but not with such exhilaration.

'Her eyes were bright—when she was dancing about—with mischief and devilry. I cannot avoid that word, thought it does not describe what I really mean. She looked wild and outlandish and full of fun, as if she knew that she was teasing the dog, and yet couldn't help herself. When you say of a child that he looks wicked, you don't mean it literally; it is rather a compliment than not. So it was with her and her wickedness. She did look wicked, there's no mistake—able and willing to do wickedness; but I am sure she never meant to hurt Bran. They were always firm friends, though the dog knew very well who was master.

'When you looked at her you did not think of her height. She was so complete; as well made as a statuette. I could have spanned her waist with my two thumbs and middle fingers, and her neck (very nearly) with one hand. She was pale and inclined to be dusky in complexion, but not so dark as a gypsy; she had grey eyes, and dark brown hair, which she could sit upon if she chose. Her gown you could have sworn was made of cobweb; I don't know how else to describe it. As I had suspected, she wore nothing else, for while I was there that first morning, so soon as the sun came up over the hill she slipped it off her and stood dressed in nothing at all. She was a regular little Venus— that's all I can say. I never could get accustomed to that weakness of hers for slipping off her frock, though no doubt it was very absurd. She had no sort of shame in it, so why on earth should I?

'The food, I ought to mention, had disappeared: the bowl was empty. But I know now that Bran must have had it. So long as she remained in the kennel or about my place she never ate anything, nor drank either. If she had I must have known it, as I used to clean the run out every morning. I was always particular about that. I used to say that you couldn't keep dogs too clean. But I tried her unsuccessfully, with all sorts of things: flowers, honey, dew—for I had read somewhere that fairies drink dew and suck honey out of flowers. She used to look at the little messes I made for her, and when she knew me better would grimace at them, and look up in my face and laugh at me.

'I have said that she used to sing sometimes. It was like nothing that I can describe. Perhaps the wind in the telegraph wires comes nearest to it, and yet that is an absurd comparison. I could never catch any words; indeed I did not succeed in learning a single word of her language. I doubt very much whether they have what we call a language—I mean the people who are like her, her own people. They communicate with each other, I fancy, as she did with my dogs, inarticulately, but with perfect communication and understanding on either side. When I began to teach her English I noticed that she had a kind of pity for me, a kind of contempt perhaps is nearer the mark, that I should be compelled to express myself in so clumsy a way. I am no philosopher, but I imagine that our need of putting one word after another may be due to our habit of thinking in sequence. If there is no such thing as Time in the other world it should not be necessary there to frame speech in sentences at all. I am sure that Thumbeline (which was my name for her— I never learned her real name) spoke with Bran and Strap in flashes which revealed her whole thought at once. So also they answered her, there's no doubt. So also she contrived to talk with my little girl, who, although she was four years old and a great chatterbox, never attempted to say a single word of her own language to Thumbeline, yet communicated with her by the hour together. But I did not know anything of this for a month or more, though it must have begun almost at once.

'I blame myself for it, myself only. I ought, of course, to have remembered that children are more likely to see fairies than grownups; but then—why did Florrie keep it all secret? Why did she not tell her mother, or me, that she had seen a fairy in Bran's kennel? The child was as open as the day, yet she concealed her knowledge from both of us without the least difficulty. She seemed the same careless, laughing child she had always been; one could not have supposed her to have a care in the world; and yet for nearly six months she must have been full of care, having daily secret intercourse with Thumbeline and keeping her eyes open all the time lest her mother or I should find her out. Certainly she could have taught me something in the way of keeping secrets. I know that I kept mine very badly, and blame myself more than enough for keeping it at all. God knows what we might have been spared if, on the night I brought her home, I had told Mary the whole truth! And yet—

how could I have convinced her that she was impaling someone with her arm while her hand rested on the bar of the bicycle? Is not that an absurdity on the face of it? Yes, indeed; but the sequel is no absurdity. That's the terrible fact.

'I kept Thumbeline in the kennel for the whole winter. She seemed happy enough there with the dogs, and, of course, she had had Florrie, too, though I did not find that out until the spring. I don't doubt, now, that if I had kept her in there altogether she would have been perfectly contented.

'The first time I saw Florrie with her I was amazed. It was a Sunday morning. There was our four-year-old child standing at the wire, pressing herself against it, and Thumbeline close to her. Their faces almost touched; their fingers were interlaced; I am certain that they were speaking to each other in their own fashion, by flashes, without words. I watched them for a bit; I saw Bran come and sit up on his haunches and join them. He looked from one to another, and all about; and then he saw me.

'Now that is how I know that they were all three in communication, because, the very next moment, Florrie turned round and ran to me, and said in her pretty baby-talk, 'Talking to Bran. Florrie talking to Bran'. If this was willful deceit it was most accomplished. It could not have been better done. 'And who else were you talking to, Florrie?' I said. She fixed her round blue eyes upon me, as if in wonder, then looked away and said shortly, 'No-one else'. And I could not get her to confess or admit, then or at any time afterwards, that she had any cognizance at all of the fairy in Bran's kennel, although their communications were daily, and often lasted for hours at a time. I don't know that it makes things any better, but

I have thought sometimes that the child believed me to be as insensible to Thumbeline as her mother was. She can only have believed it at first, of course, but that may have prompted her to a concealment which she did not afterwards care to confess to.

'Be this as it may, Florrie, in fact, behaved with Thumbeline exactly as the two dogs did. She made no attempt to catch her at her circlings and wheelings about the kennel, nor to follow her wonderful dances, nor (in her presence) to imitate them. But she was (like the dogs) aware of nobody else when under the spell of Thumbeline's personality; and when she had got to know her she seemed to care for nobody else at all. I ought, no doubt, to have foreseen that and guarded against it.

'Thumbeline was extremely attractive. I never saw such eyes as hers, such mysterious fascination. She was nearly always good-tempered, nearly always happy; but sometimes she had fits of temper and kept herself to herself. Nothing then would get her out of the kennel, where she would lie curled up like an animal with her knees to her chin and one arm thrown over her face. Bran was always wretched at these times, and did all he knew to coax her out. He ceased to care for me or my wife after she came to us, and instead of being wild at the prospect of his Saturday and Sunday runs, it was hard to get him along. I had to take him on a lead until we had turned to go home; then he would set off by himself, in spite of hallooing and scolding, at a long steady gallop, and one would find him waiting crouched at the gate of his run, and Thumbeline on the ground inside it, with her legs crossed like tailor, mocking and teasing him with her wonderful shining eyes. Only once or twice did

I see her worse than sick or sorry; then she was transported with rage and another person altogether. She never touched me—and why or how I had offended her I have no notion—but she buzzed and hovered about me like an angry bee. She appeared to have wings, which hummed in their furious movement; she was red in the face; her eyes burned; she grinned at me and ground her little teeth together. A curious shrill noise came from her, like the screaming of a gnat or hover-fly; but no words, never any words. Bran showed me his teeth too, and would not look at me. It was very odd.

'When I looked in, on my return home, she was as merry as usual, and as affectionate. I think she had no memory.

'I am trying to give all the particulars I was able to gather from observation. In some things she was difficult, in others very easy to teach. For instance, I got her to learn in no time that she ought to wear her clothes, such as they were, when I was with her. She certainly preferred to go without them, especially in the sunshine; but by leaving her the moment she slipped her frock off I soon made her understand that if she wanted me she must behave herself according to my notions of behaviour. She got that fixed in her little head, but even so she used to do her best to hoodwink me. She would slip out one shoulder when she thought I wasn't looking, and before I knew where I was half of her would be gleaming in the sun like satin. Directly I noticed it I used to frown, and then she would pretend to be ashamed of herself, hang her head, and wriggle her frock up to its place again. However, I never could teach her to keep her skirts about her knees. She was as innocent as a baby about that sort of thing.

'I taught her some English words, and a sentence or two. That was towards the end of her confinement to the kennel, about March. I used to touch parts of her, or of myself, or Bran, and peg away at the names of them. Mouth, eyes, ears, hands, chest, tail, back, front: she learned all those and more. Eat, drink, laugh, cry, love, kiss, those also. As for kissing (apart from the word) she proved herself to be an expert. She kissed me, Florrie, Bran, Strap, indifferently, one as soon as another, and any rather than none, and all four for choice.

'I learned some things myself, more than a thing or two. I don't mind owning that one thing was to value my wife's steady and tried affection far above the wild love of this unbalanced, unearthly little creature, who seemed to be like nothing so much as a woman with the conscience left out. The conscience, we believe, is the still small voice of the Deity crying to us in the dark recesses of the body; pointing out the path of duty; teaching respect for the opinion of the world, for tradition, decency and order. It is thanks to conscience that a man is true and a woman modest. Not that Thumbeline could be called immodest, unless a baby can be so described or an animal. But could I be called 'true'? I greatly fear that I could not—in fact, I know it too well. I meant no harm; I was greatly interested; and there was always before me the real difficulty of making Mary understand that something was in the kennel which she couldn't see. It would have led to great complications, even if I had persuaded her of the fact. No doubt she would have insisted on my getting rid of Thumbeline—but how on earth could I have done that if Thumbeline had not chosen to go? But, for all that, I know very well that I ought to have told her, cost what it might. If

I had done it I should have spared myself lifelong regret, and should only have gone without a few weeks of extraordinary interest which I now see clearly could not have been good for me, as not being founded upon any revealed Christian principle, and most certainly were not worth the price I had to pay for them.

'I learned one more curious fact which I must not forget. Nothing would induce Thumbeline to touch or pass over anything made of zinc. I don't know the reason for it; but gardeners will tell you that the way to keep a plant from slugs is to put a zinc collar round it. It is due to that I was able to keep her in Bran's run without difficulty. To have got out she would have had to pass zinc. The wire was all galvanised.

'She showed her dislike of it in numerous ways: one was her care to avoid touching the sides or tops of the enclosure when she was at her gambols. At such times, when she was at her wildest, she was all over the place, skipping high like a lamb, twisting like a leveret, wheeling round and round in circles like a young dog, or skimming, like a swallow on the wing, above ground. But she never made a mistake; she turned in a moment or flung herself backward if there was the least risk of contact. When Florrie used to converse with her from outside, in that curious silent way the two had, it would always be the child that put its hands through the wire, never Thumbeline. I once tried to put her against the roof when I was playing with her. She screamed like a shot hare and would not come out of the kennel all day. There was no doubt at all about her feelings for zinc. All other metals seemed indifferent to her.

'With the advent of spring weather Thumbeline became not only more beautiful, but wilder, and exceedingly restless. She now coaxed me to let her out, and against my judgement I did it; she had to be carried over the entry; for when I had set the gate wide open and pointed her the way into the garden she squatted down in her usual attitude of attention, with her legs crossed, and watched me, waiting. I wanted to see how she would get through the hateful wire, so went away and hid myself, leaving her alone with Bran. I saw her creep to the entry and peer at the wire. What followed was curious. Bran came up wagging his tail and stood close to her, his side against her head; he looked down, inviting her to go out with him. Long looks passed between them, and then Bran stooped his head, she put her arms around his neck, twined her feet about his foreleg, and was carried out., Then she became a mad thing, now bird now moth; high and low, round and round, flashing about the place for all the world like a humming-bird moth, perfectly beautiful in her motions (whose ease always surprised me), and equally so in her colouring of soft grey and dusky-rose flesh. Bran grew a puppy again and whipped about after her in great circles round the meadow. But though he was famous at coursing, and has killed his hares single-handed, he was never once near Thumbeline. It was a curious sight and made me late for business.

'By degrees she got to be very bold, and taught me boldness too, and (I am ashamed to say) greater degrees of deceit. She came freely into the house and played with Florrie up and down stairs; she got on my knee at meal-times, or evenings when my wife and I were together. Fine tricks she played me, I must own. She spilled my tea for me, broke cups and saucers, scattered my

Patience cards, caught poor Mary's knitting wool and rolled it about the room. The cunning little creature knew that I dared not scold her or make any kind of fuss. She used to beseech me for forgiveness occasionally when I looked very glum, and would touch my cheek to make me look at her imploring eyes, and keep me looking at her till I smiled. Then she would put her arms round my neck and pull herself up to my level and kiss me, and then nestle down in my arms and pretend to sleep. By and by, when my attention was called off her, she would pinch me, or tweak my necktie, and make me look again at her wicked eye peeping out from under my arm. *I* had to kiss her again, of course, and at last she might go to sleep in earnest. She seemed able to sleep at any hour or in any place, just like an animal.

'I had some difficulty in arranging for the night when once she had made herself free of the house. She saw no reason whatever for our being separated; but I circumvented her by nailing a strip of zinc all round the door; and I put one around Florrie's too. I pretended to my wife that it was to keep out draughts. Thumbeline was furious when she found out how she had been tricked. I think she never quite forgave me for it. Where she hid herself at night I am not sure. I think on the sitting-room sofa; but on mild mornings I used to find her outdoors, playing round Bran's kennel.

'Strap, our fox-terrier, picked up some rat-poison towards the end of April and died in the night. Thumbeline's way of taking that was very curious. It shocked me a good deal. She had never been so friendly with him as with Bran, though certainly more at ease in his company than mine. The night before he died I remembered that she and Bran and he had been having high games in the meadow, which had ended by their all lying down together in a heap, Thumbeline's head on Bran's flank, and her legs between his. Her arm had been round Strap's neck in a most loving way. They made quite a picture for a Royal Academician; 'Tired of Play', or 'The End of a Romp' I can fancy he would call it. Next morning I found poor old Strap stiff and staring, and Thumbeline and Bran at their games just the same. She actually jumped over him and all about him as if he had been a lump of earth or stone. Just some such thing he was to her; she did not seem able to realise that there was the cold body of her friend. Bran just sniffed him over and left him, but Thumbeline showed no consciousness that he was there at all. I wondered, was this heartlessness of obliquity? But I have never found the answer to my question.

'Now I come to the tragical part of my story, and wish with all my heart that I could leave it out. But beyond the full confession I have made to my wife, the County Police and the newspapers, I feel that I should not shrink from any admission that may be called for of how much I have been to blame. In May, on the 13 of May, Thumbeline, Bran and our only child, Florrie, disappeared.

'It was a day, I remember well, of wonderful beauty. I had left them all three together in the water meadow, little thinking of what was in store for us before many hours. Thumbeline had been crowning Florrie with a wreath of flowers. She had gathered cuckoo-pint and marsh marigolds and woven them together, far more deftly than any of us could have done, into a chaplet. I remember the curious winding, wandering air she had been singing (without any words, as usual) over her business, and how she touched each flower first with her lips, and then brushed it lightly across her bosom before she wove it in. She had kept her eyes on me as she did it, looking up from under her brows, as if to see whether I knew what she was about.

'I don't doubt now but that she was bewitching Florrie by this curious performance, which every flower had to undergo separately: but fool that I was, I thought nothing of it at the time, and bicycled off to Salisbury, leaving them there.

'At noon my poor wife came to me at the Bank distracted with anxiety and fatigue. She had run most of the way, she gave me to understand. Her news was that Florrie and Bran could not be found anywhere. She said that she had gone to the gate of the meadow to call the child in, and, not seeing her, or getting any answer, she had gone down to the river at the bottom. Here she had found a few picked wild flowers but no other traces. There were no footprints in the mud, either of child or dog. Having spent the morning with some of the neighbours in a fruitless search, she had now come to me.

'My heart was like lead, and shame prevented me from telling her the truth as I was sure it must be. But my own conviction of it clogged all my efforts. Of what avail could it be to inform the police or organise search-parties, knowing what I knew only too well? However, I did put Gulliver in communication with the head office in Sarum, and everything possible was done. We explored a circuit of six miles about Wilsford; every fold of the hills, every spinney, every hedgerow was thoroughly examined. But that first night of grief had broken down my shame: I told my wife the whole truth in the presence of the Reverend Richard Walsh, the Congregational minister, and in spite of her absolute incredulity, and, I may add, scorn, next morning I repeated it to Chief Inspector Notcutt of Salisbury. Particulars got into the local papers by the following Saturday: and next I had to face the ordeal of the *Daily Chronicle, Daily News, Daily Graphic, Star,* and other London journals. Most of these newspapers sent representatives to lodge in the village, many of them with photographic cameras. All this hateful notoriety I had brought upon myself, and did my best to bear like the humble, contrite Christian which I hope I may say I have become. We found no trace of our dear one, and never have to this day. Bran, too, had completely vanished. I have not cared to keep a dog since.

'Whether my dear wife ever believed my account I cannot be sure. She has never reproached me for my wicked thoughtlessness, that's certain. Mr Walsh, our respected pastor, who has been so kind as to read this paper, told me more than once that he could hardly doubt it. The Salisbury police made no comments upon it one way or another. My colleagues at the Bank, out of respect for my grief and sincere repentance, treated me with a forbearance for which I can never be too grateful. I need not add that every word of this is absolutely true. I made notes of the most remarkable characteristics of the being I called Thumbeline at the time of remarking them, and those notes are still in my possession.'

The Room on the Fourth Floor

RALPH STRAUS

John Chester ought never to have gone in for politics. I am quite certain that he should have sat down at a desk and written romances, and become a 'best-seller', and built himself a marble house, and married a wife, and hired a press-agent. Instead, as everybody knows, he elected to be returned to Parliament twenty-five years ago, and there he has remained ever since, always upon the fringe of the Government, though never actually entering those extraordinary precincts.

Probably succeeding Premiers have considered that Chester's duties as a raconteur at fashionable dinner-tables must for ever preclude him from undertaking anything else, though, I dare say he has refused office on his own account. He is just the kind of man to do such a thing—a man too keen about other people to look properly after his own interests.

His appearance, as you know, is military. That white moustache suggests the field-marshal, and his clothes are obviously of the dragoon cut. Also, he has a figure which, to my knowledge has changed not an inch in the last twenty years. Some people call him a phenomenon and expect you to know exactly what they mean, and somehow you do. He knows everyone and goes everywhere. He has more friends than any other man in Europe. And he is the kind of man to whom people, even the discreet people, tell things, which possibly accounts for his amazing stock of stories.

I was dining with him a week or two ago at the House of Commons. A world-famous ex-Minister was sitting in solitary state at the next table. Chester had been unusually silent, and I wondered what was troubling him; but when the great statesman hurried away, my host gave the peculiar chuckle which, with him, is the invariable introduction to some yarn or other.

'The most remarkable man in England,' he began, looking in the direction of the now empty table.

'So I am given to understand.'

'He is the only man who guessed the Farringham riddle, you know. Guessed it at once, too. Most remarkable man. Yes. And yet...'

He paused and looked at me as though I had contradicted him.

'Sometimes,' he continued, twirling the white moustache, 'I wonder whether he knew more about the affair than he pretended. He might have heard of it, of course, in his official capacity.'

'You mean when he was Prime Minister?'

'Precisely.'

'You pique my curiosity,' said I.

John Chester emptied his glass. 'You have never heard of the Farringham case, then? No, well, in the ordinary way you wouldn't. So many of these things have to be hushed up. Besides, it is thirty years old now.'

I lit a cigar and prepared for one of Chester's inimitable yarns.

❖

'Yes,' he began, 'Mrs Farringham was a beautiful widow with a passion for travelling in unusual places. She had plenty of money, and she moved from one continent to the next as you or I drive to our clubs. She never took a maid with her; but her daughter, I suppose, did much to fill the maid's place. I met them first in conference. I remember. The girl must have been about twenty then, Mrs Farringham nearly forty, though she scarcely looked older than her daughter.

'She was entertaining some Italian prince who wanted to become her son-in-law or her husband—I couldn't make up my mind which, and didn't like to ask—and I was invited to call at her London house. I fully intended to go as soon as I returned home, but—well, you shall hear why I never had the opportunity.

'It was in the year of the great Exhibition in Paris—1900. The Farringhams had been traveling in Russia and Turkey. They had spent a week in Constantinople—a detestable place—and had decided to make a tour through Asia Minor. But apparently for no reason at all Mrs Farringham suddenly took it into her head that she would like to buy new carpets for her London house, and the Asia Minor trip was indefinitely postponed.

'The ladies visited Thomas Cook, and Thomas Cook in his best English told them how to reach home in the most comfortable manner. Incidentally, he advised a night or two in Paris. The Exhibition had just opened its gates. Now I don't suppose for one moment that Mrs Farringham cared in the least whether she saw the Exhibition or not, but her daughter had not seen so much of the world as her indefatigable mother, and it was decided that twenty-four hours in Paris would make a pleasant break in a tiresome journey.

'And so it happened that three days later the two ladies, rather tired and rather irritable, arrived at the Paris terminus. It was just eight o'clock in the evening. They had already dined in the train. A porter found their baggage—three large trunks and a green bag which had accompanied Mrs Farringham from the time she had first crossed the Channel and with the help of a cabman, succeeded in placing the four pieces on the roof of the cab. Before driving off, however, the cabman altered the position of the green bag. Apparently he had got it into his head that the green bag was the last straw to break his conveyance, and he put it beneath his feet on the box.

'When they arrived at one of the big hotels—I forget for the moment which it was—the ladies asked for two adjoining rooms.

'The politest of hotel managers shrugged his shoulders many times. "Paris," said he, "is full. It flows over with *tout le monde*. It is beyond me to give madame and mam'selle two rooms in the closest adjoinment. But if madame will take an apartment on the fourth floor—of the extreme comfort—it will be well."

His manner implied that only madame's beauty had made such a favour possible.

'The ladies agreed, and signed their names in the visitors' book. One of the hotel porters took charge of the trunks, and a chambermaid showed the visitors to their rooms. Mrs Farringham's bedroom was not very large, but it looked comfortable. Her daughter's room was exactly above it.

'The porter unstrapped Mrs Farringham's trunks, and in the politest possible way hoped that the ladies would enjoy their visit to Paris. Then he received a small coin and disappeared. The chambermaid uttered a similar sentiment and followed his example. Mother and daughter were left alone. You follow so far?'

'Perfectly,' said I.

John Chester looked at up the ceiling. 'Very well, then. Here you have two estimable ladies arriving one evening in a Paris hotel of unimpeachable respectability and being given rooms one over the other. Good.

'For a short while Miss Farringham stayed with her mother and helped her to unpack a few things. Then, feeling tired, she suggested that they should both go to bed.

' "Immediately?" asked her mother. "It is not yet nine o'clock."

' "Very well," said the girl, "I will lie down for half an hour or so in my own room and then come down to help you undress."

'And she went to her room on the fifth floor.

'She was feeling particularly drowsy. Nearly two days in a continental train is enough to make anyone drowsy. She just lay down on her bed, dressed as she was, and in a minute or two was asleep.

'Again my host paused this time to refill his glass. 'Quite an ordinary story, isn't it?' he asked with a twinkle in his eye.

I knew better than to utter a word.

'Yes,' he went on, 'the girl lay on her bed and fell asleep. When she awoke it was ten minutes before midnight. She went down to the fourth floor and knocked on the door of her mother's room. There was no answer. She went in. The room was dark. She turned on the electric light. The bed was empty. Indeed, the room was obviously untenanted. It was awaiting the arrival of some visitor.

'Of course she must have made some mistake. She went out into the passage. Her mother's room would be an adjoining one. But on one side of the empty room was a bathroom, and outside the door of the other stood two unmistakably masculine boots. Added to which she was almost certain that she recalled the correct number. She rang for the chambermaid.

' "I am afraid I have made some mistake," she said. 'I thought this was my mother's room, but—this is the fourth floor, by the way, isn't it?'

'The maid looked at her curiously. "Yes, mam'selle, this is indeed the fourth floor, but what does mam'selle mean? No lady accompanied mam'selle to the hotel. Mam'selle travelled with herself!" '

John Chester looked at me across the table in much the same way as I imagined the chambermaid had stared at Miss

Farringham. It was almost a minute before he spoke again. I had no notion what was coming, but already felt in some vague way that I was no longer sitting in the dining-room of the House of Commons. I leant forward over the table. 'Go on dear man, please!'

' "Mam'selle travelled with herself," he repeated. 'Yes, that is what the chambermaid said, and Miss Farringham stared at her. "You are making a very stupid mistake," she said. "Why, surely it was you who took in my mother's bag—a large green bag. We came together, about half-past eight."

'The maid seemed completely bewildered. "Shall I ring for the porter?" she asked, more or less mechanically.

'Miss Farringham nodded. A feeling of uneasiness had suddenly come over her.

'The porter came up, and the girl recognised him. She repeated her questions. The porter allowed his mouth to open to its widest extent, which happened to be his method of expressing the completest surprise. No madame, said he, had arrived with mam'selle. He had certainly taken mam'selle's two trunks to a room on the fifth floor, but what did she mean?

'And then, I fancy, a tiny pang must have touched Miss Farringham's heart. Yet, obviously, this could only be an absurd mistake. In another moment she would be laughing with her mother. She looked hard at the two servants standing there in foolish bewilderment. "Call the manager, please," she said.

'They brought the manager to her. He was, as always, vaguely apologetic. Mam'selle was not comfortable in her room? Was there anything he could do? She had not supped? Some refreshment in her room?

'The girl explained. Her mother had been given a room on the fourth floor. Apparently this had been changed. Where was she now? She asked the questions quite calmly, but her heart was beating at a greater rate than was good for it. On a sudden it seemed to her that something was horribly, immeasurably wrong. You are probably familiar with that feeling yourself.

'The manager's manner changed ever so slightly. His tones were still suave, but a note of incredulity would not be hidden. It was as though he were angry at being summoned to the fourth floor by a possibly mad Englishwoman for no reason at all. "Mam'selle is joking?" he asked almost coldly.

'It was then that the girl realised now frightened she was. Wherever her mother might be, even though no more than a single wall was separating them, she was at that moment alone in Paris with strangers who were obviously in no mood to believe what she said. "But my mother and I, we drove from the station. You gave us the rooms yourself. Yes, and you said how sorry you were that we could not have adjoining rooms because the hotel was full. And then—of course, you remember—we wrote our names in the visitors' book."

'The manager retained his professional politeness. That is the first necessity in a hotel manager. "I cannot understand mam'selle," he said quietly. Then he turned to the porter. "Bring up the visitors' book," he ordered.

'The visitors' book was produced. You can imagine how eagerly Miss Farringham examined it. Yes, there, four or five names from the bottom of the last page, was her own; but it was sandwiched in between a victomte and an English baronet. Her mother's name was not there.

'You can picture her dismay.

' "Perhaps mam'selle is tired, and overwrought after her journey," suggested the polite manager. English girls, he knew, were often peculiar, and Miss Farringham was undoubtedly pretty.

' "But—my mother!" stammered the girl. "What does it all mean? I don't understand——"

' "There is a doctor in the hotel if mam'selle——"

'She interrupted him. "Oh, you think I am ill. But I am not. We must search the hotel. Perhaps my mother has found a friend; or she may be in the drawing-room. I am horribly nervous. You must help me."

'The manager shrugged his apologetic shoulders.

'They searched the hotel.'

John Chester handed me his cigarette-case. 'Yes,' he repeated, 'they searched the hotel.'

'And they found——'

'Everyone but the mother. In an hour's time, as you can imagine, Miss Farringham had become frantic. The manager did everything he could. As a final recourse he despatched the porter to look for the cabman who had driven the girl from the station. It was a rather forlorn hope, but the girl seemed eager to see him. She was in that state of mind in which things are no longer ordinary or extraordinary, but merely hopeful or hopeless. Fortunately the cabman was found. He was still on duty, as a matter of fact, at the terminus. And at two o'clock in the morning he was standing, hat in hand, in the foyer of the hotel.'

'It was the same cabman?' I asked.

'Miss Farringham recognised him instantly. "You remember me?" she asked eagerly.

' "But yes, mam'selle. You arrived at eight-ten—alone. I drove you to this hotel. Two trunks."

' "No, no. My mother was with me. There were three trunks and a large green bag."

'The cabman looked stupidly at her.

' "And don't you remember, you changed the position of the bag as we drove off. Perhaps you thought that it was unsafe on the roof. You put it beneath your feet on the box. Oh, you must remember, you must remember!"

'The cabman was obviously astonished. "But there was no green bag," said he. "I remember precisely. The young lady, I think, must be American or English, or she would not be travelling with herself."

'Miss Farringham stared wildly about her and fell down in a faint.

'They got her to bed and promised to send a telegram to England. Early next morning she crossed the Channel, just dazed. And she was met at Charing Cross by friends just as mystified as herself. That night she was seriously ill. Brain fever.'

'But the mother?' I asked.

'Nothing more,' said John Chester, 'was ever heard of the mother.'

The division bell was ringing, and my host excused himself. 'I must vote,' he explained. 'I shall be back in ten minutes, which will give you just sixty times as long as the ex-Prime Minister took to solve the riddle.' He nodded, and hurried away.

'I tried to exercise those faculties which the detective of fiction finds so useful. Either Mrs Farringham had arrived at the hotel in Paris, I argued, or she had not. John Chester had stated distinctly that she had arrived, and therefore....

❖

My host had returned. 'A pretty problem?' said he. 'Confess yourself completely at sea.'

'Completely,' said I.

'Come along to the terrace, then,' and we walked out and stood looking over the Thames. It was not a warm night, and we were coatless.

'I have often wondered,' he began at last, 'why Mrs Farringham had that sudden desire to buy carpets for her London house.'

I hurriedly sought for a clue in the carpets, but found none.

'Perhaps,' he continued, 'it was an excuse. Perhaps she shared in common with most of her sex the desire to practice the gentle art of self-deception. It is just possible, that is to say, that Mrs Farringham gave up the proposed trip through Asia Minor because she was not in her usual health.'

He was silent for so long that I drew his attention to the low temperature.

'Then I'll explain,' he said with a smile. 'It is all quite simple, and depends on one little fact which may or may not have escaped your notice. In France they have a peculiar way of doing things. A logical way, I admit, but sometimes peculiar. Consequently things happen in France, and particularly in Paris, which could not possibly happen anywhere else. The Farringham affair is a case in point. I will tell you exactly what happened, and then you shall come inside to hear the debate.

'Well, then, here, as I said before, you have the fact of two ladies arriving one evening in a Paris hotel. There is no question about that: they both arrived, and Mrs Farringham was given a room on the fourth floor, the actual room which her daughter found untenanted at midnight. Now I will say at once that there was nothing peculiar about this room; it was just an ordinary bedroom in a big hotel. What was peculiar was the fact that while Mrs Farringham had been in the room at half-past eight, she was not there, nor indeed anywhere in the hotel, at midnight. Consequently, at some period between these two hours she went out, or was taken out.'

'But the manager and the porter...'

'I see you will not let me tell the story in my own way,' smiled John Chester. 'I was going to show you how you might have solved the riddle. No matter. You shall have the plain sequence of things at once. A few minutes after Mrs Farringham had been shown to her room her daughter had gone up to the fifth floor and she was alone. Ten minutes later the bell in the room rang. The chambermaid appeared, and to her dismay found madame lying motionless on the floor. She rang for the porter, and the porter, hardly less frightened than herself, fetched the manager. The manager called for a doctor. Fortunately there was one in the hotel. The doctor appeared and made his examination. Mrs Farringham was dead.'

'Dead!' I repeated.

'Dead,' said John Chester. 'Now the death of a lady in a large hotel is an unpleasant event at all times, but in this case there was something so peculiarly unpleasant that the doctor, instead of notifying the police, called up one of the Government offices on the telephone, and was lucky enough to find a high official still at his post.

'What followed you may think extraordinary, and extraordinary it certainly must have been. In less than an hour's time there had arrived at the hotel a small army of men. Some seemed to be visitors, others workmen. If you had watched them at all, you might have come to the conclusion that a large quantity of furniture was being removed. As a matter of fact it was. In particular, an ottoman might have been seen being carried downstairs and placed in a furniture van, which drove rapidly away. If you had waited about the fourth floor, you might further have seen new furniture brought into the room which Mrs Farringham had occupied, and you might have been puzzled at a peculiar odour until the manager, whom you would have met casually on the stairs, informed you that a clumsy servant had upset a case of drugs destined for the Exhibition.

'At the same time, if you had been allowed into the manager's own sanctum downstairs you would have seen three or four gentlemen talking earnestly to a chambermaid and a porter, and, at a later hour, to a cabman who happened to have taken up his stand outside the hotel. The porter and the chambermaid incidentally received large sums of money, and the cabman, similarly enriched, was bidden to await instructions. Also several lessons in the art of acting had been given.'

'I am more bewildered than ever.'

'And yet,' said John Chester, 'two words whispered over the telephone had been sufficient to cause all these curious events to take place!'

Once again he paused. 'Mrs Farringham had been travelling in the East. Doesn't that suggest something to you?'

'You mean———' I was beginning; but he interrupted me. '*Bubonic plague!*'

'But I don't see———'

'At headquarters they were obliged to come to a speedy decision. In the interests of the community, my dear fellow, it was decided—the Government, that is to say, decided—that Mrs Farringham *had never arrived in Paris*. Further they were not concerned. That was the only vital point.'

'But even then———'

'Do you suppose,' asked John Chester, 'that anybody would have visited Paris if a case of bubonic plague had been reported? Even if there was no more than a rumour that———'

'No, but———'

'It was a case of one against the many. The Government, being Republican, and also patriotic, made its choice for the many. Also, being French, it did not lack the artistic temperament.'

'It's ghastly!' I murmured.

'It was Exhibition year,' said my host. 'But you are quite right,' he added; 'it is very cold. Let us go in.'

I do not remember what question was being debated that evening.

The Great French Duel

MARK TWAIN

Much as the modern French duel is ridiculed by certain smart people, it is in reality one of the most dangerous institutions of our day. Since it is always fought in the open air the combatants are nearly sure to catch cold. M. Paul de Cassagnac, the most inveterate of the French duelists, has suffered so often in this way that he is at last a confirmed invalid; and the best physician in Paris has expressed the opinion that if he goes on dueling for fifteen or twenty years more—unless he forms the habit of fighting in a comfortable room where damps and draughts cannot intrude—he will eventually endanger his life. This ought to moderate the talk of those people who are so stubborn in maintaining that the French duel is the most health-giving of recreations because of the open-air exercise it affords. And it ought also to moderate that foolish talk about French duelists and socialist-hated monarchs being the only people who are immortal.

But it is time to get to my subject. As soon as I heard of the late fiery outbreak between M. Gambetta and M. Fourtou in the French assembly, I knew that trouble must follow. I knew it because a long personal friendship with M. Gambetta had revealed to me the desperate and implacable nature of the man. Vast as his physical proportion, I knew that the thirst for revenge would penetrate to the remotest frontiers of his person.

I did not wait for him to call on me, but went at once to him. As I expected, I found the brave fellow steeped in a profound French calm. I say French, because French calmness and English calmness have points of difference. He was moving swiftly back and forth among the debris of his furniture, now and then staving chance fragments of it across the room with his foot; grinding a constant grist of curses though his set teeth; and halting every little while to deposit another handful of his hair on the pile which he had been building of it on the table.

He threw his arms around my neck, bent me over his stomach to his breast, kissed me on both cheeks, hugged me four or five times and then placed me in his own arm-chair. As soon as I got well again, we began business at once.

I said I supposed he would wish me to act as his second, and he said, 'Of course.' I said I must be allowed to act under a French name, so that I might be shielded from obloquy in my country, in case of fatal result. He winced here, probably at the suggestion that dueling was not regarded with respect in America. However, he agreed to my requirement. This accounts for the fact that in all the newspaper reports M.Gambetta's second was apparently a Frenchman.

First, we drew up my principal's will. I insisted upon this, and stuck to my point. I said I never heard of a man in his right mind going out to fight a duel without first making his will. He said he had never heard of a man in his right mind doing anything of the kind. When he had finished his will, he wished to proceed to a choice of 'last words'. He wanted to know how the following words, as a dying exclamation, struck me:

'I die for my God, for my country, for freedom of speech, for progress, and the universal brotherhood of man!'

I objected that this would require too lingering a death; it was a good speech for a consumptive, but not suited to the exigencies of the field of honour. We wrangled over a good many ante-mortem outburst, but I finally got him to cut his obituary down to this, which he copied into his memorandum book, purposing to get it by heart:

'I DIE THAT FRANCE MAY LIVE.'

I said that this remark seemed to lack relevancy; but he said relevancy was a matter of no consequence in last words—what you wanted was thrill.

The next thing in order was the choice of weapon. My principal said he was not feeling well, and would leave that and the other details of the proposed meeting to me. Therefore I wrote the following note and carried it to M. Fourtou's friend:

'Sir,—M. Gambetta accepts M. Fourtou's challenge, and authorises me to propose Plessis-Piquet as the place of meeting; to-morrow morning at daybreak as the time; and axes as the weapons. I am, sir, with great respect, Mark Twain.'

M. Fourtou's friend read this note, and shuddered. Then he turned to me and said, with a suggestion of severity in his tone:

'Have you considered, sir, what would be the inevitable result of such a meeting as this?'

'Well, for instance, what *would* it be?'

'Bloodshed!'

'That's about the size of,' I said. ' Now, if it is a fair question, what was your was your side proposing to shed?'

I had him there. He saw he had made a blunder, so he hastened to explain it away. He said he had spoken jestingly. Then he added that he and his principal would enjoy axes, and indeed prefer them, but such weapons were barred by the French code, and so I must change my proposal.

I walked the floor, turning the thing over in my mind, and finally it occurred to me that Gatling guns at fifteen paces would be a likely way to get a verdict on the field of honour. So I framed this idea into a proposition.

But it was not accepted. The code was in the way again. I proposed rifles; then double-barreled shot-guns; then Colt's navy revolvers. These being all rejected, I reflected a while and sarcastically suggested brick-bats at three-quarters of a mile. I always hate to fool away a humorous thing on a person who has no perception of humour; and it filled me with bitterness when this man went soberly away to submit this last proposition to his principal.

He came back presently and said his principal was charmed with the idea of brick-bats at three-quarters of a mile, but must decline on account of the danger to disinterested parties passing between. Then I said:

'Well, I am at the end of my string now. Perhaps you would be good enough to suggest a weapon. Perhaps you have even had one in your mind all the time?'

'Oh, without doubt, monsieur!'

So he fell to hunting in his pocket—pocket after pocket, and he had plenty of them—muttering all the while, 'Now, what could I have done with them?'

At last he was successful. He fished out of his vest pocket a couple of little things which I carried to the light and ascertained to be pistols. They were single-barreled and silver-mounted, and very dainty and pretty. I was not able to speak for emotion. I silently hung one of them on my watchchain, and returned the other. My companion in crime now unrolled a postage stamp containing several cartridges, and gave me one of them. I asked if he meant to signify by this that our men were to be allowed but one shot a piece. He replied that the French code permitted no more. I then begged him to go on and suggest a distance, for my mind was growing weak and confused under the strain which had been put upon it. He named sixty-five yards. I nearly lost my patience. I said:

'Sixty-five yards, with these instruments? Squirt guns would be deadlier at fifty. Consider, my friend, you and I are banded together to destroy life, not make it eternal.'

But with all my persuasions, all my arguments, I was only able to get him to reduce the distance to thirty-five yards; and even this concession he made with reluctance, and said with a sigh:

'I wash my hands of this slaughter; on your head be it.'

There was nothing for me but to go home to my old lion heart and tell my humiliating story. When I entered, M. Gambetta was laying his last lock of hair upon the altar. He sprang towards me, exclaiming:

'You have made the fatal arrangements—I see it in your eyes!'

'I have.'

His face paled a trifle, and he leaned upon a table for support. He breathed thick and heavily for a moment or two, so tumultuous were his feelings; then he hoarsely whispered:

'The weapon, the weapon! Quick! What is the weapon?'

'This!' and I displayed that silver-mounted thing. He cast but one glance at it, then swooned ponderously to the floor.

When he came to, he said mournfully:

'The unnatural calm to which I have subjected myself has told upon my nerves. But away with weakness! I will confront my fate like a man and a Frenchman.'

He rose to his feet, and assumed an attitude which for sublimity has never been approached by man, and had seldom been surpassed by statues. Then he said, in deep bass tones:

'Behold I am calm, I am ready, reveal to me the distance.'

'Thirty-five yards...'

I could not lift him up, of course; but I rolled him over, and poured water down his back. He presently came to, and said:

'Thirty-five yards—without a rest? But why ask? Since murder was that man's intention, why should he palter with small details? But mark you one thing: in my fall the world shall see how the chivalry of France meets death.'

❖

At half-past nine in the morning the procession approached the field of Plessis-Piquet in the following order: first came our carriage—nobody in it but M.Gambetta and myself; then a carriage containing two poet-orators who did not believe in God, and these had MS funeral orations projecting from their breast pockets; then a carriage containing the head surgeons and their case of instruments; then eight private carriages containing consulting surgeons; then a hack containing a coroner; then two hearses; then a carriage containing the head undertakers; then a train of assistants and mutes on foot; and after these came plodding through the fog a long procession of camp followers, police, and citizens generally. It was a noble turn-out, and would have made a fine display if we had thinner weather.

There was no conversation. I spoke several times to my principal, but I judge he was not aware of it, for he always referred to his notebook and muttered absently, 'I die that France may live.'

Arrived on the field, my fellow-second and I paced off the thirty-five yards, and then drew lots for choice of position. This latter was but an ornamental ceremony, for all choices were alike in such weather. These preliminaries being ended, I went to my principal and asked him if he was ready. He spread himself out to his full width, and said in stern voice, 'Ready! Let the batteries be charged.'

The loading was done in the presence of duly constituted witnesses. We considered it best to perform this delicate service with the assistance of a lantern, on account of the state of the weather. We now placed our men.

At this point the police noticed that the public had massed themselves together on the right and left of the field; they therefore begged a delay, while they should put these poor people in a place of safety. The request was granted.

The police having ordered the two multitudes to take positions behind the duelists, we were once more ready. The weather growing still more opaque, it was agreed between myself and the other second that before giving the fatal signal we should each deliver a loud whoop to enable the combatants to ascertain each other's whereabouts.

I now returned to my principal, and was distressed to observe that he had lost a good deal of his spirit. I tried my best to hearten him. I said, ' Indeed, Sir, things are not as bad as they seem. Considering the character of the weapons, the limited number of shots allowed, the generous distance, the impenetrable solidity of the fog, and the added fact that one of the combatants is one-eyed and the other crossed-eyed and near-sighted, it seems to be that this conflict need not necessarily be fatal. There are chances that both of you may survive. Therefore cheer up; do not be downhearted.'

This speech had so good an effect that my principal immediately stretched forth his hand and said, 'I am myself again; give me the weapon.'

I laid it, all lonely and forlorn, in the centre of the vast solitude of his palm. He gazed at it and shuddered. And still mournfully contemplating it he murmured, in a broken voice:

'Alas! it is not death I dread, but mutilation.'

I heartened him once more, and with such success that he presently said, ' Let the tragedy begin. Stand at my back; do not desert me in this solemn hour, my friend.'

I gave him my promise. I now assisted him to point his pistol towards the spot where I judged his adversary to be standing, and cautioned him to listen well and further guide himself by my fellow-second's whoop. Then I propped myself against M. Gambetta's back, and raised a rousing 'Whoop-ee!' This was answered from out the far distances of the fog, and I immediately shouted:

'One—two—three—*fire!*'

Two little sounds like *spit! spit!* broke upon my ear, and in the same instant I was crushed to the earth under a mountain of flesh. Bruised as I was, I was still able to catch a faint accent from above, to this effect:

'I die for…for…perdition take it, what is it I die for? ... Oh, yes—FRANCE! I die that France may live!'

The surgeons swarmed around with their probes in their hands, and applied their microscopes to the whole area of M. Gambetta's person, with the happy result of finding nothing in the nature of a wound. Then a scene ensued which was in every way gratifying and inspiriting.

The two gladiators fell upon each other's necks, with floods of proud and happy tears; the other second embraced me; the surgeons, the orators, the undertakers, the police, everybody embraced, everybody congratulated, everybody cried, and the whole atmosphere was filled with praise and with joy unspeakable.

It seemed to me then that I would rather be a hero of a French duel than a crowned and sceptred monarch.

When the commotion had somewhat subsided, the body of surgeons held a consultation, and after a good deal of debate decided that with proper care and nursing there was reason to believe that I should survive my injuries. My internal hurts were deemed the most serious, since it was apparent that a broken rib had penetrated my left lung, and that many of my organs had been pressed out so far to one side or the other of where they belonged, that it was doubtful if they would ever learn to perform their functions in such remote and unaccustomed localities. They then set my arm in two places, pulled my right hip into its socket again, and re-elevated my nose. I was an object of great interest, and even administration; and many sincere and warm-hearted persons had themselves introduced to me, and said they were proud to know the only man who had been hurt in a French duel in forty years.

I was placed in an ambulance at the very head of the procession; and thus with gratifying éclat I was marched into Paris, the most conspicuous figure in that great spectacle, and deposited at the hospital.

The Cross of the Legion of Honour has been conferred upon me. However, few escape that distinction.

Such is the true version of the most memorable private conflict of the age.

I have no complaints to make against anyone. I acted for myself, and I can stand the consequences. Without boasting, I think I can say I am not afraid to stand before a modern French duelist, but as long as I keep in my right mind I will never consent to stand behind one again.

THE RUPA BOOK
OF
HEARTWARMING STORIES

By the same author:

Angry River
A Little Night Music
A Long Walk for Bina
Hanuman to the Rescue
Ghost Stories from the Raj
Strange Men, Strange Places
The India I Love
Tales and Legends from India
The Blue Umbrella
Ruskin Bond's Children's Omnibus
The Ruskin Bond Omnibus-I
The Ruskin Bond Omnibus-II
The Ruskin Bond Omnibus-III
Rupa Book of Great Animal Stories
The Rupa Book of True Tales of Mystery and Adventure
The Rupa Book of Ruskin Bond's Himalayan Tales
The Rupa Book of Great Suspense Stories
The Rupa Laughter Omnibus
The Rupa Book of Scary Stories
The Rupa Book of Haunted Houses
The Rupa Book of Travellers' Tales
The Rupa Book of Great Crime Stories
The Rupa Book of Nightmare Tales
The Rupa Book of Shikar Stories
The Rupa Book of Love Stories
The Rupa Book of Wicked Stories
The Rupa Book of Heartwarming Stories
The Rupa Book of Thrills and Spills

THE RUPA BOOK
OF
HEARTWARMING STORIES

Edited by
RUSKIN BOND

Rupa & Co

Published by
Rupa Publications India Pvt. Ltd.
7/16, Ansari Road, Daryaganj,
New Delhi 110 002

Sales Centres:
Allahabad Bengaluru Chennai
Hyderabad Jaipur Kathmandu
Kolkata Mumbai

Typeset in 11 pts. Calisto by
Mindways Design
1410 Chiranjiv Tower
43 Nehru Place
New Delhi 110 019

Printed in India by
Gopsons Papers Ltd.
A-14 Sector 60
Noida 201 301

CONTENTS

INTRODUCTION

This is the fifteenth anthology I have compiled and edited for Rupa. It has been a stimulating experience, presenting to my readers the work of outstanding writers—some great, others unjustly neglected or forgotten. For this collection I have selected stories that warm the heart, restore one's faith in the goodness of human nature, and capture something of the joy of being alive.

Kind readers are always suggesting titles for my books. Someone suggested that I call this one *Kofta Curry for the Soul* while a young reader from the South came up with *Aloo Bonda for Everyone*. Both appetising titles but eventually I settled for plain and simple *Heartwarming Stories*—for that is what they truly are...

And these are stories that you can turn to, again and again, as one turns to a favourite piece of music or a much-loved picture. I have read several of them twice over, and my pleasure does not diminish. Familiarity breeds affection!

I keep returning to the 'Bartimeus' story, 'That Which Remained'. It always moves me, especially that last scene when all seems hopeless until three softly spoken words change everything. 'Bartimeus,' wrote almost entirely about sailors and the sea. Unlike most modern writers, he was a shy man who shunned personal publicity, and he adopted a pen-name to conceal his real identity. It took me some time to discover his true persona: he was Paymaster Commander L.A. de Costa Ricci. Rather a handful, that name! He was wise to assume a *nom-de-plume*.

Another shy, retiring writer was William Sydney Porter, who took the pen-name O. Henry. He, more than any short story writer, was responsible for that 'twist in the tail', a technique taken up by many later writers.

O. Henry was familiar with the joys and sorrows of ordinary people striving to succeed, or simply to survive, in the big cities of America. His stories have certainly survived, although he wrote many of them for newspapers and magazines. Never in robust health, he died at the age of 43, a jest on his lips. 'Don't turn down the light,' he said to those beside his bed; and then added the words of a popular song, 'I'm afraid to go home in the dark.'

Ghosts in fiction are usually evil, malignant spirits, harbingers of doom, and it is difficult to write a successful story about a harmless, ineffective ghost. But Hugh Walpole did just that. Apart from being a brilliant writer—and you must read his novel *Mr. Perrin and Mr. Traill* to find him at his best—he was a man of a sweet and gentle disposition, and this is reflected in his story of a little ghost who needed protection.

Edmund Blunder was best known as a poet, but his first love was cricket. In 'A Cricket Match of Long Ago' he captures the atmosphere of a game of cricket in a peaceful English village between the Wars. But more than the cricket, it's the quaint assemblage of characters who make for a memorable occasion.

No anthology of heartwarming tales would be complete without a couple of stories from the pen of Anton Chekhov, truly the grand master of the short story. All his stories are written with compassion and a delight in the incongruities of human behaviour.

We have gone through some famous names, but I have to confess that I had never heard of Josef Bard until I discovered his wonderful story, 'The Tale of a Child,' in an old anthology. Bard was born in Budapest, and wrote in French, English and Hungarian. This short classic was written in English. It captures perfectly the mood, behaviour and dreams of three adolescent boys who go swimming in the Danube even though, like many of our rivers today, it 'stinks'!

Robert Nathan was best known for his autobiographical novel, *The Happy Time*, which describes the life and times of a French Canadian family at the turn of the last century. It was turned into a successful play and a film. 'My Friend the Mouse' is an extract from this warm and charming book.

And that brings us to Antoine Saint-Exupery's 'Prisoner of the Sand', which I was tempted to re-title 'The Gift of Water'. But you cannot tamper with a work of art, and that is what this story is—personal experience transformed into a literary *tour-de-force*. Saint-Exupery has been called the Joseph Conrad of the air; and like Conrad, his skills as a pilot and as a writer were combined with a profound concern for man's destiny. Born in 1900, he became a full-fledged pilot at the age of twenty-one. He published his first book when he was twenty-six. His most memorable works were *Night Flight* and *Wind, Sand and Stars*. In the summer of 1944, while returning from a reconnaissance flight pursued by German planes, he disappeared over the Mediterranean.

In this intense but poetic narration of his struggle for survival after a plane crash in the desert, Saint Exupery expresses his affection for all mankind and his joy in the gift of life.

'Water, thou has no taste, no colour, no odour; cannot be defined; art relished while ever mysterious.... Of the riches that exist in this world, thou art the rarest and also the most delicate—thou so pure within the bowels of the earth!'

Reading these stories again has been a moving experience for me, as I hope it will be for you, dear reader.

Ruskin Bond
15 April, 2005

MY DATE WITH GRAYBEARD

ROBIN COLLINS

When I was a boy in Natal, South Africa, the farmers of the district organised a hunt each year in the Umzimkulu valley, using a hundred native beaters and their dogs. A variety of wildlife finds refuge in the valley—monkeys, baboons and an occasional leopard—but the creature most sought after is the wily gray bushbuck. With his speed and cunning, his ferocity when wounded or cornered, he is a quarry worthy of any hunter's gun.

There was one buck we called Graybeard, a magnificent old-timer who year after year survived the hunt. I was ten years old when I had my first glimpse of him, stepping proudly across a small clearing. His horns were long and sharp. His fur was a deep gray mottled with white. It was every hunter's desire to kill him, and from that day I could think of little else. I somehow felt that my initiation into manhood would consist of claiming Graybeard for my own.

My father had insisted that I wait until I was fourteen before I could go hunting, so I spent the next three years in a fever of anxiety, fearful that some other hunter would shoot my buck. But Graybeard survived. Once he followed silently behind a younger buck and, as it fell under a blast of shot, he jumped the clearing before the hunter could reload. Once he used a pair of legally protected does to shield him past the line of fire.

The third year the hunters chose their gun stations between the cliffs and the river so cunningly that it seemed as if no game could slip through. After the native beaters dispersed into the bush I heard their excited cries as they sighted Graybeard. I was perched on the cliffs, and from my vantage point I watched him run from their dogs straight toward the concealed hunters. I clenched my fists as I waited for the shot which would rob me of him. Then suddenly he turned, scattered the pursuing dogs and made straight for the line of beaters, who hurled their spears and knobbed throwing sticks at him. Just when I feared he had been struck down, I heard the yelping dogs pursuing him into the bush behind the beaters, and I realised that he had broken through to safety.

That evening the farmers could talk of nothing except how Graybeard had escaped into the bush for another year. I smiled, for next year I would be old enough to take my place in the line of guns.

All through that year I cherished one bright vision—the picture of myself, a skinny boy of fourteen, standing astride the magnificent creature. When my father offered me my first shotgun I rejected the light 20-gauge which would have suited my frail build and chose instead a heavy 12-gauge so that I could have a weapon worthy of Graybeard. On the day of the hunt I wanted to rush straight to the valley at dawn, but my father forced me to eat breakfast. 'Graybeard will still be there,' he said pushing me down in my chair.

In the gray light of early morning we congregated in the valley. The beaters were dispatched to the top end and we hunters drew lots for positions. The best positions were close to the cliffs, because bushbucks tend to climb in their effort to escape the pursuing dogs. To my bitter disappointment I drew a position down near the river. Then I heard my father, who had drawn a good stand, say, 'I'll change with my boy. I'd like him to have a good place for his first hunt.' As he walked past me he patted my shoulder. 'See that you get the old one,' he whispered with a smile.

I scrambled up the steep slope, determined to outdistance the others and find the best possible place of concealment. I selected an outcrop of broken boulders, well screened by bush, which gave me a line of fire across a small clearing. For a long while there was no sound. Then came the shouts of the beaters, the sound of sticks beaten against trees and the yelping of dogs.

First came a doe, blundering past me in panic-stricken flight, then a young buck. I let him pass. Graybeard might be following, and I was determined not to betray my position. But there was no further movement, and I wondered if Graybeard had crossed lower down. Then a trembling of the brush caught my eye. Not ten yards from me, Graybeard stepped to the edge of the trees, silently inspecting the clearing. I had only to lower the muzzle slightly to cover him. The ambition of my youthful life was at the point of achievement. Graybeard stood motionless before me. I had only to pull the trigger to bring him down.

Yet something made me hold my fire. The buck had turned his head now, and his great ears twitched to catch the baying of the dogs. His moist nose trembled, and his eyes, softly luminous, alert without being fearful, seemed to stare right at me. There was pride and dignity in every line of his body, and I knew suddenly that I could not destroy him. For several breathless moments he remained where he was, and then a vagary of the breeze carried my man-smell to him. In two huge leaps he crossed the clearing and was gone. I stayed where I was, silent and enraptured.

When the drive was over, my father came up the slope. I unloaded my gun and pushed the shells back into the loops on my belt. My father's quick eye took in the details of the stand I had occupied and the full belt of cartridges. 'No luck?' he asked.

I shook my head.

'That's funny,' he said. 'The boys sighted Graybeard coming in this direction, and none of the other guns saw him.'

I looked down at the ground. My reticence must have aroused his suspicions, for he walked across the clearing and paused beside the deep imprints the buck had made in the mist earth as he jumped. I walked away, unable to face the condemnation which I imagined on my father's face.

As we drove home, the thought of old Graybeard gathering his does together for another year of safety gave me a thrill of pleasure. But my father's silence had put a constraint upon us. Finally he asked. 'What happened, son?'

Shyly, stumblingly, I tried to tell him. I described Graybeard as I had seen him—majestic and fearless. I tried to explain why, when the moment had come to fire. I knew I could not buy the hunter's badge at the price of so much splendour.

My father was silent for a moment and then he said slowly, 'You've learned something today, son—something that many men live a lifetime without knowing.' He put an arm around my shoulders. 'You've learned compassion,' he said softly.

THE BIG DRUM

WILLIAM GERHARDI

The brass band played *Im Kopfle zwei Augle*, and it seemed to her that the souls of these men were like notes of this music, crying for something elusive, for something in vain. To blare forth one's love on a brass trumpet! An earnest of one's high endeavour fallen short through the inadequate matter of brass; but withal in these abortive notes one felt the presence of the heights the instrument would reach, alas, if it but could!

It touched her to the heart. She would have liked her Otto to play the trumpet instead of the big drum. It seemed more romantic. Otto was not a bit romantic. He was a soldier all right, but he looked more like a man who had started life as a shoemaker's apprentice, had grown old, and was still a shoemaker's apprentice.

The band played well—a compact synthetic body—but Otto was a forlorn figure who watched the proceedings with sustained and patient interest and was suffered by them, every now and then, to raise his drumstick and give a solitary, judicious 'Bang!'

And he—a tall gaunt man—seemed as though he were ashamed of his small part.

And as she watched him she felt a pang of pity for herself: wedded to him, she would be forgotten, while life, indifferent, strode by; and no one in the world would care whether she had her share of happiness before she died. And the music brought this out acutely, as if along the hard stone-paved indifference of life it dragged, dragged on excruciatingly its living bleeding soul. It spoke of loneliness, of laughter, of the pathos, pity and futility of life.

She watched them. The bayonets at their side. The military badges of rank. The hard discipline. And the music seemed to say, 'Stop! What are you doing? Why are you doing this?' And thoughts flowed into her mind. Of soldiers dreaming on a Sunday afternoon.

A fierce old corporal, of whom everyone was afraid, talking to her of children and of daisies. Soldiers who, too, had dreams in long waves—of what? She did not know—but not this. And the men who stood up and blew the brass trumpets seemed to say, and the shining trumpets themselves seemed to say: 'We were not born for the Army; we were born for something better—though heaven only knows what it is!'

That was so. Undeniably so. Yet she wished it were otherwise. It helped to make allowances for Otto. Whatever else he lacked, it made her think at least he had a soul. But to be wedded for life to the big drum! She did not fancy the idea. It didn't seem a proper career.

But Otto showed no sing of *wanting* to 'get on'—even in the orchestra. The most exasperating thing about it all was that Otto showed no sign of even *trying*! She had asked him if he would not, in time, 'move on' and take over—say, the double-bass: He did not seem to think it either feasible or necessary. Or *necessary*! He had been with the big drum for close on twelve years. 'It's a good drum,' he had said. And that was all.

There was no... 'go' in him. That was it: no go. It was no use denying it. As she watched him—gaunt and spectacled—she wished Otto were more of a man and less of an old maid. The conductor, a boozer with a fat red face full of pimples, some dead and dried up, others still flourishing, was a gallant—every inch a man.

He had the elasticity and suppleness and military alertness of the continental military man. She could not tell his rank from the stripes on his sleeves, but thought he must be a major. His heels were high and tipped with indiarubber, and so were straight and smart, but his trousers lacked the foot-strap to keep them in position—poor dilapidated Austrian Army! How low it had sunk! Nevertheless they were tight and narrow and showed off the major's calves to advantage. He wore a pince-nez, but a rimless kind, through which gazed a pair of not altogether innocent eyes. But a man and a leader of men.

While Otto had no rubber on his heels. His heels looked eaten away. He wore a pair of spectacles through which he peered from afar at his neighbour's music-stand, and at the appointed time— not one-tenth of a second too early—down came the drumstick with the long-awaited 'Bang!' So incidental, so contemptible was Otto's part that, in addition to handling the drum he had to turn the pages for the man who played the cymbals. It seemed to her humiliating. It was very wrong that Otto had no music-stand of his own.

He smiled shyly, and she turned away, annoyed. The little modiste walked on, meeting the stream of people who promenaded the path surrounding the bandstand; a man on high heels, three girls with a pinched look, a famous Tyrolese basso with a long ruddy beard, a *jeune premier* with whiskers and hair like a wig, whose look appeared to imply: 'Here am I.'

Innsbruck looked morose that Sunday morning, and the military band in the park executed music that was tattered, gross, a little common, yet compelling, even like the daily fare of life. Oh, why were there no heroes? Exalted, brimming over with life. These men of the Tyrol! And as for Otto? Why she could have only waved her hand!

She began to wonder whether she had not really better break it of with him. If men would but realise how little was required from them. Only an outward gesture of romance: a touch sufficed, the rest would be supplied by woman's powerful imagination. Not even so much. A mere abstention from the cruder forms of clumsiness, a surface effort to conceal one's feeblest worst. A mere semblance of mastery, a glimpse of a will.

In short, anything at all that would provide the least excuse for loving him as she so wished to do. A minute she stood, thinking. 'A minimum. Hardly as much.' There passed along the man on high heels, the three girls with the pinched look, the Tyrolese basso with the long ruddy beard, the *jeune premier* with whiskers and hair like a wig, whose look seemed to say, 'Here am I'; then again the man on high heels, the three girls with the pinched look, the Tyrolese singer, and again the *jeune premier* whose look implied, 'Here am I.' They walked round and round as if the park were a cage and there was nothing to do but walk round—with heads bent lifeless, sullenly resolute. And again there came along the man on high heels. 'The minimum of a minimum....'

The music resumed. She consulted her programme. Item 7. Potpourri from the operette *Die Fledermaus* by Johann Strauss. She returned to the stand, prepared to give her fiancé another chance. Otto's part, as before, was contemptible, more contemptible than before. He was inactive. He smiled shyly. She coloured. And, looking at him, she knew. She knew it was no use, her love could not bridge the chasm. He was despised by the rest of the band. A stick-in-the-mud. Not a man. A poor fish. Not for her....

The potpourri, as if suddenly turning the corner, broke out into a resounding march, and behold, the big drum now led the way. Bang! bang! bang! bang! Clearly he whacked, never once missing the chance; and the man with the cymbals, as if one heart and brain operated their limbs, clashed the cymbals in astounding unison, the big drum pounding away, pounding away, without cease or respite.

And the trumpeters smiled, as who might say: 'Good old big drum! You have come into your own at last!' Bang! bang! bang! bang! The big drum had got loud and excited. And all the people standing around looked as though a great joy had come into their lives: and if they had not been a little shy of each other they would have set out and marched in step with the music, taken up *any* cause and, if only because the music implied that all men were brothers, gone forth if need be and butchered another body of brothers, to the tearing, gladdening strains of the march (since it is not known from what rational cause men could have marched to the war).

And if in the park of the neighbouring town there were just such a band with just such a drum which played this same music, the people of the neighbouring town would have marched to this music and exterminated this town. The conductor, like a driver who, having urged his horse over the hill, leans back and leaves the rest to the horse, conceded the enterprise to the drummer, as if the hard, intricate work were now over and he was taking it easy, his baton moved perfunctorily in the wake of the drum, he looked round and acknowledged the greetings of friends with gay, informal salutes of the left hand, his bland smile freely admitting to all that it was no longer himself but the drum which led them to victory.

Or rather, the hard fight had already been won and these, behold, were the happy results! Bang! bang! bang! bang! Strangers passed smiles of intimate recognition, old men nodded reminiscently, small boys gazed with rapt eyes, women looked sweet and bright-eyed, ready to oblige with a kiss; while the big drum, conscious of his splendid initiative, pounded away without cease or respite.

'Wonderful! Beautiful!' said the public surrounding them. And thought: 'Noise is a good thing.'

The band had described the first circle and was repeating it with added gusto and deliberation. The big drum and the cymbals were pounding, pounding their due through the wholly inadequate blazing of brass. But these did not mind: 'Every dog has his day'—and they followed the lead of the drum. He led them. He—Otto! Her Otto was leading them. God! Merciful Virgin! What had she done to deserve such happiness? Otto!... And she had doubted him, thought there was no 'go' in him. No *go*!

She burnt red with shame at the mere thought of it. He was all 'go.' And didn't he make them go, too, the whole lot of them? How he led them! Puffing, the sweat streaming down their purple faces, they blazed away till their cheeks seemed ready to burst but Otto out-drummed them—annihilated their efforts.

He—Otto! O, God! Watching him, people could hardly keep still. But that none of them stirred and all of them wanted to, added piquancy to the illusion of motion. They stood rooted— while the drum carried on for them: Bang! bang! bang! bang!

'Marvellous!' sighed the public around them.

Her Otto—cock of the walk! She could scarcely believe her eyes. Standing in front of the crowd, only a few paces from his side and raising herself on her toes ever so gently in rhythm with the music, so that by the very tininess of her movements she seemed to be sending added impetus into the band, as if, indeed, she were pressing with her little feet some invisible pump, she scanned his face with tenderness, in dumb adoration.

And Otto at the drum must have felt it, for, at this turn, he put knew life into his thundering whacks: *Bang! bang! bang! bang!* he toiled, and the conductor, as if divining what was afoot, at that moment accelerated the pace of the march.

'Bravo, bravo!' said the people surrounding them.

There was no doubt about it. This was Art. The unerring precision. The wonderful touch. Otto!... Otto, as never before, whacked the big drum, whacked it in excitement, in a frenzy, in transcending exaltation. Thundering bangs! And now she knew— what she couldn't have dreamed—she knew it by his face. Otto was a hero. A leader of men. Something fluttered in her breast, as though a bird had flown in, ready to fly out.

'Now it's all over,' though the people, 'and we are going home to lunch.' And everyone smiled and felt very happy and gay. A sort of prolonged accelerated thundering of the big drum, and then one tremendous BANG!

The thing was over. The conductor raised a bent hand to the peak of his cap, acknowledging the applause. The bird in her fluttered more wildly than ever. She wanted to cry out, but her throat would not obey. She clutched at her heaving breast with trembling fingers. 'My love.' she thought. 'My king! My captain!——'

THAT WHICH REMAINED

BARTIMEUS

I

Oddly enough, no record exists of the origin of his nickname. 'Periwinkle' he had been all through crammer and *Britannia* days. As senior signal midshipman of the Mediterranean flagship, he was still 'The Periwinkle', small for his years, skinny as a weasel, with straight black hair, and grey eyes set wide apart in a brown face; the eyelashes, black and short, grew very close together, which gave him the perpetual appearance of having recently coaled ship and neglected to clean the dust from his eyes.

The signal midshipmen of a fleet, especially the Mediterranean Fleet, of those days, were essentially keen on their 'job'. The nature of the work and intership rivalry provided for that. But with the Periwinkle, signals were more than a mere 'job'. They formed his creed and recreation: the flag-lockers were tarpaulin-covered shrines; the semaphores spoke oracles by day as did the flashing lamps by night. And the high priest of these mysteries was the flag-lieutenant, a Rugby International and right good fellow withal, but, to the Periwinkle, a very god who walked among men.

To understand something of his hero-worship you would need to have been on the bridge when the fleet put out to sea for tactics. It was sufficient for the Periwinkle to watch this immaculate, imperturbable being snap out a string of signals apparently from memory, as he so often did, while hoist after hoist of flags leaped from the lockers and sped skywards, and the bridge was a whirl of bunting. Even the admiral, who spoke so little and saw so much, was in danger of becoming a mere puppet in the boy's sight.

But there was more than this to encourage his ardour. The flag-lieutenant, recognising the material of a signalman of unusual promise, would invite the Periwinkle to his cabin after dinner and unfold, with the aid of printed diagrams and little brass oblongs representing ships, the tactical and strategical mysteries of his craft. There was one unforgettable evening, too, when the Periwinkle was bidden to dinner ashore at the Malta Club. The dinner was followed by a dance, whereat, in further token of esteem, the flag-lieutenant introduced him to a lady of surpassing loveliness—the fairest (the Periwinkle was given to understand) of all the Pippins.

The spring gave place to summer, and the island became a glaring wilderness of sun-baked rock. For obscure reasons of policy the fleet remained at Malta instead of departing on its usual cruise, and week after week the sun blazed pitilessly down on the awnings of the anchored ships. Week by week the Periwinkle grew more brown and angular, and lost a little more of his wiry activity. The frequent stampedes up and down ladders with signals for the admiral sent him into a lather like a nervous horse; at the end of a watch his hair was wet with perspiration and his whites hung clammily on his meagre limbs. After a while, too, he began to find the glare tell, and to ease the aching of his eyes, had sometimes to shift the telescope from one eye to the other in the middle of a signal. As a matter of fact, there was no necessity for him to read signals at all: that was part of the signalman's duty. And if he had chosen to be more leisurely in his ascent and descent of ladders, no one would have called him to account. But his zeal was a flame within him, and terror lest he earned a rebuke from the flag-lieutenant for lack of smartness, lent wings to his tired heels.

It was August when the flag-lieutenant sought out the fleet surgeon in the wardroom after dinner, and broached the subject of the Periwinkle.

'P.M.O., I wish you'd have a look at that shrimp; he's knocking himself up in this heat. He swears he's all right, but he looks fit for nothing but hospital.'

So the Periwinkle was summoned to the fleet surgeon's cabin. Vehemently he asserted that he had never felt better in his life, and the most the fatherly old Irishman could extort from him was the admission that he had not been sleeping particularly well. As a matter of fact he had not slept for three nights past; but fear lest he should be 'put on the list' forbade his admitting either this or the shooting pain behind his eyes, which by now was almost continual. The outcome of the interview, however, was an order to turn in forthwith. Next morning the Periwinkle was ignominiously hoisted over the side in a cot—loudly protesting at the indignity of not even being allowed to walk—*en route* for Bighi hospital as a fever patient.

II

The news of the world is transmitted to naval stations abroad by cable, and promulgated by means of wireless telegraphy to ships cruising or out of reach of visual signalling. At Malta the news is distributed to ships present in harbour by semaphore from the Castile, an eminence above the town of Valetta, commanding the grand harbour and nearly opposite the naval hospital.

One morning a group of convalescents were sunning themselves on the balcony of the hospital, and one, watching the life of the harbour through a telescope, suddenly exclaimed, 'Stand by! They're going to make the Reuter telegram. I wonder how the Navy got on at Lord's.'

'It's hopeless trying to read it,' said another, 'they make it at such a beastly rate.'

The Periwinkle, fuming in bed in an adjacent ward, overheard the speaker. In a second he was on his feet and at the open window, a tousled-haired object in striped pyjamas, crinkling his eyes in the glare. 'I can read it, sir, lend me the glass.'

'You ought to be in bed, my son. Haven't you got Malta Fever?'

'It's very slight,' replied the Periwinkle—as indeed it was,—'and I'm quite as warm out here as in bed. May I borrow your glass?'

He took the telescope and steadied it against a pillar. The distant semaphore began waving, and the group of convalescents settled down to listen. But no sound came from the boy. He was standing with the eye-piece held to his right eye, motionless as a statue. A light wind fluttered the gaudy pyjamas, and their owner lowered the glass with a little frown, half-puzzled, half-irritated.

'I—it's—there's something wrong——' he began, and abruptly put the glass to his left eye. 'Ah, that's better...' He commenced reading, but in a minute or two his voice faltered and trailed off into silence. He changed the glass to his right, and back to his left eye. Then, lowering it, turned a white scared face to the seated group. 'I'm afraid I can't read any more,' he said in a curiously dry voice; 'I—it hurts my eyes.'

He returned the glass to its owner and hopped back into bed, where he sat with the clothes drawn up under his chin, sweating lightly.

After a while he closed his left eye and looked cautiously round the room. The tops of objects appeared indistinctly out of a grey mist. It was like looking at a partly fogged negative. He closed his right eye and repeated the process with the other. His field of vision was clear then, except for a speck of grey fog that hung threateningly in the upper left-hand corner.

By dinner-time he could see nothing with the right eye, and the fog had closed on half the left eye's vision.

At tea-time he called the sister on duty:

'My eyes—hurt...frightfully.' Thus the Periwinkle, striving to hedge with destiny.

'Do they?' sympathised the sister. 'I'll tell the surgeon when he comes round to-night, and he'll give you something for them. I shouldn't read for the present if I were you.'

The Periwinkle smiled grimly, as if she had made a joke, and lay back, every nerve in his body strung to breaking-point.

'Can't see, eh?' The visiting surgeon who leaned over his bed a few hours later looked at him from under puzzled brows. 'Can't see—d'you mean...' He picked up an illustrated paper, holding it about a yard away, and pointed to a word block type: 'What's this word?'

The Periwinkle stared past him with a face like a flint. 'I can't see the paper. I can't see you...or the room, or—or—anything... I'm blind.' His voice trembled.

To the terror by night that followed was added physical pain past anything he had experienced or imagined in his short life. It almost amazed him that anything could hurt so much and not rob him of consciousness. The next room held a sufferer who raved in delirium: cursing, praying, and shrieking alternately. The tortured voice rose in the stillness of the night to a howl, and the Periwinkle set his teeth grimly. He was not alone in torment, but his was still the power to meet it like a man.

By the end of a week the pain had left him. At intervals during this period he was guided to a dark room—for the matter of that, all rooms were dark to him—and unseen beings bandied strange technicalities about his ears. 'Optic neuritis... retrobulbar... atrophy.' The words meant nothing to the boy, and their meaning mattered less. For nothing, they told him, could give him back his sight. After that they left him alone, to wait with what patience he might until the next P. & O. steamer passed through.

His first visitor was the chaplain, the most well-meaning of men, whose voice quavered with pity as he spoke at some length of resignation and the beauty of cheerfulness in affliction. On his departure, the Periwinkle caught the rustle of the sister's dress.

'Sister,' said the boy, 'will you please go away for a few minutes. I'm afraid I have to swear—out loud.'

'But you mustn't' she expostulated, slightly taken aback. 'It's very wicked.'

'Can't help that,' replied the Periwinkle austerely. 'Please go at once; I'm going to begin.'

Scandalised and offended as well she might be—she left the Periwinkle to his godless self, and he swore aloud—satisfying, unintelligible, senseless lowerdeckese. But when she brought him his tea an hour later she found he had the grace to look ashamed of himself, and forgave him. They subsequently became great friends, and at the Periwinkle's dictation she wrote long cheerful letters that began: 'My dear Mother,' and generally ended in suspicious-looking smudges.

Everyone visited the Periwinkle. His brethren from the fleet arrived, bearing as gifts strange and awful delicacies that usually had to be confiscated, sympathising with the queer, clumsy tenderness of boyhood. The flag-lieutenant came often, always cheerful and optimistic, forbearing to voice a word of pity: for this the Periwinkle was inexpressibly grateful. He even brought the Fairest of All the Pippins, but the boy shrank a little from the tell-tale tremor she could never quite keep out of her voice. Her parting gift was an armful of roses, and on leaving she bent over till he could smell the faint scent of her hair. 'Good-bye,' she whispered; 'go on being brave,' and, to his wrathful astonishment, kissed him lightly on the mouth.

There was the admiral's wife too—childless herself—who, from long dealings with men, had acquired a brusque, almost masculine manner. As soon as he had satisfied himself that she evinced no outward desire to 'slobber,' the Periwinkle admitted her to his friendship. He subsequently confessed to the sister that, for a woman, she read aloud extremely well. 'Well, I must be going',' she said one day at parting. 'I'll bring John up to see you tomorrow.' When she had gone, the Periwinkle smote his pillow. 'John!' he gasped.

'John' was the admiral.

Even the crew of his cutter—just the ordinary rapscallion duty-crew of the boat he had commanded—trudged up one sweltering Sunday afternoon, and were ushered with creaking boots and moist, shiny faces into his ward.

'Bein' as we 'ad an arfternoon orf, sir,' began the spokesman, who was also the coxswain of the boat. But at the sight of the wavering, sightless eyes, although prompted by nudges and husky whispers, he forgot his carefully-prepared sentences.

'We reckoned we'd come and give you a chuck-up, like, sir,' concluded another, and instead of the elaborate speech they had deemed the occasion demanded, they told him of their victory in a tree-mile race over a rival cutter. How afterwards they had generously fraternised with the vanquished crew—so generously that the port stroke—" 'im as we calls 'Nobby' Clark, sir, if you remembers"—was at that moment languishing in a cell, as a result of the lavish hospitality that had prevailed. Finally, the Periwinkle extended a thin hand to the darkness, to be gripped in turn by fourteen leathery fists, ere their owners tiptoed out of the room and out of his life.

III

The Periwinkle found blindness an easier matter to bear in the ward of a hospital than on board the P. & O. liner by which he was invalided home. A naval sick-berth steward attended to his wants, helped him to dress, and looked after him generally. But every familiar smell and sound of ship-life awoke poignant memories of the ship-life of former days, and filled him with bitter woe. He was morbidly sensitive of his blindness, too, and for days moped in his cabin alone, fiercely repelling any attempt at sympathy or companionship. Then, by degrees, the ship's doctor coaxed him up into a deck-chair, and sat beside him, warding off intruders and telling stories with the inimitable drollery that is the heritage of the surgeons of P. & O. liners. And at night, when the decks were clear, and very throb of the propellers was a reminder of the home they were drawing near to, he would link his arm loosely within the boy's and together they would walk to and fro. During these promenades he invariably treated the Periwinkle as a man of advanced years and experience, whereby was no little balm in Gilead.

Many people tried to make a fuss of the boy with the sullen mouth, whose cheek-bones looked as if they were coming through the skin, and who had such a sad story. Wealthy globe-trotters, Anglo-Indians, missionaries, and ladies of singular charm and beauty, all strove according to their lights to comfort him. But by degrees they realised he never wanted to play cat's cradle or even discuss his mother, and so left him in peace.

But the boy had a friend beside the doctor, a grizzled major from an Indian frontier regiment, returning home on furlough with a V.C. tacked on to his unpretentious name. At first the Periwinkle rather shrank from a fresh acquaintance—it is a terrible thing to have to shake hands with an unknown voice. But he was an incorrigible little hero-worshipper, and this man with the deep steady voice had done and seen wonderful things. Further, he didn't mind talking about them—to the Periwinkle; so that the boy, as he sat clasping his ankles and staring out to sea with sightless eyes, was told stories which, a week later, the newspaper reporters of the kingdom desired to hear in vain.

He was a philosopher too, this bronzed, grey-haired warrior with the sun-puckered eyes: teaching how, if you only take the trouble to look for it, a golden thread of humour runs through all the sombre warp and woof of life; and of 'Hope which...

outwears the accidents of life and reaches with tremulous hand
beyond the grave and death.'

This is the nicest sort of philosophy.

But for all that it was a weary voyage, and the Periwinkle was
a brown-faced ghost, all knees and elbows and angularities, by
the time Tilbury was reached. The first to board the ship was a
lady, pale and sweetly dignified, whom the doctor met at the
gangway and piloted to the Periwinkle's cabin. He opened the
door before he turned and fled, and so heard, in her greeting of
the Periwinkle, the infinite love and compassion that can thrill
a woman's voice.

In a corner of the railway carriage that carried them home, the
Periwinkle—that maimed and battered knight—still clung to the
half to the haft of his broken sword. 'I meant to do so jolly well.
Oh, mother, I meant you to be so jolly proud of me. The flag-
lieutenant said I might have been... if only it had been an arm
or a leg—deaf or dumb... but there's nothing left in all the
world... it's empty—nothing remains.'

She waited till the storms of self-pity and rebellion passed,
leaving him biting his fingers and breathing hard. Then little by
little, with mysterious tenderness, she drew out the iron that had
entered the boyish soul. And, at the last, he turned to her with
a little fluttering sigh, as a very tired child abandons a puzzle. She
bent her head low—

'This remains,' she whispered.

THE LAST LEAF

O. HENRY

In a little district west of Washington Square the streets have run crazy and broken themselves into small strips called 'places'. These 'places' make strange angles and curves. One street crosses itself a time or two. An artist once discovered a valuable possibility in this street. Suppose a collector with a bill for paints, paper and canvas should, in traversing this route, suddenly meet himself coming back, without a cent having been paid on account!

So, to quaint old Greenwich Village the art people soon came prowling, hunting for north windows and eighteenth-century gables and Dutch attics and low rents. Then they imported some pewter mugs and a chafing dish or two from Sixth Avenue, and became a 'colony.'

At the top of a squatty, three-story brick Sue and Johnsy had their studio. 'Johnsy' was familiar for Joanna. One was from Maine, the other from California. They had met at the table d'hôte of an Eighth Street 'Delmonico's', and found their tastes in art, chicory salad and bishop sleeves so congenial that the joint studio resulted.

That was in May. In November a cold, unseen stranger, whom the doctors called Pneumonia, stalked about the colony, touching one here and there with his icy finger. Over on the East Side this ravager strode boldly, smiting his victims by scores, but his feet trod slowly through the maze of the narrow and moss-grown 'places.'

Mr Penumonia was not what you would call a chivalric old gentleman. A mite of a little woman with blood thinned by Californian zephyrs was hardly fair game for the red-fisted, short-breathed old duffer. But Johnsy he smote; and she lay, scarcely moving, on her painted iron bedstead, looking through the small Dutch window-panes at the blank side of the next brick house.

One morning the busy doctor invited Sue into the hallway with a shaggy, grey eyebrow.

'She has one chance in—let us say, ten,' he said, as he shook down the mercury in his clinical thermometre. 'And that chance is for her to want to live. This way people have of lining-up on the side of the undertaker makes the entire pharmacopoeia look silly. Your little lady has made up her mind that she's not going to get well. Has she anything on her mind?'

'She—she wanted to paint the Bay of Naples some day,' said Sue.

'Paint?—bosh! Has she anything on her mind worth thinking about twice—a man, for instance?'

'A man?' said Sue, with a jews'-harp twang in her voice. 'Is a man worth—but, no, doctor; there is nothing of the kind.'

'Well, it is the weakness, then,' said the doctor.

'I will do all that science, so far as it may filter through my efforts, can accomplish. But whenever my patient begins to count the carriages in her funeral procession I subtract 50 per cent from the curative power of medicines. If you will get her to ask one question about the new winter styles in cloak sleeves I will promise you a one-in-five chance for her, instead of one in ten.'

After the doctor had gone, Sue went into the workroom and cried a Japanese napkin to a pulp. Then she swaggered into Johnsy's room with her drawing-board, whistling ragtime.

Johnsy lay, scarcely making a ripple under the bedclothes, with her face toward the window. Sue stopped whistling, thinking she was asleep.

She arranged her board and began a pen-and-ink drawing to illustrate a magazine story. Young artists must pave their way to Art by drawing pictures for magazine stories that young authors write to pave their way to Literature.

As Sue was sketching a pair of elegant horse-show riding trousers and a monocle on the figure of the hero, an Idaho cowboy, she heard a low sound, several times repeated. She went quickly to the bedside.

Johnsy's eyes were open wide. She was looking out the window and counting—counting backward.

'Twelve,' she said, and a little latter, 'eleven'; and then 'ten,' and 'nine'; and then 'eight' and 'seven,' almost together.

Sue looked solicitously out the window. What was there to count? There was only a bare, dreary yard to be seen, and the blank side of the brick house twenty feet away. An old, old ivy vine, gnarled and decayed at the roots, climbed half-way up the brick wall. The cold breath of autumn had stricken its leaves from the vine until its skeleton branches clung, almost bare, to the crumbling bricks.

'What is it, dear?' asked Sue.

'Six,' said Johnsy, in almost a whisper. 'They're falling faster now. Three days ago there were almost a hundred. It made my head ache to count them. But now it's easy. There goes another one. There are only five left now.'

'Five what, dear? Tell your Sudie.'

'Leaves. On the ivy vine. When the last one falls I must go too. I've known that for three days. Didn't the doctor tell you?'

'Oh, I never heard of such nonsense,' complained Sue, with magnificent scorn. 'What have old ivy leaves to do with your getting well? And you used to love that vine so, you naughty girl. Don't be a goosey. Why, the doctor told me this morning that your chances for getting well real soon were—let's see exactly what he said—he said the chances were ten to one! Why, that's almost as good a chance as we have in New York when we ride on the street-cars or walk past a new building. Try to take some broth now, and let Sudie go back to her drawing, so she can sell the editor man with it, and buy port wine for her sick child, and pork chops for her greedy self.'

'You needn't get any more wine,' said Johnsy, keeping her eyes fixed out the window.

'There goes another. No, I don't want any broth. That leaves just four. I want to see the last one fall before it gets dark. Then I'll go too.'

'Johnsy, dear,' said Sue, bending over her, 'will you promise me to keep your eyes closed, and not look out of the window until I am done working? I must hand those drawings in by to-morrow. I need the light or I would draw the shade down.'

'Couldn't you draw in the other room?' asked Johnsy coldly.

'I'd rather be here by you,' said Sue. 'Besides, I don't want you to keep looking at those silly ivy leaves.'

'Tell me as soon as you have finished,' said Johnsy, closing her eyes, and lying white and still as a fallen statue, 'because I want to see the last one fall. I'm tired of waiting. I'm tired of thinking. I want to turn loose my hold on everything, and go sailing down, down, just like one of those poor, tired leaves.'

'Try to sleep,' said Sue. 'I must call Behrman up to be my model for the old hermit miner. I'll not be gone a minute. Don't try to move till I come back.'

Old Behrman was a painter who lived on the ground floor beneath them. He was past sixty and had a Michael Angelo's Moses beard curling down from the head of a satyr along the body of an imp. Behrman was a failure in art. Forty years he had wielded the brush without getting near enough to touch the hem of his Mistress's robe. He had been always about to paint a masterpiece, but had never yet begun it. For several years he had painted nothing except now and then a daub in the line of commerce or advertising. He earned a little by serving as a model to those young artists in the colony who could not pay the price of a professional. He drank gin to excess, and still talked of his coming masterpiece. For the rest he was a fierce little old man, who scoffed terribly at softness in anyone, and who regarded himself as especial mastiff-in-waiting to protect the two young artists in the studio above.

Sue found Behrman smelling strongly of juniper berries in his dimly-lighted den below. In one corner was a blank canvas on an easel that had been waiting there for twenty-five years to receive the first line of the masterpiece. She told him of Johnsy's fancy, and how she feared she would, indeed, light and fragile as a leaf herself, float away when her slight hold upon the world grew weaker.

Old Behrman, with his red eyes plainly streaming, shouted his contempt and derision for such idiotic imaginings.

'Vass!' he cried. 'Is dere people in de world mit der foolishness to die because leafs dey drop off from a confounded vine? I haf not heard of such a thing. No, I vill not bose as a model for your fool hermit-dunderhead. Vy do you allow dot silly pusiness to come in der prain of her? Ach, dot poor little Miss Yohnsy.'

'She is very ill and weak,' said Sue, 'and the fever has left her mind morbid and full of strange fancies. Very well, Mr Behrman, if you do not care to pose for me, you needn't. But I think you are a horrid old—old flibberti-gibbet.'

'You are just like a woman!' yelled Behrman. 'Who said I vill not bose? Go on. I come mit you. For half an hour I haf peen trying to say dot I am ready to bose. Goot! Dis is not any blace in which one so goot as Miss Yohnsy shall lie sick. Some day I vill baint a masterpiece, and ve shall all go avay. Gott! Yes.'

Johnsy was sleeping when they went upstairs. Sue pulled the shade down to the window-sill and motioned Behrman into the other room. In there they peered out the window fearfully at the ivy vine. Then they looked at each other for a moment without speaking. A persistent, cold rain was falling, mingled with snow. Behrman, in his old blue shirt, took his seat as the hermit-miner on an upturned kettle for a rock.

When Sue awoke from an hour's sleep the next morning she found Johnsy with dull, wide-open eyes staring at the drawn green shade.

'Pull it up! I want to see,' she ordered, in a whisper.

Wearily Sue obeyed.

But, lo! after the beating rain and fierce gusts of wind that had endured through the livelong night, there yet stood out against the brick wall one ivy leaf. It was the last on the vine. Still dark green near its stem, but with its serrated edges tinted with the yellow of dissolution and decay, it hung bravely from a branch some twenty feet above the ground.

'It is the last one,' said Johnsy. 'I thought it would surely fall during the night. I heard the wind. It will fall to-day, and I shall die at the same time.'

'Dear, dear!' said Sue, leaning her worn face down to the pillow; 'think of me, if you won't think of yourself. What would I do?'

But Johnsy did not answer. The lonesomest thing in all the world is a soul when it is making ready to go on its mysterious, far journey. The fancy seemed to possess her more strongly as one by one the ties that bound her to friendship and to earth were loosed.

The day wore away, and even through the twilight they could see the lone ivy leaf clinging to its stem against the wall. And then, with the coming of the night the north wind was again loosed, while the rain still beat against the windows and pattered down from the low Dutch eaves.

When it was light enough Johnsy, the merciless, commanded that the shade be raised.

The ivy leaf was still there.

Johnsy lay for a long time looking at it. And then she called to Sue, who was stirring her chicken broth over the gas stove.

'I've been a bad girl, Sudie,' said Johnsy. 'Something has made that last leaf stay there to show me how wicked I was. It is a sin to want to die. You may bring me a little broth now, and some milk with a little port in it, and—no; bring me a hand-mirror first; and then pack some pillows about me, and I will sit up and watch you cook.'

And hour later she said—

'Sudie, some day I hope to paint the Bay of Naples.'

The doctor came in the afternoon, and Sue had an excuse to go into the hallway as he left.

'Even chances,' said the doctor, taking Sue's thin, shaking hand in his. 'With good nursing you'll win. And now I must see another case I have downstairs. Behrman, his name is—some kind of an artist, I believe. Pneumonia, too. He is an old, weak man, and the attack is acute. There is no hope for him; but he goes to the hospital to-day to be made more comfortable.'

The next day the doctor said to Sue: 'She's out of danger. You've won. Nutrition and care now—that's all.'

And that afternoon Sue came to the bed where Johnsy lay, contentedly knitting a very blue and very useless woollen shoulder scarf, and put one arm around her, pillows and all.

'I have something to tell you, white mouse,' she said. 'Mr Behrman died of pneumonia today in hospital. He was ill only two days. The janitor found him on the morning of the first day in his room downstairs helpless with pain. His shoes and clothing were wet through and icy cold. They couldn't imagine where he had been on such a dreadful night. And then they found a lantern, still lighted, and a ladder that had been dragged from its place, and some scattered brushes, and a palette with green and yellow colours mixed on it, and—look out the window, dear, at the last ivy leaf on the wall. Didn't you wonder why it never fluttered or moved when the wind blew? Ah, darling, it's Behrman's masterpiece—he painted it there the night that the last leaf fell.'

MY FRIEND, THE MOUSE

Robert Fontaine

I made a friend of a mouse. I had never known a mouse before, and this new comradeship taught me a sad lesson in love and loyalty.

Sometimes I took shortbreads to be to keep under my pillow and munch while I read fairy tales. This was forbidden, but I knew that *Maman* expected me to do it anyway, and that her only interest in the matter was keeping her conscience and record clear. So I disregarded the injunction. The Mouse, I soon discovered, was gnawing on the shortbreads while I slept. I caught him in the act one morning. Fortunately, *Maman* had not yet had time to teach me to fear mice. I wished him to remain with me so that I might have him for a pet. Fervently I asked the Lord to make it so that no one would see The Mouse and set a trap.

But *Papa* entered my room one night and saw The Mouse. '*Hein?*' he said as a gray streak flashed across the room. 'What was that?'

'*Qu'est-ce que c'est?*' I asked naïvely.

'What was that which just now appeared and disappeared?'

'Me, I saw nothing. You promised to fix my skates.'

My father frowned and sat down slowly on the bed. But in a moment he suddenly arose with a bad light in his eyes. He was, I could see, no longer a good, kind man with music in his heart; he was now a fierce hunter. He had discovered the doorway to The Mouse's home. It was a very small hole near a corner.

'Oho!' he shouted like a savage.

'Is something the matter?' I inquired.

'Aha!' *Papa* exclaimed. He kneeled down and peeked into The Mouse's home.

'Don't let him kill The Mouse,' I demanded silently of the Lord. 'Fair is fair. I have learned already twice the number of Bible verse I am supposed to learn and You have hardly noticed *me* at all. *Papa* is *Papa* and I love and respect him, but You know and I know The Mouse is my friend.' This was the first time I had ever given the Lord orders, and I was not so sure I had used the most politic method.

I tried to engage my father in conversation. 'What do you think I learned in school today?' I asked eagerly. My father replied without looking up, 'Very little, no doubt. And that little of more harm than good.'

I tried hard to think of something else to talk about when suddenly *Papa* jumped up, holding his nose, and cried '*Nom d'un nom!*' The Mouse apparently had scratched *Papa's* long nose. I could not help but laugh. 'You, too, would be angry if someone stuck his nose in your house,' I said.

Papa rubbed his nose and came back to the bed, a little confused. He began to repair my skating boot, and I sighed happily, thinking that he had abandoned his wild-game hunt.

Perhaps he had, but The Mouse had not given up *Papa*.
Foolish Mouse! As soon as my father became comfortably seated
on the bed, The Mouse walked right out. Not only did he walk
out; he stood up on two legs and looked my father calmly in the
eye. It was as if he wished to say, 'Look here, I did not mean
to hurt your nose. It was an accident. The Boy and I are friends.
It is not easy to find a true friend in this world. For a small boy
it is difficult; for a mouse it is almost impossible. Can we not
talk this over, man to man?'

Alas, my poor father, who understood so many lovely things
so well, did not understand The Mouse. He saw only a wild
animal and lunged for it. The Mouse, who apparently knew
something of human nature, was intelligent enough to disappear.

The next day there was a trap with some cheese. I stole the
cheese in the name of my friendship with The Mouse. I could
not do otherwise.

The following day, *Papa*, seeing neither cheese nor mouse,
remarked pointedly, 'Aha! What a remarkable mouse it is we have
here, eh? He eats the cheese and yet he does not spring the trap!'

I rolled my eyes and tried to look as much as possible like
a cherub in the Sunday-school pictures. 'Such a thing is possible—
for a very smart mouse.'

Papa looked me in the eye. 'It is not possible,' he said firmly.
'But what is most possible is that a small boy with a vacant head
is removing the cheese from the trap.'

'What small boy would do such a thing?' I inquired.

'You will find him in the mirror,' said *Papa*.

He then forbade me to touch the cheese. It was a direct
command of the first degree and had to be obeyed.

Once more I prayed for The Mouse. 'Dear Lord, I saved The
Mouse once. What I can do, certainly You can do. If the worst

comes to the worst, remove The Mouse from the temptation of the cheese. Lead him not into temptation, but deliver him from the evil trap.'

Nevertheless, I awaited, with terror in my heart, the end of *mon ami*, my proven friend. I opened the subject with *Maman*. 'If you have a friend whose loyalty is proven, you stand by this friend when others wish him harm. *N'est-ce pas?*'

My mother was working a large gourd into one of *Papa's* socks. '*Mais oui,*' she replied.

'Aha!' I shouted triumphantly. 'Then why do we have to catch The Mouse?'

My mother opened her eyes wide and stood up quickly. 'Mouse?' she repeated nervously. 'What mouse? Where is The Mouse?'

Papa sipped his wine and put down his newspaper. He looked at me across the room with a wise smile. I could see I had made a fatal strategic error. *Maman* was afraid of mice.

'The Boy,' my father said quietly, 'has in his room a mouse. They are friends, these two. So the Boy claims. The Mouse has said nothing.'

'Set the trap!' cried *Maman*. 'Set the trap!'

'The trap was set,' my father explained patiently, 'but The Mouse removed the cheese without springing the trap.'

'*C'est impossible!*' my mother said. She turned to me. 'I forbid you to remove the cheese. You understand?'

'I will not remove the cheese,' I promised sadly. 'But it is only a coward who stands still while his best friend is killed with low tricks.'

'Listen to him sing!' *Papa* exclaimed, a little upset.

'*Maman* herself has said this is one of the things one does not do,' I argued.

'But a mouse,' my mother countered, 'is different.'

'A friend is a friend,' I said. 'At least, if you wish to fight my friend you could fight fair—not with traps.'

'Ho! Name of a thousand and one names!' *Papa* cried. 'Shall I make a tail for myself and get down on my hands and knees and bite The Mouse with my teeth?'

Papa went upstairs and set the trap with an unfairly large and unusually attractive piece of cheese.

I sighed. I could see it was no use. The Mouse could be saved now only by the good Lord.

When I awakened in the morning the cheese was still there. I jumped out of bed, kneeled down and told the Lord: '*Merci bien Monsieur!*' Then I dressed and bounded joyfully down to breakfast, humming gaily. I ate my oatmeal in bliss. Just as I had finished, there was a scampering above us.

'Is that,' *Papa* asked, 'perhaps The Mouse?'

I held my breath and prayed one more time. *Maman* was busy making toast and said nothing. In a few moments there was the sound of scampering again. This time it seemed very close.

'Does The Mouse know even the way downstairs?' *Papa* asked in surprise.

I did not answer him. I busied myself putting jam on my toast. Halfway through the toast I felt as if something soft had touched my feet. I looked down. There was The Mouse, reeling, wobbling, struggling toward my feet.

When he saw my friend, my father stood up hastily. I do not know what he intended to do—perhaps protect *Maman*. It does not matter. In a few seconds The Mouse rolled over at my feet, dead. He did not die, however, before he had said something to me with his eyes.

My father rushed upstairs and came back exclaiming, 'Astonishing! The cheese was removed from the trap. One imagines the trap then sprang and struck The Mouse in the jaw. Imagine it, this is a mouse who has died from a punch in the jaw!'

The wonder of it did not impress me. I knew The Mouse was a brave one. But I did not know about myself, for, with his eyes, The Mouse seemed to have said to me, 'Look, I was your friend and you have killed me. But here is the wonder—I am still your friend. See, I come to die at your feet and to forgive you. It is easy to love those who are kind to you; it is a terrible but necessary thing to love those who have betrayed you.'

Ah, perhaps The Mouse did not mean anything of the sort. Maybe it was my own heart speaking, learning, growing up.

'*Papa*,' I asked quietly, 'is there a heaven for The Mouse?'

'Yes, yes,' *Papa* said unhappily, 'there is for everyone a heaven.'

Maman, who had been white and silent through the tragedy, now spoke meekly, 'After this, let us get a large cat, so that such matters will be out of our hands.'

PRIMULA

GEOFFREY MOSS

This plant is the gem of my collection, *Primula Caspiensis Davidii*. I discovered it through a chance meeting with a Russian, a botanist who, having fled from Bolshevism, was earning his living as best he could in Jugoslavia. Here is the story:

I thought over what he had told me and decided to approach the Soviet Government for permission to undertake the expedition I had in mind. But before leaving London I found out all I could about the country he had described. The latest information about the district, I learned, had come from members of a British Military Mission which had been there just after the war. The general in charge had lost his life at the hands of the Bolshevist irregular forces, but one of his officers advised to me to visit his widow, so I went.

Her flat was out of the lower end of Sloane Street. The drawing-room, despite a big bow window, contrived to be dark. Along the window seat were Japanese dwarf trees—abortions which annoy me. She was a tall, hard, rather graceful woman, nearing fifty.

I wanted to know about the country where her husband had lost his life. She would tell me all she knew. He had written home most enthusiastically about it, for he had been an ardent fisherman.

She showed me his portrait, the usual middle-aged soldier. The eyes were all I remember, strangely humorous.

There were, too, some clever sepia drawings of calm water, a stretch of low shore, and some rough huts. Her husband had done them.... Did I see that cape? It had been on the other side of it that he had been lost, when out fishing.

'Curious,' she said. 'I always had a presentiment against his fishing.'

Surreptitiously I turned over the pages of the sketch book. Meanwhile my hostess talked on, very pleasantly, in a voice pitched just a little too high.

Yes, he had wanted to spend their honeymoon on some stream in Bohemia, while she had wanted to take him to 'beloved' Florence. The watercolours on the walls were 'mementoes of happy days.' She was no doubt a pleasant enough woman, but those Siamese cats wandered about and made that disgusting noise of their species—I don't like cats.

The general had been a good Russian scholar and on that account had been given charge of that military mission, thrust out into the wilds of Central Asia.

For months nothing happened. The mission employed agents to supply information as to what was happening still further in the heart of the Continent. Meanwhile the members of it shot, fished and amused themselves as best they could. For the general the place must have been a paradise.

Fishing! Naturally, she had never actually tried to stop it, but, when it had clashed with some social event, she had done her best to persuade him which to choose. In soldiering the social side was so important—especially in India!

Well, after some months things began to take an unpleasant turn. Disquieting rumours came from the North. Food supplies became scarcer. Once or twice the Mission's sketchy communications with its base were interrupted. Once an officer out duck-shooting heard a bullet whistle past him. For a week or so all was quiet, then a boat belonging to the Mission was burnt one night, and one morning a sentry was found dead with a knife between his shoulders.

The officers began to grow uncomfortable. They were there to observe: they had no earthly chance of putting up a fight, and the countryside, which had welcomed their arrival, was obviously turning against them.

Sometimes at night they would be conscious of people prowling around their camp. Then for days the silence of those wild lands would descend about them.

Then one evening at dusk they saw a fire somewhere northwards along the coast. The general called a conference. His instructions had been beautifully vague, freeing the higher authority from responsibility—'to observe and report upon enemy activity, political or military, in or about, etc, etc; to remain, etc, etc, but not to endanger unduly the safety of the Mission.' After a long discussion it was arranged that all should be kept in readiness for departure at an hour's notice; but that, as food was so scarce, fishing and shooting should be continued by officers—to their general relief, no doubt!

Then one day, when the general had gone up the coast, an agent from whom nothing had been heard for weeks dashed into the camp with the news that large Bolshevist forces were approaching. Preparations for retreat were made and the recall signal was given. But there was no sign of the head of the Mission. The afternoon wore on. It was time to go. They dared not risk being attacked at night. One officer undertook to stay behind till dusk, and the forlorn little band marched away.

Next morning the young fellow rejoined. He had waited till after dark, had sent up rockets, but had seen no answering ones from the general. Eventually the party reached its base. Of course, they heard rumours of how the general had come by his end, yet nothing certain was ever discovered.

Well, I took a last look at the watercolours and those cats, and I departed. And I sent flowers—from a florist; showy stuff, of no conceivable interest.

❖

Getting to the Caspian was no joke. Difficulties of every sort— dirt, delay, vile food. At length I arrived. I found a boat and a boatman. We started off.

The coast was flat; peaty wastes, forests, a desolate shore-line with an occasional wretched hut.

It was late one afternoon that a found my primula, that strangest of the whole family. The weather was threatening... intermittent rumbling of thunder. My boatman was all for getting away, but nothing could get me away. I had found this unique species, a regular meadow of these little chaps; orange against the sombre background of the forest and the grey of the sky. Extraordinary!

It's odd, but that afternoon the greyness seemed to get on my nerves. There were no birds singing. The forest grew darker and darker. My boatman, too, kept crossing himself and muttering. Eventually, an hour before dark, we launched the boat.

We hadn't gone more than a mile when the thing started— a solid wall of rain; and after it came the wind.

In a matter of minutes there was an ugly sea running. I headed in towards the shore and kept just outside the rushes. To add to our pleasure, night was descending. I held our course on the chance, and presently saw the perches of a stake-net, upright in that slantwise, windswept world. On the shore was a hut. I rounded in and beached our boat.

We scrambled to the door and hammered on it. A gaunt fisherman appeared, and eventually we persuaded him to let us in. The hut was like others: a trodden earth floor, home-made furniture and a fire; at the back a door leading to another room.

Our host was vigorous, his Russian—as far as I could judge— was pure, and it struck me that he might have once been of bourgeoisie. I tried to be pleasant to him, but he kept aloof. Outside the wind howled—the very dickens of a night!

Once I spoke of the Military Mission, for their camp must have been within a few miles of where we were sitting. On this subject our host was even less communicative. All that had been before his time, he told me. After all, I was a foreigner. Most likely he and his neighbours had helped themselves to the abandoned British stores. And that had been long ago! I turned in and slept well.

When I awoke the sun was high, the sea smooth, and my boatman was busy preparing breakfast. As for the owner of the hut, he was in the other room, for I could hear him humming some tune which seemed somehow familiar.

Presently he came in, but now that it was day he was even less communicative. He helped us to launch our boat and I persuaded him to accept some provisions in return for the night's lodging. But even before we had pushed off, he had turned back to his hut. I don't remember seeing anyone so obviously relieved to get rid of his guests.

Thus it was all the more annoying when I found I had left my camera behind and had to go back for it. I landed and walked up to the hut. Through the open door I could hear the fisherman whistling in the further room. Suddenly I knew that the tune was—'Tipperary.' I stood stock still. He must have learnt that tune from the Military Mission.

I crossed the floor and looked into the inner room. There he sat, on his bed. I got a look round before he knew that I was there. On the rough walls was evidence enough that I was right; some obviously English fishing-rods and, what was more curious still, several sketches like those I had seen in that flat in London. Then the man realised I was there and jumped up. I don't know which of us was the more surprised, for, just as he did so, two objects hanging in the corner caught my eye—a much-worn khaki greatcoat and the gold-braided cap of a British General.

He knew what I had seen and he stood there challengingly, his legs apart and his thumbs slipped through the rope which served him as a belt. Slowly his weather-beaten lips twisted into a smile and there came into his grey eyes an ironic expression which seemed to make them familiar to me.

There I stood, gaping like a duffer, while gradually in my brain a jig-saw puzzle of ideas fitted into each other. I remembered that dark drawing-room; those Japanese dwarf trees; those raucous Siamese cats; that steely woman who had tried to make her husband realise that the social side of soldiering was more important than his fishing. And, as I remembered these things, I realised all at once who the man before me was: and also the reason why he had chosen to lose himself rather than return home.

There was nothing to say. For a moment we stood so. Then without a word I went down to the boat.

Again I pushed off. The boat gathered way. Then I looked towards the shore. There at the water's edge, his hand lifted in gay and courtly farewell stood that lean, still athletic figure, once more alone, lost now for ever in the exile he had chosen.

THE BEGGAR

ANTON CHEKHOV

'Kind sir, have pity; turn your attention to a poor, hungry man! For three days I have had nothing to eat; I haven't five copecks for a lodging, I swear it before God. For eight years I was a village schoolteacher and then I lost my place through intrigues. I fell a victim to calumny. It is a year now since I have had anything to do—'

The advocate Skvortsoff looked at the ragged, fawn-coloured overcoat of the suppliant, at his dull, drunken eyes, at the red spot on either cheek, and it seemed to him as if he had seen this man somewhere before.

'I have now had an offer of a position in the province of Kaluga,' the mendicant went on, 'but I haven't the money to get there. Help me kindly; I am ashamed to ask, but—I am obliged to by circumstances.'

Skvortsoff's eyes fell on the man's overshoes, one of which was high and the other low, and he suddenly remembered something.

'Look here, it seems to me I met you the day before yesterday in Sadovaya Street,' he said; 'but you told me then that you were a student who had been expelled, and not a village schoolteacher. Do you remember?'

'N-no, that can't be so,' mumbled the beggar, taken aback. 'I am a village schoolteacher, and if you like I can show you my papers.'

'Have done with lying! You called yourself a student and even told me what you had been expelled for. Don't you remember?'

Skvortsoff flushed and turned from the ragged creature with an expression of disgust.

'This is dishonesty, my dear sir!' he cried angrily. 'This is swindling! I shall send the police for you, damn you! Even if you are poor and hungry, that does not give you any right to lie brazenly and shamelessly!'

The waif caught hold of the door-handle and looked furtively round the antechamber, like a detected thief.

'I—I'm not lying—' he muttered. 'I can show you my papers.'

'Who would believe you?' Skvortsoff continued indignantly. 'Don't you know that it's a low, dirty trick to exploit the sympathy which society feels for village schoolteachers and students? It's rivolting!'

Skvortsoff lost his temper and began to berate the mendicant unmercifully. The impudent lying of the ragamuffin offended what he, Skvortsoff, most prized in himself: his kindness, his tender heart, his compassion for all unhappy beings. That lie, an attempt to take advantage of the pity of its 'subject' seemed to him to profane the charity which he liked to extend to the poor out of the purity of his heart. At first the waif continued to protest innocence, but soon he grew silent and hung his head in confusion.

'Sir!' he said, laying his hand on his heart, 'the fact is I—was lying! I am neither a student nor a schoolteacher. All that was a fiction. Formerly I sang in a Russian choir and was sent away for drunkenness. But what else can I do? I can't get along without lying. No one will give me anything when I tell the truth. With truth a man would starve to death or die of cold for lack of a lodging. You reason justly, I understand you, but—what can I do?'

'What can you do? You ask what you can do?' cried Skvortsoff, coming close to him. 'Work! That's what you can do! You must work!'

'Work—yes. I know that myself: but where can I find work?'

'By God, you judge harshly!' cried the beggar with a bitter laugh. 'Where can I find manual labour? It's too late for me to be a clerk because in trade one has to begin as a boy; no one would ever take me for a porter because they couldn't order me about; no factory would have me because for that one has to know a trade, and I know none.'

'Nonsense! You always find some excuse! How would you like to chop wood for me?'

'I wouldn't refuse to do that, but in these days even skilled woodcutters find themselves sitting without bread.'

'Huh! You loafers all talk that way. As soon as an offer is made you, you refuse it. Will you come and chop wood for me?'

'Yes, sir; I will.'

'Very well; we'll soon find out. Splendid—we'll see—'

Skvortsoff hastened along, rubbing his hands, not without a feeling of malice, and called his cook out of the kitchen.

'Here, Olga,' he said, 'take this gentleman into the wood-shed and let him chop wood.'

The tatterdemalion scarecrow shrugged his shoulders, as if in perplexity, and went irresolutely after the cook. It was obvious from his gait that he had not consented to go and chop wood because he was hungry and wanted work, but simply from pride and shame, because he had been trapped by his own words. It was obvious, too, that his strength had been undermined by vodka and that he was unhealthy and did not feel the slightest inclination for toil.

Skvortsoff hurried into the dining-room. From its windows one could see the wood-shed and everything that went on in the yard. Standing at the window, Skvortsoff saw the cook and the beggar come out into the yard by the back door and make their way across the dirty snow to the shed. Olga glared wrathfully at her companion, shoved him aside with her elbow, unlocked the shed, and angrily banged the door.

'We probably interrupted the woman over her coffee,' thought Skvortsoff. 'What an ill-tempered creature!'

Next he saw the pseudo-student seat himself on a log and become lost in thought with his red cheeks resting on his fists. The woman flung down an axe at his feet, spat angrily, and, judging from the expression of her lips, began to scold him. The beggar irresolutely pulled a billet of wood toward him, set it up between his feet, and tapped it feebly with the axe. The billet wavered and fell down. The beggar again pulled it to him, blew on his freezing hands, and tapped it with his axe cautiously, as if afraid of hitting his overshoe or of cutting off his finger. The stick of wood again fell to the ground.

Skvortsoff's anger had vanished and he now began to feel a little sorry and ashamed of himself for having set a spoiled, drunken, perchance sick man to work at menial labour in the cold.

'Well, never mind,' he thought, going into his study from the dining-room. 'I did it for his own good.'

An hour later Olga came in and announced that the wood had all been chopped.

'Good! Give him half a rouble,' said Skvortsoff. 'If he wants to he can come back and cut wood on the first day of each month. We can always find work for him.'

On the first of the month the waif made his appearance and again earned half a rouble, although he could barely stand on his legs. From that day on he often appeared in the yard and every time work was found for him. Now he would shovel snow, now put the wood-shed in order, now beat the dust out of rugs and mattresses. Every time he received from twenty to forty copecks, and once, even a pair of old trousers were sent out to him.

When Skvortsoff moved into another house he hired him to help in the packing and hauling of the furniture. This time the waif was sober, gloomy, and silent. He hardly touched the furniture, and walked behind the wagons hanging his head, not even making a pretence of appearing busy. He only shivered in the cold and became embarrassed when the carters jeered at him for his idleness, his feebleness, and his tattered, fancy overcoat. After the moving was over Skvortsoff sent for him.

'Well, I see that my words have taken effect,' he said, handing him a rouble. Here's for your pains. I see you are sober and have no objection to work. What is your name?'

'Lushkoff.'

'Well, Lushkoff, I can now offer you some other, cleaner employment. Can you write?'

'I can.'

'Then take this letter to a friend of mine tomorrow and you will be given some copying to do. Work hard, don't drink, and remember what I have said to you. Goodbye!'

Pleased at having put a man on the right path, Skvortsoff tapped Lushkoff kindly on the shoulder and even gave him his hand at parting. Lushkoff took the letter, and from that day forth came no more to the yard for work.

Two years went by. Then one evening, as Skvortsoff was standing at the ticket window of a theatre paying for his seat, he noticed a little man beside him with a coat collar of curly fur and a worn sealskin cap. This little individual timidly asked the ticket seller for a seat in the gallery and paid for it in copper coins.

'Lushkoff, is that you?' cried Skvortsoff, recognising in the little man his former wood-chopper. 'How are you? What are you doing? How is everything with you?'

'All right. I am a notary now and get thirty-five roubles a month.'

'Thank heaven! That's fine! I am delighted for your sake. I am very, very glad, Lushkoff. You see, you are my godson, in a sense. I gave you a push along the right path, you know. Do you remember what a roasting I gave you, eh? I nearly had you sinking into the ground at my feet that day. Thank you, old man, for not forgetting my words.'

'Thank you, too,' said Lushkoff. 'If I hadn't come to you then I might still be calling myself a teacher or a student to this day. Yes, by flying to your protection I dragged myself out of a pit.'

'I am very glad indeed.'

'Thank you for your kind words and deeds. You talked splendidly to me then. I am very grateful to you and to your cook. God bless that good and noble woman! You spoke finely then. And I shall be indebted to you to my dying day; but, strictly speaking, it was your cook, Olga, who saved me.'

'How is that?'

'Like this. When I used to come to your house to chop wood she used to begin: "Oh, you sot, you! Oh, you miserable creature! There's nothing for you but ruin." And then she would sit down opposite me and grow sad, look into my face and weep. "Oh, you unlucky man! There is no pleasure for you in this world and there will be none in the world to come. You drunkard! You will burn in hell. Oh, you unhappy one!" And so she would carry on, you know, in that strain. I can't tell you how much misery she suffered, how many tears she shed for my sake. But the chief thing was—she used to chop the wood for me. Do you know, sir, that I did not chop one single stick of wood for you? She did it all. Why this saved me, why I changed, why I stopped drinking at the sight of her I can not explain. I only know that, owing to her words and noble deeds a change took place in my heart; she set me right and I shall never forget it. However, it is time to go now; there goes the bell.'

Lushkoff bowed and departed to the gallery.

WITHOUT A TITLE

ANTON CHEKHOV

In the fifteenth century, as now, the sun rose every morning and sank to rest every night. When its first rays kissed the dew the earth awoke and the air was filled with sounds of joy, ecstasy, and hope; at eventide the same earth grew still and sank into darkness. Sometimes a thunder-cloud would roll up and the thunder roar angrily, or a sleepy star drop from heaven, or a pale monk come running in to tell the brothers that he had seen a tiger not far from the monastery—and that was all. Then once again day would resemble day, and night night.

The monks worked and prayed, and their old prior played the organ, composed Latin verses, and wrote out music. This fine old man had a remarkable talent; he played the organ with such skill that even the most ancient of the monks, whose hearing had grown feeble as the end of their lives drew near, could not restrain their tears when the notes of his organ came floating from his cell. When he spoke, even if it were only of the commonest things, such as trees, wild beasts, or the sea, no one could listen to him without either a smile or a tear; the same notes seemed to vibrate in his soul that vibrated in the organ. When he was moved by wrath or great joy, when he spoke of things that were terrible and grand, a passionate inspiration would master him, tears would start from his flashing eyes, his face would flush, his voice peal like thunder, and the listening monks would feel their souls wrung by his exaltation. During these splendid, these marvellous moments his power was unlimited; if he had ordered his elders to throw themselves into the sea they would all have rushed rapturously, with one accord, to fulfil his desire.

His music, his voice, and the verses with which he praised God were a source of never-ending joy to the monks. Sometimes in their monotonous lives the trees, the flowers, the spring and autumn grew tiresome, the noise of the sea wearied them, and the songs of the birds grew unpleasing, but the talents of their old prior, like bread, they needed every day.

A score of years passed. Day resembled day, and night night. Not a living creature showed itself near the monastery except wild beasts and birds. The nearest human habitation was far away, and to reach it from the monastery or to reach the monastery from there one had to cross a desert one hundred miles wide. This only those dared to do who set no value on life, who had renounced it, and journeyed to the monastery as to a tomb.

What, then, was the surprise of the monks when one night a man knocked at their gates who proved to be an inhabitant of the city, the most ordinary of sinners, with a love of life! Before saying a prayer or asking the blessing of the prior this man demanded food and wine. When they asked him how he had got into the desert from the city he answered them by telling a long hunter's tale; he had gone hunting, and had had too much to drink, and had lost his way. To the suggestion that he should become a monk and save his soul he replied with a smile and the words: 'I am no friend of yours.'

Having eaten and drunk his fill, he looked long at the monks who were serving him, reproachfully shook his head, and said:

'You don't do anything, you monks. All you care about is your victuals and drink. Is that the way to save your souls? Think now: while you are living quietly here, eating, drinking, and dreaming of blessedness, your fellow men are being lost and damned to hell. Look what goes on in the city! Some die of starvation, while others, not knowing what to do with their gold, plunge into debauchery and perish like flies in honey. There is no faith nor truth among men. Whose duty is it to save them? Is it mine, who am drunk from morning till night? Did God give you faith and loving and humble hearts that you should sit here between your four walls and do nothing?

The drunken speech of the townsman was insolent and unseemly, yet it strangely affected the prior. The old man and his monks looked at each other; then he paled and said:

'Brothers, he is right! It is true that, owing to folly and weakness, unfortunate mankind is perishing in unbelief and sin, and we do not move from the spot, as if it were no business of ours. Whey should I not go and remind them of the Christ whom they have forgotten?'

The old man was transported by the words of the townsman. On the following day he grasped his staff, bade farewell to the brothers, and set out for the city. So the monks were left without music, without his words and his verses.

They waited first one month and then two, and still the old man did not return. At last, at the end of the third month, they heard the familiar tapping of his staff. The monks flew out to meet him and showered him with questions; but instead of rejoicing with them, he wept bitterly and did not utter a word. The monks saw that he was thin and had aged greatly and that weariness and profound sorrow were depicted on his face. When he wept he had the look of a man who had been deeply hurt.

Then the monks, too, burst into tears and asked why he was weeping and why his face looked so stern, but he answered not a word and went and locked himself in his cell. For five days he stayed there and neither ate nor drank, neither did he play the organ. When the monks knocked at his door and entreated him to come out and share his sorrow with them his answer was a profound silence.

At last he emerged. Collecting all the monks about him, with a face swollen with weeping and with many expressions of indignation and distress, he began to tell them all that had happened to him during the past three months. His voice was calm and his eyes smiled as he described his journey from the monastery to the city. Birds had sung and brooks babbled to him by the wayside, he said, and sweet, new-born hopes had agitated his breast. He felt that he was a soldier advancing to battle and certain victory, he walked along dreaming, composing hymns and verses as he went, and was surprised when he found that he had reached his journey's end.

But his voice trembled, his eyes flashed, and anger burned hot within him when he began to tell of the city and of mankind. Never before had he seen or dared to imagine what he encountered when he entered the town. Here, in his old age, he saw and understood for the first time in his life the might of Satan, the splendour of iniquity, and the weakness and despicable faint-heartedness of mankind. By an evil chance, the first house he entered was an abode of sin. Here half a hundred men with a great deal of money were feasting and drinking wine without end. Overpowered by its fumes, they were singing songs and boldly saying things so shocking and terrible that no Godfearing man would dare to mention them. They were unboundedly free and happy and bold; they feared neither God nor the devil nor death, did and said whatever they had a mind to, and went wherever they were driven by their desires. The wine, clear as amber, was surely intolerably fragrant and delicious, for everyone who quaffed it smiled rapturously and straightway desired to drink again. It returned smile for smile and sparkled joyfully, as if it knew what fiendish seduction lay hidden in its sweetness.

More than ever weeping and burning with anger, the old man went on describing what he had seen. On the table in the midst of the feasters, he said, stood a half-naked woman. It would be hard to imagine anything more glorious and enchanting than she was. Young, long-haired, with dark eyes and thick lips, insolent and shameless, this vermin smiled, showing her teeth as white as snow, as if saying. 'Behold how beautiful, how insolent I am!' Splendid draperies of silk and brocade fell from her shoulders, but her beauty would not be hidden beneath a garment and eagerly made its way through the folds, as young verdure forces itself through the earth in the springtime. The shameless woman drank wine, sang songs, and surrendered herself to the feasters.

Wrathfully brandishing his arms, the old man went on to describe hippodromes, bull-fights, theatres, and the workshops of artists where the forms of naked woman were painted and modeled in clay. He spoke eloquently, sonorously, with inspiration, as if he were playing on some invisible instrument, and the stupefied monks eagerly hung on his words and panted with ecstasy. Having described all the charms of the devil, the beauty of wickedness, and the enchanting grace of the infamous female form, the old man cursed Satan, turned on his heel, and vanished behind his door.

When he came out of his cell next morning not a monk remained in the monastery. They were all on their way to the city

ORANGE BLOSSOMS
A Story from Sri Lanka

J.A.R. GRENIER

Diru had not been to see us for over a year. But then one does not worry too much about not meeting a friend like Diru. He is a genuine friend in whose company one feels so much at home. Even after ages when you meet Diru, he falls into place like a key in a well oiled lock. Diru is a tall, lanky fellow, with a bright, pleasant face, a nice smile and steady, honest eyes. All his life Diru had no vices. He was earnest about his work, his family and his outlook in life. Diru was an engineer, who built bridges. And when he was not busy with bridges he cleared jungle and planted coconut. He also educated his younger brothers and arranged matches for his sisters. When I last saw him he was happy and contented, serious on life's affairs.

One night, like a bolt from the blue, Diru came to visit us. His hand grip was still firm, his eyes were still honest but he looked rather thin and worn out. The bright look in his face was absent and his crisp, curly hair, which covered his head in dark wavelets, had become a trifle scanty. No comments were made and though he chatted to us for some time I could see that he was rather crumpled up. And then, of course, he told us the story. He commenced by saying that after his recent experiences he was trying to find his feet once more by meeting his old friends.

Hesitantly, he told us what had happened. It was just an ordinary tale of a love affair which had misfired, but Diru felt that his world had crumbled. He had met the girl quite accidentally at a club. Now Diru is no club vallah but often these incidents pan out like that. He happened to go to the India Club, one night, for a drink with some friends. And the girl was there. She had come down from Bangalore for a holiday in the company of an Indian film star. The girl was small, demure, a pure vegetarian and according to Diru's biased judgment, kittenishly attractive.

Poor Diru. What with building bridges, educating his brothers, making matches for his younger sisters and planting coconut trees in the jungle, his experiences with women, up till that point, could have been written down in one line. He fell head over heels. For three months he poured at the girl's dainty feet his time, his money and his utter devotion. The girl led him on and Diru soaked her in. He learnt to worship the way she walked, talked, dressed, cooked her vegetarian foods and the subtle manner in which she made him dance to her every mood. She even made him a vegetarian. I always credited Diru with sober, steady judgment and I also thought he had a fine, mature mind. But the girl knocked him off his feet and who worries about a fine, mature mind in such a situation! Diru was far too honourable to play around with any woman. He proposed marriage. She made excuses but did not refuse. On a day of gloom for Diru the girl flew back to India. She left only a brief note for Diru thanking him for his wonderful attention and company. She added that she had quite recovered from the fit of blues she had developed after a dispute with her husband and told him not to worry because she would live happily ever after.

Diru brooded for days and days. I took him fishing. I gave him books to read. I did everything I could to put his mind off the one track groove into which it had fallen. It was a pretty deep groove. Diru was determined to go and spend a holiday in India when his depleted finances permitted him to do so. No, he was not going there to look for the girl. She had let him down. He would go to India and find another Brahmin girl. Only a Brahmin girl would suit his tastes after his recent experiences.

Now, I am no match-maker but I hated seeing Diru going to pieces. I knew there was one girl who could make Diru forget. That girl was Mithra. She was a real beauty, and she fitted in with the theory I expounded to Diru. Marry your own kind. Mithra was Diru's kind. She was a marvellous girl. She had received an excellent education, she was an efficient housekeeper, a good cook and most of all she was a dream to look at. Nothing old fashioned about Mithra. She used lipstick and nail polish, tied her hair in a lovely bun on the top of her shapely head and when she wore a red saree draped round her luscious figure she looked like a real film star in flesh and blood. And she was not sophisticated. That is what made her most attractive. She enjoyed the simple things in life.

But of course there was a snag. There are always snags for nice girls like Mithra. She was twenty-two. All the girls in Mithra's home town marry before they are twenty. But no one wanted to marry Mithra. Her old man had been to jail for some lark. Her old man was fond of playing larks with the tax department.

Where Mithra comes from it is a terrible crime for a man to go to jail. It's not a crime to have larks with the tax department but it was a crime for Mithra's old man to have allowed himself to be caught and put in jail. The people way up North think like that and when the people up North think in a certain way, nobody from the East, West or the South can get them to change their ways of thought.

Well, I put on my thinking cap and consulted my old lady. We are both sentimental and all that and we tried to plan it so that Diru and Mithra could meet. But the North, where Mithra lives, is a long way off. There was little excuse for us to take Diru that far without telling him the why and the wherefore. But Diru knows I am nuts on fishing and that five hundred miles is not too far for me. So one fine day we set off for the North. I wrote to Mithra and told her that I was coming to the North on business and could she kindly pose for me in her red saree. I had taken a colour picture of Mithra before and it was difficult to explain why I wanted another. But I took a chance on that and offered no explanation. Besides, Mithra knows that I am not too good in the head sometimes and maybe she just overlooked the fact that I had a picture of her in her red saree.

When Diru and Mithra met I knew that everything was all right. They had nothing to say to each other. Neither attempted to be polite and make small talk. Diru gazed his fill. I watched him with a quick side glance the moment he saw Mithra. I could scarcely suppress a smile. There was a swift, startled look in his eyes. His mental reflexes were registering some new lines of thought.

We had a superb meal with Mithra and we teased her about her concern for her figure when she ate sparingly. She gave us curried chicken, fried fish and prawn salad with tasty country rice.

We left Diru alone and were surprised to find that he too enjoyed the meal, forgetting, if you please, that he was a vegetarian by persuasion and not by conviction. We secretly hoped he would also forget his coy charmer from India.

On leaving, we asked Mithra when she would be in Colombo again. She told us that she might come down for a short holiday during Easter.

We went to see Mithra during the holidays. She stayed with her old man who had a house in the city. Diru went with us and soon he was going without us. Diru started cheering up. The brightness came back to his face and he no longer behaved like he had slipped a disc in his mind. He stopped moping and went back to building good bridges and planting coconut in the jungle. But just when my old lady and I thought everything was going right the dragons entered the arena. These, according to my old lady, are underground dragons. They work in the background. From the day Diru proposed marriage to Mithra the dragons set to work. They compared horoscope, family trees, caste and creed. In the end both sides were against the marriage. That is not unusual in the Northern land of the Palmyrah.

There was one way out of the tangle. I suggested that they should elope. My old lady bristled, all her hackles out. They must have a proper wedding, she insisted. It was no use my pointing out to her that this orange blossom mentality was the mythical basis of the feminine belief that women rule the world. She went to see Mithra's mother, who told her that a scholarship to go abroad had been arranged for Mithra and that the girl would be leaving in two months to complete her studies.

That made matters easy. At this end we fixed a scholarship for Diru in an engineering institution in the same country. We also fixed the same ship and the same date of departure, unknown, of course, to the dragons. Diru went on board with his dragons fairly early, on our advice and we saw to it that his dragons and Mithra's dragons did not meet. We saw both parties off with the usual farewells. But going back was not our responsibility. Both parties of dragons waited till the last moment to come off the ship. They had to return on the same launch. That must have been the first time a humble harbour boat became a battlefield for civilians. My old lady and I hopped a lift on the Customs launch.

Diru and Mithra were married on board. They have been away for three years. The Americans like them and they like the Americans. So they are in no hurry to come back to the dragons. They have a little boy and a little girl. The boy is like Mithra and the girl like her father. But women are perverse and my old lady says it should have been the other way round. The boy should have been like Diru and the girl like Mithra. And she says it like I am to blame. I never argue with my old lady about such complicated issues but I still don't see how I could have arranged that to her satisfaction. And besides, what does it matter? They are both bound to be handsome children with such good-looking parents.

THE TREE LOVER

RUSKIN BOND

I was never able to get over the feeling that plants and trees loved Grandfather with as much tenderness as he loved them. I was sitting beside him on the verandah steps one morning, when I noticed the tendril of a creeping vine that was trailing near my feet. As we sat there, in the soft sunshine of a north Indian winter, I saw that the tendril was moving very slowly away from me and towards Grandfather. Twenty minutes later it had crossed the verandah step and was touching Grandfather's feet.

There is probably a scientific explanation for the plant's behaviour—something to do with light and warmth—but I like to think that it moved that way simply because it was fond of Grandfather. One felt like drawing close to him. Sometimes when I sat alone beneath a tree I would feel a little lonely or lost; but as soon as Grandfather joined me, the garden would become a happy place, the tree itself more friendly.

Grandfather had served many years in the Indian Forest Service, and so it was natural that he should know and understand and like trees. On his retirement from the Service, he had built a bungalow on the outskirts of Dehra, planting trees all round it: limes, mangoes, oranges and guavas; also eucalyptus, jacaranda and the Persian lilac. In the fertile Doon valley, plants and trees grew tall and strong.

There were other trees in the compound before the house was built, including an old peepul which had forced its way through the walls of an abandoned outhouse, knocking the bricks down with its vigorous growth. Peepul trees are great show-offs. Even when there is no breeze, their broad-chested, slim-waisted leaves will spin like tops, determined to attract your attention and invite you into the shade.

Grandmother had wanted the peepul tree cut down, but Grandfather had said, 'Let it be. We can always build another outhouse.'

The gardener, Dhuki, who was a Hindu, was pleased that we had allowed the tree to live. Peepul trees are sacred to Hindus, and some people believe that ghosts live in the branches.

'If we cut the tree down, wouldn't the ghosts go away?' I asked.

'I don't know,' said Grandfather. 'Perhaps they'd come into the house.'

Dhuki wouldn't walk under the tree at night. He said that once, when he was a youth, he had wandered beneath a peepul tree late at night, and that something heavy had fallen with a thud on his shoulders. Since then he had always walked with a slight stoop, he explained.

'Nonsense,' said Grandmother, who didn't believe in ghosts. 'He got his stoop from squatting on his haunches year after year, weeding with that tiny spade of his!'

I never saw any ghosts in our peepul tree. There are peepul trees all over India, and people sometimes leave offerings of milk and flowers beneath them to keep the spirits happy. But since no one left any offerings under our tree, I expect the ghosts left in disgust, to look for peepul trees where there was both board and lodging.

Grandfather was about sixty, a lean active man who still rode his bicycle at great speed. He had stopped climbing trees a year previously, when he had got to the top of the jack-fruit tree and had been unable to come down again. We'd had to fetch a ladder for him.

Grandfather bathed quite often but got back into his gardening clothes immediately after the bath. During meals, ladybirds or caterpillars would sometimes walk off his shirt-sleeves and wander about on the tablecloth, and this always annoyed Grandmother.

She grumbled at Grandfather a lot, but he didn't mind, because he knew she loved him.

My favourite tree was the banyan which grew behind the house. Its spreading branches, which hung to the ground and took root again, formed a number of twisting passageways. The tree was older than the house, older than my grandparents; I could hide in its branches, behind a screen of thick green leaves, and spy on the world below.

The banyan tree was a world in itself, populated with small animals and large insects. While the leaves were still pink and tender, they would be visited by the delicate map butterfly, who left her eggs in their care. The 'honey' on the leaves—a sweet, sticky smear—also attracted the little striped squirrels, who soon grew used to having me in the tree and became quite bold, accepting gram from my hand.

At night the tree was visited by the hawk cuckoo. Its shrill nagging cry kept us awake on hot summer nights. Indians called the bird 'Paos-ala', which means 'Rain is coming!' But according to Grandfather, when the bird was in full cry it seemed to be shouting: 'Oh dear, oh dear! How very hot it's getting! We feel it... we feel it... WE FEEL IT!'

Grandfather wasn't content with planting trees in our garden. During the rains we would walk into the jungle beyond the river-bed, armed with cuttings and saplings, and these we would plant in the forest, beside the tall Sal and Shisham trees.

'But no one ever comes here,' I protested, the first time we did this. 'Who is going to see them?'

'We're not planting for people only,' said Grandfather. 'We're planting for the forest—and for the birds and animals who live here and need more food and shelter.'

He told me how men, and not only birds and animals, needed trees—for keeping the desert away, for attracting rain, for preventing the banks of rivers from being washed away, and for wild plants and grasses to grow beneath.

'And for timber?' I asked, pointing to the Sal and Shisham trees.

'Yes, and for timber. But men are cutting down the trees without replacing them. For every tree that's felled, we must plant *two*. Otherwise, one day there'll be no forests at all, and the world will become one great desert.'

The thought of a world without trees became a sort of nightmare for me—it's one reason why I shall never want to live on the treeless Moon—and I helped Grandfather in his tree-planting with even greater enthusiasm. He taught me a poem by George Morris, and we would recite it together:

Woodman, spare that tree!
Touch not a single bough!
In youth it sheltered me,
And I'll protect it now.

'One day the trees will move again,' said Grandfather.
'They've been standing still for thousands of years, but one day they'll move again. There was a time when trees could walk about like people, but along came the Devil and cast a spell over them, rooting them to one place. But they're always trying to move— see how they reach out with their arms!—and some of them, like the banyan tree with its travelling roots, manage to get quite far!'

In the autumn, Grandfather took me to the hills. The deodars (Indian cedars), oaks, chestnuts and maples were very different from the trees I had grown up with in Dehra. The broad leaves of the horse chestnut had turned yellow, and smooth brown chestnuts lay scattered on the roads. Grandfather and I filled our pockets with them, then climbed the slope of a bare hill and started planting the chestnuts in the ground.

I don't know if they ever came up, because I never went there again. Goats and cattle grazed freely on the hill, and, if the trees did come up in the spring, they may well have been eaten; but I like to think that somewhere in the foothills of the Himalayas there is a grove of chestnut trees, and that birds and flying foxes and cicadas have made their homes in them.

Back in Dehra, we found an island, a small rocky island in the middle of a dry riverbed. It was one of those river-beds, so common in the Doon valley, which are completely dry in summer but flooded during the monsoon rains. A small mango tree was growing in the middle of the island, and Grandfather said, 'If a mango can grow here, so can other trees.'

As soon as the rains set in—and while the river could still be crossed—we set out with a number of tamarind, laburnum and coral-tree saplings and cuttings, and spent the day planting them on the island.

When the monsoon set in, the trees appeared to be flourishing.

The monsoon season was the time for rambling about. At every turn there was something new to see. Out of earth and rock and leafless bough, the magic touch of the monsoon rains had brought life and greenness. You could almost see the broad-leaved vines grow. Plants sprang up in the most unlikely places. A peepul would take root in the ceiling, a mango would sprout on the windowsill. We did not like to remove them; but they had to go, if the house was to be kept from falling down.

'If you want to live in a tree, it's all right by me,' said Grandmother. 'But I like having a roof over my head, and I'm not going to have it brought down by the jungle!'

The common monsoon sights along the Indian roads were always picturesque—the wide plains, with great herds of smoke-coloured, delicate-limbed cattle being driven slowly home for the night, accompanied by several ungainly buffaloes, and flocks of goats and black long-tailed sheep. Then you came to a pond, where some buffaloes were enjoying themselves, with no part of them visible but the tips of their noses, while on their backs were a number of merry children, perfectly and happily naked.

The banyan tree really came to life during the monsoon, when the branches were thick with scarlet figs. Humans couldn't eat the berries, but the many birds that gathered in the tree—gossipy rosy pastors, quarrelsome mynahs, cheerful bulbuls and coppersmiths, and sometimes a noisy, bullying crow—feasted on them. And when night fell and the birds were resting, the dark flying foxes flapped heavily about the tree, chewing and munching loudly as they clambered over the branches.

The tree crickets were a band of willing artists who started their singing at almost any time of the day but preferably in the evenings. Delicate pale green creatures with transparent wings, they were hard to find amongst the lush monsoon foliage; but once found, a tap on the bush or leaf on which one of them sat would put an immediate end to its performance.

At the height of the monsoon, the banyan tree was like an orchestra with the musicians constantly tuning up. Birds, insects and squirrels welcomed the end of the hot weather and the cool quenching relief of the monsoon.

A toy flute in my hands, I would try adding my shrill piping to theirs. But they must have thought poorly of my piping, for, whenever I played, the birds and the insects kept a pained and puzzled silence.

I wonder if they missed me when I went away—for when the War came, followed by the Independence of India, I was sent to a boarding school in the hills. Grandfather's house was put up for sale. During the holidays I went to live with my parents in Delhi, and it was from them I learnt that my grandparents had gone to England.

When I finished school, I too went to England with my parents, and was away from India for several years.

But recently I was in Dehra again, and, after first visiting the old house—where I found that the banyan tree had grown over the wall and along part of the pavement, almost as though it had tried to follow Grandfather—I walked out of town towards the riverbed.

It was February, and, as I looked across the dry water-course, my eye was caught by the spectacular red plumes of the coral blossom. In contrast with the dry riverbed, the island was a small green paradise. When I walked across to the trees, I noticed that a number of squirrels had come to live in them. And a koel (a sort of crow-pheasant) challenged me with a mellow 'who-are-you, who-are-you....'

But the trees seemed to know me. They whispered among themselves and beckoned me nearer. And looking around, I noticed that other small trees and wild plants and grasses had sprung up under the protection of the trees we had placed there.

The trees had multiplied! They were moving. In one small corner of the world, Grandfather's dream was coming true, and the trees were moving again.

A CRICKET MATCH OF LONG AGO

EDMUND BLUNDEN

'Nicely.'
'Nice shot, sir.'
And again, a moment later:
'Pretty stroke.'
'Well hit.'
'Run 'em out.'
'See him open his shoulders to that one.'

It was Saturday afternoon; the place, Harmans Cricket Ground; the occasion a, say rather the, match between Harmans Second Eleven and their inevitable rivals from the next parish, Longley Street. The veterans of the Harmans side, all but 'Tardy' Gibbens, who was as usual at the wicket to open the innings and wear out the enemy with his stolid mahogany-brown pads and bat, were sitting in the small pavilion, putting on their equipment, and talking with the condescending calm expected of veterans. Their comments, chiefly stirred by the batting skill of the young hero Tom Benyon, were registered after murmured repetitions by a number of little boys, who sat with their backs against the pavilion railing; and, while it did not, of course, signify anything to such seasoned spirits, yet the effect of these judicial remarks was to leave in youthful minds the notion, 'I should say old—— —had made some runs in his time,' and even though——never made any nowadays, his name still conveyed the sense of a most valuable cricketer, and old champion. A man who, himself about to enter the arena and face the music, could speak deliberately and coolly of the struggle before him, could forget the enormous responsibilities of the hour in approving or disapproving some technical detail! To John Bowers, seated a little way apart from the veterans—the vicar's gardener, the grocer, and general dealer above the bridge, and the '& Son' of the butcher below the bridge—the attitude was not without its quiet tinge of homour; for he knew that, after their probable failure this afternoon, the impassive minds would lapse into a vein of autumn melancholy. Then it would be:

'Ah, Frank, every year after forty counts two.'

But, for the general award, their intrepidity was beyond all question.

The cricket ground was among a wide sweep of meadows, which fall easily towards the waters of the Chavender, and at one end of which you may see the church tower, with its 'candle-snuffer' atop of it, of Harmans; at the other, the modest tiled spire of Longley Street retiring among the rich greenery of midsummer. Not only was it as pleasantly situated in a girdle of tall trees, among which rose the red Jacobean chimneys of farmhouses, or the far-off hills, as cricket ground could be; nor

was it only for the sake of seeing the white pageantry of the
game pass to the cooing of doves in the deep blue shadows of
the fir-spinneys near by, that Harmans and district frequented
it. I have noticed that it was the Second Eleven which on this
day took the field; and the attendance was, from the old, old,
very old men who sat on the benches under the oak tree, to the
pale mothers who had wheeled their perambulators along-side
and rested their no less weary bones a little, in every respect the
Second Eleven's attendance. There was, it will have been remarked,
a Harmans First Eleven—a fact which explained the reverential
care with which the pitch had been prepared, and the outfield
grass not left in an intermediate stage between kempt and
unkempt as on many a country ground, but mown and rolled
with great nicety. The matches of the First Eleven resembled
a kind of levees or garden parties, to which fair ladies came
flocking, and cars swept in through the opened gates from the
byroad to bring the guests, whether more remarkable for blazer,
parasol, or the equally resplendent charm of great possessions.
Lunch and tea, then, seemed to rob the cricket of its interest;
and the cricket itself inclined to be 'to pattern,' sartorial and
immaculate.

Some signs of caste might be detected in the Second Eleven's
organisation. The grocer and general dealer, a man of five-and-
thirty, pale, brilliantined and mincing, would intimate in his manner
to the village schoolmaster, that 'clay from clay differs in dignity.'
An occasional Malapropism is not much ground lost when he
who can present a bill of £20 to him who trembles lest he receive
it, is conversing in all Christian charity with that wretch. But these
were cloudlets, and no more. Taken at all times and in all its ways,
the Harmans Second Eleven was a happy republic, and one that
had the chief intention of playing cricket. The game was not to

be half-played. It became a battle—indeed, so serious that for some of its members later battles gave less cause for personal anxiety.

And so, here were 'Tardy' and 'Tom,' treating the furious fast bowler at the benches' end and the ancient twisting-handed trundler at the river end with every promise of a noble event. The Longley Street scorer, next to Bowers, was beginning to fret; the Harmans scorer, a youth who frequently set out to keep the book and ended by playing instead of absentees, made no effort to conceal his satisfaction as he croaked, 'Thirty up'. 'Thirty up' was the chorus below the rails, as the nearest youngsters scrambled up to the scoreboard and put up the scratched numeral-plates. 'Benyon seventeen, Gibbens one,' went on the uncertain bass, 'an' twelve extras.' The Longley Street scorer sniffed.

'Ah!' 'O Lord!'

'Tom's out.'

'He shouldn't have nibbled at that.'

'I thought Smith would get him with his off theory,' smirked the Longley Street scorer, and his opposite number looked down his nose.

The gifted and popular Tom Benyon was ruefully walking back into the pavilion. The circle of veterans broke up, as the butcher, thrusting his round felt hat sternly over his eyebrows, took up his bat and, with strides like a parody of the goose-step, clumped forth to the wicket. Bowers, having still leisure enough unless things collapsed, strolled round the boundary with the schoolmaster, Scroggins, a mild man with a family. Scroggins asked, 'Is your father coming to take a look at the game?' Bowers was expecting him there at any minute. 'Some of us hoped,' continued Scroggins, 'that he might have turned out this season. We, I needn't say every one amongst us, would welcome such a return.'

'He says he's finished, except as a spectator and a Wisdenite,' answered Bowers. 'He's fifty this winter, and old for his age, he says, too.' 'O no,' said the elementary schoolmaster, vainly trying to find the right quotation. 'When he said after his game last year that he'd made positively his last appearance, we reminded him of the last appearances of the music-hall favourites. They appear as regularly after those farewells as they did before!' A misfortune had occurred at the wickets. The butcher had called the rightly named 'Tardy' for a run, and had himself done all the running. 'Tardy' maintained his ground: 'Goo back,' he said, with marble serenity, 'goo back.' It was his error, but he valued the butcher's wicket without sentiment and his own with plenty. The butcher was out, and put out too. 'All right that is, all right, ain't it? Tcha.' He stumped, yet more Prussianly, into the pavilion, asking rhetorically, 'All right, eh? St. Tut-tut-tut.'

Misfortune followed misfortune. The railway clerk, usually reliable for a hard hit or two, and the vicar's gardener had no luck whatever; Scroggins, bland and cautious, turned back to the pavilion as the bailiff from Little Green lashed the ball into the hands of a stout fieldsman at square-leg, and was succeeded by the grocer and general dealer. This gentleman had acquired something of the First Eleven's characteristic style, and urbanely placing his bat well forward, saw to his evident surprise the ball glide away behind the wicket. Two runs! ''E plays for style, does Mr Kidd,' said a youth in his working clothes, less jacket, who stood ready to follow Scroggins in this career. Again, the ball departed at an angle from the bat of the stylist, and one run ensued. Kidd, thus brought face to face with the old fellow bowling twisters, smoothed his too smooth hair, and, to the disappointment of the expectant boys, omitted to notice the fieldsman moving up behind him, into whose hands he beautifully tipped the ball. 'Bad luck, sir,' everyone ventured—and indeed, he returned answer to himself—as he sat down to remove his pads.

John Bowers, senr., came through the clap-gate, frowned at the scoreboard, and made for the pavilion. His old friend, William Dales, captain (the same who kept the 'Swan') was pacing up and down outside, bat in hand. 'Why aren't you playing, John?

'Well, for that matter, Bill, there's one John Bowers playing.'

'There ought to be two.'

'Doing none too well, I see.'

'O, Bill Dales to come in yet, y'know. Bill's to come in yet.'

'And John Bowers.'

'If John Bowers don't bowl the wickets down to-day, John, I—well, I shan't be there at church to-morrow morning.'

The score reached forty before Scroggins departed, and of these forty the indomitable 'Tardy' had made the not remarkable number, two. The stable lad with the broad mustard-coloured belt buffeted the bright air, and Bill Dales reigned in his stead. Jumping—he was a large and red-complexioned man—jumping in at the ball, he was fortunate enough to hit it, and the old men on the benches blinked as something banged against the oak bole just behind them, and leaping back on the greensward took shape and colour as the cricket ball. The fast bowler, unaccustomed to that sort of indignity, decided on a ball whose speed should surpass that of Jove's thunderbolt. There was a roar from the pavilion as this machination resulted in another mighty blow. The mothers, removing their perambulators from the oak-tree's vicinity, began to hurry. But Bill's life was short, for the next ball happened to be the fatal one, and he came away smiling. 'Some runs, boy, for the love of God,' he said, as John Bowers, junr., passed him. It was the last wicket.

Even cricket could torment John Bowers, junr. He was born with the zest of the game in him; but it implied publicities, and now, walking to the wickets, he felt his usual uncertainties of appearance. He would have liked to simulate calmness, but fearing to do that and give a false impression of *hauteur* he hurried nervously along and allowed those watching to see his true state of mind. The small boys at the pavilion rails detected the nervousness and grinned knowingly as the new batsman left a wide ball alone. That was not the way for the tail end of Harmans Second. He was too timid a batsman, altogether. The ironclad defences of 'Tardy' held out, and Bowers was again the object of criticising tongues. Why, he had made a hit—there was the ball, racing away! The boys, half-convinced, began to murmur, the veterans, re-assembled, clapped with discrimination.

'Playing 'em with confidence!'

'He's no bat. I never reckoned much of him as a bat.'

Neither did John think much of himself. But that day he felt able to eye the ball steadily and to look round him with purpose. Most days were different touching these points. He made other hits, and the fast bowler, in the last stages of diabolical genius, winked ferociously at the nearest fieldsman, and became a sort of human windmill, twirling his arm as he ran. The ball flew wildly and wide, and the bowler was motioned by his captain into temporary retirement.

By this time, several additions could be seen round the ground. Bowers observed his father and Dales taking out chairs under the shadow of the pavilion shrubbery for the curate and his wife. The curate was evidently preaching—about cricket; for the faces of Bowers senr. and Dales became bright with smiles as they looked out at the new bowler measuring his run. Then there were Mrs Scroggins, in a bulging costume known even to Bowers to be characteristic of earlier periods; and with her, forget-me-not-eyed Miss Wray. Scroggins, in his easiest manner, was explaining the state of the game.

Sixty for nine. Sixty in that stratum of cricket was a fair score, but Longley Green had the three brothers Double, whom alone sixty might not unreasonably be expected. Then, too, there was a one-armed player, who had so mastered his disability as to be a batsman of great local esteem. The oldest and wisest bowlers were apt to be uncertain what spell to put upon him.

The new bowlers, for both changes were made, were unable to tempt 'Tardy'. Grinning with horrible determination, he met each ball with a barn-door bat, and once or twice the rebound was sufficiently slow and exactly placed to enable him to call Bowers for a run. Bowers, slightly disturbed by the sight of Miss Wray, and the fact that (he thought) she had been looking at him, was becoming reckless, and his narrow escapes caused 'Tardy' to shake his head and demonstrate his own barn-door safety stroke, as though the lesson had not lasted long enough. It was evident by this time to Bowers that luck was with him, and he resolved to settle down to a batsman's innings. The score reached ninety, and the boys round the telegraph had the magic figures for the century ready to hoist, when that innings was ended by a failure in resolve, Bowers attempting to emulate the vigorous Dales, and falling short. The players left the field. 'Tardy's' grin was a little serious at first; he was mildly rebuking Bowers for his foolhardiness; and then, approaching the pavilion, he became overwhelmed with simple joy at his feat of endurance, and grinned with head erect to the chorus of 'What, my old Tardy,' and 'Well played, the old stonewaller.' No words escaped him. He had his glory; the Longley Green team had been unable to move him; and he grinned and grinned like the master of a secret, which in truth had appeared to be little else than the holding of his bat stiff, upright, and not to be moved save an inch or two fore and aft. Bowers, whose score had reached thirty-eight, while Tardy's was five, and would no doubt in eternity become infinity, felt most uncomfortable; he was glad that Tardy was interpreting the position as glowing solely with his own effulgence, but to the choice approbations of the grocer he was somehow inadequate. The grocer honestly meant to praise, but his intention was lost in a self-revealing monologue.

'You made some *dazzling* strokes, Mr Bowers. Quite classical. We never imagined—er, we had had but small conception. Do you know, I myself felt to-day as if I were to assist the fortunes of the side with a long innings? I was never more confident of the forward stroke...' He continued to a Bowers hearing an unconnected murmur, which ended, ''Ardly the thing of young Sprigg to borrow Mr Tomkins' pads without permission, I think. Noo, 'ardly the thing.'

At the moment when Dales led his Harmanians into the field, it was excitement and tension all round. The result of this ancient annual encounter would crop up in sundry places (especially the 'Grid-iron,' the public-house on the edge of Longley Street, and often claimed for Harmans by those who defied the map) throughout the next twelvemonth. For the moment, it occupied the whole stage of those engaged in it, and in many who watched it. The fates, juggling with the good luck, bad luck, indifferent luck, of this small assembly, were not desired to show their working in affairs of life and death and Death-in-Life; but what event they had in readiness for the obscure contest of an idle afternoon, was a question which loomed in the shadow of the mossy oak, in the sunny mid-circle, in every part of the field. The decline of imagination can scarcely be upheld, in face of these absorbing rivalries, for what meed?—a transient artificial glory; a stake so far beyond most of our aims, so innocent and honourable, that its pursuance is almost a religion.

Now, out came the pride of Longley Street, the two brothers Double (and the third to follow them duly). They were no novices. Their presence was immediately felt, and the score mounted. The ball seemed, no matter how sent down, to lose its speed on the way to them, or to fall short of its intended pitch. Tom Benyon was without his customary force. Dales, with his special variety of bowling that stops short, or hovers in the air, as it had appeared to do to many a victim, was no more respected by the clean-striking batsmen. Bowers, ordered to take up the story, left it as he found it. The yet grinning Tardy, whose arms seemed to be moved by mental levers, abruptly but without variation of extent or time, was able to keep the scoring without bounds, but had no other effect on the stalwart pair. Fifty was due to be signalled in a moment or two when the eldest Double made his first mistake, and the shout of the butcher, who was at present wicket-keeper, was answered by the uplifted finger of the umpire. There was yet a chance.

The excitement, considerable at the opening of this innings, became inhuman as it continued. The match was a match. With 'Soon be back, Alf,' and 'Keep y'r wicket up,' smiling nobly but not too well, the less expert men of Longley Green followed the expert to the wickets (and from the wickets with 'He bowls too straight') until there was one to go in, and still the score was a dozen short of the ninety-six runs notched by Harmans. John Bowers, fielding in the 'gully,' could not make the philosophy of 'It'll all be the same in a hundred years' time' cover the possible circumstance of his missing a catch now. Scroggins beside him felt the same, but hid the feeling under a meekly conscious, professional attitude of attention. A ball suddenly sliding between them both, it appeared that Scroggins had stiffened slightly in his alert attitude, for his hand was yards late, and Bowers had contrived to save the runs.

With eight runs separating the combatants, the one-armed batsman, who had held together the fabric almost his accustomed length of time, laid on his best powers to an over-pitched ball. The bowler was John Bowers, and by an extraordinary chance he was now clutching the ball in his right hand stretched out wide; his pose was suggestive of a Grecian dance, and occasioned an intentional dance among the urchins by the pavilion. The last man, a long, thin being, who had kept wicket for Longley Green, came, twisting his head from side to side, to provide the *explicit.* His unconventional purpose, as he met his first ball, seemed to be to scoop the ball over his left shoulder, but it struck his body, rolled to the wicket, and with delicate assurance caused a fatal bail to fall. The long man, casting a melancholy look at this, and repeating his scoop as if to express what might have been, turned away as he had come; the ground rang with clapping, and the bails having been pocketed and stumps drawn by the umpires, the victors came with modest pride from the field.

'A good match.'

'A thundering good catch by that young fellow.'

'Well, it's all over till next year.'

'Pity you didn't catch hold of that one, Smiler.'

'We never had no luck to-day.'

'Mr Double didn't reckon he was out.'

And among the victors, nothing more dramatic was said.

'I didn't half shake when the one-handed chap caught that half-volley of yours.'

'You'll be taking up batting, I 'spect, Mr Bowers.'

'We should have looked middling silly if you hadn't made them runs.'

'I think it's Mr Gibbens who made the runs for me.'

'Come on, Tardy, what you got to say to that?'

'Gentlemen, Mr Gibbens will speak.'

Not he. Grinning again, he shook his head. His increasing deafness had, also, dried up those brief springs of speech which once passed for the prime of simple wisdom. His small son, a crop-headed, hobnailed imp, carried his brown pads and bat, as he moved towards the exit of the field.

THE LITTLE GHOST

Hugh Walpole

I

Ghosts? I looked across the table at Truscott and had a sudden desire to impress him. Truscott has, before now, invited confidences in just that same way, with his flat impassivity, his air of not caring whether you say anything to him or no, his determined indifference to your drama and your pathos. On this particular evening he had been less impassive. He had himself turned the conversation towards Spiritualism, séances, and all that world of humbug, as he believed it to be, and suddenly I saw, or fancied that I saw, an real invitation in his eyes, something that made me say to myself: 'Well, hang it all, I've known Truscott for nearly twenty years; I've never shown him the least little bit of my real self; he thinks me a writing money-machine, with no thought in the world besides my brazen serial stories and the yacht that I purchased out of them.'

So I told him this story, and I will do him the justice to say that he listened to every word of it most attentively, although it was far into the evening before I had finished. He didn't seem impatient with all the little details that I gave. Of course, in a ghost story, details are more important than anything else. But was it a ghost story? Was it a story at all? Was it true even in its material background? Now, as I try to tell it again, I can't be sure. Truscott is the only other person who has ever heard it, and at the end of it he made no comment whatever.

It happened long ago, long before the war, when I had been married for about five years, and was an exceedingly prosperous journalist, with a nice little house and two children, in Wimbledon.

I lost suddenly my greatest friend. That may mean little or much as friendship is commonly held, but I believe that most Britishers, most Americans, most Scandinavians, know before they die one friendship at least that changes their whole life experience by its depth and colour. Very few Frenchmen, Italians or Spaniards, very few Southern people at all, understand these things.

The curious part of it in my particular case was that I had known this friend only four or five years before his death, that I had made many friendships both before and since that have endure over much longer periods, and yet this particular friendship had a quality of intensity and happiness that I have never found elsewhere.

Another curious thing was that I met Bond only a few months before my marriage, when I was deeply in love with my wife, and so intensely preoccupied with my engagement that I could think of nothing else. I met Bond quite casually at someone's house. He was a large-boned, broad-shouldered, slow-smiling man with close-cropped hair turning slightly grey, and our meeting was casual, the ripening of our friendship was casual; indeed, the whole affair may be said to have been casual to the very last. It was, in fact, my wife who said to me one day, when we had been married about a year or so; 'Why, I believe you care more for Charlie Bond than for anyone else in the world.' She said it in that sudden, disconcerting, perceptive way that some women have. I was entirely astonished. Of course I laughed at the idea. I saw Bond frequently. He came often to the house. My wife, wiser than many wives, encouraged all my friendships, and she herself liked Charlie immensely. I don't suppose that anyone disliked him. Some men were jealous of him; some men, the merest acquaintances, called him conceited; women were sometimes irritated by him because so clearly he could get on very easily without them; but he had, I think, no real enemy.

How could he have had? His good-nature, his freedom from all jealousy, his naturalness, his sense of fun, the absence of all pettiness, his common sense, his manliness, and at the same time his broad-minded intelligence, all these things made him a most charming personality. I don't know that he shone very much in ordinary society. He was very quiet and his wit and humour came out best with his intimates.

I was the showy one, and he always played up to me, and I think I patronised him a little and thought deep down in my subconscious self that it was lucky for him to have such a brilliant friend, but he never gave a sign of resentment. I believe now that he knew me, with all my faults and vanities and absurdities, far better than anyone else, even my wife, did, and that is one of the reasons, to the day of my death, why I shall always miss him so desperately.

However, it was not until his death that I realised how close we had been. One November day he came back to his flat, wet and chilled, didn't change his clothes, caught a cold, which developed into pneumonia, and after three days was dead. It happened that that week I was in Paris, and I returned to be told on my doorstep by my wife of what had occurred. At first I refused to believe it. When I had seen him a week before he had been in splendid health; with his tanned, rather rough and clumsy face, his clear eyes, no fat about him anywhere, he had looked as though he would live to a thousand, and then when I realised that it was indeed true I did not during the first week or two grasp my loss.

I missed him, of course; was vaguely unhappy and discontented; railed against life, wondering why it was always the best people who were taken and the others left; but I was not actually aware that for the rest of my days things would be different, and that that day of my return from Paris was a crisis in my human experience. Suddenly one morning, walking down Fleet Street, I had a flashing, almost blinding, need of Bond that was like a revelation. From that moment I knew no peace. Everyone seemed to me dull, profitless and empty. Even my wife was a long way away from me, and my children, whom I dearly loved, counted nothing to me at all. I didn't, after that, know what was the matter with me. I lost my appetite, I couldn't sleep, I was grumpy and nervous. I didn't myself connect it with Bond at all. I thought that I was overworked, and when my wife suggested a holiday, I agreed, got a fortnight's leave from my newspaper, and went down to Glebeshire.

Early December is not a bad time for Glebeshire. It is just then the best spot in the British Isles. I knew a little village beyond St Mary's Moor, that I had not seen for ten years, but always remembered with romantic gratitude, and I felt that that was the place for me now.

I changed trains at Polchester and found myself at last in a little jingle driving out to the sea. The air, the wide open moor, the smell of the sea delighted me, and when I reached my village, with its sandy cover and the boats drawn up in two rows in front of a high rocky cave, and when I ate my eggs and bacon in the parlour of the inn overlooking the sea, I felt happier than I had done for weeks past; but my happiness did not last long. Night after night I could not sleep. I began to feel acute loneliness and knew at last in full truth that it was my friend who I was missing, and that it was not solitude I needed, but his company. Easy enough to talk about having his company, but I only truly knew, down here in this little village, sitting on the edge of the green cliff, looking over into limitless sea, that I was indeed never to have his company again. There followed after that a wild, impatient regret that I had not made more of my time with him. I saw myself, in a sudden vision, as I had really been with him, patronising, indulgent, a little contemptuous of his good-natured ideas. Had I only a week with him now, how eagerly I would show him that I was the fool and not he, that I was the lucky one every time!

One connects with one's own grief the place where one feels it, and before many days had passed I had grown to loathe the little village, to dread, beyond words, the long, soughing groan of the sea as it drew back down the slanting beach, the melancholy wail of the seagulls, the chattering women under my little window. I couldn't stand it. I ought to go back to London, and yet from that, too, I shrank. Memories of Bond lingered there as they did in no other place, and it was hardly fair to my wife and family to give them the company of the dreary, discontented man that I just then was.

And then, just in the way that such things always happen, I found on my breakfast-table one fine morning a forwarded letter. It was from a certain Mrs Baldwin, and, to my surprise, I saw that it came from Glebeshire, but from the top of the county and not its southern end.

John Baldwin was a Stock Exchange friend of my brother's, a rough diamond, but kindly and generous, and not, I believed, very well off. Mrs Baldwin I had always liked, and I think she always like me. We had not met for some little time and I had no idea what had happened to them. Now in her letter she told me that they had taken an old eighteenth-century house on the north coast of Glebeshire, not very far from Drymouth, that they were enjoying it very much indeed, that Jack was fitter than he had been for years, and that they would be delighted, were I ever in that part of the country, to have me as their guest. This suddenly seemed to me the very thing. The Baldwins had never known Charlie Bond, and they would have, therefore, for me no association with his memory. They were jolly, noisy people, with a jolly, noisy family, and Jack Baldwin's personality was so robust that it would surely shake me out of my gloomy mood. I sent a telegram at once to Mrs Baldwin, asking her whether she could have me for a week, and before the day was over I received the warmest of invitations.

Next day I left my fishing village and experienced one of those strange, crooked, in-and-out little journeys that you must undergo if you are to find your way from one obscure Glebeshire village to another.

About midday, a lovely, cold, blue December midday, I discovered myself in Polchester with an hour to wait for my next train. I went down into the town, climbed the High Street to the magnificent cathedral, stood beneath the famous Arden Gate, looked at the still more famous tomb of the Black Bishop, and it was there, as the sunlight, slanting through the great east window, danced and sparkled about the wonderful blue stone of which that tomb is made, that I had a sudden sense of having been through all this before, of having stood just there in some earlier time, weighed down by some earlier grief, and that nothing that I was experiencing was unexpected. I had a curious sense, too, of comfort and condolence, that horrible grey loneliness that I had felt in the fishing village suddenly fell from me, and for the first time since Bond's death, I was happy. I walked away from the cathedral, down the busy street, and through the dear old market-place, expecting I know not what. All that I knew was that I was intending to go to the Baldwins' and that I would be happy there.

The December afternoon fell quickly, and during the last part of my journey I was travelling in a ridiculous little train, through dusk, and the little train went so slowly and so casually that one was always hearing the murmurs of streams beyond one's window, and lakes of grey water suddenly stretched like plates of glass to thick woods, black as ink, against a faint sky. I got out at my little wayside station, shaped like a rabbit-hutch, and found a motor waiting for me. The drive was not long, and suddenly I was outside the old eighteenth-century house and Baldwin's stout butler was conveying me into the hall with that careful, kindly patronage, rather as though I were a box of eggs that might very easily be broken.

It was a spacious hall, with a large open fireplace, in front of which they were all having tea. I say 'all' advisedly, because the place seemed to be full of people, grown-ups and children, but mostly children. There were so many of these last that I was not, to the end of my stay, to be able to name most of them individually.

Mrs Baldwin came forward to greet me, introduced me to one or two people, sat me down and gave me my tea, told me that

I wasn't looking at all well, and needed feeding up, and explained that Jack was out shooting something, but would soon be back.

My entrance had made a brief lull, but immediately everyone recovered and the noise was terrific. There is a lot to be said for the freedom of the modern child. There is a lot to be said against it, too. I soon found that in this party, at any rate, the elders were completely disregarded and of no account. Children rushed about the hall, knocked one another down, shouted and screamed, fell over grown-ups as though they were pieces of furniture, and paid no attention at all to the mild 'Now, children' of a plain, elderly lady who was, I supposed, a governess. I fancy that I was tired with my criss-cross journey, and I soon found a chance to ask Mrs Baldwin if I could go up to my room. She said: 'I expect you find these children noisy. Poor little things. They must have their fun. Jack always says that one can only be young once, and I do so agree with him.'

I wasn't myself feeling very young that evening (I was really about nine hundred years old), so that I agreed with her and eagerly left youth to its own appropriate pleasures. Mrs Baldwin took me up the fine broad staircase. She was a stout, short woman, dressed in bright colours, with what is known, I believe, as an infectious laugh. To-night, although I was fond of her, and knew very well her good, generous heart, she irritated me, and for some reason that I could not quite define. Perhaps I felt at once that she was out of place there and that the house resented her, but in all this account I am puzzled by the question as to whether I imagine now, on looking back, all sorts of feelings that were not really there at all, but come to me now because I know of what happened afterwards. But I am so anxious to tell the truth, the whole truth, and nothing but the truth, and there is nothing in the world so difficult to do as that.

We went through a number of dark passages, up and down little pieces of staircase that seemed to have no beginning, no end, and no reason for their existence, and she left me at last in my bedroom, said that she hoped I would be comfortable, and that Jack would come and see me when he came in, and then paused for a moment, looking at me. 'You really don't look well,' she said. 'You've been overdoing it. You're too conscientious. I always said so. You shall have a real rest here. And the children will see that you're not dull.'

Her last two sentences seemed scarcely to go together. I could not tell her about my loss. I realised suddenly, as I had never realised in our older acquaintance, that I should never be able to speak to her about anything that really mattered.

She smiled, laughed and left me. I looked at my room and loved it at once. Broad and low-ceilinged, it contained very little furniture, an old four-poster, charming hangings of some old rose-coloured damask, an old gold mirror, an oak cabinet, some high-backed chairs, and then, for comfort, a large armchair with high elbows, a little quaintly shaped sofa dressed in the same rose colour as the bed, a bright crackling fire and a grandfather clock. The walls, faded primrose, had no pictures, but on one of them, opposite my bed, was a gay sampler worked in bright colours of crimson and yellow and framed in oak.

I liked it, I loved it, and drew the armchair in front of the fire, nestled down into it, and before I knew, I was fast asleep. How long I slept I don't know, but I suddenly woke with a sense of comfort and well-being which was nothing less than exquisite. I belonged to it, that room, as though I had been in it all my days. I had a curious sense of companionship that was exactly what I had been needing during these last weeks. The house was very still, no voices of children came to me, no sound anywhere, save the sharp crackle of the fire and the friendly ticking of the old clock. Suddenly I thought that there was someone in the room with me, a rustle of something that might have been the fire and yet was not.

I got up and looked about me, half smiling, as though I expected to see a familiar face. There was no one there, of course, and yet I had just that consciousness of companionship that one has when someone whom one loves very dearly and knows very intimately is sitting with one in the same room. I even went to the other side of the four-poster and looked around me, pulled for a moment at the rose-coloured curtains, and of course saw no one. Then the door suddenly opened and Jack Baldwin came in, and I remember having a curious feeling of irritation as though I had been interrupted. His large, breezy, knickerbockered figure filled the room. 'Hullo!' he said, 'delighted to see you. Bit of luck your being down this way. Have you got everything you want?'

II

That was a wonderful old house. I am not going to attempt to describe it, although I have stayed there quite recently. Yes, I stayed there on many occasions since that first of which I am now speaking. It has never been quite the same to me since that first time. You may say, if you like, that the Baldwins fought a battle with it and defeated it. It is certainly now more Baldwin than—well, whatever it was before they rented it. They are not the kind of people to be defeated by atmosphere. Their chief duty in this world, I gather, is to make things Baldwin, and very good for the world too; but when I first went down to them the house was still challenging them. 'A wee bit creepy,' Mrs Baldwin confided to me on the second day of my visit. 'What exactly do you mean by that?' I asked her. 'Ghosts?'

'Oh, there are those, of course,' she answered. 'There's an underground passage, you know, that runs from here to the sea, and one of the wickedest of the smugglers was killed in it, and his ghost still haunts the cellar. At least that's what we were told by our first butler, here; and then, of course, we found that it was the butler, not the smuggler, who was haunting the cellar, and since his departure the smuggler hasn't been visible.' She laughed. All the same, it isn't a comfortable place. I'm going to wake up some of those of those old rooms. We're going to put in some more windows. And then there are the children,' she added.

Yes, there were the children. Surely the noisiest in all the world. They had reverence for nothing. They were the wildest savages, and especially those from nine to thirteen, the cruellest and most uncivilised age for children. There were two little boys, twins I should think, who were nothing less than devils, and regarded their elders with cold, watching eyes, said nothing in protest when scolded, but evolved plots afterwards that fitted precisely the chastiser. To do my host and hostess justice, all the children were not Baldwins, and I fancy that the Baldwin contingent was the quietest.

Nevertheless, from early morning until ten at night, the noise was terrific and you were never sure how early in the morning it would recommence. I don't know that I personally minded the noise very greatly. It took me out of myself and gave me something better to think of, but, in some obscure and unanalysed way, I felt that the house minded it. One knows how the poets have written about old walls and rafters rejoicing in the happy, careless laughter of children. I do not think this house rejoiced at all, and it was queer how consistently I, who am not supposed to be an imaginative person, thought about the house.

But it was not until my third evening that something really happened. I say 'happened,' but did anything really happen? You shall judge for yourself.

I was sitting in my comfortable armchair in my bedroom, enjoying that delightful half-hour before one dresses for dinner. There was a terrible racket up and down the passages, the children being persuaded, I gathered, to go into the schoolroom and have their supper, when the noise died down and there was nothing but the feathery whisper of the snow—snow had been falling all day—against my window-pane. My thoughts suddenly turned to Bond, directed to him as actually and precipitately as though he had suddenly sprung before me. I did not want to think of him. I had been fighting his memory these last days, because I had thought that the wisest thing to do, but now he was too much for me.

I luxuriated in my memories of him, turning over and over all sorts of times that we had had together, seeing his smile, watching his mouth that turned up at the corners when he was amused, and wondering finally why he should obsess me the way that he did, when I had lost so many other friends for whom I had thought I cared much more, who, nevertheless, never bothered my memory at all. I sighed, and it seemed to me that my sigh was very gently repeated behind me. I turned sharply round. The curtains had not been drawn. You know the strange, milky pallor that reflected snow throws over objects, and although three lighted candles shone in the room, moon-white shadows seemed to hang over the bed and across the floor. Of course there was no one there, and yet I stared and stared about me as though I were convinced that I was not alone. And then I looked especially at one part of the room, a distant corner beyond the four-poster, and it seemed to me that someone was there. And yet no one was there. But whether it was that my mind had been distracted, or that the beauty of the old snow-lit room enchanted me, I don't know, but my thoughts of my friend were happy and reassured. I had not lost him, I seemed to say to myself. Indeed, at that special moment he seemed to be closer to me than he had been while he was alive.

From that evening a curious thing occurred. I only seemed to be close to my friend when I was in my own room—and I felt more than that. When my door was closed and was sitting in my armchair, I fancied that our new companionship was not only Bond's, but was something more as well. I would wake in the middle of the night or in the early morning and feel quite sure that I was not alone; so sure that I did not even want to investigate it further, but just took the companionship for granted and was happy.

Outside that room, however, I felt increasing discomfort. I hated the way in which the house was treated. A quite unreasonable anger rose within me as I heard the Baldwins discussing the improvements that they were going to make, and yet they were so kind to me, and so patently unaware of doing anything that would not generally be commended, it was quite impossible for me to show my anger. Nevertheless, Mrs Baldwin noticed something. 'I am afraid the children are worrying you,' she said one morning, half interrogatively. 'In a way it will be a rest when they go back to school, but the Christmas holidays is their time, isn't it? I do like to see them happy. Poor little dears.'

The poor little dears were at that moment being Red Indians all over the hall.

'No, of course, I like children,' I answered her. 'The only thing is that they don't—I hope you won't think me foolish—somehow quite fit in with the house.'

'Oh, I think it's so good for old places like this,' said Mrs Baldwin briskly, 'to be woken up a little. I'm sure if the old people who used to live here came back they'd love to hear all the noise and laughter.'

I wasn't so sure myself, but I wouldn't disturb Mrs Baldwin's contentment for anything.

That evening in my room I was so convinced of companionship that I spoke.

'If there's anyone here,' I said aloud, 'I'd like them to know that I'm aware of it and am glad of it.'

Then, when I caught myself speaking aloud, I was suddenly terrified. Was I really going crazy? Wasn't that the first step towards insanity when you talked to yourself? Nevertheless, a moment later I was reassured. There *was* someone there.

That night I woke, looked at my luminous watch and saw that it was a quarter past three. The room was so dark that I could not even distinguish the posts of my bed, but there was a very faint glow from the fire, now nearly dead. Opposite my bed there seemed to me to be something white. Not white in the accepted sense of a tall, ghostly figure; but, sitting up and staring, it seemed to me that the shadow was very small, hardly reaching above the edge of the bed.

'Is there anyone there?' I asked. 'Because, if there is, do speak to me. I'm not frightened. I know that someone has been here all this last week, and I am glad of it.'

Very faintly then, and so faintly that I cannot to this day be sure that I saw anything at all, the figure of a child seemed to me to be visible.

We all know how we have at one time and another fancied that we have seen visions and figures, and then have discovered that it was something in the room, the chance hanging of a coat, the reflection of a glass, a trick of moonlight that has fired our imagination. I was quite prepared for that in this case, but it seemed to me then that as I watched the shadow moved directly in front of the dying fire, and delicate as the leaf of a silver birch, like the trailing rim of some evening clouds, the figure of a child hovered in front of me.

Curiously enough the dress, which seemed to be of some silver tissue, was clearer than anything else. I did not, in fact, see the face at all, and yet I could swear in the morning that I had seen it, that I knew large, black, wide-open eyes, a little mouth very faintly parted in a timid smile, and that, beyond anything else, I had realised in the expression of that face fear and bewilderment and a longing for some comfort.

III

After that night the affair moved very quickly to its little climax.

I am not a very imaginative man, nor have I any sympathy with the modern craze for spooks and spectres. I have never seen, nor fancied that I had seen, anything of a supernatural kind since that visit, but then I have never known since that time such a desperate need of companionship and comfort, and is it not perhaps because we do not want things badly enough in this life that we do not get more of them? However that may be, I was sure on this occasion that I had some companionship that was born of a need greater than mine. I suddenly took the most frantic and unreasonable dislike to the children in that house. It was exactly as though I had discovered somewhere in a deserted part of the building some child who had been left behind by mistake by the last occupants and was terrified by the noisy exuberance and ruthless selfishness of the new family.

For a week I had no more definite manifestation of my little friend, but I was as sure of her presence there in my room as I was of my own clothes and the armchair in which I used to sit.

It was time for me to go back to London, but I could not go. I asked everyone I met as to legends and stories connected with the old house, but I never found anything to do with a little child. I looked forward all day to my hour in my room before dinner, the time when I felt the companionship closest. I sometimes woke in the night and was conscious of its presence, but, as I have said, I never saw anything.

One evening the older children obtained leave to stay up later. It was somebody's birthday. The house seemed to be full of people, and the presence of the children led after dinner to a perfect riot of noise and confusion. We were to play hide-and-seek all over the house. Everybody was to dress up. There was, for that night at least, to be no privacy anywhere. We were all, as Mrs Baldwin said, to be ten years old again. I hadn't the least desire to be ten years old, but I found myself caught into the game, and had, in sheer self-defence, to run up and down the passages and hide behind doors. The noise was terrific. It grew and grew in volume. People got hysterical. The smaller children jumped out of bed and ran about the passages. Somebody kept blowing a motor-horn. Somebody else turned on the gramophone.

Suddenly I was sick of the whole thing, retreated into my room, lit one candle and locked the door. I had scarcely sat down in my chair when I was aware that my little friend had come. She was standing near to the bed, staring at me, terror in her eyes. I have never seen anyone so frightened. Her little breasts panting beneath her silver gown, her very fair hair falling about her shoulders, her little hands clenched. Just as I saw her, there were loud knocks on the door, many voices shouting to be admitted, a perfect babel of noise and laughter. The little figure moved, and then—how can I give any idea of it?—I was conscious of having something to protect and comfort. I saw nothing, physically I felt nothing, and yet I was murmuring, 'There, there, don't mind. They shan't come in. I'll see that no one touches you. I understand. I understand.' For how long I sat like that I don't know. The noises died away, voices murmured at intervals, and then were silent. The house slept. All night I think I stayed there comforting and being comforted.

I fancy now—but how much of it may not be fancy?—that I knew that the child loved the house, had stayed so long as was possible, at last was driven away, and that that was her farewell, not only to me, but all that she most loved in this world and the next.

I do not know—I could swear to nothing. What I am sure of is that my sense of loss in my friend was removed from that night and never returned. Did I argue with myself that that child companionship included also my friend? Again, I do not know. But of one thing I am now sure, that if love is strong enough, physical death cannot destroy it, and however platitudinous that may sound to others, it is platitudinous no longer when you have discovered it by actual experience for yourself.

That moment in that fire-lit room, when I felt that spiritual heart beating with mine, is and always will be enough for me.

One thing more. Next day I left for London, and my wife was delighted to find me so completely recovered—happier, she said, than I had ever been before.

Two days afterwards I received a parcel from Mrs Baldwin. In the note that accompanied it, she said:

I think that you must have left this by mistake behind you. It was found in the small drawer in your dressing-table.

I opened the parcel and discovered an old blue silk handkerchief, wrapped round a long, thin wooden box. The cover of the box lifted very easily, and I saw inside it an old, painted wooden doll, dressed in the period, I should think, of Queen Anne. The dress was very complete, even down to the little shoes, and the little grey mittens on the hands. Inside the silk skirt there was sewn a little tape, and on the tape, in very faded letters, 'Ann Trelawney, 1710.'

THE TALE OF A CHILD

JOSEF BARD

... To-Day it is very warm and we shall go and bathe in the Danube. We are not allowed to bathe in the Danube because it is dangerous but we know a spot where there is a bad smell because it is near a factory where they make leather from the hide of oxen. There the water is shallow and we can all stand up in the water. Jacob too can stand up though he is small but he is very wise and Andreas can swim and we all cling to the neck of Roka my dog. Jacob holds most of Roka's neck although Roka is my dog but Jacob is very frightened of the Danube and he would be punished if he drowned, because his father told him so. His father is a man with a curly long black beard and apart from that he is also our grocer and he has black rings under his eyes. I don't like Jacob's father because he always pats me on the head and then my hair smells of cheese, and I must wash always although I have washed already. But I like Jacob because he is wise. I don't know how but he is very wise. We all play at marbles after class and we all lose. But Jacob never plays because his father told him so. But he exchanges our bad marbles for better marbles and we buy them from him. Andreas says this is because Jacob is a Jew and his father told him so. I like Andreas but I think he is a liar. He told me the other day there is a dead mason hidden in the walls of every big house. The mason was alive when they walled him in but now he is dead. I don't believe it but I don't like it. Andreas' father is a gentleman who builds houses for others and he told him so.

I am sure Andreas is a liar. Now when we have all come out of the water and were drying ourselves in the grass so that nobody could tell we had been in the Danube and Roka sat down on our clothes and made them wet and we drove Roka away with stones although we all held his neck in the water, now Andreas was chewing a leaf of grass and told us he saw God yesterday early in the afternoon.

'You are a liar,' I said to Andreas. Jacob said nothing but he smiled. He is very wise when he smiles. I saw that Jacob also thought that Andreas was a little liar.

'I am not a liar. I came down to the river and I saw a big white cloud in the sky just like a feather-pillow and God flew out, dipped his feet in the water, smiled at me and flew back again.'

So we looked up into they sky. We saw white clouds, fluffy like the sheep in the village and not a bit like feather-pillows. I knew Andreas was a liar. And God simply couldn't fly out of such a cloud.

Still I was envious. I shall be ten years old after two years and I haven't seen God yet. I thought maybe Jacob had more luck. So I asked him: 'Jacob, have you see God?' But Jacob looked frightened and he said he must not speak of God because his father told him so. Then I turned to Andreas again and said to him: 'Andreas, I know you are just lying. Look in my eyes and say again that you saw God!' And Andreas who was lying on his back turned round on his belly and looked at me. Andreas is very beautiful. He has long flaxen locks and his face is very white and his eyes are like brown fruit-drops when you have sucked them and taken them out of your mouth and then hold them in your hand to see how much is left. But I could not look into his eyes as mother looks into mine. His eyes were not in his face they were just like clouds in the sky. So I just said: 'Andreas, I believe you are a liar.' Still I am not quite sure. And then we all went home, Jacob and Andreas and Roka and I and we never said another word.

❖

... to-day Father eats the marrow-bone. When Father is away I eat the marrow-bone, when he is at home he gives me a bit of the marrow, on a bit of bread, salted and peppered. I was waiting for my bit to-day but he forgot me. He often is like that. I said: 'Father—' because I am told to call him Father and not Daddie— 'Father, Andreas told me he saw God in the afternoon—do you think it is true?' But Father finished the marrow-bone and said I was a donkey. I looked sad and then Mother told Father 'don't be rude to the child.' Then Father said that Mother spoils me. Then they quarrelled. Then I stopped sulking. I love Mother. All the boys love their Mothers but they respect their Fathers. But my Mother is very beautiful. She has long hair and big eyes and a big mouth and she is soft and plump.

So we were all eating quietly in the garden under the mulberry-tree and the ripe mulberries kept dropping from the tree into my rice-pudding, so wonderful is nature. But still I wanted to know whether Andreas saw God. When Father left the table I asked Mother: 'Mother dear—do you think Andreas really saw God?' But she looked tired because Father had not kissed her when he left the table because they quarrelled and she sighed. She said: 'The questions you ask! How should I know?' And then she also left the table and followed Father into the house.

Mother is very beautiful and plump but she never answers my questions. I shall ask Kate, our cook who is plumper than Mother but not so very beautiful. She has already told me where babies come from. She will know whether Andreas, the little liar, saw God or not.

... to-day I have not spoken to Andreas in school because I am not sure whether he is a liar or not. This is a warm morning. The sun is shining and we all wanted to laugh but we had no chance because our teacher Prunk spoke only of serious things and had the birch in his hand. Jacob brought some old stamps and we are all collecting stamps because Jacob says it is the best way to learn the map of the world. Slezak sits behind me and he is the son of our washer-woman, but he hates Jacob. But Slezak is very stupid and our teacher Prunk told him so. We are all a little afraid of Slezak because he is very strong and hits us on the jaw. He says the English all hit each other on the jaw which makes them very strong. Jacob has many English stamps because he has an uncle there who sends them to him. His uncle hits nobody on the jaw but publishes books which others have written, and his father told him so. But when Slezak hit Jacob on the jaw, Jacob smiled mildly and asked him 'is this what you have learned from your Reverend Father and Jesus Christ?' And Slezak said Jacob

crucified Jesus Christ and now he must be hit on the jaw. And
we were all very excited and Prunk came in and birched Slezak
and told the class we were all Hungarians and we must love each
other because anyhow we are only few and our enemies are many.
Then he read us a poem which said that the earth is the hat of
God and Hungary is a bunch of flowers on the top of the hat.
This was written by a great poet called Petöfi, who fell in the
battle when the Hungarians were just conquering the Russians.
We Hungarians have the habit of winning all the battles but this
we lost because we were already tired by conquering the Austrians.
The Russians and the Austrians are our enemies and so are others
we haven't yet learned about and Prunk says our enemies are
many and our friends are few and we must prepare to be proud
when the moment arrives when we shall die for Hungary. But we
still have time and so we must learn Petöfi's poem by heart and
we must not forget that now the Austrians are our friends and
our King Francis Joseph rules over them too but he loves only
the Hungarians and he only rules over the Austrians because his
father told him to. Our King is hanging on the wall and he is very
dignified and hairy, and he is now very old but he was young when
he began to be a King. When we sing the National Anthem we
all look at him and he looks back at us very dignified and hairy.

We all read aloud what is called the poem and it was difficult
to remember it because the lines all end the same way, but we
were all very proud that we were so few and always conquered
our enemies who were many and Slezak wanted to go to the
lavatory, which he always wants to do when we must learn
something by heart. And Jacob stood up and asked our teacher
how could the earth be the hat of God when he told us that the
earth was round like a rubber-ball. Jacob is very wise and when
we were reading the poem we had quite forgotten that Prunk told

us the earth was round. We all looked at Prunk and we all saw
clearly he could say just nothing. But he was trying very hard.
He said Petöfi was a very great poet and very great poets are
permitted to say sometimes what is not quite true. But we all
thought that Jacob conquered Prunk. But perhaps Prunk told the
truth. And perhaps Andreas is not a little liar but only a great
poet?

… to-day grandma arrived from town. Grandma is a much older
lady than Mother but this is only natural. She is small and she
always smoothes her mouth with her fingers because her teeth
are not natural. But she was sad to-day because my Uncle Berti
came with her who is also her son and Uncle Berti is ill. I don't
know what is wrong with Uncle Berti they only say he is mad.
I like Uncle Berti because he is so funny, and he sometimes
pushes his spoon under his chin because he can't find his mouth
and pours the soup under his collar which is a good joke from
a grown-up man but Grandma looks sad and kicks me under the
table when I laugh. Uncle Berti worked in town and he was
almost a bank-director but not quite but this was before he poured
the soup under his collar. Now he lives with Grandma who is also
his Mother. And he is very big and very silent but he lies to play
with me when I play in the garden building castles from mudpies.
And Mother and Grandma sat under the mulberry tree and
watched us and we sat on the ground and when I turned round
I think Mother and Grandma were blowing their noses and I think
they wept although Uncle Berti made much better mudpies than
I did. And then they went into the house and I followed them
to wash my hands and I heard them talk although I did not want

to listen but they had not seen me. And Mother was afraid Uncle Berti would get wild one day and wanted him to go to a place where he could get wild safely. But Grandma only wept and cursed Uncle Berti's wife but he had two wives and this was unhealthy for him especially when they both loved him. And then I went to the kitchen and just heard Kate the cook say to the maid that Uncle Berti had water in his head but when they saw me they said no more.

And so I went back to Uncle Berti and he was all right doing well with mudpies. And I sat down next to Uncle Berti and looked in his eyes and they were blue but they were not there. And I thought he might perhaps know whether Andreas saw God, so I asked him. And he only said: 'Very-berry-mulberry' and then he smiled. And then he stood up and was very tall and his hair I saw was white and he said 'let us go to Church I would like to pray.' So I took him by the hand and we went into the house and I said to Mother 'Uncle Berti and I want to go to Church.' And Mother looked frightened but Grandma said it was all right. And so we walked out, I holding his hand and I took him to the Chapel although it was three o'clock in the afternoon and God is seldom at home at that hour. And it was very dark and cool in the chapel and candles burnt in the corners and I was not comfortable because Uncle Berti held my hand very tight. And I don't go to Church because Father says he hates all the priests and if there is God there is only one who also hates the priests. But it is beautiful in our chapel it smells good not like near the river where they make leather from the hide of oxen. And the lady-saints were very beautiful and they all had flowers on the altar. We just stood in the middle of the chapel and we were quite alone and it was very silent. And Uncle Berti whispered into my ear whether I could see a gentleman-saint because he would like to pray before a gentleman-saint and not before a lady-saint to-day. And I found his one in the right corner who was tied to a tree and he was very naked but there were arrows in him. And Uncle Berti let my hand go and fell on his knees and began to pray, but it seemed to have little sense and I wondered whether the saint would understand what he was saying. Then Uncle Berti wept and he wept very loud and I was afraid because it was very silent and we were alone and I had heard Mother say Uncle Berti might get wild. But it was not true because he stood up and was very quiet and stroked my hand and thanked me for taking him to the chapel. It was all right what he said, so I told him why did he let himself be called mad. Then he laughed and he laughed just as loud as he wept before, and I got frightened again. But he became quiet again and we walked out of the chapel and he said he wanted to buy me something. So I took him to Jacob's father who is the grocer and I chose a box of green lizards made of rubber-candy. And Jacob's father made big eyes and forgot to pat me on the head which made me grateful. And Uncle Berti shook hands with Jacob's father and forgot to pay and we all went back to Mother and Grandma.

Then Grandma and Uncle Berti went to the station and we accompanied them and Uncle Berti was so big and Grandma very small but she led him by the hand. And Uncle Berti was very pale and when he shook hands with me, my heart hurt because I was now sorry for him. I wished he had something better than water in his head.

❖

... to-day we went to swim in the Danube again where it stinks but it is safe and I kept my head out of water because I was afraid water might get into my head through my ears as with Uncle Berti. We are friends again with Andreas and I always like Jacob because he is wise. And we went rather late and we rolled about naked and Jacob was different because he was taken into the bosom of Abraham that way and it happened when he was eight days old and his father told him so. Jacob has very thin legs and thin arms and Andreas is much more beautiful but Andreas rolled very close to me and I told him I didn't like it because we must only love girls and Kate the cook told me so. And so Andreas rolled on his belly and his bottom was turned towards me and it seemed beautiful but it was his bottom and bottoms are ugly because my Mother told me so and you must never show it except when you are alone and the doctor asks you to. I told this to Andreas but he laughed and then he lied again because he must always lie except when he is a great poet. Andreas lied that children are made of marble and rose-leaves and they are beautiful everywhere and we only cover our bottoms because otherwise we would be too beautiful for our parents. So I called him a liar because I know babies are made by mothers and Slezak the son of our washer-woman brought me the cord which came out with him into the world and he found it in a drawer and it was wrapped in a paper and it was brown and horrid. And Jacob said we must not bother about this, but collect stamps in peace and learn the map of the world because his father told him so.

But I still called Andreas a liar because I saw our dog Roka starting to make babies to his wife and Kate, the cook told me father was not different. Andreas did not answer but smelt the daisies in the grass. Then he said he didn't care what we knew but he dreamt babies were made of marbles and rose-leaves. Now I knew he was lying again because I dreamt that uncle Berti came back and I broke a hole in his head with my hatchet and all the water flowed out and our teacher Prunk was drowned in the flood but it was not true because in the morning I saw that Prunk was still alive and teaching history. I wanted Jacob to be on my side against Andreas but Jacob is very wise and he only wants to collect stamps in peace.

So I teased Andreas who was still smelling the daisies which I know have no smell and told him if he knew everything did he know what the stars were. Andreas said he knew but he couldn't say it because he didn't know the words. So I asked him did he know what the moon was. And Andreas said the moon is a pale woman who is looking for a lost world. And then I got frightened just like in the chapel when uncle Berti wept aloud and I thought perhaps water had got into the ears of Andreas because I also see ghosts in the dark but I know they are not there because my Mother told me so. So I asked him what the sun is and Andreas lifted his head and said the sun is an angry flame which wants to burn everything and the earth is running away from him because he is frightened. And Jacob and I were also frightened and it was now dark and Jacob said we must not ask more questions from Andreas because he is perhaps a prophet and we must be happy when prophets are silent because his father told him so. And we all walked home and said no more.

... to-day I saw Kate the cook drinking rum in the kitchen but I shall not tell Mother because Kate is my friend and always answers my questions and Mother is more beautiful but she never answers my questions and Father is always angry. And Kate gave some rum to Peti the milkman who always smells of what the cows leave when they don't behave properly and who is waiting on the cows. And Peti the milkman started to be like Roka my dog when he joined his wife but Kate pushed him back and asked him whether he was not ashamed before the child which was me. And then I remembered that Lola had her birthday and she had asked me to come and have some of her birthday cake and I had not asked Mother because now it was after dinner and I had to go to bed. So I asked Kate to let me in through the kitchen door when I came back and then I went into the garden and picked white and red roses which she liked and walked to Lola's house because I think I love Lola and I would like to marry Lola if she could preserve herself till I grow up. Because Lola is already very big and her hair is perfumed when she kisses me and she lives in a big house, with a big orchard where a brook flows through and she has many young men playing the piano with her which is very musical. And when I arrived she was playing but she stopped and kissed me again and her hair was again perfumed. And there were many people and they were eating sandwiches and Lola wore a long white dress and her arms were puffed but this was only her dress and not her arms. And everybody was very nice to me though they laughed and a fat man who played with Lola pinched my cheeks, and I told him I didn't like that and I thought he was stupid. I said this because I saw him breathe down on Lola's neck when she played the piano and I love Lola. And Lola saw that I was angry and she said we two will go out into the garden, and so we went out and we sat down under a cherry tree and we sat on the grass and I put my head on Lola's white neck and kissed it which Lola said I must not do. And Lola was sad and she looked up at the moon and she sighed. And she said 'do you see the moon?' And I said 'yes, I see the moon she is like a pale woman looking for a lost world.' And then I blushed because I remembered that I had heard this from Andreas, that

little liar. But Lola did not remember it and she kissed me on
the mouth and said that it was very beautiful and asked me
whether I could say something else as beautiful. Then I said the
sun is an angry flame which wants to burn everything and the
earth is running away from him because he is frightened. Then
I blushed again because I remembered that I heard this also from
Andreas the little liar. But Lola kissed me on the mouth again
and she said how poetic children are and I saw she thought of
the fat man who was not so poetic and then she said I must come
when I had something beautiful to say and that she would always
kiss me. So we parted in the garden and I did not go back to the
house with her because I didn't like the fat man but Lola went
back and I walked to my home. I was very happy and wondered
what the stars were but then Father was waiting for me in the
kitchen and he said he would break my bones if I left the house
without permission at night and he began doing so, but Mother
came and told him not to be rude to the child and then they
quarrelled and I hurried to my room before they had finished and
I thought I hated to be beaten and I would kill whoever dares
to beat me, only fathers unfortunately can't be killed because my
Mother told me so. So I went to bed and I dreamt of Lola but
it was not true because I could not remember it in the morning.

… to-day Slezak was late for school because he said his mother
had borne him a brother which is curious because Slezak has no
father. But we did not ask questions because Prunk told us more
about our History and he said we Hungarians were somewhere
else a thousand years ago and we had the habit of multiplying
ourselves quickly so we went out to find another home so we

came to Hungary which is where we now are and we conquered the people we found here because we had the habit of winning all the battles. But it was not easy to find Hungary because it was far from the place where we multiplied ourselves, but our very own Battle-god sent us a bird and he flew ahead of us and when we arrived he flew back to our very own Battle-god and so Prunk said we have been in Hungary now for over a thousand years and had much glory and we have fought against the Turks who also belonged to our enemies but we haven't yet learnt about them and we have suffered much glory because we were only few and our enemies were many. And we were all very proud but then Jacob stood up and asked Prunk why we had so many enemies. Prunk knows much and has a big wart on his forehead but Jacob is wise and Prunk thought a little while and then said we are the bunch of flowers on God's hat and our neighbours are all envious of us. Then we all stood up and sang the National Anthem and our King Francis Joseph hanging on the wall listened to us and he listened to our promise that we would all die here because we couldn't go elsewhere. Then Prunk left us for half an hour to give us time to wash our hands and eat our bread and butter and we all stood round Slezak who was sad because now his mother can't wash for a month and he did not want a brother because they are very poor and his father died when they hit him on the head with a bottle of rum. Slezak said it was Peti the milkman who did it to his mother but he would buy a gun and shoot him. Then Andreas pulled me by the sleeve and we all left Slezak and whispered because Andreas asked us to collect money for Slezak because he is very poor. And we all promised to give him our pocket money for the week and to ask our parents to give him money. Then Slezak had to go to Prunk's room and he came back weeping because Prunk asked him to leave the school. And we all hated Prunk and called him an ugly wart which he had on his forehead. And when Prunk came back to teach history we all stood up and Jacob walked in front of us and asked Prunk in the name of the class to take back Slezak because Slezak is innocent because he did not tell Peti the milkman to do it to his mother. Then Prunk was very angry and told Jacob to go back to his place and said we should not know about such things and that Slezak was a bad influence. Then he taught us more about our glorious past and how we conquered our enemies and how our Kings helped us but I don't remember because we did not listen because we thought of Slezak. And when the class was over Prunk saw that we were all sad and he said he would talk about Slezak to the headmaster. Then we all cheered and were proud again of our glorious past.

... to-day is Friday evening and I was permitted to go to Jacob's house and have dinner with them because I gave some old stamps to Jacob and he was grateful. And it was very warm in the room and we all kept our hats on our heads because Jacob's God likes that and also we were more than thirteen because otherwise Jacob's God is not present. And Jacob's father was very clean and he had a white stole on his neck and he prayed loud and we all murmured and then we had soup with big dumplings in it and we had roast goose with much stuffings. And Jacob's relatives were there and they had beards but the women were only fat. Jacob has no mother but his aunt cooks for him and she is called Hannah and she is only half-witted but she cooks well. Jacob says Jews are wise, but when they are not they are very stupid. It was very hot and we were not happy because Jacob's God really lives in Palestine and only comes for a short visit to our village. And I said to Jacob now we will go to my garden and eat fruit from the trees.

And then we walked home which is not far because our village is small. And Jacob was sad because he had no mother and Friday night he always remembers her. So I told him stories to amuse him how the Austrian villagers carry ladders sideways through the forest and cut down the trees to make way. But Jacob was still sad and I looked up at the stars and wondered what they were and whether Andreas the little liar had found the words for them. Then I told Jacob about Lola and that I was going to marry her if she can preserve herself until I grow up but Jacob only smiled and he said I would forget her when I grew up. I know Jacob is very wise but I don't believe what he said. But when we turned into my garden we could not eat fruit because we found Kate the cook weeping under the mulberry tree and Father came out and told her she must go away, because she wanted to push the carving knife into Peti the milkman because Peti did it to Slezak's mother and he also did it to Kate, and Peti also had a wife. Peti must be very healthy because now he has three wives and has no water in his head and uncle Berti had only two wives and his head was full of water. But Mother came out and she is very kind and she patted Kate on the cheek and told her to stay and she sent Father back into the house. And then a policeman came because Kate had just scratched Peti with the carving knife and the policeman wanted Kate to go with him but Father said everything was all right and gave a cigar to the policeman and then Peti came with his head bandaged and said it was all a misunderstanding and Kate remained with us but we shall get milk elsewhere. And Father said to Peti that he would break his bones if he ever dared to come to our house again but Mother said don't be rude to the poor fellow and sent Father into the house. Then Kate went to bed weeping and Peti and the policeman left and I took Jacob to the garden gate because it was now late. And Jacob who is so wise said to me it is much better to collect stamps in peace. He said love is very unhappy always because his father told him so.

◇

... to-day when Father was eating my marrow-bone I asked him to give me money because we are collecting for Slezak in school. But Father said he had no money to throw away and I looked sad and Mother said to Father don't be rude to the child. And then they quarrelled. And when we were left alone under the mulberry-tree Mother said she would give me money but I must be nicer to Father. And I said I am very nice to him but he never talks to me. Mother said Father works for us and he is tired and we must cheer him up. All fathers must be cheered up. They all work for their wives and children and when they don't they are not happy. So I must not forget to greet Father when I see him in the morning which I always do. So I asked Mother why she married Father and she said the questions children ask and left me alone. Mother is plump and beautiful but I don't understand her. I understand Kate much better who is now very plump. But I love Mother and she gave me money for Slezak. Slezak is now back in school with us and he wanted to give me his cord which is in a tissue paper because he is grateful because I collected for him but I did not want his cord because it is horrid. Slezak is very stupid and he hit Jacob on the jaw because he said it will make him strong because the English all hit each other on the jaw which makes them strong. But Jacob always says he hates violence because his father told him so.

Slezak is also very happy because the brother his mother bore him recently died yesterday and now Slezak is again his mother's only orphan. And he asked us to come and see him because he is now in a coffin over the washing-tub and candles burn. And in the afternoon we all went to see Slezak's brother, Jacob and Andreas and Roka and I but Roka had to wait outside in the courtyard. And Slezak's brother was in a small white coffin and Slezak's mother who is our washer-woman when she has no babies gave rum to her friends who came to see her and she wanted to give rum to us too but we did not want it. So we just stared at the candles and we were silent and Jacob was sad because he remembered his mother as on Friday evenings and Andreas was very pale and he whispered something but I could not hear it. Then we all coughed because we wanted to go out and Slezak's mother thanked us for coming and thanked us for collecting money for Slezak who is only a silly bully. Then she wept and her cheeks were all very red like apples and when she wiped her tears I saw her hands were all red from washing. So we coughed again and blew our noses and went out into the courtyard because the room opens on a courtyard which is not clean. And Roka was chewing an old bone which he had found on the dustheap and we took it away from him. But Slezak only stood there leaning against the door and he looked on the ground and he forgot to hit Jacob on the jaw to make him strong which he always does.

... to-day we are very excited because Aunt Leonie arrived who is also my Mother's sister. And she married an Austrian who lives in Vienna where also lives our King Francis Joseph when he rules over the Austrians. But Aunt Leonie married long ago and now she has children and she brought one called Pamperl which sounds silly but is Austrian because the Viennese are also Austrian. Aunt Leonie married Uncle Pepi because he was beautiful and he sang songs about Vienna which is also beautiful and he was very funny and because she thought Uncle Pepi was almost a bank-director but he was only a great traveller for business and he always was travelling when Aunt Leonie had the babies. So we all sat under the mulberry-tree and Aunt Leonie wept and she had anyhow watery eyes and Father said why did she marry Uncle Pepi and she must go back to Uncle Pepi because now they had four children and then Aunt Leonie finished her cake and wept some more and Mother said to Father don't be rude to my sister and then we were left alone.

Then Mother asked Aunt Leonie what she intended to do and Aunt Leonie said the children should go for a walk. And I took Pamperl by the hand which is very soft and we walked out and Pamperl who has a sallow face and a lace collar talked to me but it was Austrian or Viennese and it sounded funny but I could not understand it. So we walked to the river and I led Pamperl through the dam where the water is very wild and I thought it was a pity the Austrians were our friends now and our King Francis Joseph rules over them also, because otherwise I would push Pamperl into the water and then Uncle Pepi and Aunt Leonie would have only three children and we would all be happier. But I hurried through the dam and I took Pamperl to where we bathe and I wanted Pamperl to bathe in the river because I thought Pamperl might drown without my help and then we should have one enemy less when the Austrians will be our enemies again, because we are only few and our enemies are many. But Pamperl shrieked and so I walked back with him to our house. And there we found Uncle Pepi who is very bald but has a lovely beard and a moustache like our King Francis Joseph but he is not so dignified because he always laughs. And Uncle Pepi followed my Aunt from Vienna because he thought now that he loved her better than Gullash and beer which he loves very much. And he took Pamperl on his knees and gave him beer and he sang a song about a Viennese cab which all Viennese sing and is also loved by our King Francis Joseph when he rules over the Austrians. Mother was sad and told Aunt Leonie that she must go back to Vienna tomorrow. And we went to bed but I slept only little because Uncle Pepi sang about the Viennese cab all night long.

... to-day Slezak hit the butcher's son on the jaw who called him a bastard and then Slezak hit him again and Jacob asked Slezak whether he had learnt this from his Reverend Father and Jesus Christ our Saviour because Jacob hates violence and wants us all to collect stamps in peace. Slezak hit Jacob on the jaw but only to make him strong. But I stood up for Slezak because he was called a bastard which was true but not very beautiful. And Slezak wanted to give me his cord again but I did not want it because it is horrid. Then he wanted to give me holy pictures which he got from our Reverend Father because Slezak has very good marks in religion and the Reverend Father calls him a lost sheep who is now back with the flock. And the holy picture was very beautiful and the Virgin Mary on it looked like Lola whom I love only Lola has no baby. But I did not take the holy picture because if there is a God there is only one who hates the priests because my Father told me so. Then Slezak who is very grateful because I have also collected money for him said he would tell me a secret but I must swear not to tell it to anybody else. And he told me there is a house in our village which stands alone in a meadow and which is always shut with green shutters during the day because the ladies who live there always sleep during the day and only wake up at night. And they are all very beautiful because they are all painted and perfumed and he knows one lady called Amanta who looks like the Virgin Mary on the picture only she is not a virgin although she has no baby. And they have many visitors during the night but they are all men who want no babies. And I thought Slezak was lying to me and I told him so but Slezak swore it was all true because his mother is washing for the ladies who sleep during the day and it is all very beautiful and full of mirrors and he went one day with his mother to help with the laundry and his mother told him not to look but he looked very much. And now I remembered I had seen the house with the green shutters alone in the meadow but I did not know ladies lived there who were sleeping during the day just like in the fairy-tales. So when I went home from school I asked mother to come with me for a walk and she was happy because I always go with Jacob and Andreas. And then I wanted to go where the house with the green shutters stood and we saw it standing alone in the meadow. I told Mother to look what a beautiful house it was. But she blushed and said it was an ugly house and I must never go near it. And I said I thought it was the house of the Sleeping Beauty which I read in the tales. But Mother said this was a very bad house and I must promise never to go near it. Mother is plump and very beautiful but she never answers my questions. Kate the cook always answers them. So I went to the kitchen to ask Kate about the fairy castle which stands alone in the meadow because I also dreamt of the fairies but I can't remember.

But Peti the milkman was there although my Father will break his bones because he told him so. Peti still smells of cows but Kate our cook loves him again. He also gave me a whistle which he brought for me but I will wash it because Peti made it wet with his mouth. And Kate is now very plump and she weeps but she says she loves Peti again because the baby died which Peti did to Slezak's mother and Peti's wife has also the dry rot and she will die soon and then Peti will marry Kate. And we were all very happy and Kate gave him goose-liver. And I wanted to ask Kate about the house but I thought she would not know because she is only a cook and she cooks well but she never told me a good fairy-tale. I think I shall not ask anyone about the house standing alone in the meadow because all the people I know sleep during the night and they would know nothing about the ladies who sleep during the day.

... to-day it is almost summer and now we know already how to add up and subtract and multiply and divide and we have learnt about most of our enemies and of our glorious past and how the Austrians have always swindled us after we have so often conquered them. And we have learned many poems and I think Petöfi wrote better poems than the one about God's hat and I have learned some and I have won a prize for reading poetry. And now we sing the anthem in tune to our King who hangs on the wall. And soon school will be over and then Mother and I shall go to the Lake Balaton which is the most beautiful lake in the world where all the Hungarians go and the Jewish Hungarians live on one end and the Roman Catholic Hungarians on the other and scattered in between are the rest. But I am not very happy because Lola whom I love will marry the fat man whom I hate and she will kiss the fat man with the same mouth with which she kissed me and she will not wait for me and preserve herself. And I am sad because Grandma came and told us that Uncle Berti is now very wild and he wants to eat his collar-buttons with his breakfast and he will die because now he has more water in his head. So I went out with Roka and looked for Jacob and then we went to find Andreas to ask him to bathe with us in the Danube. Andreas lives in a big house called a villa and he sat in the garden with his mother who has very soft hands which I like. So we kissed her hands and Roka misbehaved on the flowers and we asked Andreas to come with us. And Andreas was reading a book of poems by a poet called Shelley who was also loved by our poet Petöfi. Andreas got the book to-day because he only wants to read poetry and he said Shelley died very young and he was English but very frail, but that was perhaps because they did not hit him on the jaw to make him strong. And the father of Andreas came out into the garden and smiled at us because he is very kind and he builds houses for others and when you do that you can build some for yourself. So we all went to the Danube where it smells but it is safe and we went into the water holding Roka's neck. And I said the Danube was very beautiful this afternoon because the water was blue and green and when the leather did not stink the acacia-trees smelt sweet on the banks. But Andreas says the Danube is not very beautiful and the people who love along the Danube are all very unhappy. Andreas has travelled much already because his father takes him along with him and he has seen high mountains and he told us stories of beautiful lakes in Italy. So I was sad that the Danube was not very beautiful and we scampered back to the riverside to dry in the grass and I told Andreas to move away because we must love only girls because Kate the cook told me so. And Jacob was also very sad because his father has a bad heart and that is why he has rings under his eyes and I thought of Lola who was not faithful to me. And we all ate grass and lay on our bellies and I said when we grow up we shall also have rings under our eyes and bad hearts and perhaps water in our heads like uncle Berti and how nice it would be to preserve ourselves. And Andreas rolled on his back and looked into the clouds which were swimming over the sky and he said everything passes away only the clouds pass and stay and I thought this was very beautiful and I could easily have told it to Lola and she would have kissed me on the mouth but now she has married the fat man who is not so poetic as we are. And I also thought this Danube river comes from Vienna where Uncle Pepi and Pamperl live and where our King Francis Joseph enjoys to hear the song of Uncle Pepi. But I got tired of thinking and I played with Roka who rolled on his back and watched Andreas who always looks into the clouds when he finds some in the sky, and I asked Andreas whether he had seen God fly out again because perhaps he said the truth after all and Andreas said he wanted to fly with the wind and hold the whole world against his heart. And he said he hated to think that one day he must die and he said there were many Gods and most of them hated us and that is why we must die. But Jacob who is very wise said that he must not say such things and there is only one God who punishes those who call him names and we must all collect stamps in peace and learn the map of the world, because his father told him so. But Andreas was not listening to him because he still watched the clouds swimming in the blue sky and I pinched him to wake him up and then he rose and we all walked home very silent and said no more.

PRISONER OF THE SAND

ANTOINE DE SAINT EXUPERY

We had been flying for three hours. A brightness that seemed to me a glare spurted on the starboard side. I stared. A streamer of light which I had hitherto not noticed was fluttering from a lamp at the tip of the wing. It was an intermittent glow, now brilliant, now dim. It told me that I had flown into a cloud, and it was on the cloud that the lamp was reflected.

I was nearing the landmarks upon which I had counted; a clear sky would have helped a lot. The wing shone bright under the halo. The light steadied itself, became fixed, and then began to radiate in the form of a bouquet of pink blossoms. Great eddies of air were swinging me to and fro. I was navigating somewhere in the belly of a cumulus whose thickness I could not guess. I rose to seventy-five hundred feet and was still in it. Down again to three thousand, and the bouquet of flowers was still with me, motionless and growing brighter.

Well, there it was and there was nothing to do about it I would think of something else, and wait to get clear of it. Just the same, I did not like this sinister glitter of a one-eyed grog-shop.

'Let me think,' I said to myself. 'I am bouncing round a bit, but there's nothing abnormal about that. I've been bumped all the way, despite a clear sky and plenty of ceiling. The wind has not died down, and I must be doing better than the 190 mph I counted on.' This was about as far as I could get. Oh, well, when I got through the cloud-bank I would try to take my bearings.

Out of it we flew. The bouquet suddenly vanished, letting me know I was in the clear again. I stared ahead and saw, if one can speak of 'seeing' space, a narrow valley of sky and the wall of the next cumulus. Already the bouquet was coming to life again. I was free of that viscous mess from time to time but only for a few seconds each time. After three and a half hours of flying it began to get on my nerves. If I had made the time I imagined, we were certainly approaching the Nile. With a little luck I might be able to spot the river through the rifts, but they were getting rare. I dared not come down, for if I was actually slower than I thought, I was still over high-lying country.

Thus far I was entirely without anxiety; my only fear was that I might presently be wasting time. I decided that I would take things easy until I had flown four and a quarter hours: after that, even in a dead calm (which was highly unlikely) I should have crossed the Nile. When I reached the fringes of the cloud-bank the bouquet winked on and off more and more swiftly and then suddenly went out. Decidedly, I did not like these dot-and-dash messages from the demons of the night.

A green star appeared ahead of me, flashing like a lighthouse. Was it a lighthouse? or really a star? I took no pleasure from this supernatural gleam, this star the Magi might have seen, this dangerous decoy.

Prévot, meanwhile, had waked up and turned his electric torch on the engine dials. I waved him off, him and his torch. We had just sailed into the clear between two clouds and I was busy staring below. Prévot went back to sleep. The gap in the clouds was no help; there was nothing below.

Four hours and five minutes in the air. Prévot awoke and sat down beside me.

'I'll bet we're near Cairo,' he said.

'We must be.'

'What's that? A star? or is it a lighthouse?'

I had throttled the engine down a little. This, probably, was what had awakened Prévot. He is sensitive to all the variations of sound in flight.

I began a slow descent, intending to slip under the mass of clouds. Meanwhile I had had a look at my map. One thing was sure—the land below me lay at sea level, and there was no risk of conking against a hill. Down I went, flying due north so that the lights of the cities would strike square into my windows. I must have overflown them, and should therefore see them on my left.

Now I was flying below the cumulus. But alongside was another cloud hanging lower down on the left. I swerved so as not to be caught in its net, and headed north-northeast. This second cloud-bank certainly went down a long way, for it blocked my view of the horizon. I dared not give up any more altitude. My altimeter registered 1200 feet, but I had no notion of the atmospheric pressure here. Prévot leaned towards me and I shouted to him, 'I'm going out to sea, I'd rather come down on it than risk a crash here.'

As a matter of fact, there was nothing to prove that we had not drifted over the sea already. Below that cloud-bank visibility was exactly nil. I hugged my window, trying to read below me, to discover flares, signs of life. I was a man raking dead ashes, trying in vain to retrieve the flame of life in a hearth.

'A lighthouse!'

Both of us spied it at the same moment, that winking decoy! What madness! Where was that phantom light, that invention of the night? For at the very second when Prévot and I leaned forward to pick it out of the air where it had glittered nine hundred feet below our winds, suddenly, at that very instant...

'Oh!'

I am quite sure that this was all I said. I am quite sure that all I felt was a terrific crash that rocked our world to its foundations. We had crashed against the earth at a hundred and seventy miles an hour. I am quite sure that in the split second that followed, all I expected was the great flash of ruddy light of the explosion in which Prévot and I were to be blown up together. Neither he nor I had felt the least emotion of any kind. All I could observe in myself was an extraordinary tense feeling of expectancy, the expectancy of that resplendent star in which we were to vanish within the second.

But there was no ruddy star. Instead there was a sort of earthquake that splintered our cabin, ripped away the windows, blew sheets of metal hurtling through space a hundred yards away, and filled our very entrails with its roar. The ship quivered like a knife-blade thrown from a distance into a block of oak, and its anger mashed us as if we were so much pulp.

One second, two seconds passed, and the plane still quivered while I waited with a grotesque impatience for the forces within it to burst it like a bomb. But the subterranean quakings went on without a climax of eruption while I marvelled uncomprehendingly at its invisible travail. I was baffled by the quaking, the anger, the interminable postponement. Five seconds passed; six seconds. And suddenly we were seized by a spinning motion, a shock that jerked our cigarettes out of the window, pulverised the starboard wing—and then nothing, nothing but a frozen immobility. I shouted to Prévot:

'Jump!'

And in that instant he cried out:

'Fire!'

We dove together through the wrecked window and found ourselves standing side by side, sixty feet from the plane. I said:

'Are you hurt?'

He answered:

'Not a bit.'

But he was rubbing his knee.

'Better run your hands over yourself,' I said; 'move about a bit. Sure no bones are broken?'

He answered:

'I'm all right. It's that emergency pump.'

Emergency pump! I was sure he was going to keel over any minute and split open from head to navel there before my eyes. But he kept repeating with a glassy stare:

'That pump, that emergency pump.'

He's out of his head, I thought. He'll start dancing in a minute.

Finally he stopped staring at the plane—which had not gone up in flames—and stared at me instead. And he said again:

'I'm all right. It's that emergency pump. It got me in the knee.'

Why we were not blown up, I do not know. I switched on my electric torch and went back over the furrow in the ground traced by the plane. Two hundred and fifty yards from where we stopped the ship had begun to shed the twisted iron and sheet-metal that spattered the sand the length of her traces. We were to see, when day came, that we had run almost tangentially into a gentle slope at the top of a barren plateau. At the point of impact there was a hole in the sand that looked as if it had been made by a plough. Maintaining an even keel, the plane had run its course with the fury and the tail-lashings of a reptile gliding on its belly at the rate of a hundred and seventy miles an hour. We owed our lives to the fact that this desert was surfaced with round black pebbles which had rolled over and over like ballbearings beneath us. They must have rained upward to the heavens as we shot through them.

Prévot disconnected the batteries for fear of fire by short-circuit. I leaned against the motor and turned the situation over in my mind. I had been flying high for four hours and a quarter, possibly with a thirty-mile following wind. I had been jolted a good deal. If the wind had changed since the weather people forecast it, I was unable to say into what quarter it had veered. All I could make out was that we had crashed in an empty square two hundred and fifty miles on each side.

Prévot came up and sat down beside me.

'I can't believe that we're alive,' he said.

I said nothing. Even that thought could not cheer me. A germ of an idea was at work in my mind and was already bothering me. Telling Prévot to switch on his torch as a landmark, I walked straight out, scrutinising the ground in the light of my own torch as I went.

I went forward slowly, swung round in a wide arc, and changed direction a number of times. I kept my eyes fixed on the ground like a man hunting a lost ring.

Only a little while before I had been straining just as hard to see a gleam of light from the air. Through the darkness I went, bowed over the travelling disk of white light. 'Just as I thought,' I said to myself, and I went slowly back to the plane. I sat down beside the cabin and ruminated. I had been looking for a reason to hope and had failed to find it. I had been looking for a sign of life, and no sign of life had appeared.

'Prévot, I couldn't find a single blade of grass.'

Prévot said nothing, and I was not sure he had understood. Well, we could talk about it again when the curtain arose at dawn. Meanwhile I was dead tired and all I could think was, 'Two hundred and fifty miles more or less in the desert.'

Suddenly I jumped to my feet. 'Water!' I said.

Gas tanks and oil tanks were smashed in. So was our supply of drinking-water. The sand had drunk everything. We found a pint of coffee in a battered thermos flask and half a pint of white wine in another. We filtered both, and poured them into one flask. There were some grapes, too, and a single orange. Meanwhile I was computing: 'All this will last us five hours of tramping in the sun.'

We crawled into the cabin and waited for dawn. I stretched out, and as I settled down to sleep I took stock of our situation. We didn't know where we were; we had less than a quart of liquid between us; if we were not too far off the Benghazi-Cairo lane we should be found in a week, and that would be too late. Yet it was the best we could hope for. If, on the other hand, we had drifted off our course, we shouldn't be found in six months. One thing was sure—we could not count on being picked up by a plane; the men who came out for us would have two thousand miles to cover.

'You know, it's a shame,' Prévot said suddenly.

'What's a shame?'

'That we didn't crash properly and have it over with.'

It seemed pretty early to be throwing in one's hand. Prévot and I pulled ourselves together. There was still a chance, slender as it was, that we might be saved miraculously by a plane. On the other hand, we couldn't stay here and perhaps miss a near-by oasis. We would walk all day and come back to the plane before dark. And before going off we would write our plan in huge letters in the sand.

With this I curled up and settled down to sleep. I was happy to go to sleep. My weariness wrapped me round like a multiple presence. I was not alone in the desert: my drowsiness was peopled with voices and memories and whispered confidences. I was not yet thirsty; I felt strong; and I surrendered myself to sleep as to an aimless journey. Reality lost ground before the advance of dreams.

Ah, but things were different when I awoke!

In times past I have loved the Sahara. I have spent nights alone in the path of marauding tribes and have waked up with untroubled mind in the golden emptiness of the desert where the wind like a sea had raised sandwaves upon its surface. Asleep under the wing of my plane I have looked forward with confidence to being rescued next day. But this was not the Sahara!

Prévot and I walked along the slopes of rolling mounds. The ground was sand covered over with a single layer of shining black pebbles. They gleamed like metal scales and all the domes about us shone like coats of mail. We had dropped down into a mineral world and were hemmed in by iron hills.

When we reached the top of the first crest we saw in the distance another just like it, black and gleaming. As we walked we scraped the ground with our boots, marking a trail over which to return to the plane. We went forward with the sun in our eyes. It was not logical to go due east like this, for everything—the weather reports, the duration of the flight—had made it plain that we had crossed the Nile. But I had started tentatively towards the west and had felt a vague foreboding I could not explain to myself. So I had put off the west till tomorrow, In the same way, provisionally, I had given up going north, though that led to the sea.

Three days later, when scourged by thirst into abandoning the plane and walking straight on until we dropped in our tracks, it was still eastward that we tramped. More precisely, we walked east-northeast. And this too was in defiance of all reason and even of all hope. Yet after we had been rescued we discovered that if we had gone in any other direction we should have been lost.

Northward, we should never have had the endurance to reach the sea. And absurd as it may appear, it seems to me now, since I had no other motive, that I must have chosen the east simply because it was by going eastward that Guillaumet had been saved in the Andes, after I had hunted for him everywhere. In a confused way the east had become for me the direction of life.

We walked on for five hours and then the landscape changed. A river of sand seemed to be running through a valley, and we followed this river-bed, taking long strides in order to cover as much ground as possible and get back to the plane before night fell, if our march was in vain. Suddenly I stopped.

'Prévot!'

'What's up?'

'Our tracks!'

How long was it since we had forgotten to leave a wake behind us? We had to find it or die.

We went back, bearing to the right. When we had gone back far enough we would make a right angle to the left and eventually intersect our tracks where we had still remembered to mark them.

This we did and were off again. The heat rose and with it came the mirages. But these were still the commonplace kind—sheets of water that materialised and then vanished as we neared them. We decided to cross the valley of sand and climb the highest dome in order to look round the horizon. This was after six hours of march in which, striding along, we must have covered twenty miles.

When we had struggled up to the top of the black hump we sat down and looked at each other. At our feet lay our valley of sand, opening into a desert of sand whose dazzling brightness seared our eyes. As far as the eye could see lay empty space. But in that space the play of light created mirages which, this time, were of a disturbing kind, fortresses and minarets, angular geometric hulks. I could see also a black mass that pretended to be vegetation, overhung by the last of those clouds that dissolve during the day only to return at night. This mass of vegetation was the shadow of a cumulus.

It was no good going on. The experiment was a failure. We would have to go back to our plane, to that red and white beacon which, perhaps, would be picked out by a flyer. I was not staking great hopes on a rescue party, but it did seem to me our last chance of salvation. In any case, we had to get back to our few drops of liquid, for our throats were parched. We were imprisoned in this iron circle, captives of the curt dictatorship of thirst.

And yet, how hard it was to turn back when there was a chance that we might be on the road to life! Beyond the mirages the horizon was perhaps rich in veritable treasures, in meadows and runnels of sweet water. I knew I was doing the right thing by returning to the plane, and yet as I swung round and started back I was filled with portents of disaster.

We were resting on the ground beside the plane. Nearly forty miles of wandering this day. The last drop of liquid had been drained. No sign of life had appeared to the east. No plane had soared overhead. How long should we be able to hold out? Already our thirst was terrible.

We had built up a great pyre out of its of the splintered wing. Our gasoline was ready, and we had flung on the heap sheets of metal whose magnesium coating would burn with a hard white flame. We were waiting now for night to come down before we lighted our conflagration. But where were there men to see it?

Night fell and the flames rose. Prayerfully we watched our mute and radiant fanion mount resplendent into the night. As I looked I said to myself that this message was not only a cry for help, it was fraught also with a great deal of love. We were begging for water, but we were also begging the communion of human society. Only man can create fire: let another flame light up the night; let man answer man!

I was haunted by a vision of my wife's eyes under the halo of her hat. Of her face I could see only the eyes, questioning me, looking at me yearningly. I am answering, answering with all my strength! What flame could leap higher than this that darts up into the night from my heart?

What I could do, I have done. What we could do, we have done. Nearly forty miles, almost without a drop to drink. Now there was no water left. Was it our fault that we could wait no longer? Suppose we had sat quietly by the plane, taking suck at the mouths of our water-bottles? But from the moment I breathed in the moist bottom of the tin cup, a clock had started up in me.

From the second when I had sucked up the last drop, I had begun to slip downhill. Could I help it if time like a river was carrying me away? Prévot was weeping. I tapped him on the shoulder and said, to console him:

'If we're done for we're done for, and that's all there is to it.'

He said:

'Do you think it's me I'm bawling about?'

I might have known it. It was evident enough. Nothing is unbearable. Tomorrow, and the day after, I should learn that nothing was really unbearable. I had never really believed in torture. Reading Poe as a kid, I had already said as much to myself. Once, jammed in the cabin of a plane, I thought I was going to drown; and I had not suffered much. Several times it had seemed to me that the final smash-up was coming, and I don't remember that I thought of it as a cosmic event. And I didn't believe this was going to be agonising either. There will be time tomorrow to find out stranger things about it. Meanwhile, God knows that despite the bonfire I had decidedly given up hope that our cries would be heard by the world.

'Do you think it's me...' There you have what is truly unbearable! Every time I saw those yearning eyes it was as if a flame were searing me. They were like a scream for help, like the flares of a sinking ship. I felt that I should not sit idly by: I should jump up and run—anywhere! straight ahead of me!

What a strange reversal of rôles! But I have always thought it would be like this. Still, I needed Prévot beside me to be quite sure of it. Prévot was a level-headed fellow. He loved life. And yet Prévot no more than I was wringing his hands at the sight of death the way we are told men do. But there did exist something that he could not bear any more than I could. I was perfectly ready to fall asleep, whether for a night or for eternity. If I did fall asleep, I could not even know whether it was for the one or for the other. And the peace of sleep! But that cry that would be sent up at home, that great wail of desolation—that was what I could not bear. I could not stand idly by and look on at that disaster. Each second of silence drove the knife deeper into someone I loved. At the thought, a blind rage surged up in me. Why do these chains bind me and prevent me from rescuing those who are drowning? Why does our conflagration not carry our cry to the ends of the world? Hear me, you out here! Patience. We are coming to save you.

The magnesium had been licked off and the metal was glowing red. There was left only a heap of embers round which we crouched to warm ourselves. Our flaming call had spent itself. Had it set anything in the world in motion? I knew well enough that it hadn't. Here was a prayer that had of necessity gone unheard.

That was that.

I ought to get some sleep.

At daybreak I took a rag and mopped up a little dew on the wings. The mixture of water and paint and oil yielded a spoonful of nauseating liquid which we sipped because it would at least moisten our lips. After this banquet Prévot said:

'Thank God we've got a gun.'

Instantly I became furious and turned on him with an aggressiveness which I regretted directly I felt it. There was nothing I should have loathed more at that moment than a gush of sentimentality. I am so made that I have to believe that everything is simple. Birth is simple. Growing up is simple. And dying of thirst is simple. I watched Prévot out of the corner of my eye, ready to wound his feelings, if that was necessary to shut him up.

But Prévot had spoken without emotion. He had been discussing a matter of hygiene, and might have said in the same tone, 'We ought to wash our hands.' That being so, we were agreed. Indeed already yesterday, my eye falling by chance on the leather holster, the same thought had crossed my mind, and with me too it had been a reasonable reflex, not an emotional one. Pathos resides in social man, not in the individual; what was pathetic was our powerlessness to reassure those for whom we were responsible, not what we might do with the gun.

There was still no sign that we were being sought; or rather they were doubtless hunting for us elsewhere, probably in Arabia. We were to hear no sound of plane until the day after we had abandoned our own. And if ships did pass overhead, what could that mean to us? What could they see in us except two black dots among the thousand shadowy dots in the desert? Absurd to think of being distinguishable from them. None of the reflections that might be attributed to me on the score of this torture would be true. I should not feel in the least tortured. The aerial rescue party would seem to me, each time I sighted one, to be moving through a universe that was not mine. When searchers have to cover two thousand miles of territory, it takes them a good two weeks to spot a plane in the desert from the sky.

They were probably looking for us all along the line from Tripoli to Persia. And still, with all this, I clung to the slim chance that they might pick us out. Was that not our only chance of being saved? I changed my tactics, determining to go reconnoitering by myself. Prévot would get another bonfire together and kindle it in the event that visitors showed up. But we were to have no callers that day.

So off I went without knowing whether or not I should have the stamina to come back. I remembered what I knew about this

Libyan desert. When, in the Sahara, humidity is still at forty per cent of saturation, it is only eighteen here in Libya. Life here evaporates like a vapour. Bedouins, explorers, and colonial officers all tell us that a man may go nineteen hours without water. Thereafter his eyes fill with light, and that marks the beginning of the end. The progress made by thirst is swift and terrible. But this northeast wind, this abnormal wind that had blown us out off our course and had marooned us on this plateau, was now prolonging our lives. What was the length of the reprieve it would grant us before our eyes began to fill with light? I went forward with the feeling of a man canoeing in mid-ocean.

I will admit that at daybreak this landscape seemed to me less infernal, and that I began my walk with my hands in my pockets, like a tramp on a highroad. The evening before we had set snares at the mouths of certain mysterious burrows in the ground, and the poacher in me was on the alert. I went first to have a look at our traps. They were empty.

Well, this meant that I should not be drinking blood today; and indeed I hadn't expected to. But though I was not disappointed, my curiosity was aroused. What was there in the desert for these animals to live on? These were certainly the holes of fennecs, a long-eared carnivorous sand-box the size of a rabbit. I spotted the tracks made by one of them, and gave way to the impulse to follow them. They led to a narrow stream of sand where each footprint was plainly outlined and where I marvelled at the pretty palm formed by the three toes spread fanwise on the sand.

I could imagine my little friend trotting blithely along at dawn and licking the dew off the rocks. Here the tracks were wider apart: my fennec had broken into a run. And now I see that a companion has joined him and they have trotted on side by side. These signs of a morning stroll gave me a strange thrill. They were signs of life, and I loved them for that. I almost forgot that I was thirsty.

Finally I came to the pasture-ground of my foxes. Here, every hundred yards or so, I saw sticking up out of the sand a small dry shrub, its twigs heavy with little golden snails. The fennec came here at dawn to do his marketing. And here I was able to observe another of nature's mysteries.

My fennec did not stop at all the shrubs. There were some weighed down with snails which he disdained. Obviously he avoided them with some wariness. Others he stopped at but did not strip of all they bore. He must have picked out two or three shells and then gone on to another restaurant. What was he up to? Was he nurseryman to the snails, encouraging their reproduction by refraining from exhausting the stock on a given shrub, or a given twig? Or was he amusing himself by delaying repletion, putting off satiety in order to enhance the pleasure he took from his morning stroll?

The tracks led me back to the hole in which he lived. Doubtless my fennec crouched below, listening to me and startled by the crunching of my footsteps. I said to him:

'Fox, my little fox, I'm done for; but somehow that doesn't prevent me from taking an interest in your mood.'

And there I stayed a bit, ruminating and telling myself that a man was able to adapt himself to anything. The notion that he is to die in thirty years has probably never spoiled any man's fun. Thirty years ... or thirty days: it's all a mater of perspective.

Only, you have to be able to put certain visions out of your mind.

I went on, finally, and the time came when, along with my weariness, something in me began to change. If those were not mirages, I was inventing them.

'Hi! Hi! there!'

I shouted and waved my arms, but the man I had seen waving at me turned out to be a black rock. Everything in the desert had grown animate. I stopped to waken a sleeping Bedouin and he turned into the trunk of a black tree. A tree-trunk? Here in the desert? I was amazed and bent over to lift a broken bough. It was solid marble.

Straightening up I looked round and saw more black marble. An antediluvian forest littered the ground with its broken tree-tops. How many thousand years ago, under what hurricane of the time of Genesis, had this cathedral of wood crumbled in this spot? Countless centuries had rolled these fragments of giant pillars at my feet, polished them like steel, petrified and vitrified them and induced them with the colour of jet.

I could distinguish the knots in their branches, the twistings of their once living boughs, could count the rings of life in them. This forest had rustled with birds and been filled with music that now was struck by doom and frozen into salt. And all this was hostile to me. Blacker than the chain-mail of the hummocks, these solemn derelicts rejected me. What had I, a living man, to do with this incorruptible stone? Perishable as I was, I whose body was to crumble into dust, what place had I in this eternity?

Since yesterday I had walked nearly fifty miles. This dizziness that I felt came doubtless from my thirst. Or from the sun. It glittered on these hulks until they shone as if smeared with oil. It blazed down on this universal carapace. Sand and fox had no life here. This world was a gigantic anvil upon which the sun beat down. I strode across this anvil and at my temples I could feel the hammer-strokes of the sun.

'Hi! Hi, there!' I called out.

'There is nothing there,' I told myself. 'Take it easy. You are delirious.'

I had to talk to myself aloud, had to bring myself to reason. It was hard for me to reject what I was seeing, hard not to run towards that caravan plodding on the horizon. There! Do you see it?

'Fool! You know very well that you are inventing it.'

'You mean that nothing in the world is real?'

Nothing in the world is real if that cross which I see ten miles off on the top of a hill is not real. Or is it a lighthouse? No, the sea does not lie in that direction. Then it must be a cross.

I had spent the night studying my map—but uselessly, since I did not know my position. Still, I had scrutinised all the signs that marked the marvellous presence of man. And somewhere on the map I had seen a little circle surmounted by just such a cross. I had glanced down at the legend to get an explanation of the symbol and had read: 'Religious institution.'

Close to the cross there had been a black dot. Again I had run my finger down the legend and had read: 'Permanent well.' My heart had jumped and I had repeated the legend aloud: 'Permanent well, permanent well.' What were all of Ali Baba's treasures compared with a permanent well? A little farther on were two white circles. 'Temporary wells,' the legend said. Not quite so exciting. And round about them was nothing... unless it was the blankness of despair.

But this must be my 'religious institutions'! The monks must certainly have planted a great cross on the hill expressly for men in our plight! All I had to do was to walk across to them. I should be taken in by those Dominicans....

'But there are only Coptic monasteries in Libya!' I told myself.

... by those learned Dominicans. They have a great cool kitchen with red tiles, and out in the courtyard a marvellous rusted pump. Beneath the rusted pump; beneath the rusted pump... you've guessed it!... beneath the rusted pump is dug the permanent well! Ah, what rejoicing when I ring at their gate, when I get my hands on the rope of the great bell.

'Madman! You are describing a house in Provence; and what's more, the house has no bell!'

...on the rope of the great bell. The porter will raise his arms to Heaven and cry out, 'You are the messenger of the Lord!' and he will call aloud to all the monks. They will pour out of the monastery. They will welcome me with a great feast, as if I were the Prodigal Son. They will lead me to the kitchen and will say to me, 'One moment, my son one moment. We'll just be off to the permanent well.' And I shall be trembling with happiness.

No, no! I will *not* weep just because there happens to be no cross on the hill.

The treasures of the west turned out to be mere illusion. I have veered due north. At least the north is filled with the sound of the sea.

Over the hilltop. Look there, at the horizon! The most beautiful city in the world!

'You know perfectly well that is a mirage.'

Of course I know it is a mirage! Am I the sort of man who can be fooled? But what if I *want* to go after that mirage? Suppose I enjoy indulging my hope? Suppose it suits me to love that crenelated town all beflagged with sunlight? What if I choose to walk straight ahead on light feet—for you must know that I have dropped my weariness behind me, I am happy now.... Prévot and his gun! Don't make me laugh! I prefer my drunkenness. I am drunk. I am dying of thirst.

It took the twilight to sober me. Suddenly I stopped, appalled to think how far I was from our base. In the twilight the mirage was dying. The horizon had stripped itself of its pomp, its palaces, its priestly vestments. It was the old desert horizon again.

'A fine day's work you've done! Night will overtake you. You won't be able to go on before daybreak, and by that time your tracks will have been blown away and you'll be properly nowhere.'

In that case I may as well walk straight on. Why turn back? Why should I bring my ship round when I may find the sea straight ahead of me?

'When did you catch a glimpse of the sea? What makes you think you could walk that far? Meanwhile there's Prévot watching for you beside the *Simoon*. He may have been picked up by a caravan, for all you know.'

Very good. I'll go back. But first I want to call out for help.

'Hi! Hi!'

By God! You can't tell me this planet is not inhabited. Where are its men?

'Hi! Hi!'

I was hoarse. My voice was gone. I knew it was ridiculous to croak like this, but—one more try:

'Hi! Hi!'

And I turned back.

I had been walking two hours when I saw the flames of the bonfire that Prévot, frightened by my long absence, had sent up. They mattered very little to me now.

Another hour of trudging. Five hundred yards away. A hundred yards. Fifty yards.

Good Lord!'

Amazement stopped me in my tracks. Joy surged up and filled my heart with its violence. In the firelight stood Prévot, talking to two Arabs who were leaning against the motor. He had not noticed me, for he was too full of his own joy. If only I had sat still and waited with him! I should have been saved already. Exultantly I called out:

'Hi! Hi!'

The two Bedouins gave a start and stared at me. Prévot left them standing and came forward to meet me. I opened my arms to him. He caught me by the elbow. Did he think I was keeling over? I said:

'At last, eh?'

'What do you mean?'

'The Arabs!'

'What Arabs?'

'Those Arabs there, with you.'

Prévot looked at me queerly, and when he spoke I felt as if he was very reluctantly confiding a great secret to me:

'There are no Arabs here.'

This time I know I am going to cry.

A man can go nineteen hours without water, and what have we drunk since last night? A few drops of dew at dawn. But the northeast wind is still blowing, still slowing up the process of our evaporation. To it, also, we owe the continued accumulation of high clouds. If only they would drift straight overhead and break into rain! But it never rains in the desert.

'Look here, Prévot. Let's rip up one of the parachutes and spread the sections out on the ground, weighed down with stones. If the wind stays in the same quarter till morning, they'll catch the dew and we can wring them out into one of the tanks.'

We spread six triangular sections of parachute under the stars, and Prévot unhooked a fuel tank. This was as much as we could do for ourselves till dawn. But, miracle of miracles! Prévot had come upon an orange while working over the tank. We share it, and though it was little enough to men who could have used a few gallons of sweet water, still I was overcome with relief.

Stretched out beside the fire I looked at the glowing fruit and said to myself that men did not know what an orange was. 'Here we are, condemned to death,' I said the myself, 'and still the certainty of dying cannot compare with the pleasure I am feeling. The joy I take from this half of an orange which I am holding in my hand is one of the greatest joys I have ever known.'

I lay flat on my back, sucking my orange and counting the shooting stars. Here I was, for one minute infinitely happy. 'Nobody can know anything of the world in which the individual moves and has his being,' I reflected. 'There is no guessing it. Only the man locked up in it can know what it is.'

For the first time I understood the cigarette and glass of rum that are handed to the criminal about to be executed. I used to think that for a man to accept these wretched gifts at the foot of the gallows was beneath human dignity. Now I was learning that he took pleasure from them. People thought him courageous when he smiled as he smoked or drank. I knew now that he smiled because the taste gave him pleasure. People could not see that his perspective had changed, and that for him the last hour of his life was a life in itself.

We collected an enormous quantity of water—perhaps as much as two quarts. Never again would we be thirsty! We were saved; we had a liquid to drink!

I dipped my tin cup into the tank and brought up a beautifully yellow-green liquid the first mouthful of which nauseated me so that despite my thirst I had to catch my breath before swallowing it. I would have swallowed mud, I swear; but this taste of poisonous metal cut keener than thirst.

I glanced at Prévot and saw him going round and round with his eyes fixed to the ground as if looking for something. Suddenly he leaned forward and began to vomit without interrupting his spinning. Half a minute later it was my turn. I was seized by such convulsions that I went down on my knees and dug my fingers into the sand while I puked. Neither of us spoke, and for a quarter of an hour we remained thus shaken, bringing up nothing but a little bile.

After a time it passed and all I felt was a vague, distant nausea. But our last hope had fled. Whether our bad luck was due to a sizing on the parachute or to the magnesium lining of the tank, I never found out. Certain it was that we needed either another set of clothes or another receptacle.

Well, it was broad daylight and time we were on our way. This time we should strike out as fast as we could, leave this cursed plateau, and tramp till we dropped in our tracks. That was what Guillaumet had done in the Andes. I had been thinking of him all the day before and had determined to follow his example. I should do violence to the pilot's unwritten law, which is to stick by the ship; but I was sure no one would be along to look for us here.

Once again we discovered that it was not we who were shipwrecked, not we but those who were waiting for news of us, those who were alarmed by our silence, were already torn with grief by some atrocious and fantastic report. We could not but strive towards them. Guillaumet had done it, had scrambled towards his lost ones. To do so is a universal impulse.

'If I were alone in the world,' Prevot said, 'I'd lie down right here. Damned if I wouldn't.'

East-northeast we tramped. If we had in fact crossed the Nile, each step was leading us deeper and deeper into the desert.

I don't remember anything about that day. I remember only my haste. I was hurrying desperately towards something—towards some finality. I remember also that I walked with my eyes to the ground, for the mirages were more than I could bear. From time to time we would correct our course by the compass, and now and again we would lie down to catch our breath. I remember having flung away my waterproof, which I had held on to as covering for the night. That is as much as I recall about the day. Of what happened when the chill of evening came, I remember more. But during the day I had simply turned to sand and was a being without mind.

When the sun set we decided to make camp. Oh, I knew as well as anybody that we should push on, that this one waterless night would finish us off. But we had brought along the bits of parachute, and if the poison was not in the sizing, we might get a sip of water next morning. Once again we spread our trap for the dew under the stars.

But the sky in the north was cloudless. The wind no longer had the same taste on the lip. It had moved into another quarter. Something was rustling against us, but this time it seemed to be the desert itself. The wild beast was stalking us, had us in its power. I could feel its breath in my face, could feel it lick my face and hands. Suppose I walked on: at the best I could do five or six miles more. Remember that in three days I had covered one hundred miles, practically without water.

And then, just as we stopped, Prévot said:

'I swear to you I see a lake!'

'You're crazy.'

'Have you ever heard of a mirage after sunset?' he challenged.

I didn't seem able to answer him. I had long ago given up believing my own eyes. Perhaps it was not a mirage; but in that case it was a hallucination. How could Prévot go on believing? But he was stubborn about it.

'It's only twenty minutes off. I'll go have a look.'

His mulishness got on my nerves.

'Go ahead!' I shouted. 'Take your little constitutional. Nothing better for a man. But let me tell you, if your lake exists it is salt. And whether it's salt or not, it's a devil of a way off. And besides, there is no damned lake!'

Prévot was already on his way, his eyes glassy. I knew the strength of these irresistible obsessions. I was thinking: 'There are somnambulists who walk straight into locomotives.' And I knew that Prévot would not come back. He would be seized by the vertigo of empty space and would be unable to turn back. And then he would keel over. He somewhere, and I somewhere else. Not that it was important.

Thinking thus, it struck me that this mood of resignation was doing me no good. Once when I was half drowned I had let myself go like this. Lying now flat on my face on the stony ground, I took this occasion to write a letter for posthumous delivery. It gave me a chance, also, to take stock of myself again. I tried to bring up a little saliva: how long was it since I had spit? No saliva. If I kept my mouth closed, a kind of glue sealed my lips together. It dried on the outside of the lips and formed a hard crust. However, I found I was still able to swallow, and I bethought me that I was still not seeing a blinding light in my eyes. Once

I was treated to that radiant spectacle I might know that the end was a couple of hours away.

Night fell. The moon had swollen since I last saw it. Prévot was still not back. I stretched out on my back and turned these few data over in my mind. A familiar impression came over me, and I tried to seize it. I was... I was... I was at sea. I was on a ship going to South America and was stretched out, exactly like this, on the boat deck. The tip of the mast was swaying to and fro, very slowly, among the stars. That mast was missing tonight, but again I was at sea, bound for a port I was to make without raising a finger. Slave-traders had flung me on this ship.

I thought of Prévot who was still not back. Not once had I heard him complain. That was a good thing. To hear him whine would have been unbearable. Prévot was a man.

What was that! Five hundred yards ahead of me I could see the light of his lamp. He had lost his way. I had no lamp with which to signal back. I stood up and shouted, but he could not hear me.

A second lamp, and then a third! God in Heaven! It was a search party and it was me that they were hunting!

'Hi! Hi!' I shouted.

But they had not heard me. The three lamps were still signalling me.

'Tonight I am sane,' I said to myself. 'I am relaxed. I am not out of my head. Those are certainly three lamps and they are about five hundred yards off.' I stared at them and shouted again, and again I gathered that they could not hear me.

Then, for the first and only time, I was really seized with panic. I could still run, I thought. 'Wait! Wait!' I screamed. They seemed to be turning away from me, going off, hunting me elsewhere! And I stood tottering, tottering on the brink of life when there were arms out there ready to catch me! I shouted and screamed again and again.

They had heard me! An answering shout had come. I was strangling, suffocating, but I ran on, shouting as I ran, until I saw Prévot and keeled over.

When I could speak again I said: 'Whew! When I saw all those lights...'

'What lights?'

God in Heaven, it was true! He was alone!

This time I was beyond despair. I was filled with a sort of dumb fury.

'What about your lake?' I rasped.

'As fast as I moved towards it, it moved back. I walked after it for about half an hour. Then it seemed still too far away, so I came back. But I am positive, now, that it is a lake.'

'You're crazy. Absolutely crazy. Why did you do it? Tell me. Why?'

What had he done? Why had he done it? I was ready to weep with indignation, yet I scarcely knew why I was so indignant. Prévot mumbled his excuse:

'I felt I had to find some water. You... Your lips were awfully pale.'

Well! My anger died within me. I passed my hand over my forehead as if I were waking out of sleep. I was suddenly sad. I said:

'There was no mistake about it. I saw them as clearly as I see you now. Three lights there were. I tell you, Prévot, I saw them!'

Prévot made no comment.

'Well,' he said finally, 'I guess we're in a bad way.'

In this air devoid of moisture the soil is swift to give off its temperature. It was already very cold. I stood up and stamped about. But soon a violent fit of trembling came over me. My dehydrated blood was moving sluggishly and I was pierced by a freezing chill which was not merely the chill of night. My teeth were chattering and my whole body had begun to twitch. My hand shook so that I could not hold an electric torch. I who had never been sensitive to cold was about to die of cold. What a strange effect thirst can have!

Somewhere, tired of carrying it in the sun, I had left my waterproof drop. Now the wind was growing bitter and I was learning that in the desert there is no place of refuge. The desert is as smooth as marble. By day it throws no shadow; by night it hands you over naked to the wind. Not a tree, not a hedge, not a rock behind which I could seek shelter. The wind was charging me like a troop of cavalry across open country. I turned and twisted to escape it: I lay down, stood up, lay down again, and still I was exposed to its freezing lash. I had no strength to run from the assassin and under the sabre-stroke I tumbled to my knees, my head between my hands.

A little later I pieced these bits together and remembered that I had struggled to my feet and had started to walk on, shivering as I went. I had started forward wondering where I was and then I had heard Prévot. His shouting had jolted me into consciousness.

I went back towards him, still trembling from head to foot—quivering with the attack of hiccups that was convulsing my whole body. To myself I said: 'It isn't the cold. It's something else. It's the end.' The simple fact was that I hadn't enough water in me. I had tramped too far yesterday and the day before when I was off by myself, and I was dehydrated.

The thought of dying of the cold hurt me. I preferred the phantoms of my mind, the cross, the trees, the lamps. At least they would have killed me by enchantment. But to be whipped to death like a slave!...

Confound it! Down on my knees again! We had with us a little store of medicines—a hundred grammes of ninety per cent alcohol, the same of pure ether, and a small bottle of iodine. I tried to swallow a little of the ether: it was like swallowing a knife. Then I tried the alcohol: it contracted my gullet. I dug a pit in the sand, lay down in it, and flung handfuls of sand over me until all but my face was buried in it.

Prévot was able to collect a few twigs, and he lit a fire which soon burnt itself out. He wouldn't bury himself in the sand, but preferred to stamp round and round in a circle. That was foolish.

My throat stayed shut, and though I knew that was a bad sign, I felt better. I felt calm. I felt a peace that was beyond all hope. Once more, despite myself, I was journeying, trussed up on the deck of my slave-ship under the stars. It seemed to me that I was perhaps not in such a bad pass after all.

So long as I lay absolutely motionless, I no longer felt the cold. This allowed me to forget my body buried in the sand. I said to myself that I would not budge an inch, and would therefore never suffer again. As a matter of fact, we really suffer very little. Back of all these torments there is the orchestration of fatigue or of delirium, and we live on in a kind of picture-book, a slightly cruel fairy-tale.

A little while ago the wind had been after me with whip and spur, and I was running in circles like a frightened fox. After that came a time when I couldn't breathe. A great knee was crushing in my chest. A knee. I was writhing in vain to free myself from the weight of the angel who had overthrown me. There had not been a moment when I was alone in this desert. But now I have ceased to believe in my surroundings; I have withdrawn into myself, have shut my eyes, have not so much as batted an eyelid. I have the feeling that this torrent of visions is sweeping me away to a tranquil dream: so rivers cease their turbulence in the embrace of the sea.

Farewell, eyes that I loved! Do not blame me if the human body cannot go three days without water. I should never have believed that man was so truly the prisoner of the springs and freshets. I had no notion that our self-sufficiency was so circumscribed. We take it for granted that a man is able to stride straight out into the world. We believe that man is free. We never see the cord that binds him to wells and fountains, that umbilical cord by which he is tied to the womb of the world. Let man take but one step too many... and the cord snaps.

Apart from your suffering, I have no regrets. All in all, it has been a good life. If I got free of this I should start right in again. A man cannot live a decent life in cities, and I need to feel myself live. I am not thinking of aviation. The airplane is a means, not an end. One doesn't risk one's life for a plane any more than a farmer ploughs for the sake of the plough. But the airplane is a means of getting away from towns and their bookkeeping and coming to grips with reality.

Flying is a man's job and its worries are a man's worries. A pilot's business is with the wind, with the stars, with night, with sand, with the sea. He strives to outwit the forces of nature. He stares in expectancy for the coming of dawn the way a gardener awaits the coming of spring. He looks forward to port as to a promised land, and truth for him is what lives in the stars.

I have nothing to complain of. For three days I have tramped the desert, have known the pangs of thirst, have followed false scents in the sand, have pinned my faith on the dew. I have struggled to rejoin my kind, whose very existence on earth I had forgotten. These are the cares of men alive in every fibre, and I cannot help thinking them more important that the fretful choosing of a night-club in which to spend the evening. Compare the one life with the other, and all things considered this is luxury! I have no regrets, I have gambled and lost. It was all in the day's work. At least I have had the unforgettable taste of the sea on my lips.

I am not talking about living dangerously. Such words are meaningless to me. The toreador does not stir me to enthusiasm. It is not danger I love. I know what I love. It is life.

The sky seemed to me faintly bright. I drew up one arm through the sand. There was a bit of the torn parachute within reach, and I ran my hand over it. It was bone dry. Let's see. Dew falls at dawn. Here was dawn risen and no moisture on the cloth. My mind was befuddled and I heard myself say: 'There is a dry heart here, a dry heart that cannot know the relief of tears.'

I scrambled to my feet. 'We're off, Prévot,' I said. 'Our throats are still open. Get along, man!'

The wind that shrivels up a man in nineteen hours was now blowing out of the west. My gullet was not yet shut, but it was hard and painful and I could feel that there was a rasp in it. Soon that cough would begin that I had been told about and was now expecting. My tongue was becoming a nuisance. But most serious of all, I was beginning to see shining spots before my eyes. When those spots changed into flames, I should simply lie down.

The first morning hours were cool and we took advantage of them to get on at a good pace. We knew that once the sun was high there would be no more walking for us. We no longer had the right to sweat. Certainly not to stop and catch our breath. This coolness was merely the coolness of low humidity. The prevailing wind was coming from the desert, and under its soft and treacherous caress the blood was being dried out of us.

Our first day's nourishment had been a few grapes. In the next three days each of us ate half an orange and a bit of cake. If we had had anything left now, we couldn't have eaten it because we had no saliva with which to masticate it. But I had stopped being hungry. Thirsty I was, yes, and it seemed to me that I was suffering less from thirst itself than from the effects of thirst. Bullet hard. Tongue like plaster-of-Paris. A rasping in the throat. A horrible taste in the mouth.

All these sensations were new to me, and though I believed water could rid me of them, nothing in my memory associated them with water. Thirst had become more and more a disease and less and less a craving. I begin to realise that the thought of water and fruit was now less agonising than it had been. I was forgetting the radiance of the orange, just as I was forgetting the eyes under the hat-brim. Perhaps I was forgetting everything.

We had sat down after all, but it could not be for long. Nevertheless, it was impossible to go five hundred yards without our legs giving way. To stretch out on the sand would be marvellous—but it could not be.

The landscape had begun to change. Rocky places grew rarer and the sand was now firm beneath our feet. A mile ahead stood dunes and on those dunes we could see a scrubby vegetation. At least this sand was preferable to the steely surface over which we had been trudging. This was the golden desert. This might have been the Sahara. It was in a sense my country.

Two hundred yards had now become our limit, but we had determined to carry on until we reached the vegetation. Better than that we could not hope to do. A week later, when we went back over our traces in a car to have a look at the *Simoon*, I measured this last lap and found that it was just short of fifty miles. All told we had done one hundred and twenty-four miles.

The previous day I had tramped without hope. Today the word 'hope' had grown meaningless. Today we were tramping simply because we were tramping. Probably oxen work for the same reason. Yesterday I had dreamed of a paradise of orange-trees. Today I would not give a button for paradise; I did not believe oranges existed. When I thought about myself I found in me nothing but a heart squeezed dry. I was tottering but emotionless. I felt no distress whatever, and in a way I regretted it: misery would have seemed to me as sweet as water. I might then have felt sorry for myself and commiserated with myself as with a friend. But I had not a friend left on earth.

Later, when we were rescued, seeing our burnt-out eyes men thought we must have called aloud and wept and suffered. But cries of despair, misery, sobbing grief are a kind of wealth, and we possessed no wealth. When a young girl is disappointed in love she weeps and knows sorrow. Sorrow is one of the vibrations that prove the fact of living. I felt no sorrow. I was the desert. I could no longer bring up a little saliva; neither could I any longer summon those moving visions towards which I should have loved to stretch forth arms. The sun had dried up the springs of tears in me.

And yet, what was that? A ripple of hope went through me like a faint breeze over a lake. What was this sign that had awakened my instinct before knocking on the door of my consciousness? Nothing had changed, and yet everything was changed. This sheet of sand, these low hummocks and sparse tufts of verdure that had been a landscape, were now become a stage setting. Thus far the stage was empty, but the scene was set. I looked at Prévot. The same astonishing thing had happened to him as to me, but he was as far from guessing its significance as I was.

I swear to you that something is about to happen. I swear that life has sprung in this desert. I swear that this emptiness, this stillness, has suddenly become more stirring than a tumult on a public square.

'Prévot! Footprints! We are saved!'

We had wandered from the trail of the human species; we had cast ourselves forth from the tribe; we had found ourselves alone on earth and forgotten by the universal migration; and here, imprinted in the sand, were the divine and naked feet of man!

'Look, Prévot, here two men stood together and then separated.'

'Here a camel knelt.'

'Here...'

But it was not true that we were already saved. It was not enough to squat down and wait. Before long we should be past saving. Once the cough has begun, the progress made by thirst is swift.

Still, I believed in that caravan swaying somewhere in the desert, heavy with its cargo of treasure.

We went on. Suddenly I heard a cock crow. I remembered what Guillaumet had told me: 'Towards the end I heard cocks crowing in the Andes. And I heard the railway train.' The instant the cock crowed I thought of Guillaumet and I said to myself: 'First it was my eyes that played tricks on me. I suppose this is another of the effects of thirst. Probably my ears have merely held out longer than my eyes.' But Prévot grabbed my arm:

'Did you hear that?'

'What?'

'The cock.'

'Why ... why, yes, I did.'

To myself I said: 'Fool! Get it through your head! This means life!'

I had one last hallucination—three dogs chasing one another. Prévot looked, but could not see them. However, both of us waved our arms at a Bedouin. Both of us shouted with all the breath in our bodies, and laughed for happiness.

But our voices could not carry thirty yards. The Bedouin on his slow-moving camel had come into view from behind a dune and now he was moving slowly out of sight. The man was probably the only Arab in this desert, sent by a demon to materialise and vanish before the eyes of us who could not run.

We saw in profile on the dune another Arab. We shouted, but our shouts were whispers. We waved our arms and it seemed to us that they must fill the sky with monstrous signals. Still the Bedouin stared with averted face away from us.

At last, slowly, slowly he began a right angle turn in our direction. At the very second when he came face to face with us, I thought, the curtain would come down. At the very second when his eyes met ours, thirst would vanish and by this man would death and the mirages be wiped out. Let this man but make a quarter-turn left and the world is changed. Let him but bring his torso round, but sweep the scene with a glance, and like a god he can create life.

The miracle had come to pass. He was walking towards us over the sand like a god over the waves.

The Arab looked at us without a word. He placed his hands upon our shoulders and we obeyed him: we stretched out upon the sand. Race, language, religion were forgotten. There was only this humble nomad with the hands of an archangel on our shoulders.

Face to the sand, we waited. And when the water came, we drank like calves with our faces in the basin, and with a greediness which alarmed the Bedouin so that from time to time he pulled us back. But as soon as his hand fell away from us we plunged our faces anew into the water.

Water, thou hast no taste, no colour, no odour; canst not be defined, art relished while ever mysterious. Not necessary to life, but rather life itself, thou fillest us with a gratification that exceeds the delight of the senses. By thy might, there return into us treasures that we had abandoned. By thy grace, there are released in us all the dried-up runnels of our heart. Of the riches that exist in the world, thou art the rarest and also the most delicate—thou so pure within the bowels of the earth! A man may die of thirst lying beside a magnesium spring. He may die within reach of a salt lake. He may die though he hold in his hand a jug of dew, if it be inhabited by evil salts. For thou, water, art a proud divinity, allowing no alternation, no foreignness in thy being. And the joy that thou spreadest is an infinitely simple joy.

You, Bedouin of Libya who saved our lives, though you will dwell for ever in my memory yet I shall never be able to recapture your features. You are Humanity and your face comes into my mind simply as man incarnate. You, our beloved fellowman, did not know who we might be, and yet you recognised us without fail. And I, in my turn, shall recognise you in the faces of all mankind. You came towards me in an aureole of charity and magnanimity bearing the gift of water. All my friends and all my enemies marched towards me in your person. It did not seem to me that you were rescuing me: rather did it seen that you were forgiving me. And I felt I had no enemy left in all the world.

This is the end of my story. Lifted on to a camel, we went on for three hours. Then, broken with weariness, we asked to be set down at a camp while the cameleers went on ahead for help. Towards six in the evening a car manned by armed Bedouins came to fetch us. A half-hour later we were set down at the house of a Swiss engineer named Raccaud who was operating a soda factory beside saline deposits in the desert. He was unforgettably kind to us. By midnight we were in Cairo.

I awoke between white sheets. Through the curtains came the rays of a sun that was no longer an enemy. I spread butter and honey on my bread. I smiled. I recaptured the savour of my childhood and all its marvels. And I read and re-read the telegram from those dearest to me in all the world whose three words had shattered me.

'So terribly happy!'

A JOURNEY WITH DICKENS

KATE DOUGLAS WIGGIN

> The child who made this journey, by the side of the idol who,
> until then, she had hardly realised could smile and breathe like
> an ordinary human being, was Kate Douglas Wiggin, the author
> of *Rebecca of Sunnybrook Farm*. It is taken from her autobiography,
> *My Garden of Memory*.

It seems to me that no child nowadays has time to love an author
as the children and young people of my generation loved Dickens;
nor do I think that any living author of to-day provokes love in
exactly the same fashion. From our yellow dog, Pip, to the cat,
the canary, the lamb, the cow, down to all the hens and cocks,
almost every living thing was named, sooner or later, after one
of Dickens's characters; while my favourite sled, painted in brown,
with the title in brilliant red letters, was 'The Artful Dodger'. Why
did we do it? We little creatures couldn't have suspected that 'the
democratic movement in literature had come to town', as Richard

Whiteing says; nevertheless, we responded to it vigorously, ardently, and swelled the hero's public.

We never read newspapers save the weekly *Portland Transcript,* so that there was a moment of thrilling excitement when my mother, looking up from the *Portland Press,* told us that Mr Dickens was coming to America, and that he was even then sailing from England. I remember distinctly that I prayed for him fervently several times during the next week, that the voyage might be a safe one, and that even the pangs of seasickness might be spared so precious a persónage. In due time we heard that he had arrived in New York, and had begun the series of readings from his books; then he came to Boston, which was still nearer, and then— day of unspeakable excitement—we learned that he had been prevailed upon to give one reading in Portland, which was only sixteen miles away from our village.

It chanced that my mother was taking me to Charlestown, Massachusetts, to pay a visit to an uncle on the very day after the one appointed for the great event in Portland. She, therefore, planned to take me into town the night before, and to invite the cousin, at whose house we were to sleep, to attend the reading with her. I cannot throw a more brilliant light on the discipline of that period than to say that the subject of my attending the reading was never once mentioned. The price of tickets was supposed to be almost prohibitory. I cannot remember the exact sum; I only know that it was mentioned with bated breath in the village of Hollis, and that there was a general feeling in the community that anyone who paid it would have to live down a reputation for riotous extravagance forever afterwards. I neither wailed nor wept, nor made any attempt to set aside the parental decrees (which were anything but severe in our family), but if any martyr in Fox's 'Book' ever suffered more poignant anguish than I, I am heartily sorry for him; yet my common sense assured me that a child could hardly hope to be taken on a week's junketing to Charlestown and expect any other entertainment to be added to it for years to come. The definition of a 'pleasure' in the State of Maine, county of York, village of Hollis, year of our Lord 1868, was something that could not reasonably occur too often without being cheapened.

The days, charged with suppressed excitement, flew by. I bade good-bye to my little sister, who was not to share my metropolitan experiences, and my mother and I embarked for Portland on the daily train that dashed hither and thither at the rate of about twelve miles an hour. When the august night and moment arrived, my mother and her cousin set out for the Place, and the moment they were out of sight I slipped out of the door and followed them, traversing quickly the three or four blocks that separated me from the old City Hall and the Preble House, where Dickens was stopping. I gazed at all the windows and all the entrances of both buildings without beholding any trace of my hero.

I watched the throng of happy, excited, lucky people crowding the streets on their way to the hall, and went home in a chastened mood to bed—a bed which, as soon as I got into it, was crowded with Little Nell and the Marchioness, Florence Dombey, Bella Wilfer, Susan Nipper, and Little Em'ly. There were other dreams, too. Not only had my idol provided me with human friends, to live and laugh and weep over, but he had wrought his genius into *things*; so that, waking or sleeping, every bunch of holly or mistletoe, every plum pudding was alive; every crutch breathed of Tiny Tim; every cricket, and every singing, steaming kettle, had a soul.

The next morning we started on our railroad journey, which I remember as being full of excitement from the beginning, for both men and women were discussing the newspapers with extraordinary interest, the day before having been the one on which the President of the United States had been formally impeached. When the train stopped for two or three minutes at North Berwick, the people on the side of the car next the station suddenly arose and looked eagerly out at some object of apparent interest. I was not, at any age, a person to sit still in her seat when others were looking out of windows, and my small nose was quickly flattened against one of the panes. There on the platform stood the Adored One! It was unbelievable, but there he was in the flesh; standing smiling, breathing, like ordinary human beings. There was no doubt, then, that 'angels and ministers of grace', called authors, had bodies and could not only write David Copperfields, but could be seen with the naked eye. That face, known to me from many pictures, must have looked in some mysterious way into the face of Dora, of Agnes, of Paul Dombey, of Little Dorrit! My spirit gave a leap and entered a new, an unknown world.

Dickens's hands were plunged deep in his pockets (a favourite gesture), but presently one was removed to wave away laughingly a piece of famous Berwick sponge cake, offered him by Mr Osgood, of Boston, his travelling companion and friend. I knew him at once!—the smiling, genial, mobile face, rather highly coloured, the brilliant eyes, the watch-chain, the red carnation in the buttonhole, and the expressive hands, much given to gesture. It was only a momentary view, for the train started, and Dickens vanished, to resume his place in the car next to ours, where he had been, had I known it, ever since we left Portland.

When my mother was again occupied with her book, I slipped away, and, borne along by some resistless and hitherto unrecognised force, I entered the next car; which did not seem at all to me a vehicle carrying Tom, Dick, and Harry to Boston, but a sort of travelling shrine or altar. I took a humble, unoccupied seat near the end, close by the much patronised tank of (unsterilised) drinking-water and the train-boy's basket of popcorn balls and molasses candy, and gazed steadily at the famous man, who was chatting busily with Mr Osgood. I remembered gratefully that my mother had taken the old ribbons off my grey velvet hat and tied me down with blue under the chin, and I thought, if Dickens should happen to rest his eye upon me, hat he could hardly fail to be pleased with the effect of the blue ribbon that went under my collar and held a very small squirrel muff in place. Unfortunately, however, his eye did not meet mine, and my toilette made no sensation in any quarter, but some family friends espied me, and sent me back to ask my mother to come in and sit with them. I brought her back, and, fortunately, there was not room enough for me with the party, so I gladly resumed my modest seat by the popcorn boy, where I could watch Dickens, quite unnoticed.

There is an Indian myth which relates that when the gaze of the Siva rested for the first time on Tellatonea, the most beautiful of women, his desire to see her was so great that his body became all eyes. Such a transformation, I fear, was perilously near to being my fate! Half an hour passed, perhaps, and one gentleman after another came from here or there to exchange a word of greeting with the famous novelist, so that he was never for a moment alone, thereby inciting in my breast my first, and about my last, experience of the passion of jealousy. Suddenly, however, Mr Osgood arose, and with an apology went into the smoking-car. I never knew how it happened; I had no plan, no preparation, no intention, certainly no provocation; but invisible ropes pulled me out of my seat, and, speeding up the aisle, I planted myself breathlessly and timorously down, an unbidden guest, in the seat of honour. I had a moment to recover my equanimity, for Dickens was looking out of the window, but he turned suddenly and said with justifiable surprise:

'God bless my soul, child, where did you come from?'

My heart was in my mouth, but there was still room to exercise my tongue, which was generally the case. I was frightened, but not so completely frightened as if I had been meeting a stranger. You see I knew him, even if he did not know me; so I became immediately autobiographical, although palpitating with nervousness. I had to tell him, I thought, where I came from, who I was, where I was going, or how could I account for myself and my presence beside him in Mr Osgood's seat? So I began, stammeringly, to answer his question.

'I came from Hollis, Maine, and I'm going to Charlestown to visit my uncle. My mother and her cousin went to your reading last night, but of course three couldn't go from the same family, it was so expensive, so I stayed at home. Nora, that's my little sister, is left behind in Hollis. She's too small to go on a journey, but she wanted to go to the reading dreadfully. There was a lady there who had never heard of Betsey Trotwood, and had only read two of your books!'

'Well, upon my word!' he said; 'you do not mean to say that *you* have read them!'

'Of course!' I replied; 'every one of them but the two that we are going to buy in Boston, and some of them six times.'

'Bless my soul!' he ejaculated again. 'Those long thick books, and you such a slip of a thing.'

'Of course,' I explained conscientiously, 'I do skip some of the very dull parts once in a while; not the short dull parts, but the long ones.'

He laughed heartily. 'Now, that is something that I hear very little about,' he said. 'I distinctly want to learn more about those very long dull parts.'

And, whether to amuse himself, or to amuse me, I do not know, he took out a notebook and pencil from his pocket and proceeded to give me an exhausting and exhaustive examination on this subject; the books in which the dull parts predominated; and the characters and subjects which principally produced them. He chuckled so constantly during this operation that I could hardly help believing myself extraordinarily agreeable, so I continued dealing these infant blows, under the delusion that I was flinging him bouquets.

It was not long before one of my hands was in his, and his arm around my waist, while we talked of many things. They say, I believe, that his hands were 'undistinguished' in shape, and that he wore too many rings. Well, those criticisms, must come from persons who never felt the warmth of his handclasp! For my part, I am glad that Pullman chair cars had not come into fashion, else I should never have experienced the delicious joy of snuggling up to Genius, and of being distinctly encouraged in the attitude.

I wish I could recall still more of his conversation, but I was too happy, too exhilarated, and too inexperienced to take conscious notes of the interview. I remember feeling that I had never known anybody so well and so intimately, and that I talked with him as one talks under cover of darkness or before the flickering light of a fire. It seems to me, as I look back now, and remember how the little soul of me came out and sat in the sunshine of his presence, that I must have had some premonition that the child, who would come to be one of the least of writers, was then talking with one of the greatest;—talking, too, as it were, of the author's profession and high calling, for were we not discussing books? All the little details of the meeting stand out as clearly as though it had happened yesterday. I can see every article of his clothing and of my own; the other passengers in the car; the landscape through the window; and above all the face of Dickens, deeply lined, with sparkling eyes and an amused, waggish smile that curled the corners of his mouth under his grizzled mustache. A part of our conversation was given to a Boston newspaper next day, by the author himself, or, by Mr Osgood, and was long preserved in our family archives, while a little more was added a few years after by an old lady who sat in the next seat to us. (The pronoun 'us' seems ridiculously intimate, but I have no doubt I used it, quite unabashed, at that date.)

'What book of mine do you like best?' Dickens asked, I remember; and I answered with the definite assurance of childhood, 'Oh, I like *David Copperfield* much the best. That is the one I have read six times.'

'Six times—good, good!' he replied; 'I am glad that you like Davy, so do I;—I like it best, too!' clapping his hands; and that was the only remark he made which attracted the attention of the other passengers, who glanced in our direction now and then, I have been told, smiling at the interview, but preserving its privacy with the utmost friendliness. I had never looked behind to see how my mother was faring. There are great crises in life when even mothers must retire to the background. For the moment I had no mother, family, friends, or acquaintances, no home, no personality; I was a sort of atom floating in space, half conscious that I could not float forever, but must come to earth again.

'I almost said *Great Expectations*,' I added presently, 'because that comes next in our family. We named our little yellow dog "Mr Pip" out of your book. They told Father when they gave him to us that he was part rat terrier, and we were all pleased, because, if he was, he wasn't all mongrel. (That means mixed-up.) Then one day Father showed him a trap with a mouse in it. The mouse wiggled its tail just a little, and Pip was so frightened that he ran under the barn and stayed the rest of the day. That showed that there wasn't enough rat terrier in him to be right, and the neighbours made fun of him and used to call 'Rats!' when he went down the street. We loved him just the same and he had as hard a time as Pip in *Great Expectations*.'

Here again my new friend's mirth was delightful to behold, so much so that my embarrassed mother, who had been watching me for half an hour, almost made up her mind to drag me away before the very eyes of our fellow passengers. I had never been thought an amusing child in the family circle; what, then, could I be saying to the most distinguished and popular author in the universe?

Dickens here told me little stories about English dogs, but I remember them too vaguely to repeat them or give them their inimitable mingling of fact and nonsense. 'Have you only one dog' he asked.

'We had another,' I answered, 'a big curly one called John Brent, out of a novel, but he died, and we take all our names from your books now. We know a dog who stays with us most of the time. He doesn't belong to anybody and he likes to visit Pip, so we named him Mr Pocket after Mr Pip's friend. The real Mr Pip and Mr Pocket met first in Miss Havisham's garden and they had such a funny fight it always makes Father laugh till he can't read properly! Then they became great friends. Perhaps you remember Mr Pip and Mr Pocket?' And Dickens thought he did, which, perhaps, is not strange, considering that he was the author of their respective beings.

Mr Harry Furniss declares that *Great Expectations* was Dickens's favourite novel, but I can only say that to me he avowed his special fondness for *David Copperfield*. I can never forget that and never be mistaken in my remembrance of it.

'Did you want to go to my reading very much, child?' was another question. Here was a subject that had never once been touched upon in all the past days—a topic that stirred the very depths of my disappointment and sorrow, fairly choking me, and making my lip tremble by its unexpectedness, as I faltered, 'Yes, I did, more than tongue can tell! I know how I feel when I read one of the books, but I wanted to hear how it sounded.'

I looked up a second later, when I was sure that the tears in my eyes were not going to fall, and to my astonishment saw that Dickens's eyes were in precisely the same state of moisture. That was a never-to-be-forgotten moment, although I was too young to appreciate the full significance of it.

'Do you cry when you read out loud, too?' I asked curiously. 'We all do in our family. And we never read about Tiny Tim, or about Steerforth when his body is washed up on the beach, on Saturday nights, for fear our eyes will be too swollen to go to Sunday School.'

'Yes, I cry when I read about Steerforth,' he answered quietly, and I felt no astonishment. 'I cried when I wrote it, too! That is still more foolish!'

'Where do you cry the worst?' I asked. 'Our time is when it says, "*All the men who carried him had known him and gone sailing with him and seen him merry and bold*"'; and here I grew tearful and reminiscent.

We were now fast approaching our destination—the station in Boston—and the passengers began to collect their wraps and bundles. Mr Osgood had two or three times made his appearance, but had been waved away with a smile by Dickens—a smile that seemed to say, 'You will excuse me, I know, but this child has the right of way.'

'You are not travelling alone?' he asked, as he arose to put on his overcoat.

'Oh! my goodness!' I said, coming down to earth for the first time since I had taken my seat beside him—'certainly not; I had a mother, but I forgot all about her.' Whereupon he said, 'You are past-mistress of the art of flattery!'

But this remark was told me years afterwards by the old lady who was sitting in the next seat, and who overheard as much of the conversation as she possibly could, so she informed me. Her pencilled notes, read to me when we met by chance in South Reading, Massachusetts, have helped me greatly in the minor details of the interview and my own phraseology, which amused her because of its chatterbox fluency and the amazing response it elicited from so great a man.

Dickens took me back to the forgotten mother, and introduced himself, and I, still clinging to his hand, left the car and walked with him down the platform until he disappeared in the carriage with Mr Osgood.